PRIMAL DEITY

2

Crisis Management

ALLEN OZARK

Edited by Bella Fox

Published by Sumner House Publishing

ISBN: 978-1-7334656-2-5

Experience the Primal Deity Series…

1 THE CHAOS ENGINE

- 2 CRISIS MANAGEMENT -

3 CONTAINMENT

4 EARLY DETECTION

5 ONE FEDERAL PARKWAY

www.primaldeity.com

Acknowledgements

I would like to give a heartfelt thank you to:

God, for without His love and mercy, nothing is possible in the Universe;

My family and friends, who have my heart and always will—always and forever; and

Every Alex Southerland fan, who bought the first book in the series, *The Chaos Engine*.

Thank you so much for supporting Alex and giving me all your positive feedback—I love you all.

Dedication

The title of this book is *Crisis Management*, and despite what I wrote in the opening chapter, I think a better definition of the term is a single mom raising five kids—yes, five kids on her own with no complaints and no regrets. Somehow, amazing just doesn't say it. The good part about being a son is you can say you have the best mom ever. For me and my siblings, nothing could be more truthful. You're beyond awesome mom, and I love you more than you can ever imagine.

PRIMAL DEITY

2

Crisis Management

Chapter 1

I always wondered what comes to mind when the average person thinks of the simple life, if there is such a thing. When I was growing up, I used to hear family members talking about it all the time, how they love waking up to the smell of country air. In my mind, all I could imagine was some dilapidated farmhouse that reeked of hog balls, but they made it seem like it's the best thing since sliced bread. I just couldn't seem to get beyond the word *simple*. Even back then, nothing in my life was remotely simple. At the same time, it wasn't that complicated either. Complicated means you're doing something important like feeding the hungry or finding a cure for cancer. Complicated is when you have a loving family or friends who want your time even when you don't have a second to spare. No, my life isn't complicated at all. It's just screwed up. For the first time in a while though, I can honestly say it's not my fault. You see, it's not who I've become, or even where I come from—it's what I have to do.

Every day, I wake up and attempt to limit the impact of unforeseen problems, which is the textbook definition of my job. It sounds good in theory, but whoever wrote that never worked kidnapping in a city where criminals rule. New York problems are always unforeseen and generally bad for your health—sometimes even deadly. Forget about colors, or gangs, or protection because this city is chockfull of dirty cops, murderers, friends, and foes who all know only the strong survive. And, there's no such thing as loyalty anymore. They'll turn on each other in a second and won't think twice about it.

In this godforsaken land of high fashion and big-time wheelers and dealers, the weak are more than just prey.

They're slaves to sadistic, unreasonable masters. There's no such thing as negotiating with them either. Forget about it. The rules are strict, the self-guided training is brutal, and the punishment's always unforgiving. It doesn't matter who you are or how much money you make—you don't even need a condition, just step outside your front door and, nine times out of 10, you will have a serious situation on your hands.

I laugh every time I hear a manager, or some pencil-dick rookie, utter the words *crisis management*. It's all a big joke. Naturally, the head honchos at the Agency of Female Bashing Imbeciles, or the FBI as they prefer to call it, bounce that term around only after the job's done, and only if the outcome makes them look good. Let one recovery goes south, and suddenly *crisis management* turns into *disaster recovery*, which is basically a one-sided witch-hunt. I know this because on one or more occasions, I played the part of the witch, and my ass played the part of the hunted.

I found out the hard way losing a case is like when I used to come home as a child from school with anything less than an A+ grade on an assignment. I never got a B or C but let me bring home one A- and it was disaster recovery in the Southerland house, which meant I had to recover what was left of my bruised-up ass after Momma mopped the floor with it. The Bureau is no different. Sad to say, but one way or another, it always ends up bad for the only one in the bunch who gives a damn about the victim—the negotiator.

In my line of work there are no heroes. We do our job well because we train hard, but one screw up and we know we're automatically getting hung out to dry. Sure, it's no way to work, and yes it kills morale, but that's the way it is. It's what happened to me the last time, and this recent debacle is no different. As we speak, the powers that be are shining up the biggest hook money can buy, just for me. The Office of Professional Responsibility is always itching for one of them good ole fashion Salem, Massachusetts style lynchings, and they want my head. Sad to say, but with each new inquiry, they get closer and closer to their objective.

So, there I sat in a poorly lit room, alone at a table with only a microphone, a drinking glass, and a pitcher of water within arm's reach. I probably could have gone on and on about all the things I did to close the case in question without incident, but it was irrelevant. I was at the mercy of OPR, and there ain't no two ways about it, what OPR wants, OPR gets. Over the course of my time with the Bureau, I've come to know them intimately, and in return, they've become quite fixated on me. I don't want to sound like the victim here, but despite my best efforts, it's never enough.

Hard as it was, I managed to hold my peace as members of the review panel, a bunch of underpaid, egotistical pencil-pushers, gazed upon me with judging eyes. They ogled me for more than five minutes. Then, it was right down to business. You should've seen them, digging through mounds of paperwork all in unison with the precision of Olympic synchronized swimmers. I could tell by the expressions on their faces, they were searching for any reason to rip my life apart and end what little career I had left. Funny thing is, they didn't have to look very hard. I'd given them everything they needed. If they'd just dug a little deeper the last time, it would've been game over for me. Unlucky for them, they were careless and too busy thinking about their own reputations instead of just doing their jobs. *I hate bureaucrats.*

So, knowing all this, why was I still chipper? Well, things had been going downhill, but my luck was starting to change for the better. Unlike the last time, I had a few things in my corner that made it harder for them to throw the book at me. First, I had over seven years of service. Second, my boss, Tony Crane, was on the review panel and he always had my back. Last but not least, the evidence was on my side, and there's nothing anyone could do about that. If I wasn't such a fuckin' lady, I would rip off my top, jump up on the desk, and growl like a wild jungle animal as I beat my chest. However, I figured it was a good idea to try and contain myself in case someone important was watching. By the way ... I'm FBI Special Agent Denise Alexandria Southerland, but my friends call me Alex.

There I sat in that review panel. I swear those idiots were sweating me all hard, and they weren't being nice about it either. They took turns, turning their nose up at me like I was a piece of mud under the heels of their boots. Of course, I know I'm supposed to always keep my cool in situations like that, but if I could have my cake and eat it too, I would've snuck a flame-thrower past security and had myself a good ole fashion weenie roast.

Despite their futile looks of disgust, with all my ducks in a row, I already knew how that scenario was going to play out. I'd get a slap on the wrist—one of those gingerly executed slaps—and I'd be on my way out of town in no time. But then, the unspeakable happened. Assistant Director Amanda Cross, ringmaster of Cirque du OPR, showed up out of the blue, and my confidence dropped straight to hell.

For all the tea in China, I couldn't imagine who invited Amanda the Hun to the party. I wasn't an executive, so as far as I knew there was no need for her to be on the review panel, but she and I had history. I guess it was time for some payback.

Cross was of a special breed, evil and rotten to the core. I know I've said that about a lot of people, but I really mean it about her. She had it in for me from the beginning, and I could tell how she plopped down in her seat she wouldn't back off without a fight or at least a goddamn heart attack. *If only I could be so lucky.*

Director Cross grabbed her microphone and pointed it to her mouth. "Agent Southerland," she bellowed, her voice echoing about the room, "it seems only yesterday when you last appeared before this disciplinary review board under similar circumstances."

"Ma'am if I may, I'd like to ask why you are-"

"No, you may not!" exclaimed Cross. "You had your opportunity to provide testimony in a sworn statement. Now, you will give this panel the proper respect."

Tony looked to his left at Cross. His expression suggested he didn't like her tone, but his hands were tied. I had only myself to thank for that.

"Quite frankly, your behavior concerns me," Cross confessed. "Despite the remote possibility your actions may be genuine in nature, it is incumbent upon us to ensure all agents, including you Agent Southerland—especially you as a supervisor—we have to make sure you operate within the parameters of our Manual of Administrative Operations and Procedures. Let's get down to brass tacks here ... you may have rescued that little boy, but you also eliminated the possibility of him ever having a normal life. His parents have filed suit against the government, and they intend to pursue civil action against you. Agent Southerland, do you understand the nature and seriousness of this situation?"

I leaned forward closer to the microphone. "Yes, I do."

Like clockwork, Tony spoke up in my defense. "On behalf of the leadership team, I'd like to remind this review panel that Agent Southerland's actions, though somewhat unorthodox, were consistent with FBI field guidelines. And, although the boy must undergo physical therapy, he is alive as a direct result of Agent Southerland's efforts."

"Thank you, SAC Crane. I concur with your assessment, and I'll add that it is this reason alone you're still here, Agent Southerland." Suddenly, Cross changed the subject. "Truthfully, this panel is no longer concerned with the details of this isolated incident. We are, however, concerned about your conduct as an FBI Agent. When I look at your record, I see a history of violence and constant disregard for proper protocol and procedures. With so many border-line code-of-conduct violations, the question I submit to you today, Agent Southerland, is how can we in good conscious trust you to behave in the field?"

"Assistant Director Cross," I said, clearing my throat as I leaned forward in my chair, "while I hesitate to dwell on my individual achievements, I believe it would be unfair for this review board to ignore them. I have given years of unwavering loyalty to the Bureau, and I'm committed to my charge as an agent. I have reviewed the case in question and identified several areas of opportunity within my team.

Unfortunately, field operations happen fast, and we have to make the best decisions we can with the information we have. I'm an FBI agent, but I am also human. You ask if you can trust me. The answer is, absolutely yes. I understand your concerns about the outcome of the case in question, and I too agree there are things we could've done better, but if we simply respond to the emotions in the aftermath, we'll give power to the criminals who continue to commit these horrible crimes. Kidnappings in New York are on the rise, and our team is short on resources. I implore you to reinstate me, so I can continue my work."

"Well said, Agent Southerland," Cross replied. She took off her glasses and sat up in her chair. "As we carefully consider the current proposal for termination, we note this inquiry has not developed facts warranting harsh administrative action. However, this panel has a single concern ... allow me to rephrase, we have a single requirement, and pardon my bluntness, but Agent Southerland you're like a mad dog."

Uh, did that croissant-eatin' heifer just call me a mad dog? THAT WAS RACIST!

Cross finished sneering at me, cleared her throat, and said, "I'm not sure how you've managed to slip through the cracks so many years," she said. "In my opinion, you're spiraling out of control, and we can no longer allow you back in the field without a leash." She paused for a moment and looked down. Then, she stared back up at me. "Immediately following the incident in Atlanta that led to ASAC David Chandler's death, you were required to attend sessions with a therapist. I am of the opinion treatment ended prematurely. I'm sure other members of this panel would agree. You're currently on 15-day suspension ... ... it is the recommendation of this review board you be reinstated with provisions. Our requirement is simple. You must resume therapy with a qualified psychologist. This committee may reconvene in six months for a follow-up based on your reported progress." She looked over at Tony for a brief second, and then refocused her attention on me. "SAC Crane has indicated you require time to attend to a rapidly developing family situation. I understand your mother is terminally ill, is that correct?"

"Yes," I solemnly replied.

"I'm sorry to hear that, Agent Southerland. I recommend you use this week to handle your affairs and return to the office next Monday with a new attitude." She flipped through some more papers, and then wrote something down. "I'll downgrade your suspension to a letter of censure. In addition to returning to therapy, OPR may conduct appropriate ongoing investigations to determine the use of illegal drugs. Do you have any questions for this review board?"

Letter of censure? Illegal drugs? This is some bullshit! Like I said, it was just a witch hunt. It's not like I'd lost a weapon or had a vehicle stolen from me. I didn't do anything wrong. All I did was my job, but I guess Cross had to make her point. She had to make an example out of me.

"Agent Southerland, do you have any questions?" Cross asked again.

"No, I do not, Assistant Director Cross." I responded.

"Then this review board is adjourned ... dismissed, Agent Southerland."

I stood up and darted out of the room, walking as fast as my long slender legs could carry me.

"ALEX, WAIT!" yelled Tony, running to catch up to me.

I stopped midway down the hall and sighed. "What, Tony?"

"You know you're not making this easy for me, right?" he asked.

"Oh, so what, I just make your life hard every day?" I shook my head. "Look I'm thinking about quitting anyway," I said softly.

"Don't say that!" he exclaimed.

"Tony, I'm always first on the scene, and I'm the last one there with the family, not just when everything goes well, but when it's all screwed up too. Nobody gave a damn that kid got burned. Me? I was with him every night in the hospital. Where the hell were his parents then? Now they wanna sue me? See, none of that shit-"

"Keep your voice down," he warned.

I whispered, "None of that shit ever comes into play, does it? OPR just wants to fuck with me. It's bullshit man!" I turned to walk away.

Tony grabbed my arm. "Listen," he whispered, "I know ... trust me, I know. Look, all I'm saying is, if you could be a tad more sensitive to the politics, it'd be a hell of a lot easier to avoid situations like this, but you tie my hands behind my back every time."

I played dumb. "I don't know what you're talking about."

"You don't? How about your statement? Alex, you all but called Cross the Wicked Witch of the East. You didn't think you'd get a reaction from that? You didn't even need to mention her. It's like you're looking for trouble."

I rolled my eyes. "That why she showed her dumb ass up?"

"See, that's exactly my point," he said, waving his finger in my face. "Look, don't take this the wrong way Alex, but you need to reel it in, okay?"

"Tony, I appreciate everything you do, but it's not worth it. I'm done ... I'm going home to see my-"

"Listen-"

"No, you listen to me, Tony. You can't sweettalk this Bureau utopia bullshit to me anymore. The dream's dead man. I'm broke, this apartment's wearing a hole in my pocket, and I really can't deal with the stress anymore. I'm out."

"Wait, what are you-"

"I'll call you when I get to Atlanta." I unclipped my ID badge from my jacket and shoved it in his hand.

"Wait a minute!" he whispered, desperately trying to hold me back, but I struggled free and walked off.

The entire time we were talking, Tony had this confused look on his face. I understood where he was coming from though. I all but begged Cross to let me stay, but not because I wanted to get back to work. Truth is I wasn't planning on going back at all. I just didn't want a termination at the hands of OPR on my record, hence the begging.

I hated Cross slid that letter of censure in my file, but nobody cares what she says anyway. She's just an old bag of wind. As for Tony, I didn't care what he thought about my leaving. My mind was made up, and Jesus himself couldn't change it. He didn't realize it, but the day I got word my mother was sick, I'd planned on leaving the Bureau. Cross' letter was just the icing on the cake.

Despite my typical poor disposition, sometimes I try to look for the silver lining in things. So, even though I couldn't stand that old, white hag, Cross, she actually gave me the rest of the week off. Thanks to her, I had plenty of time to get down to Atlanta and sort out an ancient part of my life once and for all before turning in my resignation. It was a good thing because that meant I had an extra week of pay that would be coming to me.

When I walked out of the office, I exhaled and literally left every bit of the job behind me. On the way down to the parking garage, all I could think about was my mother. I hadn't seen her in over 10 years. Naturally, I was still bitter as a bowl of lemons, but I also knew she was on her way out, literally. I needed to lay eyes on her one last time before she died. The way I saw it, this was her last chance to do right by me. She at least owed me that.

I pulled out of the garage and drove straight to JFK International. I parked my little beat up rusty BMW 325 in the pay-by-day lot and walked into the American Airlines terminal. I didn't even bother to pack, I just went straight from the office. I knew my family wouldn't be rolling out the welcome mat, so there was no reason to hang around. I figured I'd be there a few hours, or a day at the most, and then catch the first flight back out.

I'd given my ID to Tony back at the office, but I was smart enough to keep my badge and gun. So, after I bought my plane ticket, I flashed my credentials and cut right through the lines at all the security checkpoints. Then, I waited inside a café in the terminal until it was time to board. I had the sandwich salad special with a glass of water. I wanted a big glass of wine, but my last-minute ticket for the flight to Atlanta broke the bank, so I just shut up and tried to enjoy the food. The salad wasn't bad at all, but the grilled chicken sandwich left something to be desired. Actually, it reminded me of how my dad used to make sandwiches, all wet and drippy. *YEESH!*

I finished eating about 10 minutes before it was time to board. I paid for my meal and headed down to the terminal. I guess eating took longer than I thought in my mind because by the time I got down there everybody was already on the plane. I hustled onboard and took my seat. It didn't take long before we were taxiing down the runway and jetting off southbound to Hartsfield-Jackson International.

Spending the day with OPR was draining to say the least. By the time we reached cruising altitude, the plane wasn't the only thing running on autopilot. I didn't even order a drink. It's even hard for me to imagine myself flying sober, but that's exactly what I was doing that day. I had become quite the lush, but honestly, everything I had going on in my life was probably enough to keep me off the sauce for a few hours. Besides, if I arrived in Atlanta drunk and my family got started with me, there's no telling what would come out of my mouth. I had decades of pain built up, ready to eat some poor, unfortunate, unsuspecting soul alive.

I was in rare form on that flight. I didn't even go to sleep. I just sat there, gazing out the window at the clouds, my mind traveling faster than the speed of light. Maybe I had the strength to survive dealing with my family for a day, but beyond that, it was hard to tell. The prospect of being jobless again wasn't helping either. On the outside I looked normal, but anyone, who knew me well enough, could see I was barely holding on. Thinking about everything was starting to make me tear up. I had to pull it together fast. I didn't want anyone to see me like that, especially not my sister. Actually, I was hoping to avoid her all together. They say time heals, but they never tell you how much time it takes. At that point, the whole time-healing thing just wasn't cutting the mustard because I still wanted to kick my sister in her throat for what she did to me.

The flight was a little over two hours. After we touched down in Hartsfield and deplaned, I took the tram down to the other side of the airport. I ran through the baggage claim area and went straight out the door, no stops. I just wanted to get my visit done and over with because I was starting to feel weird about the whole situation, maybe even a little guilty, although I'm not sure why.

It had been ages since I last spoke with my family, but I always kept tabs on their whereabouts. I lost track of my sister, and had no clue how to find her, but I made a point to keep a good address for my mother. She and I didn't speak, but I thought it was important for both of us to know where the other was just in case. Whenever I moved, I mailed a self-addressed envelope to her. She actually wrote me, which is how I learned she'd been sick for a while. In the letter, she didn't say what hospital she was in though. I had precious little cab fare, and I didn't want to run around the city, hoping I'd get lucky, so I headed to her home in Atlanta. Even if she wasn't there, surely someone would be able to point me in the right direction.

My cabdriver pulled up at Momma's house around 7 p.m. I got out and pushed the call button at the gate. I could see the house through the big black wrought iron bars, and what a hell of a sight it was. The two-story traditional brick home was nestled into a partially wooded lot with a perfectly sculpted landscape of trees, shrubbery and flowers. There was a string of lights strategically positioned up the driveway on both sides, illuminating what seemed to be a quarter-mile-long path. Obviously, Mom spent Dad's insurance money well.

"How may I help you?" came a man's voice over the speaker.

"Yes, I'm here to see, Ezola Southerland."

"And, your name?" he asked.

I hesitated to say.

"Your name please?" he repeated.

"Alex Southerland," I replied, but the man didn't respond. I waited for a few seconds, and then buzzed him again, but there was no answer. I thought about pressing the call button one last time, but then decided to just leave.

"I knew this was a bad idea," I said to myself. If I could've turned the plane around mid-flight I probably would have and just said, *Hey I tried*. That was enough for me. I got back into the cab. "Turn it around," I told the driver. "Head back to the airport, so I can catch the next flight out."

"You got it," he replied, pulling the column shifter of the car into reverse.

We were just about to turn around when suddenly, the gate opened. My driver looked back over his shoulder. "You want me to go on in?" he asked.

"...Yeah, I guess so."

"Look lady, what you wanna do?" he asked in a frustrated tone.

"Go ahead, but hang around out front until I come back out, okay?"

"Sure", he replied, leaning over the steering wheel, looking up at the house. "Meter's running," he casually warned. He waited until the gate was fully open, and then drove up the driveway and parked near the front door.

I got out and just looked around for a second. "Damn!" Momma was living all lavish with shiny, brand new Mercedes and BMWs lined up out front. All I could think about was me up in New York in that subterranean shit-hole of an apartment of mine, scraping beanie weenies out of the can while she was eating good off of Daddy's life insurance money. I was so pissed.

I slowly walked up the stairs to the front door. Then, I rang the doorbell a few times and just stepped back a little.

A very short Latina woman, who I assumed was the maid based on her all black dress and bright white apron, answered the door. "Señorita," she greeted. "Come, wait here...."

"Is Mrs. Southerland home?" I asked.

"Come, wait," she repeated, beckoning for me to enter further into the home.

I followed her into the dining room, which seemed as long as a football field. In the center of the room was a table big enough to seat at least twenty people. I walked around and looked at the art hanging on the walls. After a while, a man came in. As fate would have it, this particular man had a very familiar face—one I hoped to never see again for as long as I live.

"I thought you might need a drink, Alex," he said, carrying a bottle of scotch and two small glasses.

"The hell you doing here, Bill?"

"You've been gone a long time, Alex. A lot's changed. Can I pour you one?"

I rolled my eyes. "Whatever, nigga."

"Well, maybe not everything's changed." He took the top off the bottle and poured a little bit of scotch into each glass. "I take it you still hate me for what I did?"

I walked over and snatched the drink from him. "Where's my mother?"

"Hospital," Bill replied. "I paid your cab driver and told him he could leave. I'm on my way back to the hospital now. I'm getting ready to leave here in just a few, so you can ride with me if that's alright."

I took a sip of my drink. "I didn't ask you to pay for my cab, Bill. I don't need anything from you."

"You never did," he retorted. "Maybe that's why we had so many problems. Maybe I wanted you to need me just a little sometimes."

"FUCK YOU!" I exclaimed. "You crossed the line. It had nothing to do with how I treated you, so don't put your shit on me. You're right, nothing's changed! I knew coming here was a bad idea, and seeing your black ass only makes it worse." I slammed the glass down on the table and walked out of the room.

I wandered around aimlessly, looking for the front door, so I could leave. I needed to call another cab, but couldn't get a signal on my cell, so I figured I'd call as soon as I got back outside. Unfortunately, I got lost in that house and ended up in front of another big room. I heard footsteps approaching in the hall, so I ducked inside. After a few seconds, I zoomed in on something hanging on the wall that nearly brought me to tears. I heard Bill walk up, but I was frozen in time, so choked up I couldn't move an inch.

"That's her favorite painting," said Bill, standing beside me.

It was amazing. It looked like an artist used different pictures of us, including one with Dad dressed in his Sheriff's uniform, and put them all together in one huge collage. It seemed so real, like we were all right there, taking that picture together. In all our years, we never took a single-family photo. Every time we attempted, my mother started trippin', so it never happened. I guess she was trying to make up for it with that painting. Staring at that thing on the wall, a thousand emotions hit me all at once. I couldn't help but think about how great our family could've been—should've been—and suddenly, I burst into tears.

Bill put an arm around me. I fought him at first, but then I fell into his big strong arms. Even then, after all that time, I still felt safe with him. I stood there and cried on his chest for nearly five minutes until his shirt was completely soaked with my tears.

"You okay?" he asked, rubbing my back.

I pulled away from him. "Yes, I'm fine. I'm sorry, I just-"

"Look, it's alright, Alex."

"I know she doesn't love me, but I love her ... and I miss my dad."

Bill touched my shoulders and looked deep into my eyes. "Baby, you can hold a grudge for the rest of your life, or you can go and tell her how you feel."

I got quiet for a second.

Bill smiled. "Come on Alex ... let me take you to her. She keeps talking about you. I know she wants to see you."

I wiped my tears and nodded.

"You're doing the right thing," said Bill.

I gave him a half-ass smile.

"Give me a few, I just gotta go upstairs and change my shirt, okay?" He chuckled a little.

"So ... you live here too?"

He looked a little strange. "Well, yeah. Look, Alex ... Theresa and I ... we, uh ... we got married!" He smiled big.

He caught me off guard a little with that. I almost cried because, quite frankly, he gave her something he never thought to give me—a wedding ring. But far as I was concerned, what she'd done to me wasn't even half the treachery that whore's capable of. Bill had something coming. If she'd do something like that to her own sister, she'll do anything.

Like I say, that news almost brought me to tears, but when I thought about what he got for what they did, the feeling passed quickly. I didn't feel like crying, but I was still stewing about the situation. Bill, on the other hand, was all juiced up. He had this really big stupid grin on his face, like I was gonna slap him high-five or something, but honestly, I didn't give a tinker's damn about him and Theresa. I didn't really care about anything anymore. A big ass garbage truck could've run me down in the street that night, and I wouldn't have even flinched.

"Yeah, we've been married for three years now," he said proudly. "We sold our house and moved in with Mom when we found out how sick she was last year." Bill looked up and around. "Yeah, when I'm not at the shop, I'm here helping Theresa with Mom."

Hearing him call my mother *Mom* almost made me sick to my stomach. I just shook my head and said, "Well, I guess congratulations are in order."

I stuck my hand out, but Bill smacked it away and hugged me tightly.

"I miss talking to you," he said, "I'm glad you're here Alex. Just give me a few minutes and I'll be ready to go, okay?" He kept smiling.

I pushed away from him again. "Please hurry," I said, emotionlessly, looking down.

Bill took off and came back downstairs in record speed. And, I don't mean to be a bitch about it, but he moved faster than he'd ever moved for me while we were together. I guess knocking up, and then marrying your girlfriend's sister changes a brother. He came back in the room with some books, magazines and other miscellaneous items under his arm, and all I could think about was what a dick he'd been with me versus what a thoughtful little husband, slash father, slash son-in-law he'd become for my folks. My pissivity was growing rapidly.

Bill put everything in a little bag, and then led me through that maze of a house back out to the front entryway.

"Maria!" he yelled, "hey, Maria!"

"Señor...?" Maria came running around the corner.

"We're leaving. I'll be at the hospital tonight."

"And, your guest, Señor Bill?"

"She's coming with me, but we'll be back later."

"Okay," replied Maria, "but you bring the misses back home soon. Hospital no good for her condition, okay?"

Bill smiled and nodded. "Come on Alex, this way."

We walked out and my mind continued wondering. It's funny I was being called a guest in my own mother's home. I guess I deserved it though me being a bad daughter and all. Maybe I should've just gotten over it, but I'm sorry, for me that was easier said than done. My mother hurt me in ways I never even told Bill. Sure, she's sick now, and yeah, she took the first step in writing me, but that didn't excuse the horrible things she did to me growing up.

I followed Bill out to a silver Benz. He unlocked the doors and we got in.

"You can push the seat back if you need to," he told me.

"I'm fine ... thanks." I put my seatbelt on, but he didn't. Bill never wore his seatbelt, but I knew better than to take that risk. Years back, I proved their usefulness beyond a shadow of a doubt. Seatbelts mean the difference between life and death. If he'd seen my mustang after that crash on the freeway, he might've buckled up too, but as usual, I didn't know anything. I couldn't tell that nigga shit if I had a glowing mystical staff in my hand. Bill's about as stubborn as me and my momma put together.

Bill started the car, shifted into drive and pulled down to the gate. Then, he all of a sudden got extremely chatty. "Mom's down at Emory Crawford Long," he said.

"Oh, okay."

Bill pressed the button for the gate. While we waited for it to open, he turned to me and smiled. "I know it doesn't mean much at this point ... but, I really am sorry about what happened between us."

I sighed. "I don't wanna talk about it, Bill."

"You think you could ever find it in your heart to forgive me?"

"I don't know. You broke my heart, and-"

"I was a fool," he confessed, "a fool for listening to my boys and messing around with Theresa. I was acting like an idiot. I should've never hurt you like that, and I'm sorry, I really-"

"STOP IT BILL!" I shouted.

"No, I really am sorry." He sounded so sincere. It was pitiful.

"Just stop saying you're sorry!" I yelled. "I wasn't exactly an angel, you know? I did my fair share of dirt, so save your guilt-bag for somebody who deserves it. We're just jacked up together, always have been."

"Yeah, but it was still good wasn't it?" he asked.

We both started laughing.

"I don't know whether to laugh or cry about all this ... let's just change the subject, alright?"

Bill nodded. "Cool." He made a left out of the driveway and headed down the main street. After a few turns, he merged onto I-75 North.

"You know when I said earlier that you haven't changed, I was lying," Bill confessed.

I looked at him and twisted my lips up. "Yeah, whatever."

"No, I'm serious," he said.

"How so?" I asked.

Bill laughed a little. "I mean, just look at you...."

"What?"

"You're so ... uh, well...."

"Oh, spit it out, Bill."

"You're so girly now." He drew over to his side of the car as if I was gonna hit him.

"Uh, and just what is that supposed to mean?" I asked.

Bill laughed hard as hell. "I don't know, it's just, you actually look like a girl, and you don't talk like ... ... like one of the boys-"

"Oh, you'd be surprised," I interrupted.

He smiled. "Well, you have makeup on, your hair's done up, and you know ... you aren't acting so ... what's the word I'm looking for...."

"Mannish?"

"Hey, that's your word not mine Alex!" He continued chuckling.

I sighed. "Whatever boy ... so, you still up at the plant?"

"No," he replied, "I took your advice and started my own auto repair shop. Can you believe that?"

"No shit?"

"I'm serious Alex. It's not a big operation, but it's enough to keep me busy. I got a few guys working for me now, so it's a good deal for us."

"I'm very proud of you. I always believed in you. I knew you could do it, which is why I was always pushing you, man."

He smiled, "Yeah, we've been open for a few years and now we have a loyal customer base from all over the city."

"Well, good for you Bill."

"You still with the FBI?" he asked.

"Yeah."

"Mom said you're up in New York."

"I transferred up a while back."

"Man, you been working for them for a minute now, that's good," said Bill.

I smirked a little. "Almost eight years."

"That's awesome, Alex. You'll be running the place soon."

I frowned. "I doubt it ... too much BS and competition. They're like ill-tempered crabs in a barrel. And, if that ain't enough, I got OPR riding my ass like I owe them money."

"OPR?" he asked.

"Yeah, they're like internal affairs for the FBI."

"Gotcha."

"Job completely sucks," I said. "I think I'm gonna quit when I get back up there. Maybe go back to school or something, but ... I don't know."

Bill got off on 10th Street and made a right. "Well, whatever you decide to do, I got your back. I never changed my cell phone number, so you know you can give me a call if you need me."

"Thanks ... that's sweet Bill ... but ... I think I'll be fine."

"Listen, I meant to tell you, your mom's been in Jamaica for a while. Before she got really bad, she was down there doing a lot of stuff in her home town. Somewhere along the line, she seemed to have reverted back to her native language—that or she just doesn't feel like speaking English anymore. Anyway, I figured I'd give you a heads-up. Sometimes it's hard for me to understand what she's saying, and I'm around her quite a bit, ya know? "

"Well ... I appreciate the heads-up."

Bill turned and looked at me. "I gotta be straight with you ... it's not looking good at all. She's got stage four lung cancer."

"From all the smoking?" I asked.

"Maybe ... hard to say, but the doctors are telling us it spread from her lungs to her liver, spine and other parts of the body. Mom's in bad shape. She's done the chemotherapy and everything. We thought the cancer was going into remission, but this year it came back in full force. I know it's a lot to take in. If I could spare you from hearing it I would, but I wanted you to be prepared for what you see up there."

"How long?"

"Days, maybe hours," he shook his head, "we just don't know."

We continued down Peachtree towards Crawford Long, and Bill kept talking, but I drowned him out. All I could think about was seeing my mom again, what she looked like, and what I was gonna say to her. I had so many things bouncing around in my head. There were so many things I wanted to get off my chest, but the closer we got, the more it all got jumbled together.

We drove up to the front of the hospital and I got out. Bill pulled into the valet parking line and hopped out too. The guy handed him a ticket, and then we walked inside together. I wanted to buy some flowers, so we stopped at the gift shop and I got a very nice floral arrangement. It was beautiful. I paid for the flowers, and then we walked to the elevators and got in. We rode up to the fifth floor, got out and Bill led the way to Mom's room. He walked inside, but I just kind of stuck my head in the door and watched.

"Mom, I see you're still awake," said Bill.

"Yes ... come here ... mi look at you, Son."

He walked over and kissed her forehead. "You eat yet?"

"Mi nuh like di food," she snapped.

"I know, I know, but you gotta eat now. Promise me, okay?" Bill put the bag he was carrying down in a chair. "I brought you a few more magazines and a couple of books for you to read."

"Bless you, child."

"I also brought someone with me ... you feel like having a visitor?"

"Oh nuh..." She covered her mouth with both hands. "Denise?"

Bill turned around and pointed at me standing by the door. I wanted to duck back out and run, but I didn't. I walked slowly into the room and stood a few feet away from the foot of the bed.

I spoke up. "Momma?"

"Oh Jah, child, please come!"

Bill was right. Her accent was much thicker than I remember, but she was so weak and frail I didn't even recognize her. She held her little skinny arms up, beckoning me to come closer, and suddenly I felt all warm and full of joy.

I walked around, sat down on the bed and gave her a big hug. She wrapped her arms around me and kissed my face over and over again.

"Mi thought mi neva see you," she said. "You look so tin, you look good."

"Thank you, Momma. I missed you."

"Miss you too, baby." Then, she gave Bill a very strange look. "Leave us, Bill."

"Okay, I'll go down and look for Theresa. I'll be back in a while."

As soon as Bill left the room, my mother did what I never knew she was capable of—she apologized.

"Child, mi gone tell you something that make you sad. But, mi tink you undastand why ya madda treat you so bad-"

I touched her hand. "No, you don't have to-"

"Hush now, child. Madda know what ya need to hear. Cuya, mi love your fadda. He mi puttus, mi precious mon. Mi love him. But he love dis matey, dis odda woman too. She tall, bruck up, ya know a model, nuh one cyaan test. Wa'ppen, he say, he wan' be wit mi, but he be wit her too ... it was truly dred. Even now, when mi see you, mi see him too ... see him face. When mi hold you, mi know you nuh fi. All dis time mi love you, but mi hate you too."

I squeezed her hand and tried to hold back my tears.

"We be together, but when ya madda die, he say we bring you home. Mi say mi nuh, nuh, but he insist. He insist we make you fambly, but mi hate him for dat. Dat why mi send fa ya now ... wan' ya to know what in mi heart." She reached up and touched my face. "It don' matta who ya madda is ... dis a fi mi - ya understand?"

I nodded, sniffling.

"Mi tink mi love ya more dan' ya sista and ya brudda," she laughed, "but don' you tell 'em none, okay? You like a lil baby angel. Mi love ya, but mi know da truth about ya fadda, and it hurt mi bad."

"I love you," I said, teary eyed. "I missed you so much Momma." I leaned down and kissed her face. Then, I pressed my cheek against hers and we lay there and cried together for a while.

The last time I cried like that, Bill had just broken my heart into a bunch of pieces. That day's events had already been extremely emotional for me, and seeing my mother was no different. It was enough having to see Bill again, but what she told me was too much for words. *What was I supposed to do?* After all these years, I learn the woman I needed to feel motherly love from wasn't my real mother at all. *How could they do this to me?* I felt like my dad betrayed me. I felt like the whole family had betrayed me, but even though it made me sad, I was kinda relieved she finally told me the truth. Just for a moment, I felt like we'd connected like never before, and that meant a lot to me.

Her kindness and this gesture of honesty made me remember that not every day at home was bad. Despite the truth, I didn't care who she was. I still loved her and was glad I had the chance to see her again.

I helped her sit up and drink some water. I looked in her eyes and she looked in mine. Suddenly, I felt really special. I believe she did too. It was as if we were never apart, and never at odds. For that brief tender moment, years of anger and distance meant absolutely nothing. We may not have been blood, but for almost an hour, we were mother and daughter again. It was the most precious gift she could've ever given me before leaving this earth.

Eventually, she fell asleep in my arms. I got up and pulled her blanket up to her neck to keep her warm. Then, I sat in the chair near the bed and watched her rest. She was so peaceful, and as usual, strong; stronger than I could ever be. I could see it took a lot for her to show me a side I'd rarely seen before—her sweet side.

I believe I now understand what she was trying to tell me. In a lot of ways, I feel sorry for her, and I feel terrible about the way I had treated her all this time. I'd been so pig-headed, staying away from the family and not doing everything I could to be an integral part of their lives. As for Mom, we were different in a lot of ways, but at the same time, we were so much alike it was hard to believe she wasn't my biological mother. Honestly, I didn't know what to believe, but in her condition, I don't think she would've lied to me. I had so many questions, but there was no way I was gonna ask. Momma was in such bad shape, it was like I could see her life slowly fading away, and I just wanted her to be at peace, you know?"

Bill came back in to the room. "Hey ladies-"

"Shhh!" I pointed to Mom. "She's asleep," I whispered.

Bill lowered his voice. "Oh, sorry."

"You find Theresa?" I asked.

"Yeah, she's downstairs talking to a friend. I told her you were here. She said she'd be up soon."

"Really?" I asked. "So, she's okay with me being here?"

"Yeah," he replied, looking confused as to why I might ask.

"Well, look, I'm a little beat up. I need a shower and I need to get some rest. Maybe I can come back in the morning. I'll visit with Theresa then. I'm just gonna check into a hotel and-"

"No!" whispered Bill. "Here, take the Mercedes. I'll call and let Maria know you're on the way. You can get cleaned up at the house and then ride back here with us in the morning."

I shook my head. "No, I couldn't-"

"Hey, look at Mom, she's smiling in her sleep," Bill said, pointing.

'I love her so much," I said, smiling right along with her.

"Go to the house Alex ... Mom would want it that way."

"And, what about Theresa?" I asked. "What does she want?"

He sighed, and both his eyebrows went straight up. "Theresa's a big girl. She knows the deal. Look, we got a lot to be thankful for. I can't imagine her having a problem with it. There's plenty of space, and besides she seemed just fine downstairs a few minutes ago when I told her you were up here."

I sat all the way up. "You sure?"

"Give Maria your clothes so she can clean and press them. She'll give you a robe, and I'll have her fix some dinner too. She doesn't speak much English, but she's good. Oh, wait you speak Spanish, don't you?"

"Where's she from?" I asked.

"Guatemala, I think...." Bill handed me his car keys.

"Yeah, I'm a little rusty, but I'm pretty sure I can work with her."

"Oh, and you'll need this for the valet. You got money?"

I took the keys and the parking slip from him. "Yeah, I've got some cash ... I'm good."

I stood up and hugged him. "Thank you, Bill ... I'm serious, thank you for this."

"We're family," he said, "this is how it's supposed to be, right?"

I smiled.

"We'll be back home either tonight or early in the morning, so maybe we can have breakfast together and catch up before we leave again for the hospital."

"Alright, thanks Bill."

"You know your way home?" he asked.

"I think I'm good. I've got your cell phone number if I get lost."

"Never changes," he reminded. "Go home, Alex."

I liked the way he said that, *go home.* He made me feel like I was actually at home, home with my family. I was glad Bill was being so cool even with me being the usual stubborn ass I am. He didn't seem to care about me busting his balls either. In his own way, I think he still loved me.

It had been a long day. I was completely drained. I sped back to the house and Maria let me in through the gate. When I walked in the door, she'd already set me up with a room and just ran me a bubble bath. I got undressed and she took my clothes to clean them. If there's one word to describe Maria, it'd be *fucking awesome.* She had everything set for me like I was some kind of royalty. It felt good.

I soaked my bones for a while and got nice and clean. I don't know what Maria put in that bath water, but I smelled so good and I felt relaxed. I finished bathing, put on the robe she left for me, and then went downstairs to meet her in the kitchen.

I didn't know where the kitchen was, but all I had to do was follow the smell. Maria put together one hell of a late snack—some kind of shrimp and lobster stuff, which was delicious to say the least. We had some nice wine too. Maria was kind enough to eat with me and we chatted for a minute. After we finished, I thanked her for the meal, and then went back upstairs to my room. I was growing more tired with each passing moment. It was time to get some serious rest.

"That's funny I don't remember turning the light off," I said softly. I walked into my room and flipped the light switch on. "Shit, Theresa!" I grabbed my chest. "The fuck you doing sitting here in the dark? You scared the hell outta me ... I thought you were at the hospital anyway ... T...? T...?"

"Aaaahhhh!!!" she screamed, lunging right at me with my gun in her hand. She ran up and pushed me against the wall. "I'm gonna fuckin' kill you bitch!" she yelled, gasping for air and swinging the gun around. She was completely out of breath, but that didn't stop her from pressing that pistol right into my chest.

"It's loaded," I said calmly, "so, put the gun down T, and-"

"You killed my baby you fuckin' whore!" She put her finger on the trigger, gripping it tightly.

"I didn't shoot you!" I snapped.

"FUCKIN' BITCH, I HATE YOU!" she screamed.

"You know what Theresa, if you weren't in my bed, fuckin' my man, your dumbass would've neva got shot. Now put the fuckin' gun down before I do something both of us regret!"

"What is all the screaming about?" yelled Maria, running into the room. One look at the gun and she started screaming too.

Theresa took her eyes off me for a split second, just long enough for me to act. I spun around, grabbing her wrist and pulling her into me to strip the gun away. She started screaming again, slamming her other fist into me one after the other. I turned around and pushed her down on the floor. I wanted to bash her fucking face in, but then I noticed her belly was big and swollen. It looked like she had a basketball stuffed under her shirt. Theresa was pregnant, and from the looks of it, ready to pop any minute.

"YOU'RE GONNA GET YOURS, BITCH!" she yelled, slamming both her hands down on the hardwood floor. "You can stay here if you want tonight. I'm gonna kill you in your fucking sleep!"

"Please, Señora, you must be calm," said Maria, "you stress baby. Come, I help you to your room. I call Señor Bill, no?"

"FUCK YOU MARIA! AND FUCK THIS SCRAGGLY BITCH TOO!" She swatted Maria's hand away. "This is my house I know where the fuck my room is." She pulled herself up and pointed in my face, bobbing her head from side-to-side. "Better sleep wit' yo' fuckin' eyes open, bitch!"

I didn't say a word. I just stood there, my gun down by my side. I watched as Theresa waddled out like a butterball turkey. I took a deep breath and tried to stop my heart from racing.

"I so sorry, Señorita," Maria apologized. "Her hormones you know, baby come soon."

"No se preocúpe por ello."

Maria smiled and lowered her head a little. "Gracias, Señorita," she replied.

"De nada." I locked the door behind Maria, turned off the lights, and walked over to the bed. The moon illuminated every square inch of the room, bathing it in a soft white-blue. I took my robe off and laid it across the foot of the bed. Then, I stuck my gun under my pillow, pulled back the covers and climbed in.

I lay there in the bed, rewinding the situation in my mind. That's when it hit me like a big bag of bricks. My own sister just tried to put me six feet under. I think, deep down inside, that psycho really wanted to kill me. She seemed bitter as hell, but after all the things I'd done for her over the years, versus all the dirt she'd done to me, I just didn't get it.

I pulled my arms from under the covers and held my hands up to the moonlight. They were still shaking. I don't think I was scared—probably more disappointed than anything. I was ready to bring all this to its logical conclusion. I'd been ready for a long time. I thought Theresa was gonna finally put me out of my misery, but I lost hope the minute she stuck my gun to my chest. I sniffed the air in the room several times but couldn't smell a thing. Death was nowhere to be found. I knew the moment she drew down on me Theresa wasn't woman enough to send me to hell. She was always such a coward. That baby would've dropped before she ever pulled the trigger.

When I think of all the situations I been in—all those close calls—I keep coming to the same screwed up conclusion. I've been cursed with immortality, a gift from the incompetents of the world. Everyone hates me and wants me dead. The problem is dumb fucks like Theresa seem to be the only ones up to the task. Unfortunately, they all tend to fail miserably. If you're gonna kill me, just do it and get it over with. Stop all that talky, talky bullshit and pull the trigger. And by all means, don't shoot me in the chest because you just might miss my heart. Just blow my goddamn brains out all over the wall so there's no coming back.

I tried to stop thinking about dying and started concentrating on the next best thing; getting out of that house. As soon as the sun came up, I planned to get my clothes and get the fuck outta there. I'd done what I'd come to do, and it was time to go.

As for my mother, I was getting over her real fast. Sure, she'd been straight with me back at the hospital, but honestly, it was too little too late. For a moment there, I felt extremely close to her, but that small bit of truth after all these years of lies seemed to put even more distance between us.

I had to get the hell away from that goddamn circus act before someone actually got hurt and I got blamed yet again. Speaking of someone being hurt, I was gonna get me some answers the minute my feet touched back down on New York soil, and I knew just who to ask.

I stayed up as long as I could, my eyes fixated on the door, but eventually I dozed off. It was the first time I'd slept for more than fifteen minutes at a time in weeks. As if I didn't have enough problems already, my insomnia was becoming more than just a figment of my imagination, but I managed to sleep off and on throughout the night.

The next morning, I got up early and the first thing I did was track down Maria to get my clothes back. They were starched to perfection. My suit looked brand new. Maria was amazing. I got dressed and called for a cab.

"You come back later?" asked Maria.

I shook my head and smiled. "No, I'm going home now, but thank you for taking care of my mother, Maria … mucho gracias."

"De nada," she replied.

"Tell Bill I said goodbye, okay?"

"Okay, Señorita," she replied. "Bye-bye now."

I snuck out the house, being careful to avoid another incident. Thankfully, my cab was waiting for me when I got down to the gate. I approached the car with caution. I didn't really believe Theresa had the balls to kill me, but you never know. Her fat ass may have been folded up in the back of the cab, waiting on a bitch. Soon as I let my guard down, she'd pop out and stab me with her rusty fork or try and strangle me with some soggy spaghetti noodles. *Fat ass!*

I opened the back door of the cab and took a peek. The coast was clear, so I climbed on in. Before we pulled off, I looked back at the gate, and there Theresa was on the other side in her PJs with her tummy poking out of her robe. She stood there staring at me as if she were plotting my demise with every ounce of hatred in her body.

It's funny, I was able to forgive Theresa for her treachery, but she couldn't find a way in her little pea brain to accept the fact I didn't attack her. Why on earth would I shoot my own sister in the chest? Just what kind of woman threatens her family's life? Then again, what kind of a woman gets knocked up by her sister's man? When I frame it like that, I can see exactly where she's coming from. People always think you'll do to them what they're more than willing to do to you without batting an eye.

"Where to, Miss?" asked the driver.

"Airport. And, I'm kinda in a hurry."

"You got it," he replied.

He drove me straight to the airport—no stops—just like I asked. He dropped me off right in front of the American Airlines terminal. I paid him and then did my thing, you know, badge-flashing, cutting through the ticket line and security checkpoints. If you didn't know any better, you would've thought it was a national emergency the way I rolled up through there. I paid for a one-way ticket back to New York and boarded the plane a few hours later. Bill called my cell several times, but I just ignored him. I'd had enough drama to last the rest of the week. I was going home.

Chapter 2

I called Tony from my cell as soon as I got off the plane at JFK. He didn't answer, so I called a few more times as I made my way through the terminal and out to the parking deck. When I got to the car, he finally answered.

"FBI, Crane."

"Tony, it's me."

"Alex, what the hell happened? I thought you were going to call me once you got down to Atlanta. I was worried."

"I'm fine, Tony. Look, I just need some time to-"

"Alex," he interrupted, "meet me somewhere, so we can talk ... you think you can do that?"

After all that had gone down, I was beat. I didn't even care about trying to get Tony to fess up to lying just like my mom and dad— and evidently David too. "It's been a long day, Tony," I replied. "I'm tired."

"It's important," he replied.

"I don't know, I-"

Tony said, "Look it'll just take a few minutes ... tell you what, I can pick you up from the airport and we'll go over together."

I was quiet for a minute.

"Alex...?"

"No, I've got my car. What's the address?"

"55 Wall Street," Tony responded. "Just go in and tell the door man who you are, and he'll tell you where to go, alright?"

"Wall Street...? Tony, what's this about, I don't have time for-"

"Look Alex, I can't talk about it right now I've got some people in my office. Just meet me there in say two hours, got it?"

"Fine. I'll be there." I hung up. I'd been on planet earth long enough to know where Wall Street was. But I was tired and the last thing I wanted to do was go all the way up to the Financial District. At the same time, I was so pissed with Tony I was compelled to go. Tony's punk ass knew what was going on. I ain't no fool. All these years he been hovering around. It's like David told me before he died, he, Tony, and my dad were all tight, so something like this ... Wait ... this means I really am a bastard child ... hmm ... bygones. Anyhow, like I was saying, Tony and them were all tight, so you mean to tell me he didn't know about my real mother? I don't buy it for a second. One way or another I'm gonna get me some answers.

And, just like that, I was fired up again. I drove out to the lot cashier and paid my parking bill. Then, I left JFK and took the Van Wyck Expressway towards New York. It was late, but traffic was still heavy. I jumped off on the Long Island Expressway, and then took the Brooklyn Bridge and merged onto Park Row. I turned off Park Row onto Broadway and made a left onto Wall Street. The place Tony was talking about was on the left, the Cipriani Club Residences.

"Dayum!" I shouted, gazing up at the building.

I pulled into the parking garage, parked in a visitor spot in front of the gate, and got out.

"I'm early," I said softly.

I didn't want to hang out in the garage, so I took the elevator up to the lobby. Honestly, I didn't know why Tony wanted to meet there, but it was nice as hell inside like one of those fancy apartment buildings you see in the movies. I casually walked over to the man behind the desk.

"Miss Southerland?" he greeted.

I cocked my head to the side and raised an eyebrow. "Uh, yes...?"

"It's an honor to finally meet you. Here...." He opened a drawer and started rummaging through it. He took out a key and handed it to me.

"Seventh floor," he said.

"I don't-"

"705," he interrupted, "just take the elevator up, you can't miss it. Name's Ralph. You need anything, anything at all, you let me know."

"Okay...? Thanks Ralph."

I have to admit, I was a little confused. Ralph already seemed to know who I was as if he'd been expecting me. Maybe Tony called him or something though. No matter what was actually going on, it was New York, so there was no telling what Tony had gotten me into. Maybe he's really the mob playing FBI. *Imagine that.*

I followed Ralph's directions and went up to apartment number 705. I looked in both directions down the hall and then tried the door, which surprisingly was already unlocked. I drew my gun and pushed the door open, creeping inside the apartment slowly and cautiously.

The bedroom was directly across from the entryway. I peeked in, and then looked down the hall where I saw the shadow of a man. Someone beat me there, and I doubted seriously if it was Tony. He never moves that fast. I pointed my gun straight ahead and slowly walked into the kitchen area.

"You planning to use that?" Tony asked with his hands in the air.

"Depends...."

"On what?" he asked.

"On your answers to my questions," I retorted cleverly.

"Come on Alex, put the gun away."

I sighed and holstered my weapon as I walked over to the sofa. I sat down, leaned back and crossed my legs. "Did you know, Tony?" I asked.

He walked over and sat next to me. "Listen Alex, I-"

"Did you know about my mother?" I asked slowly.

"It's complicated," he replied.

"What's the complication? It's a simple question." I looked him dead in the eye. "Did you know she was not my mother?"

He dropped his head. "Alex, your dad-"

"OH GOD, YOU'RE SO FULL OF SHIT, TONY!" I yelled.

"You gonna let me talk or what?" he asked in a frustrated tone.

"FUCK YOU, TONY!"

"Your dad didn't want you to know. I'm sorry, but that's the way he wanted it. He didn't want you to be hurt. Your real mother's been dead for a long time. There was nothing any of us could have done about it."

"ONE OF YOU ASSHOLES SHOULD'VE TOLD ME!" I exclaimed.

"Told you what...? That he cheated on his wife with a model and a drug addict who overdosed on heroine? Now, how do you think that would've gone over?"

"It would've gone over like the goddamn truth, Tony!"

"Alex, I'm sorry if you think it was wrong, but he ... we did what we thought was best for you ... to protect you."

"Fuck you and fuck him too!" I shot him a bird. "You treat me like some little frail girl that can't fend for herself. In case you haven't noticed, Tony, I'm a grown woman. Hell, you could've told me this shit before I went all the way down to Atlanta, wasting my goddamn time with those people."

"If I had, you and I both know you wouldn't have gone, and you needed to see your family-"

"They ain't my family, Tony!"

He smiled. "Sure, they are Alex. Look, it doesn't matter who gave birth to you. Your family is who you love ... do you love them?"

I closed my eyes for a few seconds. "Yes."

"Then, I hope you understand why I did what I did."

I looked around the room. The apartment was small, but it was nicer than anything I'd seen in the city. The kitchen was over to the left where I first walked in, and there was a nice table set near the back wall. On my right were two big windows, and straight across from me was a nice shelf with a boat load of drawers. The place was extremely well decorated.

"What are we doing here, Tony, and how'd that Ralph guy downstairs know my name? You told him I was coming or something?"

"He knows this is your place," Tony replied.

"Look, I'm really tired," I stood up, shaking my head, "and I don't have time for this shit ... I'm going home."

He jumped up and blocked my path. "I'm serious," he said, chuckling.

I rolled my eyes. "Tony, what the fuck are you talking about? Look, I'm just gonna go 'cause you're obviously smoking something."

He laughed. "No, look sit down, okay...? Come on, have a seat."

I stepped back over to the sofa and sat down again.

"Yesterday you told me you were having some money trouble."

"No, I told you I was broke ... and I am. What can I say? The trip down to Atlanta set me back a little."

He looked completely disgusted. I smirked at him and crossed my arms to keep my middle finger reflex locked down.

"What are you making now, about seventy, seventy-five?" he asked.

"What's your point, Tony?"

"My point is what the hell are you doing with your money?"

"Truthfully?"

Tony's eyebrows shot up. "Please."

"Well, I have an expensive, shitty apartment, my raggedy-ass BMW keeps falling apart, I can't stop buying clothes, oh, and I also happen to be a fuckin' alcoholic. Those are just the highlights."

He shook his head. "Jesus Alex, you've gotta cut your spending back."

"Tony, I love you, and you're the boss's boss, but unless you plan on giving me a suitcase full of cash, please keep your big nose outta my business. How I spend my money is my-"

"LOOK SMARTASS, I'M TRYING TO HELP YOU!" Tony exclaimed. "Christ, you're just like your father. Here's the deal, your dad spent a fortune on life insurance ... I guess it was just one of his things ... nevertheless it's what he did."

"So what? My mother took all the life insurance money when he died."

"Not all of it," he said, "he left some to David. We took the money, invested it, and I've been managing it for the past 15 or so years."

"So, what exactly are you saying, Tony?" I was starting to get excited.

"Well, I don't want you to get all amped up and go crazy, but you've got quite a bit saved up. I'll give you the account information."

"Oh, well thanks for clearing that up for me!" I exclaimed sarcastically. "I guess this apartment's mine too, huh? Tony, you're such a joker ... who put you up to this? Dom? It's a trick, right?"

"No, I'm not joking," he responded in the most serious of tones. "We've put aside somewhere around $300,000 a year in discretionary funds. That puts your spending account at about $4.5 million, well minus this apartment. We bought the apartment last year ... purchase price was around $1.5 million, so I think right now, you've got around $3 million liquid."

"STOP LYING!" By then I was on the edge of my seat. "HOW THE FUCK YOU-"

"I can't take all the credit," Tony confessed. "You've got a really good financial advisor and investment banker. Our investments have grown steady over the years. I don't really know what's in the portfolio because I lost track of it, but everything's set up in your name. I've had power of attorney, but I can relinquish it at this point. The apartment's yours and so's the money. If I knew you were having trouble, I would've done this sooner, but I was under the impression everything was okay. Why didn't you say something?"

"I didn't want to bother you with it...." I stood up and walked around the apartment in disbelief. Tony followed me. The more I looked around, the giddier I got.

"This has gotta be a joke man. You fuckin' with me?"

"Nope it's all yours. You have your dad to thank for this."

I went into the bedroom and sat down on the bed. Then, I laid back and started crying a little. "I miss him, Tony ... David too."

He sat down on the edge of the bed and put his hand on my knee. "I miss him too, kid," he confessed.

I smiled. "David used to call me kid all the time."

"He was a good man," said Tony, "and, he was a great friend to a whole lot of people who didn't deserve it ... people like me. Sometimes I wonder-"

"Don't say it ... I don't wanna think about it right now ... today's a good day." I wiped my tears and changed the subject. "My goodness, Tony, the Financial District...? What on earth were you thinking, man?"

He chuckled softly. "Well, I didn't exactly pick the place," he confessed. "Your investment banker claimed it was a solid purchase, so we went for it. Personally, I would've put you in Harlem so you could get back in touch with your roots." He laughed a little, poking fun at me.

I smiled and shot him another bird. "Fuck you very much, sir! I'm way blacker than a lot of real black folks."

"All the floors are mahogany," he said, laughing. "You've got the high ceilings—I think they're 22 foot, oh and there's a fitness center, library, spa, and a bar downstairs ... I'm sure I know where to find you if I need you."

Without hesitation, I punched him in the arm, and we both laughed.

"I mean seriously man, is this real?" I asked.

"You're killing me, Alex. I'm not going to answer that. Let's talk about something else...." He pulled my ID out of his pocket and laid it on the bed.

I got up and walked over to the window.

"You can't quit," said Tony, "your father didn't raise a quitter."

I sighed. "I'm tired."

"Yeah, but you're not retired, Alex. Listen, we're all tired of having to fight the bureaucracy, but you and I got work to do."

"And...?"

"And, what would David do?" he asked.

"That's hitting below the belt, Tony," I said, peeking out at the city through the blinds.

"Look Alex, Johnson transferred to Miami last week. That leaves your team a man short. OPR's cleared you for duty, and I need a new ASAC."

I spun around. "No shit? Seriously?"

Tony nodded. "I never joke about promotions. So, what's the deal? You going back down to Atlanta for your mother's funeral?"

I rolled my eyes. "Well, she ain't gone yet, but I'll send flowers when the time comes."

"Give Ralph the address. He'll take care of it for you."

"Really?" I asked.

"Yep," he replied. "So, what's the deal, you coming back or what?"

"ASAC, huh?"

"That's right ... Alpha Team. You'll run the show on K&R, and report directly to me."

"And, I get to pick my cases?" I asked.

He frowned. "Hey, don't push it!"

"Okay, okay..."

"So?" He put his hands up.

"Hmm, let me think ... um...."

Tony grabbed a small throw-pillow and hurled it at me.

"Okay, I'll come back," I giggled, "on one condition...."

"Anything," he said.

"Keep those OPR bastards off my back and get that letter out of my file."

Tony sighed. "I tell you what. You start behaving ... be a little more diplomatic and keep a low profile, and I'll see what I can do. How's that?"

"I can work witcha," I replied. "So, how does this whole money thing go down?"

"However you want it to," said Tony. "It's yours. Just don't spend it all in a day. You're having trouble with the BMW, so get a newer one and get some clothes if you need to, but keep it simple, alright? No point in drawing undue attention to yourself, especially at the office. Go ahead and move your stuff in if you want, and I'll send over your banking information."

"Thank you, Tony!" I walked over, wrapped my arms around his waist and gave him a big teddy bear hug.

"I told you if you needed something to come to me first, remember?" He squeezed me tight.

"I'm sorry ... I just didn't want to bother you with all my bullshit."

"You gonna be alright?" he asked.

"Yeah, what about you? You need a loan?" I laughed loudly.

"Not exactly," he said, chuckling a bit. "I've been pulling a management fee, so I've got something stashed away."

I tugged at his suit lapel. "That explains a lot Mr. G.Q."

"Do me a favor," he said, "just keep all this to yourself. I've got enough to deal with as is. Best thing to do is act like you don't even have any money. Don't flaunt your wealth. I assure you it'll save you a whole lot of trouble in the long run. Listen, I'm about to go, so make sure you lockup."

"Yes, Sir!" I saluted him. We laughed one last time, and then I walked him to the door.

Tony stopped short on his way out. "Oh, and kid?"

"Yeah?"

"Try to stay out of trouble," he reminded.

"God, does everybody think I'm a trouble maker?"

"Well-"

"Hey, don't answer that, man!" I smiled big. "I'll see you next Monday."

"Enjoy the apartment. I'll talk to you later."

I closed the door and locked the dead bolt. Honestly, I didn't know what to say. I was speechless. I felt like a millionaire—wait, I was a millionaire— BWAAHAAHAAHAA. I couldn't believe it. I ran around the apartment from room to room, jumping up and down on the sofa and bed, screaming like an adolescent. I even opened a window and screamed at the top of my lungs, "I'M RICH MOTHAFUCKAS!"

After a few more yells, screams and cartwheels, I finally calmed down and got settled in. I took off all my clothes and jumped right into bed, grinning like a little girl on

Christmas morning. After all the bullshit I'd been dealing with since David died, that was one of the happiest days of my life. I stretched across the bed and lost myself in that big pillow-top mattress. By then, I'd totally forgotten about all the problems I left behind in Atlanta. My life was definitely looking up.

Chapter 3

I said it before, and I'll say it again; Tony is a man of his word. He said I'd get my package the next day, and I did. It came right on time. Inside were checks, an American Express Black Card—whatever that is—plus cash and a bunch of banking paperwork. Turns out, Tony and the crew set up some kind of holding company in my name. I didn't understand how all of it worked, but honestly, I didn't care. I had plenty of time to learn about stocks and stuff like that later; much later. All I needed to know was how much I had to spend. Besides, I had betta fish to fry.

Speaking of frying, I wanted so desperately to put a nickel in that rusty piece of shit BMW and roll it off a cliff. Don't get me wrong now, I was in a much better mood than before, but watching that heap of Euro-trash go up in flames would be the icing on one fine, tasty cake.

However, to my insurance agent's presumed delight, I finally came to my senses and decided to let the BMW live another day. Still, I couldn't keep bumming around in that thing. I needed a new ride and bad, so I got dressed and marched out of the apartment with a plan. I was gonna catch a cab down to a local dealer and roll back in something off the showroom floor. I took the elevator down to the lobby and walked up to Ralph.

"Miss Southerland how are you today?" he asked.

"Fine Ralph, call me Alex."

"Thank you, Alex," he replied. "What can I do for you?"

"I need a new car," I said, smiling a big toothy grin.

"What are you looking for?" he asked.

"Something sporty."

"Well, how about a BMW, they're-"

"Ralph, no! No BMWs," I said, shaking my head. "I said sporty, not sorry."

He laughed. "Okay, okay Alex, how about-"

"Ooh, James Bond," I interrupted. "You see the Bond movies?"

"Yes," said Ralph.

"What's the car he drives in those movies?"

Ralph laughed hard. "He drove a BMW in-"

"RALPH!"

"I'm just teasing ... well, he had a Lotus back in the 80's ... that's sporty."

"No, I don't want a little boxy thing...." I played with my hair and thought hard. "What's the other one, the old looking silver car?"

Ralph smiled. "Oh ... yes, I think you're talking about the Aston Martin."

I made double six-shooters with my hands and pointed them at him. "Yeah that's it! With the little wings?"

He nodded. "I believe so. Tell you what, I'll call Aston Martin in Long Island and have them bring a few cars over."

"You can do that?" I asked.

"Absolutely, Alex."

"Ralph, you're awesome! I'll be around for the next few days pretty much all day long, so can you just give me a call whenever they come?"

"Sure, I'll call you once they arrive."

I went back up and just enjoyed my new crib. By then I'd forgotten all about my old apartment. I was living in luxury for sure. Somewhere in my mind, it was like I'd always lived there though—like I was supposed to be there. I don't mean that in an arrogant way either. I guess I'm just saying it felt right. I felt right. You'd be amazed what moving into a decent place and getting a new car will do to a gal. I was in a real good space.

I figured it'd take a few days to get the car thing sorted out, but much to my surprise, three hours later and here come Ralph calling me down to the parking garage. He was down there chatting up a representative from the dealership. And, get this; the man brought three different cars with him. Talk about customer service. I walked up to them and smiled.

"Miss Southerland, I'm Ira, how are you?" asked the man wearing a shiny suit with, standing with Ralph. He had a British accent.

We shook hands. "I'm fine, call me Alex."

He smiled. "Alex, I understand you're looking for a quality vehicle."

"I am."

"You need anything else from me?" asked Ralph.

"No," I replied. "Thanks for your help though man, you're the best."

Ralph smiled his perfect smile, and then headed back to the elevator.

I immediately turned my attention to the cars. I walked slowly around them looking closely at every little detail. The two other drivers that came with Ira stepped out of their vehicles and held the door open for me.

"That's a DB9," Ira said. "Carbon black, V-12."

"Is it fast?" I asked.

"Fast, but luxurious as well," he boasted.

"I need the fastest ... what about that one?"

"Yes, that's a V-8 Vanquish."

I said, "It's cute... how much is it?"

"Oh, don't worry about it."

I rolled my eyes. "No seriously, how much?"

"A little over a hundred."

"Thousand?"

"Yes. The DB9 over there is around one-ninety."

"And, what about the one on the right?"

"Ah, the DBS," Ira responded. "It's completely new, V-12, 510 horsepower ... it's the 5th made out of a scheduled 300 for release in a couple of years. It will be featured in an upcoming James Bond movie. This one's about 260."

"Dude! That's over a quarter of a million! Will it pinch my nipples for me?"

I thought Ira was gonna bust a gut laughing at me. "I don't think so," he replied trying desperately to regain his fine, British composure, "but, it has some very nice features." He opened the door. "This is somewhat of a rough and rugged sports car, but it is still quite elegant. Of course, it has very unique styling both inside and out. As you can see, it has large wheels and brakes with carbon ceramic cross-drilled rotors, so you have quite a bit of stopping power. It comes with a six-speed manual transmission and does zero to 60 in about four seconds. Top-speed is approximately 190, and of course it is fully loaded. I think you'll find the interior exquisite. Please, have a seat."

I bent down to have a look inside. The leather around the dashboard was stitched perfectly. It looked like a goddamn Coach bag. The shift gear knob was silver and so were all the other accents throughout the interior. The seats were like Recaro or something—shit I don't know—basically, that car was totally ridiculous.

"Ira, did you know there's a fire extinguisher back there?" I asked.

"Well, it's an extremely powerful vehicle," replied Ira. "You can never have too many safety features."

I sat down and pushed back into the driver seat, gripping the steering wheel and rolling my wrists up and down. "So, you're saying it's not in production yet?"

"No, this one came over as a demo. It was a favor to me, but I'd be more than happy to sell it to you. Now, it's a little tricky to start. I assume you can operate a manual transmission?"

I frowned.

Ira laughed a little. "Good. Now, this one is not like the older shiftless transmissions, which is a good thing because the software never really performed at its best. This model has a standard clutch with a stick in the floor. You have six forward gears. Reverse is all the way to the left and up. To start the motor, you want to have the clutch down, put the key into the ignition, and turn it to the on position. You're going to get a ready light on the key ... press the start button and you're good to go. To stop the motor, just turn the key back and remove it."

"Oh, wow, so you're actually gonna let me drive it?"

"I'll do you one better," said Ira. "Keep it till Saturday. If you like it, I'll send over the paperwork. If not, then we'll try one of the others. You seemed to prefer the DB9 over the V-8 Vanquish. Am I right?"

"Yes, I think so. Yeah, I like the big one." I stood up out of the car and closed the door. "Wait ... you know what ... maybe that's not such a good idea. I mean, I probably shouldn't spend this kind of money." I shoved the key back in his hand.

"Let me ask you something, Alex...."

"Yes Ira?"

"If you could afford to treat yourself to this car, would you?"

I cocked my head to the side. "This is a trick question isn't it?"

Ira held the key up. I smiled really big and took it from him.

"Here's my business card," he said, slipping it into the palm of my hand like a smooth operator. "Call me if you have any questions."

"And, what if I wreck the car?"

He grinned. "We'll get another one for you. They'll have more ready soon."

I burst out laughing. "Ira, you're too much—we'll get another one—good grief man!"

"Okay...?"

"Wait, you're serious?" I asked.

"Alex, I never joke about cars." He gave me one last firm handshake. "Enjoy it ... gentlemen!" He gave a swift nod, and he and the guys loaded up in the other cars and rolled out.

"THESE MOTHAFUCKAS ARE OUT THEIR MINDS!" I shouted. "HOLY SHIT!"

I opened the door again and sat down in the driver seat. I stepped on the clutch and put the key in, turning it forward. It lit up bright red. I took a deep breath and then pressed the start button. I didn't know what to expect, but that car was unbelievable. When the motor started, it was quiet as a church mouse, but when I tapped the gas, it felt like the ground was opening up around me. I had to take that baby for a spin.

I slid both arms into the seatbelt harnesses and buckled up. Then, I shifted into first gear. Everything about that ride was hot, but the dashboard setup was kinda weird. The speedometer was normal, meaning the needle moved clockwise, but the tachometer went in the opposite direction. I'd never seen a layout like that before. I figured it was gonna be irritating for a second, but truthfully, I didn't give a damn how the dials were set up. That car was hot like freeway sex in the HOV lane. It was seriously crazy. Man, after shredding my 89 5.0 Mustang years back, I never thought I'd be driving an exotic fly-ass Aston Martin like that. She was just as tight as my Stang too—glossy, black on black and plenty of power only the DBS was like a fuckin' space ship inside, which definitely bumped it up a notch or two in my book.

After a few minutes, the low decibel rumble from the ample V-12 motor was beginning to get to me. I couldn't wait any longer. I had to put her out on the road where she belonged.

I was already in first gear, so I eased out of the clutch until the car started rolling forward. The big twenty-inch wheels squeaked through the garage as I pulled around to the exit and stopped. I looked both ways to make sure it was clear, tapped the gas a few times and popped the clutch, spinning the wheel to the right. I almost came up out of my seat trying to hold on as I burned out of the parking garage onto Wall Street. I ran first gear out and then slammed into second. The rear wheels chirped as the car lunged forward. I don't know how fast I was going, but it was damn sure fast. I had the pedal to the metal and was aching for a long stretch of road as I started daydreaming about-

"OH SHIT!" I slammed on the brakes and came to a screeching halt just a few feet away from an endless sea of gridlocked traffic.

"FUCKING NEW YORK!" I yelled, as if anyone could actually hear me. The cockpit for the most part was soundproof.

I laid down on the horn. I wasn't exactly committed to the honk, I just wanted unsuspecting motorists to look in their rearview and picture a sexy bitch like me behind the wheel of a $260,000 car.

"Don't hate the playa, hate the game baby!" I said laughing out loud. I was on a serious high.

But then, I spent the next hour driving around the city mostly in first gear. The traffic was extremely frustrating, but eventually I was able to get her up to fourth gear on the Brooklyn Bridge. I was passing people like they were standing still. It felt like I was dreaming—like I'd wake up any minute back in my old apartment trying to pour coolant in that goddamn piece of shit BMW in a foot of snow. All of this was just so sudden it was wild to me. And, I couldn't believe how that salesman from the dealership was acting either. I guess I draw a lot of water 'round these parts. *Sorry, but I don't get to use phrases like that often.*

I kept rolling around, but then finally got fed up with all the traffic and decided to head home. I drove back to the apartment and carefully parked my new DBS in the garage. I almost felt nervous about leaving it down there until I looked around and realized I was at the bottom of the totem pole. Somebody had an eggshell white Rolls Royce Phantom parked over in the corner. Heaven knows what that thing cost, but you can bet it's more than a quarter-mill.

I didn't go upstairs. I had my little Black card in my back pocket, so I got Ralph to hail me a cab and I went straight to Saks Fifth Ave—no stops. I looked like a bum, but the folks in Saks didn't seem to care. I guess they can smell money a mile away. They were so helpful. I picked up some new suits, dresses, oh and a shitload of shoes. To date, men have not been able to reconcile in their feeble minds the link between woman and shoe. Because I am a humanist, and I want to help my brothers as much as possible, that day I set out to document the intricacies of the direct correlations between girl and shoe, one receipt at a time. Right there, sitting in that store, I tried on shoe after shoe, discovering the mythical power of designer footwear, and I never looked back. Say whatever you want, but shoes make or break the woman.

I've always liked nice shoes, but suddenly, I had a new fetish and a wide range of designer options—Manolo Blahniks, Gucci, Stuart Weitzman, oh my. I had them pack everything up and I handed the girl my new credit card. I didn't know how much all that shit cost and for the first time ever, I didn't care. I'd been depressed enough to drive into a lake. As it turns out, spending truckloads of cash was the only therapy I needed. The evil OPR snow queen Cross told me to come back to work with a new attitude, and I was convinced shopping like a rock star was the best way to make that happen.

Back at the apartment, Ralph had a few guys help me lug everything upstairs. Then, I found a use for my old dented up, barely running BMW—a grocery store run. I ran back out and picked up everything I needed from toothpaste to food and of course a boatload of liquor to keep the demons at bay. I'm not kidding either—alcohol is a viable solution.

With all my running up and down, I thought Ralph might be getting tired of my black ass, but he helped me with my groceries and was just as pleasant and helpful as the first time we met. Ralph was the man.

Just as soon as I finally got settled in, Bill called my cell phone for the 50th time. I finally answered in an aggravated tone.

"Hello!"

"Alex...?"

I sighed. "Yeah, hey Bill."

"What happened?" he asked.

"Nothing ... I ... I got an emergency call from work and had to fly out early," I lied.

"Well, I hope everything's alright," he said.

"It will be soon," I snapped.

"Good. Yeah, Theresa asked about you."

"Did she now?"

Bill was silent for a second. "Yeah, she-"

"Well, I hope she's okay with the baby and all." It was hard for me to say that without completely twisting myself inside out.

"You're gonna be back down for the funeral, right?" asked Bill.

"Funeral...?"

"Oh dang, I'm sorry Alex, my mind is moving a thousand miles per hour ... you didn't get my message?"

"No, I haven't checked messages yet. Did she-"

"She's gone, Alex," he said, "she passed away earlier this morning."

I was quiet for a moment. I wasn't sure whether to be angry, sad or happy. Sad seemed to be the right emotion, but oddly enough, I didn't feel sad at all. I wanted to be angry, but I couldn't be pissed with her either. Maybe I was just happy. I mean, obviously she'd suffered quite a bit, and no matter how I felt about the way she treated me, no one deserved her fate.

Bill asked, "Alex, you there...? Hey, Alex...?"

"I'm still here."

"Are you okay?" he asked.

"Yeah, I'm fine ... hey, look, don't, don't worry about me ... I'm ... I'm alright."

"Listen, I know you may be tied up at work," said Bill, "but I think it'd mean a lot if you were here ... you think you can catch a flight back tonight?"

"No, it'd probably be better for everyone if I stayed here Bill. But, get me the funeral home information, and I'll send something down."

He was quiet for a moment. "I guess I don't understand why you just don't-"

"Bill...."

"Yeah...? What?"

"How long were we together?"

He replied, "All our life it-"

"Most of our life," I reminded. By then, the bitch in me was oozing to the surface. "Before you fucked my sister, who, by the way, would prefer me dead despite your delusions—and don't gimmie any of that we are the world horse shit either. Before then ... before you stuck your cock up in her pussy OVER AND OVER AGAIN BEHIND MY BACK, you and I were running on the same frequency. Remember that?" After I said that, Bill got really quiet.

"Yeah, that's what I thought. So, when I tell you I got good reason not to be there, you should just respect my wishes and drop it. You at least owe me that ... wouldn't you say so?"

"Yes. I respect your position, but I wish you would reconsider. I'll send you the information you need and-"

"EXCELLENT, HAVE A GOODIN!" I was just about to hang up on him.

"Wait, Alex...?"

"What?" He was really irritating me by then.

"I know I can't change what happened," Bill said, "but, please don't shut us out. You may hate me, and I don't even know what's going on between you and Theresa right now, but my child needs an aunt, and Christopher needs his big sister."

I sighed. "Chris already has his big sister ... and a big happy home far as I could tell."

"No, he doesn't have his oldest sister, and you know what I'm talking about, so stop being difficult. Just give it some thought." He sighed heavily. "I'm not going to call you except to maybe let Chris leave a message or something like that. He's doing well in school nowadays and he's always asking about you. I'm not going to change my phone number, so you can call anytime ... listen, I want you to be safe up there, and please talk to your brother. It's been too long. He remembers you, and he misses you like crazy ... we all do."

When he said that, I just hung up on him. Aside from sticking his dick in that cow-whore I call a sister, Bill was always reasonable. He always made sense to me. In a lot of ways, I needed him in my life, but I was still bitter as hell when it came to him. He was the only man I'd given the keys to my heart, and he walked all over me, just like my mother. Yeah, I wasn't sad she died. We were closer the night back in the hospital than we'd been the entire time we lived together. Still, not being around my family was becoming more than I could bear. Being away from Bill, Chris and even Theresa, it was tearing me apart. Maybe now that momma's gone, things will get better. Who knows?

I fixed myself a cocktail, which I mean was literally a cocktail. Basically, I just poured drink after drink of whatever I could find in the same glass until I settled down with a bottle of my favorite in the bunch. I dimmed the lights and climbed deeper into my dark pit, desperately looking for a way to cope with the pain from the huge barrier between me and the people I love. Halfway on my journey from insane to drunk outta my mind, I started to resent my mother again, but for a whole new reason. She took me away from my brother and sister, and I still believe she had a hand in Bill fucking Theresa behind my back. What's worse is she did nothing to try and fix all that before she died. Everything was just one big mess. I felt so heartbroken. All I could do was drink myself towards a soothing loss of consciousness that only hard liquor could bring about. Drinking was the one thing I was still really good at, and I was sticking to it.

That night, I fell asleep in a chair in the living room, still gripping the bottle of scotch I'd polished off without breaking a sweat. I was out like a light bulb, and I'd drunk enough to forget all my woes—at least for the night.

Chapter 4

It's very possible, with the amount of booze I consumed, I dipped into a coma at some point through the night. When I finally woke the next day, I felt like I'd been sleeping in a greenhouse. I was sweaty all over. It was one o'clock in the afternoon, and the sun was shining bright through the big open windows in the living room. If I didn't know better, I would've thought little elves had been working in my mouth all night, building a castle with big blocks of dry ice. I felt super dehydrated. As soon as I stood up, the urge to pee hit me and I had to go like never before. There was only one bathroom in the apartment, and it was all the way in the back past the bedroom. I was so desperate to go, I looked over at the kitchen sink for a second, but then I quickly came to my senses.

My roommate in college used to pee in the sink. She was a filthy bitch. After drinking all night, she'd pass out naked on the floor. The next morning, she'd jump up, running to the sink with pee streaming down her legs. I was shampooing my side of that carpet every week. That girl was strange, but she knew how to party her ass off. Needless to say, there was no way I was gonna bring myself down to her level, so I pulled it together and sprinted down the hall.

For a second there, I was afraid I couldn't hold it long enough, but I managed to get my panties down and hop on the toilet just in the nick of time; a trick I'd come to master over the years. As one who habitually exceeds normal social drinking limits, the secret to holding your water is to make sure you don't think about how hung-over you feel, and never ever think of anything funny because that'll be all she wrote. Just act like a lifeless zombie, only one that runs really, really fast.

I sat there on the toilet with my head down. The room was spinning, and I felt woozy. All I could think about was how I planned to start planning to plan to stop drinking one day before I die. With the way I felt, I knew I'd be committed to that plan in no time, and it'd last forever or at least until nighttime.

After I finished peeing and lying to myself, I washed up and stumbled into the kitchen to make coffee and nothing else—no more booze. Anyway, whoever designed my apartment was a certified genius. That or they somehow knew I'd watch TV in every room. Just my luck, there was a 60-inch Phillips plasma in the living room and a little matching 30-inch in the kitchen next to the table. I desperately needed coffee, but it was taking way too long to brew, so I did what I had to do ... I had a shot of bourbon to tide me over. I needed to ignore the fact I'd just broken a promise I made to myself less than five minutes ago, so I switched on the small TV. I turned straight to CNN and watched the news while I tried to screw my head back in place. Just my luck, I started watching right in the middle of a breaking news report of another kidnapping.

"...Again, there have been no ransom demands, but our sources confirm Charles Miller, son of New York City District Attorney, Janice Miller, has been kidnapped. Charles, who also responds to Chip, was last seen wearing a baseball cap, red t-shirt and blue jeans. In recent news, Miller announced she was working to build a case against Kaamil Qalat, leader of an Islamic extremist group believed to have been responsible for a number of foiled terrorist attacks in Brooklyn. Though Qalat maintains his innocence, it's quite clear there is a connection between this kidnapping and the ongoing trial. D.A. Miller was unavailable for comment, but her assistant told us Miller will make a statement in a press conference scheduled later today. This is Craig Mitchem, reporting live from City Hall."

Coffee was finally ready, so I turned the TV off, and not a moment too soon. Just thinking about that mess-to-be was bugging me out. I didn't see any good end to that scenario 'because Miller was the special kind of asshole any sane person could do without. Hell, I'd just gotten promoted, so why let her get me fired? *I hate it for the unlucky bastard who gets that case.* Of course, I was sorry to hear her son was missing, but I worked with Miller before, and getting her to climb off her high horse was like trying to push a two-ton bull around with gobs of Vaseline on the sole of your shoes. It just ain't happening.

I grabbed the phone and called my new money manager, Josh Goldman, the man behind the fancy paperwork. Obviously, he was Jewish, but I sure as hell wasn't complaining. See, I got this standard rule in life— you need good food, fly clothes, the low-low on some electronics, go see a brotha. But, if you need a diamond, a money man, or good attorney, do yourself a favor and hook up with a smart-looking Jew. Yes, I said it. Now, do I sound like a racist, insensitive idiot? Why, yes, yes I do ... and, I'll do it again, and again, and again. You can think whatever you want about me, but you've been warned by a woman who's escaped disaster, more than the law should allow with my smart-looking Jew-lawyer by my side. The life you save may be your own--I'm just sayin'. I grabbed the phone and gave Mr. Goldman a ring.

"Josh Goldman," he answered.

"Josh, Alex Southerland, I'm-"

"Ah yes, it's good to finally meet you, even if it's over the phone. How are things going?"

"Just fine Josh, may I call you Josh?"

"Yes, you may," he replied.

"Good. Josh, Tony Crane just gave me access to my accounts, and-"

"Excellent," he interrupted. "I trust you're happy with our investment strategy?"

"Well, honestly, I don't know ... I mean, I wanna be straight with you Josh I'm not a wiz at finances, I just want some basic idea of how all this works."

"Alex, it's simple. I've spent the past ten years working your portfolio. My predecessor did a good job, but he wasn't as aggressive as he could have been in certain areas. When I was hired by Mr. Crane and Mr. Chandler, rest his soul, they gave me specific goals. Basically, I work every single day to make sure we meet those goals. As long as I'm on the job, you don't ever have to worry about all that stuff. Here's how it works for you ... you have your accounts, which are all discretionary accounts. I divide about five-hundred thousand dollars between them and the holding company that has majority share in approximately eight businesses. For all intents and purposes, you own those businesses. Collectively, they generate approximately 25 million annually, which is reinvested in the businesses or the stock market. You follow me so far?"

"I think so."

Josh continued explaining, "With dividends and discretionary allocations, it leaves you with about $300,000 a year to spend. We've allowed some carry over, so you've built up about $3.5 million in liquid assets and you have an apartment now worth about $1.5 million ... uh, did Mr. Crane tell you about that too?"

"Yes, I'm staying here now."

"Excellent!" Josh said. "The short story is, I'm your financial manager, not your boss, so you spend as you see fit, but I ask that you alert me of any expense over $50,000-"

"Well, if it's my money, why do you need to know what I buy?" I asked.

"Good point," he responded, "but anything you buy of significance should be negotiated. We can do some tradeoffs to make sure we keep the majority of your liquid assets intact."

"Oh, shit ... I mean, shit, I'm sorry, Josh." I giggled a little.

"What's the matter?" he asked.

"Well, it's not that big of a deal, but I think I'm committed to buying a car, and I bought some other things this week with my black card ... sorry, but I got a little excited."

"What kind of other stuff?" he asked.

I told him, "Clothes, shoes, purses, stuff like that."

"Alright, I'll send someone by to catalog everything and increase the insurance on the apartment."

"Seriously?"

"You pay us well," he said, "so we're happy to oblige."

"You really are Jewish aren't you Josh?" I giggled. "You wouldn't happen to be a lawyer, would you?"

"Yes, I'm an attorney too," he revealed.

"I was just joking with you ... sorry, shameless joke."

"No need to apologize Alex, I actually happen to be an attorney, I wasn't joking."

I smiled. "Well, how 'bout that?"

Josh laughed a bit. I think I was loosening him up some.

"Alright, so tell me about the car," he said.

"Well, I'm driving it ... the guy just dropped it off the other day."

"What kind of car is it?" he asked.

"Oh, it's a new DBS."

Josh paused for a moment. "Is that a Mercedes?"

"No, Aston Martin. He said it was a special limited edition."

"What's the sticker price?" he asked.

"It doesn't have a sticker, but he said he'd sell it to me for 260."

"And, you agreed?" asked Josh.

"Uh, well ... yeah ... is that bad?"

"Not at all," he replied. "Now Alex, is that the Long Island Aston Martin, or did you go to a private owner?"

"That would be the Long Island one. The guy's name is Ira."

"Very well," Josh responded, "I don't know what a DBS is valued at, but I'll check around and follow up with Ira. If he calls back, send him over to me. In the future, just treat us like a procurement department at your job. If you want something, call me and I'll sort out the details. Again, we can do some tradeoffs like stock, advertising, appearances, and endorsements. You're one of the few biracial, woman-owned holding companies in the city, so as you're living your life, we're building a damn good story based off your name."

"I think I follow you, Josh, but what's up with the appearances?"

"For example, with the car, we may give the dealer stock in the holding company and promise him you'll appear at a few of his special events, you follow?"

I sighed. "So, basically, you're pimpin' me out Josh, and how much do I pay you exactly?"

"Don't worry about it," he replied.

"Do you know this Ira dude or something? He said the exact same thing. And, what does that even mean, don't worry about it?"

Josh chuckled. "Well, it means you have enough money not to worry about prices. It means we'll work it out for you. You just keep doing what you do and get some help. Don't think I don't know about the drinking, Alex."

I gasped. "What?"

"Mr. Crane's a little worried about you, and frankly so am I."

"Is that so?"

"Alex, we have discrete, private programs to help get you back on track. I'll make a few calls and-"

"Josh, are you going to get in my personal business too, or are you just hired to run my company?"

"Listen Alex, all I'm saying is that now that we've talked, we're going to give you more visibility. Folks are going to know who you are and what you do, so remember, not only are you an FBI agent, but you're the face of a fairly successful small business ... you have to find a way to balance those parts of your life. Look, I gotta run. Are you good to go?"

"Long as you're gonna take care of my car, yes."

Josh said, "Drive it, it's yours, don't worry. Oh, and I'll send a company car over too, that way you've got some options. That DBS thing doesn't sound like an ideal car to drive around the city. You want a hard top or convertible?"

"Convertible I guess."

"I'll have someone bring it over today," he said. "Any questions?"

"Not right now."

"Alright kid, pat yourself on the back 'cause you're one wealthy gal. Be sure to thank your dad and his friends for it, and remember don't get carried away with the spending."

"Okay, thanks."

"Talk to you later." He hung up.

Josh was a serious fast talker. He really moved. I imagined him being this little short guy with a bowtie and some glasses, wearing his hair in a slicked back style. Regardless of how he looked, I liked the way his little Jewish ass worked.

Now, I probably said it before, but just in case I didn't, allow me to reiterate—every single day of that particular week was like Christmas morning. I was totally set. I had money, a fly ride and all the right gear—not to mention the fact I was an instant prominent businesswoman and hadn't lifted a fucking finger to get there. It was a good thing too because I didn't know the first thing about running a company. However, I know how to read between the lines. And, if I was reading between the lines correctly, it sounded to me like Josh's biggest concern was me ending up in the tabloids. Guess what? He was right. There really was no telling with me. Drama seems to follow me everywhere I go. But I figured they went through all the trouble, so the least I could do was try and act right sometimes.

The rest of the week was fairly uneventful. By the time Saturday rolled around, I realized I actually had to go back to work the next week. I know Tony wanted me to stay, but honestly, I just wanted to hang out and shop. I'd been living like a hermit for years because I was broke. Once I had access to money, the last thing I wanted to do was go work all day. "I'M NOT GOING BACK!" I yelled repeatedly, but then I finally came to grips with reality and started pulling myself together. Tony needed me, and after all he'd done, I had to make good on my end of the deal.

I stayed in the house the rest of the weekend just winding down and getting ready for my first week back in the danger zone. I started watching cooking shows, trying to learn something new and actually got inspired to make dinner Sunday. In hindsight, I should've ordered takeout. Actually, the salad was good, but the lamb chops ended up tasting like a rubber band, and don't think I don't know what a rubber band tastes like. Trust me, it's not good.

After dinner, I read a short romance novel, and then turned in early. I figured a responsible FBI agent, slash businesswoman, such as myself should set an example for the other young aspiring women of New York. There was no telling how long I could keep up the front, but I think it was worth a try. How hard could it be. Hell, I'd been undercover half my life. Playing myself, or the normal, nice respectable version of me, should be no hill for a climber.

I lay in bed, looking up at the ceiling without giving it all another thought. I was destined for greatness. I knew I had it in me to make this all work and not screw it up. It wasn't a matter of hope, it was just a matter of time before I proved all my worst critics wrong. I was damn sure looking forward to that day.

Chapter 5

I'm not sure if it was because I'd been out on suspension for weeks or just that I dreaded going back, but it was hard as hell waking up Monday morning. I literally had to drag myself out of bed. I finally got up, showered and put on one of my new suits from Saks—the dark brown one with the long jacket and short skirt. I topped my ensemble off with a pair of strappy Gucci heels and my lucky gold anklet. Satisfied with my new look, I strapped on all my gear—cell phone, radio, badge, gun, extra magazines, cuffs, flashlight and anything else I could either fit on my belt or inside my jacket pockets.

I ate a light breakfast—toast and grapefruit—and then went downstairs to the garage. I was just about to hop in the DBS when I noticed Josh had made good on his promise. Parked to the right of the Aston Martin was a black Mercedes Benz AMG 600 SL. It was nice, but not as nice as the Aston Martin. I didn't care though, it wasn't mine. *No, wait a minute, it actually was mine ... hey, talk about sticking it to the man ... I am the man.* I giggled hard and opened the driver side door of the Benz. The keys were in the ignition, so I hopped in. Evidently, our garage was one of the few places in New York you could leave the keys in an expensive car and expect it to be there when you came back to it. I adjusted my mirrors, cranked up and headed to the office.

One extremely good thing about my new apartment was it was only about six miles away from the office, but any good New Yorker knows that equates to a 30-minute trip on a good day. I headed down Wall Street and turned left onto South. Then, I followed St. James Place around to

Federal Plaza. I parked the car in the garage and went inside.

After clearing security, I took the elevator up to my area on the 23rd floor. Once again, Tony had proven he was the poster boy for the Bureau because he was already in. I stopped by his office and knocked on the door, which was partly open.

Tony looked up. "Hey, good morning," he said, "come on in."

I shut the door, and then walked over and sat down across from him.

He leaned over his desk, looking me up and down. "Wow, you look really great."

"Few million'll do that ... from busted to sexy all in a day."

He frowned a little. "If you say so ... alright, so you want the good news or the bad news first?"

"What, I can't be ASAC? OPR up to their old tricks again?"

"No, you're good there," he replied, "I already got your paperwork processed. As of 8:00 a.m. this morning, you're officially my new ASAC. Like I said, you got Alpha Team all to yourself."

"So, is that the good news or the bad news?"

"Neither."

"Shit Tony," I shook my head. "I guess gimmie the bad news first."

He frowned. "Bad news is I can't let you back in the field 'til you go see the shrink."

I shook my head. "You gotta be kidding me man."

"No, I'm not," he replied, "I'm to suspend you again if you don't go."

"I don't have time to deal with this shit right now, Tony."

He looked like he agreed but dared not utter the words. "Listen, you just gotta do what you gotta do Alex."

"Whatever man ... so, what's the good news?"

"Alpha Team's got the Chip Miller case," he replied.

I tried to maintain my composure. "No!" I shook my head. "You call that good news, uh, uh ... I'll pass."

"Not on your life!" exclaimed Tony. "This is an open and shut case. You go over, make contact, do a little baby sitting and do what you do best."

"What get the kid half blown up?" I asked, sarcastically.

"Don't be so hard on yourself," Tony said, "that wasn't your fault."

"Look, I know this woman. I worked with her before. Miller's got issues. She never listens to anything. Jesus Christ, this is gonna be a disaster!"

Tony promised, "I'm going to personally introduce you and make sure we have an understanding. She's got a press conference at the courthouse today. The charges she's bringing against this guy are pretty light anyway, so she's going to announce she's dropping the charges. Then, she'll release Qalat into our custody for questioning on a non-related matter. We'll release him, pin a tail on him and find out where they're keeping Chip. Once we get the boy back, we'll get Qalat back off the streets along with any accomplices we can connect to the kidnapping."

I thought about it for a moment. "Sounds like a good plan. You mean Miller's actually gonna go for that?"

"She doesn't have a choice," Tony replied. "Like I said, it's an open and shut case and a good one for you to spring back on. OPR says you're righteous again, you're coming off suspension to promotion, and the first thing you'll do is close a high-profile case. It doesn't get any better than that, Alex."

"So, you're suggesting I should be grateful?"

"I don't want to put words in your mouth," said Tony, "but you seem to be spitting this golden opportunity back in my face. If I were you, I'd find a way to be a little more appreciative." He smiled and nodded slightly. "This is a good thing."

"Then, why do I feel like I'm gonna get fucked again?"

"That's simple," said Tony, "you're paranoid, Alex. He stood up, walked over to a tall file cabinet and opened the top drawer. "At some point you have to learn to trust people to do what they say they'll do and just move on." A file caught his eye and he pulled it out of the drawer.

"You know Boss, the old me would've said something like, you're full of shit, or easy for you to say, but no, not the new me. ASAC Southerland's gonna say, thank you, sir ... hope I'm up to the task, sir ... anything to please the Bureau, sir!" I smirked.

"Fuckin' wise ass." He smacked me on the head with the file, and then handed it to me. "I should've never told you about that damn money, it's making your head get even bigger than it was the last time I saw you."

"So, you like my outfit?" I hopped out of my seat and spun around, sticking my right leg out and pointing my toe as if I were standing at the end of a fashion show runway.

Tony just shook his head and smiled. "Guess we should've set up a trust fund, huh?"

"Why's that?" I asked.

He burst out laughing. "So, you couldn't touch the money till you turned 40."

I shot him a bird.

"Hey!" He pointed his finger at me.

"Sorry, couldn't help myself." I held up the file. "Everything here?"

"Yeah, but remember you need to go see OPR first."

"Rrrrrright."

"I'm serious," Tony said, "don't give me any shit on this. You see them before you go see Miller, okay?"

I stood there quiet for a second. I hated lying to Tony, but I wasn't feeling that shrink shit at all. "Fine, I'll go see Miller after lunch."

"Don't wait too long, Alex. Miller's got that press conference coming up this afternoon."

"I'm on it." I tucked the folder under my arm and headed for the door.

"Welcome back, ASAC Southerland."

I turned around and smiled. "Good to be back, Sir." I walked out of his office and headed straight for my crew. Everyone was already in.

"Congratulations, Alex," said Dominic Harris, a transfer from the San Diego, California field office. Harris was a loyal, hard worker. He'd only been with the team a short while, but he fit right in. It seemed like he'd been there all along. When things went down, he was my wingman, and there was no doubt about it, he was a Bureau man to the core, dedicated and willing to go the distance.

"Thanks, Dom."

"Johnson really went to Miami?" asked Deborah.

I nodded. "It certainly seems that way."

"Lucky son-of-a-bitch," she smiled.

"Alright guys. Johnson's moving up the food chain, so that moves me from Supervisor to ASAC ... anybody got a problem with that...?" I paused for a moment. "Fantastic! Okay, good news." I laughed for a quick second. "You're all gonna love this one."

"Let me guess," said Dom, "we got the Miller case."

"I'm gonna bake you some hero cookies later," I retorted. "That's right, we just got the Miller case, it's official."

The entire team groaned, and then sighed in unison.

"Yup." I nodded and smirked a little. "My sentiments exactly people, but we got a job to do, and this is my first time as ASAC, so I need your best performance out there. I want you to pull all of the preliminary together and schedule a briefing in Situation Room A in one hour. Make sure Tony's got availability 'cause he's making the introductions onsite at the command center this time."

"Are we supposed to get you coffee now or something?" asked Carlos.

I grinned. "Get to work smart ass. I'll be down in admin for the next hour."

Everyone immediately hopped to it. Our team, me included, probably had the most mouth out of everyone on the floor, but when we settle down, we produce mad work. I walked off the floor and down the hall to the admin area. I figured I'd get that stupid OPR shit out of the way, but halfway there, my cell phone rang. The number was restricted, but I picked up anyway.

"Hello, this is Southerland," I answered.

"Agent Southerland, we need to talk." The voice was altered to disguise the identity of the caller.

"Who's this?" I asked, abruptly.

"I have information regarding the Miller case."

"Fine," I replied, "come into the office and we'll talk."

"Meet me behind the courthouse in five minutes," said the caller.

"Can't do it, I-"

The caller hung up.

"Shit!" I snapped, checking the time. "Goddammit!"

I took off running for the elevators. I mashed the down button repeatedly, but it didn't seem to get the elevator up any faster. I kept looking at my watch. I was racing against time. I only had a few minutes. As soon as the doors cracked open, I squeezed inside and rushed everyone out. I got down to the lobby and ran outside around the back of the courthouse building. It was deserted back there, so I crept down the alley with my hand on my gun, cautiously inspecting every possible hiding place.

"Over here," came a whisper.

I walked around a dumpster, and there was a man standing back there in the corner wearing a hat and trench coat. The sight of that made me burst out laughing. "You gotta be kidding me, man!"

"No joke Agent Southerland," he said.

I kept my distance from him. "Who the fuck are you? And, how'd you get my number?"

"I'm a friend," he replied.

I noticed a bulge in his coat and in a flash, I drew down on him. "Okay Mr. Friend, let me see some I.D."

"Drop the gun," came a deep voice from the side.

I looked to my right and saw a man in a ski mask with his gun pointed at the side of my face. Evidently, he'd snuck up on me when I wasn't looking. He had me dead bang too. I looked up to the sky and shook my head.

"Shit!"

"Hands!" the man commanded.

I slowly raised my hands.

The masked man reached up and took my gun. "Thank you for your cooperation," he said. His voice was deep and slithery like a Saturday morning cartoon villain. He circled around and stood behind me. "Put your hands down," he said, taking my cuffs.

I complied. "You know, I've got people waiting for me upstairs, so why don't we go up to my office and we can talk."

"For security reasons I cannot reveal my identity," said the man in the trench coat. "You must know my primary concern is the boy. My sources indicate D.A. Miller is not going to release Qalat. If she doesn't comply with the kidnapper's demands, the boy will surely die. This is an unacceptable loss. You are to go see Miller at once and convince her to proceed as planned."

"Miller's a smart woman," I said. "She knows what's at stake, and-"

"This way Agent Southerland." He pointed towards the street.

The man behind me nudged me forward with the tip of his gun.

I raised my hands a little and started walking. "I can't make her do anything."

"Shut up." He pushed me.

"I'm a Federal agent, this is kidnapping!"

"It'll be murder if you don't shut your fuckin' mouth," said the man with the gun in my back.

We walked closer to the end of the alleyway.

"It's broad daylight," I said, "you think you can get away with this shit and nobody notice?"

He dug his pistol into my right shoulder. "You wanna go in one piece or not?"

I nodded, "I... I prefer one piece actually, thank you."

"Then, shut up! I'm not gonna tell you again."

"Alright, alright!" I exclaimed.

By the time we got to the end of the alley, a black limo pulled up to a screeching halt, close enough to the buildings to block me from getting away on foot. The back door of the limo swung open. My options were limited—no fuck that—I didn't have any options at all. Escaping was out of the question. I either had to turn and face the big overgrown fucker in the ski mask or get my lil ass into the car. I thought about it for a second and then quickly realized it made sense for me to get in the car. The alleyway was wide open. They'd shoot me and roll off. But, in the confines of that vehicle, I just might have a fighting chance.

"Hold it," the man said.

I stopped in my tracks. Then, the man pulled my arms behind me and zip-tied my wrists together. Well, that pretty much marked the end of my fighting chance.

"Get in," he grumbled.

I climbed in and sat down on the back seat. Inside there was another masked man sitting on the left with his gun on me. My kidnapper pushed me over and sat on my right. Then the man in the trench coat climbed in and closed the door. He moved past us and sat with his back against the driver's partition. Then, he knocked three times against the window and the car started moving.

"Who are you guys supposed to be, CIA? What, you friends of the D.A.?" No one said a single word. "The ex-husband, you're working for him, right...? You got me tied up, so fuckin' say something you dickless mothafuckas!"

"What a filthy mouth you have, Agent Southerland."

I looked at the man in the coat. "Fuck you, where are you taking me? I WANNA KNOW NOW!"

"This'll all be over soon," he said, "all you have to do is your job, and it'll be over before you know it. Get the boy back and everyone'll be fine."

"UNTIE ME!" I exclaimed. "UNTIE ME RIGHT NOW, OR I'LL TELL THAT BITCH TO FRY QALAT. LOOK ME IN THE EYE AND TELL ME IF I'M BLUFFING."

"Oh, I believe you," he replied, "but you won't do it."

"What makes you so sure?" I asked.

He held up a photo of the kid from my last case. Even in the picture, you could see the entire right side of his body was destroyed. His charred skin, or what little was left, was just hanging off of his body. He was a bloody mess. A tear streamed down my cheek.

"I know you remember him, don't you?" he asked.

I got quiet.

"He'll never be the same," he said, slowly and callously. "You know, they say he might make it through if he doesn't get infection. I can't even begin to imagine the pain from all the skin grafts, you know all the treatments. I did hear they have this new artificial skin, but I think the family's too poor to afford it. Maybe you can help them out, Agent Southerland ... you just came into a lot of money recently, didn't you?"

He kept blabbing, but I zoned out and started thinking about that night—the night little Percy Gordon got burned. It was horrible. Despite OPR's rendition of what happened, it wasn't my fault, but I still take the blame. We setup command in the Gordon home and had been negotiating with the kidnappers all week back and forth. As we collected and processed evidence, ASAC Johnson stalled the kidnappers, asking for proof of life and haggling about the ransom amount—all kinds of standard FBI playbook tactics. Most kidnappers run a serious operation, but those assholes were amateurs at best. We all had a bad feeling about the deal. Somehow, we knew they weren't going to let Percy go no matter what we did.

After extensive negotiations, we finally had an agreement. The money was in the bags and the boy's father was making the drop, but everything went south fast. The kidnappers didn't deliver what they promised, which was the location of the child. There were agents from another team backing us up, and they were doing their job, shadowing the drop. Problem is they ended up getting into a high-speed pursuit with the kidnappers, who naturally crashed their van. The two men inside died, but it was obvious they were just runners. To this day, it amazes me how those two dumbass agents never got disciplined, but I ended up getting suspended. If they'd done their jobs, I wouldn't have had to do what I did.

I remember we got a call from the man in charge. He was livid; pissed he didn't get his money. He told us he was gonna kill the kid. The powers that be thought he was bluffing, but I could tell he was dead serious.

Against orders, I recruited a few of my teammates to go find the man in charge. ASAC Johnson felt searching the grid was a waste of time, especially since agents had already checked the area, but I wasn't convinced.

There was only one location they could've been operating out of—an abandoned warehouse about five miles away from the drop point. So, we geared up and checked out the location that night. Four of us infiltrated the warehouse and just as I suspected, the kidnappers were there and so was Percy.

We took out their security fast. Unfortunately, the last man standing had a hand grenade and was using Percy as a human shield. The man's speech patterns matched the voice we'd been hearing all week. He was definitely the man in charge. He didn't have a chance in hell of getting out of there. All four of us were drawing down on him from every angle. He had nowhere to go, but he was holding a grenade, which I guess he thought was his bargaining chip. It meant nothing to me. He removed the pin and held the grenade up in the air, which proved to be a horribly bad move in more ways than one. He was struggling hard, keeping his eye on us and trying to hold onto the boy who was squirming to break free, so I took a chance. I fired one shot into the man's left shoulder.

The grenade flew back out of his hand and he let go of the boy. We yelled for Percy to run to us and he started to at first. The man was down, and the grenade was rolling on the floor; it was live, so the other agents dropped and took cover, but I stood there waving my arms, beckoning Percy to come to me. I screamed and yelled, and I was sure he'd make it before the grenade went off, but for some reason, he turned back and ran towards it. Even today, I still don't understand what he was going back for. I took off after him, but sadly, I didn't make it in time.

The grenade rolled over right between the man I shot and his guards who were already down. It all happened in seconds, but when the grenade exploded, body parts flew everywhere, and the blast knocked me onto my back. The air was filled with smoke and my ears were ringing. I struggled to crawl over to Percy. Blood and human limbs were scattered about in all directions, but they weren't Percy's. He was still in one piece, badly burned, but still in one piece.

I used my jacket to put the fire out on his body and we immediately called for a rescue ambulance. He wasn't breathing at first, so I administered CPR. Each time I pressed on his little chest, I could feel his flesh moving around under the palm of my hand. I had to be careful not to hurt him any more than he already was, but I also had to get him breathing again. I worked on him for nearly five minutes, and finally, he coughed a few times. By the grace of God, Percy was back among the living.

When he came to, he immediately started screaming. He was in agony; the kind of pain a young boy should never have to experience. All I could see was sheer terror in his eyes. He thought he was going to die, and so did I.

I sat there with him and held his little hand, doing everything I could think of to make him comfortable until the paramedics arrived. Even the EMTs were horrified by the site of his body. They couldn't believe he'd survived. Sometimes when I lay still at night, I hear him screaming, and I-

"Agent Southerland!" the man yelled, breaking my train of thought. "We're here."

The man sitting next to me pushed me over on my side. After cutting my restraints, he quickly put his arm around my neck, pulling me into a fierce chokehold.

"Move it," he said, pushing me over to the door. "Open it!" he commanded.

"I can't breathe." I struggled to move with his arm cutting off my air supply.

"Shut up and do it!" He squeezed tighter.

I reached down, pulled the handle and kicked the door all the way open. The man pushed me to the edge, still gripping my neck tightly. I put my feet out of the car down on the ground and got ready to stand up. Then, he reached behind me, pulled my jacket up and put my cuffs back in place. He also reached around my waist and holstered my gun. I immediately felt the barrel of his pistol in my back again.

"Remember, get the boy back," he whispered. "Now, get the fuck out."

He slowly loosened his grip on my neck, and I slid out of the car.

As soon as I was clear of the door, they peeled off down the street. I rubbed my neck and wrists, and then drew my gun to check it. To tell you the truth, I felt violated. At that point I knew firsthand what it was like to be kidnapped. At least my assailants were civil for the most part though. I imagine it's no picnic for the real victims.

They'd dropped me off in front of a residence, but I didn't know where I was or what the hell I was doing there. I could only assume it was the Miller residence because it was crawling with police. There was a huge gate at the edge of the driveway. About ten feet inside the gate were a few officers standing guard, or at least they were supposed to be standing guard. I couldn't understand for the life of me how they didn't see a gang of masked assailants manhandling a woman in a car. What the hell were they there for?

"FBI," I yelled, holding my badge up.

An officer ran over and opened the gate for me. "Yes ma'am?"

"This the Miller residence?" I asked.

He nodded. "Yes."

"I'm the ASAC on this case."

"Oh, yeah, they been expecting you," he replied. "Go on up, I'll radio you're coming."

"Thank you." I casually walked up the driveway past another group of officers, and up to the front of the home. I flashed my badge again at the front door, and they let me in.

"They're in the living room to the right," said a nearby officer.

I nodded at him. "Thank you." Then, I walked through the entryway towards the living room. There was a group of people standing around D.A. Miller talking. As soon as she noticed me, she cut the conversation short.

"Come with me," she said, pointing and snapping her fingers.

I followed her to the back of the home where her office was.

"Please have a seat, Agent Southerland."

I sat down at the table with her.

"I trust you know why you're here?" asked Miller.

"I know what happened to your son, and I'm sorry, but I don't know why I've been brought here."

She grinned a little. "I apologize for this. It is quite unorthodox."

"Yes, it is," I replied. I was pissed. I wanted to drag her ass down and lock her up for obstruction. I mean, how the fuck your son gets kidnapped, and then you go kidnap the bitch who supposed to be helping you?

"I'm terribly sorry, but I need your counsel," she said.

I asked, "Why me?"

"We've crossed paths before, and you didn't back down from me. I also heard what you did in the Gordon case, and I admire your courage. The bottom line is...." She sighed heavily. "I need your help, Agent."

I stood up. "Look Ms. Miller I-"

"Please call me Janice." She handed me the ransom note, which was neatly preserved in a clear plastic bag.

The note was short, sweet and to the point. It read, *release him or the boy dies.*

"Look, Janice, best thing I can do for you right now is get prepped and get my team set up in here. Your goons drug me down here prematurely, and ... hey, what the hell is this...?" Outside the window, I noticed a mob of reporters and camera crews. "Janice ... what's this about?"

"Your perception is powerful," she replied, "and your suspicions are correct, but I didn't send anyone to bring you here. If my people or my idiot ex did something inappropriate, I need to know about it, and they will be held accountable."

"Forget about it ... what's going on outside?" I asked, sternly.

"Qalat is a dangerous man," she said. "It's taken us years to build a shaky case on him. If I let him go ... if we let him go now, he'll go deep underground and further fuel these Islamic terrorists your office has been unable to track, capture, or even get a whiff of to date." She shook her head. "No, I can't risk letting him go."

I responded, "With all due respect ma'am, we're going to have surveillance up on Qalat immediately. I promise you he's not getting away. This isn't Counterterrorism, this is K&R ... we get our man."

"I'm sorry Agent Southerland, but your promises are worthless to me right now."

"Then, if you're not going to listen to me, Janice, why ask for my counsel?"

"I need you to do what you did before," she replied sharply.

I raised an eyebrow. "I don't follow you."

"What I'm about to do will put my son's life in jeopardy. I need you to find Chip, get him home, and then give him some kind of witness protection."

I put my hands up. "Whoa ... what are you about to do?"

"I'm going to announce that we will not release Qalat. We're going to be seeking the death penalty."

"No," I shook my head vigorously. "No, you can't do that, I-"

"There's nothing you can do to stop this from happening." She put her hands on her hips. "Agent Southerland, we must first uphold the law, even if-"

"EVEN IF IT MEANS THE DEATH OF YOUR SON? YOUR ONLY SON? NO ... HELL NO...! I'M SORRY, BUT I CAN'T LET THAT HAPPEN. Look, we've got a good plan. Let's stick to the plan. Now, I'm about to-"

"PARDON ME FOR BEING BLUNT AGENT SOUTHERLAND, BUT IF YOU DON'T HELP ME, THEN MY SON'S DEATH WILL BE ON YOUR FUCKING HEAD. NOW, YOU CAN EITHER HELP ME OR GET THE HELL OUT OF MY WAY, AND I'LL FIND SOMEONE WHO WILL."

"No, you won't ma'am ... I'm sorry Janice, but you're going to have to come with me."

She looked surprised. She started backing up to her desk. Then, she took the phone off hook and pressed a button.

"Don't do this. Put the phone down, Janice."

"I need you in here right away!" she exclaimed. Then she slammed the phone back down.

I cocked my head to the side. "What do you call yourself doing?"

"Agent Southerland, I cannot allow you to stop this press conference from taking place ... I'm truly sorry."

Before I could get a word out of my mouth a mob of anxious officers burst into the room. They all took one look at me and suddenly seemed extremely confused. I pulled my jacket back to show my badge and shook my head at them. They lowered their weapons.

"Sergeant Graham take this woman into custody," Janice ordered.

The officer stood up from his firing stance and bravely asked, "Um ... well, what's the charge?"

"Obstruction and tampering with evidence," she replied.

I looked down at my hand. Naturally, I was still holding the ransom note.

"Ms. Miller ... I ... this is highly irregular ma'am," Officer Graham said. "I gotta call it in."

"NO!" exclaimed Janice. "There's no time. The press conference is about to begin, and I need your officers to protect me and my staff. You are to detain her, and we'll deal with the charges in question after the press conference."

He still hesitated to act. He knew it was a bad move, and I think if he'd known exactly what she was up to, he would've stopped her too. Honestly, I was kind of in shock the bitch had flipped on me like that. I was trying to formulate what to say in my mind, but I couldn't.

"D.A. Miller, I think we just need to calm down," said Officer Graham. "She's an FBI agent, she has jurisdiction, and-"

"Take her into custody or lose your job!" Janice exclaimed.

Graham dropped his head and sighed. Then, he walked over to me.

"It's okay," I said. I turned around and he cuffed me. As Graham was relieving me of my gun and radio, I stared Janice in the eye and said, "Nothing good will come of this ... I implore you to reconsider."

She pointed to the door. "Get her out of here, dammit!"

While we were on the way out, Janice opened the back door and invited the reporters in. Out in the hallway, Officer Graham apologized.

"Agent Southerland, I ... I don't know what to say, I'm sorry about all this. As soon as I call my Captain, we'll get this sorted out, alright?"

I thought about telling him what she was planning, but it wouldn't have made a damn bit of difference. Obviously, she was in charge.

"I gotta put you in the car," Graham said, as we approached his cruiser parked in front of the home. Graham opened the back door.

I didn't say a word I just got in. Anything I said would've been a waste of breath because Janice's press conference was already underway. Basically, the damage was done, so there was no sense in getting Graham in trouble too. He was just trying to do his job—in the face of stupidity I might add.

I sat down on the back seat. That was the second time that day I found myself tied up in the back of a car. Obviously, I was having a bad experience. All things considered though, I was extremely calm. Guess I really didn't care anymore. Hell, it was my first day back in the office, so I was just going through the motions.

"Just sit tight and I'll call my Captain now." Graham shut the door and used his radio to request a callback from his superior. I saw him pacing around a bit, and after about five minutes, he got a call on his cell. He walked off to take it. I just sat back and relaxed. Yeah, it was some bullshit, but I was doing what I was supposed to do, so I wasn't the least bit worried.

Thirty minutes passed and finally, Graham showed back up, but he had a friend with him, Tony. I smiled as Graham opened the door and helped me out of the car. He uncuffed me, and then scattered with his tail between his legs. I couldn't blame him though. I probably would have run off too because Tony had this wild, disgusted expression on his face. That joker was fit to be tied as my Nana used to say.

I rubbed my wrists and stretched a little. Tony looked at me like never before. He kept shaking his head, but I think he just really couldn't find the right words to say.

"Before you say anything Tony, I was on my way to OPR and these fuckin' guys conked me over the head and brought me here ... I didn't-"

"You see the report?" he asked.

"I've been in the back of this car for the past half hour! No, I didn't see any report."

Tony said, "Miller just announced she won't be dropping the charges against Qalat. What the hell happened, Alex?"

"Okay ... see, I know how this looks, but it's not my fault. So, I walk in, then she tells me she's gonna do this unscheduled press conference and refuse the demands, and so I told her-"

"Wait, you knew she was going to do this?" Tony asked.

"Well, yeah but I tried to talk her out of it."

Tony covered his face with his hands. "God, I don't need this today, Alex."

"Alex...? I got abducted, and then she had her little henchmen lock me up in the back of this car, just how the hell is that my fault?"

"What did she say to you?" he asked.

"She wants me to go do some rogue shit and rescue and protect her son, but I told her I couldn't do that. She's crazy. I told you before she won't listen to a goddamn thing, Tony! This shit is not my fault. I told that bitch-"

"Hey!" He put his hand up for a second.

"Sorry, I told Miller to say that she was going to release Qalat, but she ran off and did exactly whatever she wanted. And, on top of that, she had me locked up. I oughta take her in for obstruction."

He looked at me and squinted. "You sure it went down like that? I don't need any more surprises."

I stared him right in the eyes. "Yes, that's exactly how it went down."

He sighed. "Give me your badge."

"What?"

"Come on," he held out his hand, "give me your badge!"

"This is fuckin' bullshit Tony," I whispered, "what the fuck, are-"

"Hey, you're talking to a superior kid!" he exclaimed. "Watch your mouth!"

"Yes, Sir." I unclipped my badge and frowned up hard as I put my shield in the palm of Tony's hand. I was hoping the pitiful look on my face would have some kind of effect, but it didn't. For once, he stuck to his guns.

Tony held my badge up. "You want this thing back, you go see OPR. I'll try to clean up this mess while you're gone. Where's your car?"

"At work," I replied. "I told you the bitch kidnapped me!"

Tony laughed.

I shook my finger at him. "THAT'S NOT FUNNY, TONY!"

"Here...." Tony gave me his keys. "Take my car back to the office. You can come back for me once OPR clears you. Hopefully by then Miller and I will be on the same page. In the interim, we'll start setting up command. Team's already here. I'll be in charge until you get back. You cool?"

"Yeah, where the hell did that little fat fucking-"

"ALEX!" Tony exclaimed.

"Sorry." I cleared my throat. "I NEED MY GUN AND GEAR BACK FROM SERGEANT GRAHAM!" I yelled loudly.

Tony spun around and gave me an assist. "SERGEANT GRAHAM...?" he yelled. "ANYBODY SEEN GRAHAM?"

"OVER THERE!" yelled an officer.

I spotted Graham and ran over to him. He gave me back my stuff and apologized three or four more times. I told him not to sweat it. I knew he was just following orders. I walked down the driveway and located Tony's car. I hopped in and drove straight back to the office.

It had already been a long day. I could only hope Tony would be able to talk some sense into Miller's thick skull, but I think we had a better chance of peace in the Middle East. That woman was hopeless. I felt bad for her son, but deep down, I knew there wasn't much I could do to help him.

Back in the office I went straight to the admin area. The girl in Assistant Director Cross's office told me where to go. She said she'd send someone down to meet with me.

I went down the hallway and into the office on the right. I sat down on the couch and took a breather while I waited for my big waste of time to walk through the door. It took so long, I almost fell asleep. The day had been the worst Monday I'd had in some time, and from where I was sitting, I figured it was gonna get a whole lot worse. As far as Tony's easy, open-and-shut case was concerned, so far, I was batting zero.

I continued to wait, impatiently. Fifteen minutes later, a woman walked in. As soon as I caught a glance of her, my jaw dropped. I looked at her and pointed. "I KNOW YOU!"

"I'm afraid so," said the woman. "The last time we spoke you were in a lot of trouble, Agent Southerland."

I kept pointing at her and thinking. Finally, I remembered. "Stephens ... Dr. fuckin' Stephens. The fuck are you doing here?"

"I see you haven't changed much," she retorted.

"I assure you I'm not the same little girl you pushed around in the showers years back."

"Ah, I see you remember our little encounter." she said.

"I remember you tried to fuck me over. I've gotta meet with my shrink now, so again I ask, what do you want? I promise you, Stephens, I've grown in a lot of ways, but my patience is still lacking."

"You mean your patience is non-existent, don't you?" she responded.

I rolled my eyes at her.

"Agent Southerland, I reviewed your sessions from when you first arrived here in New York."

"What happened to doctor patient privilege? Don't you little rats take an oath or something."

Dr. Stephens responded, "You're a recently promoted FBI agent. Your file's an open book with OPR."

"So, you're my shrink?" I asked.

"I'm your therapist," she replied. "As I was saying, I reviewed your sessions and I believe your therapist did not do a complete and thorough assessment. Based on recent events and your record to date, OPR needed a more experienced doctor to provide some insight, and I'm the only one who has experience with you."

"I don't believe this shit. Look lady, I've had a long day, and I'm tired. What could you and I possibly have to talk about?"

Stephens walked around her desk and sat down. "I'm here to help you more than you know. I'm your friend; not your enemy."

"I don't need a friend. I need to be cleared for duty. I have to see a shrink so I can get back to work."

"Well, you see me, and I see you," she said. "I heard about the Miller case, so please go back to work. I'll see you back here in two weeks." She looked at her appointment book. "Say, next Friday?"

I rolled my eyes at her. "Whatever."

"Friday at 10 it is," she smiled, "I'll see you here."

I got up and stomped out of the room. Stephens was the same psychiatrist that screwed me over back in Atlanta. She lied her ass off to gain access to my Navy records and proceeded to try and soil my slightly good name. I should've sued her ass for defamation of character. She had nothing on me but kept me in holding for weeks before she finally changed her stripes and cleared me for duty. Her popping back up here in New York years later was definitely not a coincidence. I wasn't sure what was going down, but with her involved, I knew I had to watch my back.

Chapter 6

I left the office and drove back to District Attorney Miller's home. By the time I arrived, the command center was online, and everything seemed to be going as well as it could—everything except Tony's talk with Miller. As soon as I walked into the room, she gasped for air as if she'd just seen a ghost.

"Agent Southerland, I-"

I held up my hand. "Don't. I saw the news report ... you just killed your son."

She sighed. "I don't think you understand my position."

"Honestly, I don't care!" I snapped. "I have a job to do, and so far, you've been playing games with me. We're talking about your son's life. I need you to go back on TV and, I don't know, say you made an error in judgment." I looked over at Tony, who at the time was nodding in agreement. "Tell 'em you're gonna release Qalat and let us get back to work so we can bring Chip home."

She dropped her head. "I can't do that."

"And, why not?" I asked.

"There are things at stake here that go far beyond my family and your pay grade."

"Now you're talking in code," I replied. "Look, I don't care what's going on. Let us help Chip."

I thought she was going to start crying. I would've if it was my child, but she was one tough broad. She just sat there quiet. I knew she was holding something back from us. I didn't know what it was, but evidently it was worth her son's life.

"Janice, do you understand what you've done to our investigation?"

She looked up at me. "My decision is final. I know what's at stake, and I don't have to explain myself to you or anyone else." She crossed her arms and gave me a stern look.

I glanced over at Tony. "Tony, can you give us a few minutes?"

"Sure." He left the room.

I walked over and kneeled next to Janice. "There's a way for us to win this thing for everybody involved," I said softly. "I gotta be honest with you, I don't have kids ... I don't know what it's like. The only thing I know is how I feel when I find a dead kid and I know we didn't do everything humanly possible to bring him home alive. I don't want to feel that way about Chip, and I know you don't either."

"You don't know my son!" exclaimed Janice. "My son is strong."

"I suspect he gets that from his mother."

She smiled a little.

"Janice, I don't understand why you won't let me do this the right way."

"As a mother, my heart tells me to give in," Janice said. "But ... but, my spirit tells me nothing great happens without sacrifice. I'm not sure how, but I don't believe Chip will have to suffer at all. I don't think I'll have to sacrifice him. I believe the sacrifice will be for you to make. I'm confident you will not rest until Chip is home safely. That's why I chose you. Now, I need you to be strong and do your job while I do mine."

I just sat there with my mouth wide open. She was certifiable, but for some reason, what she said made perfect sense. I was torn between following protocol and fulfilling my desire to bust down some doors and get Chip back alive before the stroke of midnight. She didn't say it—she didn't have to—we both knew they'd kill Chip whether she complied with the demands or not. What made it even worse is the FBI's chance to intercept and rescue the boy successfully was estimated somewhere around seventy percent. And, how about the other thirty percent?

Unknown. So, ask yourself this, would you trust your son's life to an unknown thirty percent? I couldn't.

For about five minutes, I sat with her. I'm not a mother, but I knew where she was coming from. I kinda felt the same way she did. I think we had a better chance of getting Chip back running around like a bunch of lawless psychos, luckily stumbling over clues and evidence. If I told Janice how I really felt, the Bureau would have my black ass hung up on the wall somewhere. I couldn't say a word, but I felt like even though we'd been at odds previously, in that single moment of clarity, we were jacked in on the same frequency; one of tough love and protection at all costs. After a few moments, I finally broke the uncomfortable silence.

"Janice ... I don't know what to say."

"Help me," she pleaded.

"And, what happens to me when I get busted back down for breaking protocol?" I asked.

"I'm sorry, Agent Southerland, but that's not my problem."

See, she just fucked up right there. She almost had me, but when she said that, she pushed me over the edge.

"You know what Janice-"

"What?" she interrupted.

"Under normal circumstances ... I mean, if you'd caught me on any other day, I might buy this whole guilt trip you're trying to send me on, but you picked the wrong fuckin' day."

Janice did a double-take, looking at me as if I'd just lost my mind.

"If you don't release Qalat, then you've tied my hands," I said. "We'll do our best to stay out of your way here. I expect the kidnappers will try to establish contact soon. I hope you'll do the right thing when they call. I'll be outside." I walked towards the door.

"Agent Southerland...."

I stopped but didn't turn around.

"The opportunity to do the right thing is in your hands. I know in my heart you'll do what's best for everyone."

I walked out and grabbed Tony. We went out front and talked under a tree.

"You were right, Alex."

"I usually am, you know?" I said, sarcastically.

Tony sighed and scratched his chin. I could tell he was frustrated. "I hate to say it, but you are right more than you're wrong. This woman's lost it. What options do we have?"

"I don't know, Tony. All I can do is work on her until they call. If she doesn't have a change of heart by then ... shit man, I don't know. Maybe we try to find a way to track these jokers and move in before they have time to do anything."

It was kind of warm out. Tony took his jacket off and slung it over his shoulder. "What are the odds these guys hang on to the kid?" he asked.

"Slim to none," I replied. "They aren't your average kidnappers for cash. They're not businessmen. They're extremists. They're trying to make a point here, and I bet you a dollar to a doughnut they're prepared to lose this battle. Hell, Qalat's already in custody ... say we don't give in to their demands, what have they lost?"

"Nothing," Tony replied.

"Exactly. But, what does Miller stand to lose?"

"Everything ... her only son... Alex, I don't understand where she's coming from, but this is gonna get bad real fast."

I leaned up against the tree. "It probably already has. For all we know, Chip could be dead now."

Tony said, "Okay, let's do this ... I'll pull some other teams in along with some NYPD officers, and we'll hit the streets and see what we turn up. You stay here with Miller and try to convince her to retract her statement."

"I'll see what I can do," I responded, "but frankly I think we got a better chance on the streets than with her."

"Do what you can," Tony said, "I'll check back with you later."

"Be careful out there," I said.

"I hate it when you say that kid. Be good, I'll see you shortly. Oh, shit ... I almost forgot." He took my shield out of his pocket. "You see OPR?"

"Yeah, but we gotta talk about that shit."

"What?" he asked.

"We'll talk later. Can I have my badge back now please, Mr. Crane, sir?"

He smiled and gave it to me.

"Thanks, boss."

"Get Miller in line," said Tony. Then, he left.

I went back inside. My whole team was there getting settled in, checking the equipment, verifying the phone lines were up and clear, and hooking up some coffee. I grabbed a cup and just watched their little busy asses for a few. We were the poorest excuse for a kidnapping squad ever. I'm not sure any of us had a major serious bone in our bodies. To make matters worse, they trusted me to lead them for some odd reason. It was a sad sight to see.

I looked around the room desperately trying to figure out just what the hell Tony was thinking when he put us misfits together and threw us on the front line. The real reason Johnson left probably was because he was just sick and tired of us. With him gone, we were an official hot mess. But we all had major passion and were serious about the job. That was gonna have to be enough too because, yet again, we were right in the thick of shit, and nothing was going as planned. No time for doubts or second guessing.

I remember Cross calling me a loose cannon, and you know what, now that I think about it, she's right, I am. At that very moment, I wanted to bust into Miller's office, pop her in the head and call it a day. If only my life were that simple.

I think criminals really have it the best. They take what they want and when they come across people who don't dance to their tune, boom, they blow 'em away. *What a life.* Soon as I realized I had zoned out for a moment, I snapped my attention back to the task at hand—protecting that idiot Miller, who, by all reasonable assessments, was sure to get her son killed.

The first day on a case like this is always tough because your adrenaline's pumping, but nothing is going down. That always makes it hard to get through, so you have to keep your mind busy, so you don't lose it. The harder trick is trying to get the parents of the victim to do the same thing. We didn't seem to have that problem with Miller though. She was cool as a cucumber for some reason. What the hell did she know? I had to find out—one way or another.

We waited and waited for the kidnappers to make contact, but it didn't happen that day. In fact, we didn't hear anything the rest of the week. The weekend was approaching, and the situation was starting to look bad on all fronts. I talked to Miller over and over, trying to convince her to do the right thing, but she never budged. Tony's ground search wasn't turning up anything either. Friday, I had one last conversation with Janice, but it was an utter waste of time. After that, I just did my best to avoid her. I told her I didn't want to see her face unless she was ready to give up Qalat. I'm still waiting for that to happen.

I sat there in her house and watched the live news feed inside the courtroom as Miller argued the state's case against Qalat. It was brilliant. She was brilliant. It was as if she poured every ounce of fear, hate, anger, and any other emotion she had over her son's kidnapping into convicting that murderous son-of-a-bitch. And, guess what, it worked. Qalat was convicted on twelve counts of offenses from arson to murder, kidnapping and possession of illegal weapons. Miller didn't get the death penalty, but Qalat was slammed with five consecutive life sentences and extradited to Afghanistan to face war crime charges there. Plain and simple, Miller whooped his ass in court, a victory that cost her everything.

Unfortunately, the kidnappers never made contact again. The fax Miller received was their only warning. Six weeks after the trial ended, we received confirmation. Even at that late date, we were still hopeful, camped out in the Miller home, checking phone calls, visitors and all deliveries. One day, a small suspicious package arrived by courier. It was about one foot square and had some weight to it. To be on the safe side, I called the bomb squad. They inspected it thoroughly and determined there were no explosives inside, so I ordered everyone out of the room except my best guy, Dominic. Together, he and I carefully opened the package.

"Fuck me!" I closed my eyes and almost fell on the floor crying.

Our worst nightmares had come true. When Dom opened the top all I saw was black, bloody hair. Even without further examination, I knew exactly what it was. Dom cut down the side of the box to reveal the severed head of young Chip Miller in a plastic bag.

Dominic dropped his head, mumbling under his breath. I think he was praying for Chip. I stood up and walked into the next room. Janice was already in hysterics, screaming and yelling.

"What is it?" she cried out, "what's in the package?"

I shook my head but didn't say anything. I just walked over and put my arms around her.

"Oh God," she screamed, hitting my shoulders with her fists.

She fought me, but I didn't let her go. I pulled her close, holding her tighter and tighter until she gave in and laid her head on my shoulder. She sobbed for her only son, another sacrificial lamb in the war on terror.

District Attorney Janice Miller had done America a service by putting Qalat away, but she paid the ultimate price. Unfortunately, there was nothing anyone could've done about it. We did the best we could, considering the circumstances. With Janice in my arms, all of a sudden, I felt sad and alone. It was a heartbreaking feeling I don't wish on anyone. I couldn't hold my tears back. I felt so sad for Chip. His life ended before it even began really. It was a tragedy no matter how you looked at it.

I knew—in my heart I knew when we didn't get a call from the kidnappers it was just a matter of time before we found Chip's body. But this was a helluva a lot worse than finding a dead kid dumped in the woods. These sick mothafuckas took his head. That was just pure evil.

I hung around the Miller home for weeks after. I'm not sure why. In my mind, it was just something that had to be done. It was weird too because Janice and I never spoke again. Whenever we saw each other in the house, we just stared for a brief moment and then moved on. Five more deliveries came, first his torso, and then each of his limbs. If there was any way to see some kind of good in it, at least she could bury him all together.

I don't generally hate people, but with all I have, I hate anyone who'd even think about hurting a hair on an innocent child's head. I've never been the religious type, but I swear every day when I hit the clock, I pray God will just burn 'em all in hell before lunch and save me a bunch of time, heartache, and paperwork.

After about a month, I finally vacated the Miller residence and went back to my apartment. I took some time off to recover before going back to work. I left Dominic in charge of the crew, and they were working backup for Bravo Team. The whole time I was out, I didn't even think about work. However, I was careful and smart enough to keep my follow up sessions with Dr. Stephens. It didn't take long to realize she was intentionally making matters worse. Stephens was trying to fuck me again, and unlike Cross and the others, she'd dug up enough dirt on me to make her move.

I was falling apart fast. I'd been able to fight off my urges for years, but after the Miller case, I lost control again. I thought about going to church a few times, but it never happened. I hadn't been to church in forever. Besides, it probably would've been a waste of time anyway. I thought about checking into a program like Josh said, but how would that look on my record? OPR would have a field day with that. What's the point anyway? I already have a pretty good idea where I'm headed. Between the alcohol, illicit sex, foul language, and all the other fucked up things I do to people, I don't have a snowball's chance in hell of getting even a hand-me-down halo.

Sometimes, when I'm really high or drunk—I mean just completely wasted—I wish the rapture would come and I get left behind. That way I know most everyone else still here is bad, and I won't have to worry about making a mistake and killing an innocent. I'd speed through the streets of New York, plowing down all those evil bastards. Then, after tallying up the death toll, I'd blaze one and run my activity log upstairs to management to see if it scores me a few points with the Big Man.

It's possible you may have just missed that little gem, so I'll help you out. I've started smoking again only it's marijuana this time. Imagine that, an FBI agent on drugs. What a new revelation! Hell, I'm high right now! Way I see it it's just another vice to add to my overcrowded naughty list. I know what you're thinking, and yes OPR's going to be screening for drugs, but I once read this extremely clever shit. It said you must be willing to make an intelligent compromise with perfection, and that it's still a good idea to cross some bridges when you get there. Now at this particular moment in time, everything's kinda hazy and I don't remember who said that, or even what the fuck it means, but I assure you it's relevant.

I treated myself the last day I was off. I pretty much just laid in bed all night, puffing away on my little joint until I couldn't remember my name or the name of the strange man beside me. Honestly, I didn't give a shit who he was. Sure, he was kind of short, and he seemed to have a Napoleon complex about it, but his body was gorgeous. He was muscular as hell, and the sex was mind blowing, angry and nasty—just how I like it. Or, maybe it was just the weed. Hell, I don't know. Who cares? I woke that nigga's ass up in the middle of the night, horny as ever. I was still stratosphere too—high as hell—trippin' on weed and alcohol.

When he woke up, I was giggling under the covers, trying to choke myself on his thick, stiff cock. He wasn't very long, but he was damn sure wide, and I was having a ball with that. Soon as he realized what was happening, he sprung back into action, taking full advantage of the situation. He used his strong arms to pull me up on top of him, and then he kissed me, flipped us both over with his lil Mighty Mouse ass, and proceeded to knock the bottom out of my pussy for the next hour. My head banged against the headboard with each thrust, but I didn't feel a thing. I was completely numb.

"Fuck me," I moaned.

"I got you mami," he said, "shut up and take this big ass muthafuckin' dick, bitch!" He grabbed my ass with both hands and thrust deeper.

He said he wanted to cum inside, and for some reason I dared not resist. By then I was sailing on Blondie-pilot, and El Capitan was hell-bent on steering the ship into the Bermuda Triangle.

We clawed at each other for a few more minutes, exchanging dirty talk like the pros do. Then, we both shook and shivered as Mr. Universe filled me up. After he came, he had this big grin on his face—one of complete satisfaction—but, as always, it just wasn't enough for me.

I got up and poured myself four drinks. Then, I helped my little boy toy get ready to play again, teasing his member until it was back at attention. Next, I washed my pain away with Hennessey, and then proceeded to achieve multiple, leg-splitting orgasms at the hands of that little sexy, black stallion. The last time we did it, he fucked me hard doggy style and was acting like he'd die the next morning unless he found a way to fit his thick, rock-hard cock balls-deep in my ass. It was simply amazing. He knew exactly how to treat me. He fucked me like I was a streetwalker, and then afterwards wrapped me up in his big, strong, tattooed arms. Passionately, he kissed my shoulders. Then, we both passed out together in bed. He was just what the doctor ordered. He put a half grin on my face, and I slept good that night.

Chapter 7

After hours of senseless lust and passion, I was good again. I don't know any better way to say it other than I'd finally found the reset button and was able to get back to normal. I don't care what anyone says, the whole drunk, promiscuous sex thing works for me. Hell, I couldn't even remember why I was so depressed before. I quickly kicked my new best friend out of my apartment. He all but proposed to me, and I answered him quickly by tossing his clothes out into the hallway. For a second, I thought I was going to have to fight him to get him up out of there, but he took it rather well all things considered. He was actually laughing. *Who knew?*

I showered and got dressed. I was in a hurry to get moving, but after being off for so long again, I was screwing up simple things. Like, it took me half an hour to find my badge and gun. I finally found them wedged between the cushions on the sofa in the living room. That apartment was a mess. I needed to clean up but didn't have time to fool around. It was my first day back, so I had to get in on time.

I went down to the garage and fired up the DBS. Honestly, the first day I saw it, I fell in love. I really thought I wanted that thing, but the luster's starting to wear out fast. Josh worked out a deal so I could have it for free, and of course that seemed like a good idea at the time, but the kicker was I had to drive that fucker everywhere I went. That, plus they wanted me to take it up to the dealership when they had some kind of special event. Truth is the whole situation made me kinda feel like a model or movie star, but after driving that monster around New York every day it was like a goddamn Greek tragedy. At least I had sense enough to register it with the Bureau. They wired up some flashing blue lights and all the stupid cop gear, which got me through traffic better, but it made the cockpit grow even smaller. I just couldn't seem to win with that car.

I asked Josh what happened if I was on a case and the damn thing got smashed up. He told me Ira was ordering another one exactly like mine, just in case. Turns out having a sexy, rich FBI lady drive your top of the line sports car around the city gives you a serious boost in the marketing and advertising department. *Learn something new every day.* Oh, and it's funny because they even stuck a big billboard up with me in the car and my hair blowing in the wind. Every time I drive past that thing, I think of Tony telling me to keep a low profile and I just bust out laughing. Honestly though, I don't think anybody even realized it was me up there, so it was cool—at least I hoped they didn't notice it was me.

I went straight into the office and snuck up onto my floor. I was desperately trying to get to my desk unnoticed, but I didn't make it that far. Everyone stood up and started clapping. They caught me while I was crouching down, damn near in a prone position. I slowly stood up straight and looked around. They were all just cheering and clapping. I looked out the corner of my eye and saw Tony and his admin approaching with a cake. I was a little confused. I knew it wasn't my birthday, so I wasn't sure what was up.

"CONGRATULATIONS ON EIGHT YEARS!" exclaimed Tony.

I cocked my head to the side for a second. Then, I smiled really big and giggled the silliest way I knew how. With all that had been going on, I totally forgot my eight-year service anniversary was coming up. I guess I was too busy just trying to stay employed.

"Who knew I'd make it this long?" I joked, cheesing big.

Everyone laughed. Tony and several other teammates walked over and gave me a hug, which I greatly appreciated. I thanked them all and told them it was a pleasure working together. I really enjoyed being around them. After that, they cut up the cake and everyone got back to their work.

I followed Tony into his office to catch up. We sat down at his conference table and ate our cake while we talked.

"I hear you're still an FBI agent," Tony teased.

"Yeah ... at least for a day or so."

"You alright?" he asked.

"Not bad," I replied, "just ready to get back into the groove of things, you know?"

Tony grinned. "K&R's been pretty uneventful while you were out. Either all the criminals went on vacation, or you really are a bad luck magnet." He slid a file across the table to me. "We got this yesterday ... Rahid Amadi ... 46-years-old. Wife's dead ... no family here. Amadi's one and only son, Keon, went missing three days ago."

"I take it he's rich?" I asked.

"Net worth is off the charts," Tony replied, "imports and exports. Got a law degree at Cambridge and has his hands in just about everything that comes out of Nigeria."

"Shit man, Nigeria?"

Tony gave me an odd look. "What's up?"

I shook my head. "Why is it every time there's a senator, priest or fuckin' ayatollah involved, I end up having to take the case? Remind me who's making whose job hard!"

"Relax Alex, this guy seems pretty normal. Son goes to school here in New York."

"How old is he?" I asked.

"Nineteen," Tony responded, wiping his mouth with a napkin. He'd finished his cake, but I was still picking over mine.

"Any chance the boy just ran off with a white girl? Ya know, Mandingo meets-"

"ALEX!" Tony's face turned beet red.

"I'm just-"

"STOP IT!" he exclaimed.

I laughed. "I'm just asking man ... you know how it is in college."

"Yes, I do." Tony chuckled and said, "I remember all too well."

"That was like in 1940 or something, right?" I joked.

"Smartass!" Tony balled up his napkin and threw it at me. It hit me right in the forehead. "Kidnappers have already made contact with Amadi. They refused proof of life, so I imagine you're going to have to work on them a while."

"What do they want?" I asked.

Tony replied, "Ninety million in cash for Keon's safe return."

I held my fork up to my lips and thought for a minute. "This guy have any private security?"

"Not that I'm aware of," Tony replied.

"No driver or anything?" I asked.

"We've got a statement from the driver. He was scheduled to pick Keon up from school, but the kid never showed. Mr. Amadi called NYPD after 24 hours. Missing persons got involved about a day later and then kicked it over to us when the kidnappers made contact yesterday."

"Anybody at the school see anything?"

Tony shook his head. "Cops haven't turned up anything yet."

I pushed my little plate aside and took the file from Tony. "Any priors on Amadi?"

"Just some INS stuff, but nothing major."

"None of that rebel freedom fighting bullshit?" I asked just to be sure.

"No, I think we're okay in that department, but I've got one of your folks running background on the boy and the father just in case."

"Who's working it?"

"Deborah," he replied.

"You should've put Dom on it. Deborah's too damn slow."

"Yeah, but she's thorough," Tony replied.

"Very true ... very true ... okay, so we'll pack it up and go see Mr. Amadi."

"Excellent. First though, how are you doing, really?"

"Tony, you already asked that, and I already answered you."

He leaned back in his chair. "Yeah, but you lied to me."

I smiled. "Am I that transparent?"

Tony smirked. "Uh, yeah."

"Well, I'm having a bit of a hard time right now. I just ... sometimes, I just feel so isolated you know, and I ... I miss David too. I don't even wanna talk about it, I ... I'll start crying again."

"Okay then, how about your sessions with OPR?" he asked.

"Oh shit, yeah remember that shrink that did my assessment back in Atlanta before David died?"

"Stephens?" he replied.

"Yeah, she showed up as my OPR approved therapist. I swear she's trying to build a case against me."

"You're probably right," Tony replied. "Watch your six with her ... she and I have history."

"Really? Oh, do tell Mr. Crane."

"Not much to tell, but she's got a bad habit of trying to advance her career off other agents' misfortune. Far as I know, she isn't even posted here. I thought she was in Virginia."

"Well, she must've got wind of my situation and took the first damn train to New York."

"Like I say, watch your six, Alex," Tony repeated. "As a matter of fact, don't even talk about our relationship outside the office or your business or anything. Keep it professional, and by all means watch what you say in there. I don't have to tell you this is-"

"Yeah, I know it's off the record."

Tony said, "Listen, a few of us are going to get together for drinks later on-"

"What time?" I asked.

"About seven," he replied.

"Count me in, I...." I stood up. "What the hell are they up to?"

Tony stood up too and looked through the glass wall of his office. Everyone out on the floor was gathered around the television monitors on the far back wall.

"What the hell's going on now?" Tony walked out of the office, and I followed him.

We both walked up and stood behind the crowd of agents.

"What's going on guys?" Tony asked.

"They found District Attorney Miller's body this morning in her home," replied Thomas.

"FUCK ME!" I yelled. Everyone turned and looked. I'd meant to say that to myself, but evidently the shock from that news disabled my inner-monologue. I flipped a hand up in the air. "Sorry ... what happened?" I asked.

"They believe it's suicide," said Deborah. "That's just sad."

"She lost her son and now this," I added.

"Come on guys, get back to work," Tony bellowed.

Slowly, everyone returned to their desks. Tony and I stood there watching the news report.

"This is fucked up," I whispered out the corner of my mouth.

Tony touched my shoulder. "You gonna be alright?" he asked.

I took a deep breath, and then nodded.

"Nothing we can do about that now," Tony said. "Let's help the next one ... you ready?"

"I'm on it." I left him back at the TVs and joined my team.

"What's up, Top?" greeted Dominic.

"How's everybody holding up?" I asked.

"We're good," he replied, "ready to kick some ass."

I smiled. "Well, you're about to get your chance. Guys, we got another one—Keon Amadi. Kid's been missing for three days. Kidnappers made contact yesterday ... Deborah, how's the background coming?"

"It's on your desk, and I'm sending it to the monitors in the primary briefing room now."

"Good job Deborah." I checked my watch. "Let's do it in ten."

I walked over to my desk to check my email and voicemail, or at least that's what I wanted to look like I was doing. Inside, I was falling apart over Janice Miller taking her own life. She must've been in complete hell. I felt sorry for her and Chip, but after two bad cases, one after the other, I had to pull myself together and get back in the zone. We desperately needed to win one for the home team.

After a few minutes, my crew was assembled in the briefing room all eager and raring to go. I walked in and stood behind the podium. As promised, Deb already had the backup info on Amadi and his family on the screens directly behind me. I dropped my notes down and started the briefing.

"Alright team, thanks for being on time. Three days ago, 19-year-old Keon Amadi, went off the grid. The father Rahid Amadi, Nigerian businessman from Port Harcourt, southern Nigeria, is heavy into exporting petroleum to the U.S., Spain and Italy. Yesterday, at 1500, Amadi received a communication from a man who calls himself Aker. He claims to represent interested parties and has requested $90 million dollars in unmarked U.S. currency on their behalf for Keon's safe return. We'll be helping Amadi negotiate directly with this Aker character. At this point we don't know how the kidnapping occurred, but we need to try and pick up a trail fast. Right now, Amadi's working diligently to raise the money just in case. Our priority-one right now is proof of life, but we also need to take an in-depth look into Rahid and anyone he moves with or has moved with. Find out who his enemies are, who the competition is, any pissed off girlfriends, the whole nine. At first glance, this case looks routine, but stay sharp, people. We've all seen the report on District Attorney Janice Miller...." I paused for a brief moment. "We can't afford another messy recovery. First task is setting up command in the Amadi residence. We'll split into two teams ... Dominic, take Deborah and put together an onsite team, then get me a deployment plan. Everyone else is running background from here ... any questions?"

"Yes." Melvin Woods, a five-year K&R agent raised his hand.

"Go ahead, Woods."

"I've seen the preliminary on this guy, Amadi ... I mean, he's worth a lot. What kind of security are we going to have to deal with?"

"Good question, but I'm not sure. From what I understand he doesn't move with any private security."

"No body guards, nothing?" Melvin looked confused.

"Let's assume we have to deal with someone, and we'll update OPSEC as required ... anything else...?"

Dom raised his hand.

"Yes, go ahead Harris."

"Uh, yeah, are you going to replace yourself as supervisor?"

I smiled. "I already have ... give yourself a pat on the back if you like. I want everybody to give Dominic Harris your full support ... he's our new sup."

The entire team clapped and the agents sitting beside Dominic slapped him on the back. That's what I liked about my team most. No matter the situation or who got what, everyone was supportive and didn't hesitate to do what was best for the team. As for Dominic, he was truly one of the best. I knew it wouldn't take long for him to move up the ranks. He was smarter, faster and far more behaved than I'd ever be, and that's saying a helluva lot. I admired him greatly.

"Okay guys," I said, "split into your teams, get comms up and let's plan to be on site by 1300. Deb, make contact with Amadi's people and NYPD. Let them know we're on the way."

"Yes ma'am." She spun around and picked up the phone at her station. Everyone else followed suit and got to work.

By noon, we were equipped and ready to roll out. I followed the team in my car. Amadi lived in Nassau County, one of the richest parts of New York east of the city. The area's said to be one of the safest in the world, and I think I know why. It's nothing but old-ass rich white people living out there. Kidnapped my ass. I bet Keon's dancing around right now with his dick poking out a grass skirt giving the neighbor's daughter his spear chucking routine. Yes, I know that was a tasteless remark made at some poor unfortunate schmuck's expense, but after spending all that time with the late distinguished David Chandler, I can't help myself. I like to think he would've been proud of that one too, rest his soul. Sometimes I do stuff like that just to pay homage to him.

When we pulled up to the home, there were a few NYPD officers standing outside talking to Mr. Amadi. As always, we approached with our lights flashing, but this time we kept the sirens off. Amadi seemed to be just fine until I pulled up in my Aston Martin and got out. He took one look at me and you would've thought his kid was already dead. Men never cease to amaze me—especially Africans. The team hung back while Dom and I walked up to meet with Amadi. We stepped to him and did our standard dynamic duo bit.

"Gentlemen, I'm Special Agent Harris, FBI," announced Dom, flashing his credentials, "and, this is Assistant Special Agent in Charge Southerland. I know this is a difficult situation Mr. Amadi, but time is always against us, so pardon me for being short. Here's how this works ... my team will establish a command center inside your residence. Agents will occupy some parts of your home 24 hours a day until your son is returned safely. We'll control all incoming and outgoing landline calls and will also be monitoring cell phone signals. If a call comes in, we will screen, monitor, and attempt to identify the caller. Sometimes this can be a bit frustrating with us being so visible in your life, but it's important we be right there in the mix so we can get your boy home, and I promise you we will get your boy back home."

"Like District Attorney Miller's son?" Amadi retorted. His accent was heavy, but he spoke English fluently.

I smirked a little.

Dom didn't skip a beat. "It's unfortunate what happened to the Miller family," he said, "but it's also a good example of what happens when people ignore our recommendations. We're expert investigators, and we get nine out of ten victims back home safe and unharmed. You make it easy for us to do our job, we'll get Keon home, and this whole thing will all be behind us."

I was more than impressed with Dom's response. It was spot on.

"Do what you must," Amadi snapped, "I want my son back!" He turned around and walked into the house.

"Sergeant...?"

"Yeah, I'm Sergeant Rick Sharpe," said the officer.

"Okay Rick, anything we need to know?" asked Dom.

"We've been on site since yesterday after the detectives came through. We can stay if-"

"No need, Rick. See that van right there?" Dom pointed to the black van in our convoy. "Go to the back of that van and ask for Special Agent Deborah Moss. Once you brief her, you can pull your team out and get back to doing what you do best."

"Alright ... it's your show."

Dom shook his hand. "Thanks Rick, you're a good man."

Rick pushed the button on his radio. "Alright guys, FBI's here, let's pack it up. Rovetti, make sure you get these guys a copy of our logs."

"Copy that Sarge," Rovetti replied over the radio.

After about a half hour, the cops had cleared out and my guys were getting set up in Amadi's office on the first floor. I watched as they moved stuff around and did their thing. I think ASAC Johnson always had a problem with the way I work, but I never gave a shit. He moved way too slow for me. I was glad he transferred to Miami because I felt like he was holding us back. Doing it by the book is one thing, but further perpetuating all the bureaucracy and bringing our activity to a screeching halt right in the middle of a crisis is another.

There was no reason in hell for Johnson to slowpoke around with us. We had a pretty good team all things considered—I mean, there were a couple of bad apples—but for the most part we had a good crew, and Dominic was a gift from the gods themselves. I didn't have anything to worry about with him on the case. Our team needed to be able to move when we had to, and not wait for some old geezer to give the okay on every little micromanaged detail. I was glad Johnson bounced because that was his M.O. He had to know every little thing before it happened. Don't get me wrong, he's a good agent, but after he punked out on the Gordon case, I just couldn't deal with him anymore.

Dominic was a short guy, about 5' 10", but what he lacked in height he made up for with attitude. He was my kind of guy; confident, but smart enough to not be uselessly arrogant. He and I made a good team. He graduated top of his class in the academy and became one hell of an investigator, even though he was only 30. He had a close haircut, a thin goatee, and was always dressed very nicely; nothing out of place. Like I told Tony, I'm always the first and last one on the scene, but one thing I forget to mention when I say that is Dom's always right by my side. One day soon, I think he's going to make a good SAC, maybe even Assistant Director. He's definitely a good kid.

Now Deborah, she's a whole nother story. I'm always conflicted about her because she really is a good worker, but she is slow as molasses. Naturally, she and Johnson got along just fine, which irritated the shit outta me. She was funny as hell though, an older black woman about 45 years old. She'd been in the Army for over ten years before she joined the Bureau. She reminded me of Lieutenant Uhura on Star Trek, you know old in the face, but she got a banging body? The thing that really kept her in the game was she had serious skills. Even still, she was an enigma to me because she looked like she'll put yo' ass in a figure-four, or some other painful wrestling hold, but then she moves around like she's sleepwalking—mysterious indeed.

Deb was sweet, but she just didn't seem to have any reasonable sense of urgency. And, the thing is, she had an impeccable file. She probably could've taken Tony's job if she wanted to, but she never went for it. She just seemed to want to do her thing behind the scenes and go home. All and all, I definitely liked her. I just had to check myself because I move fast, so sometimes I be ready to go off on her slowpoke ass.

Dom and Deborah picked their field team fairly quickly. Ray Santos, Michael Eaton, and Chuck Warren made the cut plus the three of us for a six-man team.

Ray Santos is definitely a good agent, confident in his work and a science superfreak. When it comes to processing crime scene evidence, he wrote the book. I learned a ton of stuff from him over the past few years.

He's my Latin brother from Miami. I like hanging around Ray because I get a chance to practice my Spanish, but when he gets to talking fast and using all that damn slang, I just can't keep up.

Ray's cool, but Michael, or Mike as he likes to be called— well Mike's one of those sons-of-bitches I could do without. Oh, he's as friendly as they come, but he be on some shit. He's one of those sneaky bastards that pops up out of thin air and you don't know where the fuck he came from. I mean, you can be having the most private conversation on the planet. Suddenly, you look down and these little scaly white fingers will be crawling up over your shoulder like a spider, and there his ass is, right on your back like a goddamn monkey, hanging on to every word you say. I swear that fucker is a snitch for OPR.

Unfortunately, Mike was one of the three agents I took on the Gordon raid. I thought I could trust him, but after everything went belly-up, he got really quiet. I asked him if he talked to OPR, but he just beat around the bush and bullshitted me. I wanted to whoop his tall pasty white ass, but I couldn't prove he ratted me out. Honestly, I think he's feeding OPR info so he can get bumped up the ranks. That kind of mess makes me sick to my stomach. You really have to watch your peers more than OPR. Some of these cats will cut you for the next salary grade.

Last, but not least was Chuck Warren, who seemed to be a pretty good guy, but he and Mike were tight like two peas in a pod. Every time I do something Mike doesn't like, they have to run off in a corner like two little bitches and meet on it. Now that I'm ASAC, all that's gonna have to cease. Chuck was an older guy, but he seemed easily influenced, like he'd spent his life following the crowd. Still, we got along for the most part. Actually, despite the fact I bitch and moan about them, we all get along pretty well even when we're at odds.

So, there you have it. That's our crew. Soon as we got in the Amadi house and got the lay of the land, we jacked into the network and brought communications online. I walked around to check the cameras outside, and then made a test call. Everything seemed to be working fine.

"Dom...?"

He ran over to me. "Yeah, boss?"

"Get Amadi ready."

"Give me five minutes and meet us in the kitchen."

I smiled. "Did I tell you I love you?"

"Hey, I'm married!" Dom laughed, and then he took off.

I waited for five minutes and then casually made my way into the kitchen. Dom and Amadi were standing near the stove talking. Naturally, I interrupted. I walked right up to Amadi and shook his hand.

"Mr. Amadi, I'm Alex. How are you holding up?"

With both hands, he gripped mine tightly. "I am concerned for my son's safety. I am also concerned that the FBI has sent you to oversee this crisis instead of a more qualified agent. I feel they are not taking this matter seriously."

"Twenty-four hours," I replied.

He frowned. "I don't understand."

"Twenty-four hours is just one day, but I promise you a lot can happen in a day. Our kidnappers are smart, capable, and they took your son without leaving a shred of evidence behind. They have a three-day head start. Forget about the last 24 hours and let's think about the next 24 hours it's going to take to pull me off this case and get another negotiator here, if he's available. I'm assuming your problem is that I'm a woman. Well, I may be a woman, but I assure you I'm quite capable. Right now, I need you to make a decision ... you wanna waste the next 24 hours on red tape...? Or, do you wanna get your boy back?"

He sighed heavily. "I am at your mercy, Agent Southerland, but my brother will be here soon. He is head of security for my business in Nigeria, and I expect for you to give him the proper respect. I trust him, but I do not trust you."

"We'll see what we can do ... is there anything I can get you?"

He looked at me strange. "No."

"Good ... no more phone calls without me knowing, okay?" I tapped his shoulder.

That seemed to piss him off. He pointed his finger in my face. "I WANT MY SON BACK!" Then, he stormed out of the kitchen.

"Well, that went well," Dom joked.

I smiled. "Tell me about it."

"Don't worry about it, I'll run interference. We actually gonna let his brother get involved, Top?"

I thought about it carefully for a second. "If it'll calm his ass down, yeah. We'll just have to keep 'em isolated."

"N.T.K.?"

"Did I tell you-"

"I know I know," he interrupted, "you love me ... oh yeah, by the way, I got Deborah on coffee detail.

"I bet that's killing her."

"Not this time," Dom said, "she wanted to get out and get some fresh air. I think she might be having some trouble at home or something."

"Okay," I responded nodding, "I 'preciate the heads up on that Dom. Come on, let's get back in there."

We walked back around into Amadi's office. He was at his desk working, and the rest of the guys were monitoring from their respective workstations. Dom sat down and got to work too. I just kind of paced around, studying the room, especially Amadi. He and I traded a few mean looks, but he kept working and so did I. For the most part the rest of the day was uneventful.

Chapter 8

Much to my surprise, the rest of the week was extremely slow. I spent most of my time watching Amadi and taking notes on his general behavior, which left a lot to be desired if you ask me. At first, I thought maybe we'd luck up and he'd turn out to be one of those nice, friendly foreigners. Man was I wrong. Like Rick James would say, *He was cold as ice!* Dom and I took turns, sitting with him, slowly chipping away at the iceberg to see what was beneath the surface, but that was a full-time job in itself. Amadi was a good-looking man, and so was his son and his late wife—oh my goodness, she was unbelievably gorgeous. There were pictures of her all over the house. It was obvious she was missed.

With the size of Amadi's wallet, I was really surprised at the lack of staff and security personnel around him. For the most part, he was self-sufficient, which was most impressive. Anybody else would've had an entire entourage, but not him. He was actually pretty cool. All he needed was a good old fashion personality adjustment, and I was the right girl to help him in that department.

Thankfully, by the time the weekend came, he was finally starting to come around. It was Saturday morning around 7:30. Everyone else was asleep, but he was up, and by then sleep was just a fantasy for me, so I was up too. In fact, I already had my sweats on to go running around the property. I bumped into Amadi coming down the stairs.

"Good morning Mr. Amadi," I whispered.

He looked at me and frowned at first. Then, he gave me a fake smile. I think he was forcing himself to be cordial—that or he just wasn't much of a morning person.

"I have made coffee," he said. "We can drink it in the kitchen."

"That's where I do some of my best drinking," I responded. I was joking, but he didn't laugh.

"Come with me."

He always seemed so serious.

I dipped into the office and grabbed a cordless phone, and then met Amadi in the kitchen. "You have a lovely home," I complimented.

"Thank you," he replied. "I fear it is too much for my son and me."

"Perhaps you just need a woman's touch."

He smiled. "Can't you see it? My wife has touched everything here."

"She did a good job ... I'm sorry for your loss."

Suddenly, he stopped smiling. "This way, Agent Southerland."

"Please, call me Alex."

"That's very kind of you, Alex. May I return the favor?"

"Yes, please."

"I am Rahid," he said, "please, call me Rahid. Sit," he commanded.

I sat down at the breakfast bar and put the phone in my pocket. Rahid walked over to the cabinet and took out two cups. He removed the pot from the coffee maker and filled both cups. He fumbled around over there at the counter for a second before joining me at the bar. The coffee smelled delicious. It was some kind of hazelnut or something. But when I picked up my cup, I had to study the coffee for a moment because it looked a little funny. I raised an eyebrow as soon as I realized that sneaky bastard snuck some cream and sugar in there when I wasn't looking. I hate that stuff, but I needed to make some progress with Amadi, and offending the man over his coffee habits wouldn't have been a good start. I finally gave in and took a sip. It wasn't too bad, but it tasted more like dessert than breakfast.

"Is there something wrong with the coffee?" he asked.

I shook my head. "No, no, it's fine ... I'm just used to drinking black coffee."

He raised an eyebrow. "How strange."

I smiled. "Are you calling me strange, Rahid?"

"No, I'm sorry...." He took a few sips of his coffee. "Did you know that coffee is originally from Ethiopia?"

I put my cup down. "I didn't know that ... I thought we got it from the Arabs."

"It's true, central Ethiopia," he said, "it still grows there. The Arabs got it from Ethiopia. It just became popular in Arabia Qahveh houses in the 13th century."

"That's very interesting, Rahid. Tell me something else...."

"Yes...?"

"How do you do it?" I asked.

He looked at me strange. "What do you mean?"

"Well, you're an oil billionaire, but you seem so ... well, you just seem normal."

He laughed out loud. "Normal?"

"Yes, aside from the whole coffee story, you seem like a pretty normal guy."

"You did not like my story?" he asked, still chuckling. He spoke so proper it was damn near sickening.

"I've heard better pickup lines." I winked at him and drank a little more coffee. I must've hit a nerve because all of a sudden, his entire posture changed.

He put his cup down. "Why have they not called?" he asked. I could hear the frustration in his voice.

"Rahid, these things take time. It's a game to-"

"This is no game!" he exclaimed. "This is my only son's life you speak so callously of!"

"You're right, it's no game to us, but to them it's a big game. It's like going to gamble at the casino only they're playing with a set of loaded dice. You understand what I'm saying?" I got two chirps on my radio, but I didn't look down. I knew what that signal meant; Dom was up and mobile and just in time too because Shaft in Africa was starting to get on my fucking nerves.

"I'm an educated man," he said, "and I understand how this works."

I drank a little more coffee and just looked at him for a moment. Then I responded, "Patience is the word of the day Rahid. Now, I know that's tough for you … anybody can see you love your son, and you're in pain, but we have to take our time and do this the right way, alright?" I smiled.

"Enjoy the coffee." He walked over, put his cup in the sink and left the kitchen.

I picked up my radio, pressed the talk button and said, "House is yours Dom. I'll be back in twenty … see if you can get the subject to dial it down a few notches."

"Copy that, Top," he replied, "I'll do what I can, but I can't make any promises."

"See what you can do, over and out."

I walked out through the front of the house so I could get a good look at the street. Everything was copacetic, so I stretched and started jogging. I took my time and warmed up. Then, I kicked it up to a nice, brisk run.

Rahid's home was fairly large, a six-thousand square foot Victorian on about a five-acre lot. The landscape was just as beautiful and immaculate as the inside of the home. A small trail circled the perimeter. I went down by the front edge of the lot and then towards the back into a cluster of trees. I always made it a point to run, every day, no matter where I was or what was going on. I'd already run that trail several times before, but that day, something caught my eye—footprints—fresh footprints.

"Dom," I radioed.

"Go ahead," he responded.

"Code four, I repeat code four!" I pulled my backup gun from inside my sweat pants and cut across the yard to the back of the house. I ran as fast as I could. It took less than a minute for me to get to the backdoor. I turned the doorknob and pushed the door open. I could hear Rahid yelling at the top of his lungs. I peeked inside, before entering, gun first. By the time I made my way into Rahid's office, I had a pretty good idea why he was so agitated. If Rahid had an identical twin, then the man kicking and screaming, handcuffed to a chair with his mouth duct taped would be him. Those guys looked identical. I automatically assumed it was his brother, the security specialist.

"WE'RE CLEAR!" yelled Dom over his shoulder.

Mike and Chuck were standing near Dominic with their guns drawn too. Dominic reached back, handing me the intruder's firearm.

"THIS IS AN OUTRAGE!" exclaimed Rahid, pointing at me.

"Everyone okay?" I asked. I wanted to laugh, but I kept it to myself

"NO!" Rahid exclaimed. "Your agents have detained my brother for no reason. Are you here to protect me and my family or are you here to-"

"Come with me please," I interrupted.

Rahid looked over at Dom, who naturally nodded his head suggesting Rahid comply with my request or face his wrath. I turned around and walked out of the room. Rahid reluctantly followed. Outside in the hallway, I just let him vent for a minute.

"YOU HAVE NO RIGHT TO DO THIS!" he exclaimed. "I WILL CALL THE EMBASSY! I WILL CALL YOUR SUPERIOR AND HAVE YOU REMOVED FROM THIS HOME TODAY! DO YOU NOT HAVE ANYTHING TO SAY TO ME?"

"I figured I'd give you time to finish," I retorted.

"I have nothing further to say." He stood tall and stared me in the eye. "RELEASE MY BROTHER NOW!"

"No."

"WHAT...? HOW CAN YOU DO THIS, AGENT SOUTHERLAND?"

"Alex, call me Alex. And, I can do this because your brother unlawfully breached our perimeter. I call that obstruction of justice. Not to mention the fact he's carrying a concealed weapon," I held the gun up, "which makes this an official crime scene. I'm gonna have one of my agents take him in for questioning, and we'll hold him for as long as the law will allow. Then, I'll have him deported, how'd that be?"

Rahid frowned.

"Now, I know the charges won't stick, and he'll be back soon, but not before I make contact with the kidnappers, and I will make contact with the kidnappers. Now, you can make your calls and try to get me pulled, but with all due respect, Rahid, you don't wanna fuck with me."

He gasped and tried to respond, but I didn't give him the chance. I kept right on selling my wolf-tickets.

"You and your brother wanna play games? I know a whole lot of games ... we can do this all day long."

"This is outrageous, my brother is here to help, and so far, you have done nothing to get my son back. You need to let my brother do his job."

"And, what is that exactly?"

"I NEED HIM TO FIND MY SON!" he exclaimed.

I sighed deeply. "Here's what's gonna happen. My agents are going to step out of your office and guard the doors. What's your brother's name?"

"Gamba," he replied.

"Okay, Gamba ... so, you'll go into your office, you'll remove the duct tape from Gamba's mouth, and you will tell him to be cool ... you know why you're gonna tell him to be cool?"

He just stared at me, still frowning.

"You're gonna tell him to be cool because if he's not cool, I'll spend an entire day coming up with bullshit charges that are gonna land his ass in Gitmo while the State Department sorts everything out, which under normal circumstances could be about a year. Do we understand each other?"

"Fine."

He started to walk off, but I put my hand on his chest and stopped him. I held up my radio. "Dom...?"

"Go ahead, Top," he replied.

"We're code six."

"Copy that, we're coming out now."

I nodded towards the door. "Make sure Gamba understands."

Rahid pushed me out of his way and ran back into his office.

"Top...?" Dom radioed.

"I'm here."

"Setting up a perimeter, I'll be on you in five."

"Copy that ... stay sharp."

Five minutes passed and Dom was on me as expected. "They're still in there," he said.

"Yeah, I know." I gave him a disgusted look. "Duct tape, Dom?"

He smiled. "The man was resisting."

"Whatever!" I slapped his arm. "You think he's gonna play ball?"

"I dunno," he replied, sighing heavily. "I don't get these guys man. Why the hell won't they just let us do our job?"

"You got kids, Dom?"

"You know I do boss," he replied, "I got a little girl."

"Well, I don't, but...."

"What?" he asked.

"Back in Atlanta, years ago, I was working undercover on a case. We'd been tryin' to catch this serial killer for a long time. Turns out he wasn't even a real serial killer, but that's another story. I went deep under cover but fucked up real bad ... ended up compromising the case, but that wasn't the whole of it. I exposed my boyfriend too. Killer tracked him down and got to him before I did. I was drunk that night— totally blitzed out of my mind. When I got back home and walked through the door, my boyfriend fell out onto the floor right in front of me, and the killer took me down before I could move a muscle. Right then, right there in that dark apartment while he was smacking me upside my head with a bat, the only thing I could think about was the fact he had my boyfriend. I thought he was gonna take him away and kill him or hurt him real bad, and there was nothing I could do about it. The last time that guy swung and hit me, I blacked out. When I woke up in the hospital, my boyfriend was right there with me in the room. I was glad to see he was still alive and okay, but that 30 or so seconds when I was coming to was complete hell. Here's what I'm saying ... the family members of kidnapping victims have the same feeling I did for that brief 30 seconds, only it's there every day when they wake up, when they eat, when they go to bed—24 hours a day, seven days a week—they never stop thinking about it. If I were Rahid, I'd be trying everything I could, and I'd only trust the people I know. What about you?"

Dom rubbed his head. "Damn Top, that's deep. I guess I'd do whatever I had to for my baby girl ... so, whatever happened to your boyfriend?"

"Awe fuck 'em, he cheated on me! I should've let his ass get killed, you ready?"

He chuckled. "Yeah come on."

Dom led the way back into the office. Rahid was standing with his arms crossed right beside his brother Gamba, who of course was still cuffed to the chair. Obviously, the two of them had spoken. Dom walked over and stood in front of Rahid as I walked up to Gamba and dropped down to his level.

"I'm Assistant Special Agent in Charge Alex Southerland."

"I am Gamba," he responded.

"Gamba," I said, smiling, "pleasure to meet you ... now, you gonna play nice, Gamba?"

"We have many kidnappings in Nigeria. These men know everything about you, and they will not deal with a half-breed. They will kill Keon if you do not allow me to negotiate with-"

"Okay, cowboy," I interrupted, "calm down and listen carefully ... I have every right to detain you after that 007 bullshit you just pulled sneaking onto this property past my agents. So, you have two options ... stay, and do everything you can to take care of your brother. Mr. Amadi's already gone through a lot and it's gonna get worse. So, you stay here, you help him around the house, you talk to him and be a good brother. Or, you go back to Nigeria and you don't look back. You see, I just lost a kid, and I'm not gonna allow you to make me lose another. You screw around with me on this, and you'll be looking over your shoulder for the rest of your short-lived life. I will hunt your ass down."

Gamba seemed shocked when I said that, but I think he knew I was dead serious.

"Now, you're welcome to stay Gamba, but you can leave at my discretion. You understand what I mean?"

Gamba replied, "Yes, Agent Southerland of the FBI."

I smiled. "Please, call me Alex. Now, what can you tell me about Aker?"

"Agent Southerland, he is cooperating," Rahid said calmly. "Please remove his restraints."

I looked over at Dom and gave him a slight nod. He immediately moved over and began removing the cuffs. Before Dom freed both hands, he warned Gamba to remain calm. As soon as Gamba was loose, he rubbed his wrists and sat up in his chair.

"I apologize, but I needed to see my brother, and I was afraid your agents would redirect me."

"You're right Gamba," I replied, "we would've taken you to the office to question and brief you first. We have to maintain control of this environment because that's all we have control over during this entire process. Remember, they have Keon, which means they have the upper hand."

"I appreciate your honesty," Gamba responded. "I will tell you of Aker now ... he is South African. He works for no one but is paid by everyone. He is everywhere and nowhere. He negotiates for so-called freedom fighters all over Africa and South America. The IGP has dedicated an Anti-Corruption team to finding and killing the man, who calls himself Aker, god of man, but no one knows what he looks like-"

"IGP?"

"Yes," he replied, "the Inspector General of Police."

"Oh yeah, I got it. So Gamba, why do you think we haven't heard from this god character yet?"

Gamba thought about it for a moment. "Kidnappings in Nigeria have increased. He is thorough, and he will only negotiate one at a time."

"So, basically, we're queued up."

"I do not understand," Gamba replied.

Rahid clarified for him. "Brother, she is saying our time is coming soon."

"Yes," said Gamba, "I understand. Alex, you must delay Aker long enough for me to find Keon. Please, let me help you."

I shook my head. "You're not getting this Gamba. You stay here. If you sneak out, I'll have you arrested. This is nonnegotiable. I assure you, our primary objective is to bring Keon home alive. You're gonna have to trust me."

"Trust must be earned," Gamba retorted.

"Then you better start working hard to earn mine 'cause you're starting out in the red. Now, are there any questions, gentlemen?" I looked back at Rahid.

"No," Rahid replied.

"Do we have an understanding?"

"Yes," said Rahid.

I turned back to Gamba. "Gamba?"

He reluctantly replied, "Yes."

"Fantastic!" I looked over at Dom. "I'm gonna finish running ... house is yours."

Dom held up his radio. "Team, all clear ... stand down."

As I walked outside, the other agents filed back into the house, all except Chuck, who continued to roam the property.

It's no secret, I don't like Nigerians. I think they're some of the most crooked, heinous mothafuckas on the planet. Every dollar they make I imagine somehow is directly associated with a severed head, an arm, or titty, or an email scam, and the list goes on. Bottom line, I didn't trust either brother as far as I could throw them. For all I knew, they could've had the boy kidnapped themselves. However, Gamba knew more about this Aker god joker than I did, so for the moment, I let him hang around. Still, I knew we had to keep an eye on him. Perhaps he meant well, but I couldn't risk him poking around and blowing the case. There was a lot at stake—more than just Keon's life. This was my chance to get righteous again.

I got on the trail and sprinted to get my heart rate back up. I jogged about 30 minutes and then went back inside to get cleaned up. By the time I finished showering and got dressed, everyone seemed to have calmed down, including Gamba. It would seem he finally accepted the fact he wasn't running the show. I'm sure for him that was like getting reamed up the butthole with a broomstick coming from a light skinned half-breed like me. *Arrogant ass Africans!* I should've just kicked him in the throat, and we could've called it square. As passionate as I felt about getting Keon home unscathed, part of me wanted to just say the hell with it and let those snooty charcoal-looking mothafuckas figure it out for themselves. I think Dom felt the same way. His attitude was getting worse by the moment. I sat down beside him and touched his shoulder.

"You good?" I asked.

"Yeah, Top, I'm fine." He rubbed his face with both hands. "I just hate waiting around doing nothing."

"Me too."

"Oh, yeah, here's the backup you asked for." He handed me a file.

I asked him, "How's the rest of the team holding up?"

"Solid," he replied. "Since they're done with the backup, Crane pulled them over to help with another investigation."

"Good ... I know they hate being idle too. I'm gonna go check this out in my room."

"We'll hold the fort down," he said.

I walked down the hall to the guest room I was set up in. I sat down at the desk and opened up the file Dom had just given me. It was kinda dim in there, so I turned the lamp on. Then, I started reading to myself softly in hopes of countering the dead silence in the house. "Let's see here ... Rahid Amadi, 46, six feet tall, 190 pounds, muscular build, brown eyes ... he's got a serious scar on his neck from where someone tried to rob him with a machete. Wonder why I didn't notice that earlier ... guess I haven't gotten that close to him. Arrested by Interpol in 1989 for export noncompliance but was released without being charged. Mother, Monifa, was killed in a car bombing ... uh, hmm ... Father, Oba, cocoa exporter, survived a kidnapping, and turned the family cocoa business over to sons Rahid and Gamba. Looks like Rahid moved them into petroleum right after the father died. Hmm ... nothing out of the ordinary here." I flipped through the pages, still mumbling aloud to myself. "Financials ... shit this fucker's rich, I mean for chrissake! And, I thought I had loot, this man makes me look like a goddamn hobo."

I leaned back in my chair and just let my mind wander. But, after a while, all I could think about was Bill and my little brother Christopher. I missed them. I wondered what

Chris looked like. All I knew was he was enrolled as a freshman at Princeton University if you can imagine that. I didn't doubt it for a second. He was always smart as hell.

New Jersey was just a hop, skip, and a jump away from New York. I wanted to go down and see him, but I didn't know if he would even recognize me. There's no telling what Theresa and Mom had been telling him all those years. *Evil bitches.* I've prayed about it over and over again, but the result's still the same. I have nothing but hate in my heart for the pair of them. Amazingly though, for some reason, I'm willing to give Bill a pass. *Who would've thunk it?* I treat him badly because he hurt me, but honestly, I was hoping Bill would simply ignore my bullshit and keep calling me anyway.

"Come on Alex get back on the clock sweetie we got work to do," I mumbled.

I was definitely with Dom on the whole waiting thing. I hate waiting around for anything, but all we could do was wait—wait for the bad man to make the first move, so we could do what we do best—get the victim home safely and do it quickly.

The thing about this case that really bugged me was we had zilch on the people that took Keon. Usually, we could spend this time doing some research on the kidnappers, but we didn't have anything to go on. We had to just wait until Aker made contact, and then hopefully we could get busy and turn up something that would give us an edge. I've found the smallest detail can help turn things around and give us the upper hand. Sometimes it even pushes the kidnappers into making a mistake or two. There would be plenty to get done when the time came, but until then, all we could do was wait it out and try not to let anxiety get the best of us.

Chapter 9

Another week passed and everyone was starting to get edgy, especially Rahid and Gamba. At one point, I overheard them speaking in their native tongue, and I thought they were just gonna strip down to their drawers and start yelling and roaring in some kind of primal rage. Thankfully, they managed to hold it down.

I continued my daily running routine, taking my time outside to reflect on things and of course do what I had to do to remain patient and calm. My job during that time was to keep everyone focused, but all the waiting was getting to me too. After weeks of no contact from Aker, I had the strange feeling Keon was already dead. I think the others did too, but no one dare utter the words.

It was late Tuesday night, almost 11 p.m. The sky was clear, and the moon lit up the cityscape like the sun on a mid-summer day. All of New York was bathed in blue. It was a scenic sight serene enough to turn even the most savage of beasts into a calm, compliant pushover. The entire house was quiet and at a complete standstill. We'd been complaining about the downtime for weeks. It seemed like the harshest kind of torture. I didn't realize it at the time, but before long, we'd all be begging for some peace and quiet.

I'd just finished writing my report to Tony. It was a short one. Basically, there was nothing new to report, but as soon as I pressed the send button, everything changed. The phone rang the instant my email went out. I sprung up from my desk, tripping over the leg of my chair and nearly knocking down the lamp. I opened the door and ran full speed to Rahid's office. Just before I got there, I slowed down and walked briskly into the room. Rahid, Gamba, and the rest of the team were waiting for me. It was late, and Rahid's telephone patterns didn't involve inbound calls after 9 p.m. Everyone had that look on their face like they knew exactly who was on the other end. I had a pretty good idea myself.

"We ready?" I asked.

Dom gave me a thumbs-up, and Michael held up a wireless headset, so I walked over and took it from him. I put on the headset and Dom pointed for Rahid to pick up. He grabbed the receiver and put it up to his ear slowly.

"Hello," Rahid answered.

"Mr. Amadi, do you love your son?" The man had a European accent.

"Yes," Rahid replied, "with all my heart, please do not hurt my son."

"Do you believe in God, Mr. Amadi?"

"Yes. I am a God-fearing man."

"Then, you understand that God giveth and God taketh away, yes?" the man asked.

Rahid begged, "Please Sir ... I beg you, do not hurt my son Keon. Please."

"You know that I am a god too, don't you Mr. Amadi? I am the god of deliverance ... you may call me Aker-"

"Gatekeeper of the Underworld," replied Rahid.

"Ah, an educated man," said Aker, "most impressive."

"Can you help me Aker? Can you give me my boy back?"

"That depends, Mr. Amadi," he replied. "I'm afraid my job is quite simple. I control the gate that gives you passage into a dark world. I am your son's keeper of life. I hold his in the palm of my hand. Listen carefully Mr. Amadi ... there's nothing about this transaction you will be familiar with. This is not a feature film at a theatre. We do not ask for money and then tell you to not involve the authorities. The people I represent are professionals. They will deliver as agreed as long as you supply the money. Do you understand?"

"Yes," replied Rahid.

"This will be the last time that you and I speak Mr. Amadi," said Aker. "If I hear your voice on the line, I will have young Keon raped, ravaged, and beheaded. I will broadcast it over and over again on the internet, and the footage will be as clear as a bell so you may experience his pain up close and personal. Do you understand?"

"Yes." Rahid's voice trembled.

"Fabulous. Now, put Assistant Special Agent in Charge Denise Alexandria Southerland on the line, and as for you my friend ... you may fuck off!"

I started pacing around a bit. Clearly, this guy had his shit together, and I had about 30 seconds to work on mine. I took a deep breath and then snapped my finger at Dom. He muted Rahid's phone and turned my mic on.

"This is Agent Southerland," I said.

"May I call you Alex?" asked Aker.

"Yes, you may," I replied politely.

"Do you think you are here to negotiate, Alex?" he asked.

"I'm here to help you," I replied. "I'm only interested in helping you close this transaction quickly, effectively, and on a positive note."

Aker cleared his throat. "Perhaps we should first discuss how I work."

"Please."

"Your mother just died of a horrible cancer," he said. "Your ex-boyfriend is alive and well, living with his new wife—your half-sister, who's with child. Personally, I think it's an adulterous shame what she did to you, but that's just my opinion. You have a younger brother, Christopher Southerland, currently enrolled in Princeton ... excellent school by the way ... I hear he's made the Dean's list again. You don't have much family, which is unfortunate and at the same time quite a blessing. Allow me to explain ... if you deviate from my instructions in any way, I will annihilate your entire family. However, in your case, you'll only mourn the loss of four family members. That is your blessing and mine too. I just as soon not murder 30 or 50 people as it makes for a difficult thing to schedule. Now, would you say we have agreeable terms?"

I was cool as hell. "It would seem we do, Aker."

"You are both intelligent and wise," he replied. "Now, what is your schedule?"

"I'm available 24 hours a day ... again I'm here to help."

"You will have your day to do as you please, but you will give your nights to me. I know that your men are attempting to trace this call, however, I assure you there's no need to waste valuable agency resources on that. The number on your display is my can-be-reached number. You will see it is a local number, but there is nothing you can do about it. You may call me at night, or I will call you. Do you have any questions Alex?"

"Yes."

"Please, go ahead." He was so polite.

"You know everything about me, so you should know what I can do with a phone number ... why so open?"

"I would've been terribly disappointed had you not asked, young lady. I work in the South African Consulate here in New York. However, I command a limitless number of soldiers and personnel in the Nigerian Embassy where Keon is being held. Naturally, you will put surveillance on the embassy, but you will not breech its security. Such an attempt would be considered an act of war on sovereign Nigerian soil and my soldiers will kill your men ... then, I will kill your family. If you arrest me, you'll achieve nothing. I have diplomatic immunity and will in a worst-case scenario be deported, but Keon's fate will be an atrocity on CNN. This is check-mate, and your only move is to do exactly as I say, or you will pay the price for your lack of cooperation. Today is Friday, Alex... sleep well this weekend, and we will talk again Monday."

The call disconnected. I pulled off my headset and went out the back. I took a few deep breaths and then called Tony from my cell.

"Crane," he answered.

"Tony, it's Alex."

"What's going on?" he asked.

"We need to talk, now."

"Okay."

"No, in person!"

Tony sighed. "How soon can you be here?"

"Give me-"

"Wait," he interrupted. "No, I'll meet you at your apartment, alright? Give me an hour."

"I'll see you there." I hung up and walked back inside. "Dom," I waved.

He ran over to me and whispered slowly, "What do you want us to do?"

I shook my head. "I don't know yet ... I've gotta go meet with Tony. Lock this place down until I get back."

"I'm on it, Top." He turned around. "Mike, Chuck, Deborah, Ray ... I need two on full perimeter and two roaming. I'll cover the inside. No one gets in or out without my say. Call up NYPD and get some backup on the perimeter. Get me a unit on both ends of the street, got it?"

"Yes, sir," replied Deborah.

"I'll take the front," Mike volunteered.

"I'll cover the back," Deborah said.

"Okay, that puts Chuck and Ray roaming," said Dominic. "Radio silence with half hour stat-reps ... Go! Go! Go!"

I watched as Dom walked over to Rahid and Gamba, who were on pins and needles.

"Mr. Amadi," said Dom.

"What is going on?" Rahid desperately asked.

"Sir, this was an unusual initial contact," Dom replied. "We need to invoke certain authority before we can proceed. Our Chief Negotiator, Agent Southerland, is going to meet with FBI leadership to discuss options. Meanwhile, I need for both of you to remain calm and inside the home ... please, allow us to do our job and protect you."

"We will do our part," said Gamba.

Rahid nodded.

Then, Gamba looked over at me. "You are surprised by Aker, no?"

I didn't show any emotion at all. "I don't put anything past these criminals, Gamba."

Gamba said, "I beg you to reconsider."

I ignored him and looked at Dom. "No one gets in or out."

"Copy that, Top," he replied.

I stormed out to the car and got inside. I cranked up, and then turned the car around in the driveway. I put it in first and headed for the front gate. Mike was already in place controlling access. I heard him radio Dom to tell him I was leaving the grounds. As I pulled out onto the street, I couldn't help but think about Aker and how he knew so much about me. More than that, why the hell would they be so bold as to use the Embassy to operate out of? Obviously, he was well connected, but how and to whom? Far as I could tell, the whole situation was growing worse by the moment. It was as if we were already 20 points down and the ballgame hadn't even started yet.

Unless Aker was bullshitting me, and I doubt he was, we knew where Keon was, which is why I needed to see Tony. We had to find a way to get into that Embassy. I figured somebody above my pay grade should be able to make some contacts and get the President of Nigeria to play ball with us. Unfortunately, that idea just seemed a little too simple for U.S. government style foreign affairs.

I turned on my warning lights and plowed through traffic, running red lights and cutting down every alley possible to get over to my apartment fast. I wheeled into the parking deck, jumped out and ran into the elevator. I went up to my floor and walked down the hallway towards the apartment. Tony was waiting for me outside.

"I thought you said an hour."

"I was able to get away sooner than expected," Tony replied.

"Don't you have a key?" I asked.

"Yeah, but I didn't want to be rude."

"Shit man, you should be used to all my empty beer bottles by now."

Tony smiled.

I unlocked the door and we walked in. I took my jacket off and threw it over one of the kitchen chairs. Then, I poured myself some vodka and sat down next to Tony on the sofa. I was so busy drinking and pouring, I didn't even notice what he was holding in his hand. Finally, I looked over at him. He had such a serious look on his face.

"I can explain that," I said, choking down a glass full of liquor.

"Please ... explain." Tony frowned, holding up the little Ziploc bag of high-dollar weed I obviously forgot to conceal in my haste to leave the apartment. I left it out in plain sight on the coffee table.

"Yeah ... well, I started smoking again."

He squinted. "But this is marijuana ... I'm confused, Alex."

For some reason I started blinking uncontrollably. "Like I said, I started smoking again." I stood up and snatched the bag of weed from him. "You weren't supposed to see that." I walked over and stuffed the bag into one of the drawers on the other side of the living room. I looked back and Tony was sitting there just shaking his head. He was at a complete loss for words.

"Tony ... hell, I don't know what to say."

"You know, I ... I just don't know what I was thinking," he confessed, putting his face in his hands.

"I know what you're thinking, Tony-"

"Do you?" he interrupted.

"Well, yeah ... you think I'm ungrateful and foolish ... and a pain in the ass, right?"

"Go on," he responded.

"But, there's one thing you're overlooking."

"Alex, what ... what on earth could that be?"

"I'm a good agent."

"Yeah, a good agent that's about to be suspended yet again for drug use. As soon as you're done with the Amadi case, you've got an unannounced piss test."

"What?" I almost jumped up out of my skin.

"You're making my head hurt," he said, "I'm starting to regret I gave you access to that money. It's like I'm enabling you."

I shook my head and smiled. "Tony, I'm just going through some things and-"

"I can't deal with this right now," Tony said. "We'll talk about this later ... what's going on with the case?"

I sat back down on the sofa. "The negotiator for the kidnappers is up on his game, but he's crazy. He knows everything about me, and I can tell he doesn't play around. Claims to be working out of the South African Consulate and has soldiers running out of the Nigerian Embassy. Get this...."

"What?"

"They're holding the boy in the Embassy."

"He told you that?" asked Tony.

"Yes."

"And you believed him?" he asked.

"Yes," I replied, "I really do."

Tony reached over and took the bottle of vodka from me. He poured himself a double into my glass, picked it up and gulped it down. "So, you want me to give you authorization to search the Embassy?" he speculated.

I turned and leaned back against the throw pillow, pulling my left leg up onto the sofa. "I don't know. I don't think we have a chance in hell to get the kid out alive. I think we need to put surveillance on the Consulate and Embassy, and maybe try to figure out the identity of this negotiator, this uh Aker dude."

"There's gotta be something we can do," Tony said. "That's a bold move to snatch a kid and use the Embassy to ransom him. I can check with the Deputy Director and see what kind of cards we're holding."

"Yeah, but how long's that gonna take?" I asked.

"Weeks, maybe months," he replied.

"Tony, the kid'll be dead by then." I picked up the vodka again. "Here you want another?"

"Yeah," he replied.

I filled his glass and we continued talking. I was too lazy to get another glass, so I just drank from the bottle.

"Is there any other way we can do this?" asked Tony. "What does this guy call himself again?"

"Aker."

"Hmm ... Isn't that a Greek god?" he asked.

"No, I think it's Egyptian, GATEKEEPER OF THE UNDERWORLD!" I exclaimed in a spooky voice.

Tony gulped down his drink and put the glass back on the coffee table. He leaned back against the sofa and closed his eyes.

"What's wrong, Tony?"

He looked over and stared at me for a second, contemplating whether he'd clue me in or not. He sighed and said, "Girlfriend's driving me nuts ... nice little Italian girl, but she's talking marriage. Not sure I'm ready for that. Oh, while I'm thinking about it, Josh says you have to do a photo shoot for Long Island Aston Martin. What's that about?"

I shook my head and frowned. "It's a long story."

Tony said, "Try to keep a low profile while we're sorting this Amadi thing out ... you think you can handle that?"

"Alright...." I thought for a second. "You think we should try to get a warrant or somethin'?"

"It's not gonna help," Tony replied. "Technically, the Consulate isn't U.S. territory ... we don't have jurisdiction ... give me a few days, and I'll see what I can come up with. Meanwhile, I'll give you one team for surveillance, but you can't have any contact with them at all."

"Why?" I asked.

Tony replied, "If this Aker's as good as you say he is, he's already got eyes on you. We don't want to spook anyone and end this thing prematurely. I'll put together some kind of operation that's not connected and personally share any intel with you. Stall Aker as long as you can, but not too long ... just make sure you get proof of life."

"Yeah, we're concerned the boy may already be dead. The other issue is the brother."

"The security specialist?" asked Tony.

"Yes. Of course, he thinks he can deal with Aker better than we can. We've got him under control for now, but I can see he might be a problem."

"Just handle him with kid gloves," Tony recommended. "You remember how to do that, right?"

I smiled. "If he gets in my way, I'M TAKING HIM DOWN!"

Tony chuckled. "Look, just watch your six. We're in political space now. Meanwhile, I'll see what I can do from the top."

"So, you're getting married?" I asked.

Tony frowned like never before. "I don't wanna talk about it. Look, I gotta go. I'm authorizing you to do what you need to do, but please use your best judgment ... I know I keep asking if you can handle stuff, but based on what I see here, I gotta do what I gotta do. So, you think you can handle that?"

"Done."

"Good," Tony replied, "now, how are you really doing?"

I ran my fingers through my hair. "I try to stay busy, but I get pretty lonely sometimes, you know?"

"I know how you feel," Tony said. "When Barbra left, I was in pieces, but I promise you it'll get better. You've still got people, who love you and you're unbelievably gorgeous."

I started cheesing really big. Tony's compliment was either super flattering or the vodka was working a number on me.

Tony said, "You got nothing to worry about in the friend department, we love you ... but Alex, I need you to be a little smarter in other areas."

"What, like the weed?" I asked, sheepishly.

"I'll push the piss test back six months," he responded, "but you're gonna have to walk the straight and narrow, understand?"

"You always take care of me, Tony," I said softly.

"Forgetaboutit," he responded, smiling. "Come on." He reached over for a hug.

I crawled across the sofa and all but jumped on him. He smelled so good, just like a real man should. We embraced, and I held on as tight as I could. Somehow in the process, I managed to make it over into his lap. I wrapped my arms around his neck and continued to hug him. Then, I closed my eyes and moved around until my lips were about an inch from his.

"Alex...?"

"Yes Tony," I whispered, seductively.

"I can't breathe," he said.

"OH SHIT!" I pulled back and fell onto the floor, bumping my head on the end of the coffee table.

Tony quickly grabbed my arm and pulled me back up. "You okay?" he asked.

I just threw my hands up in sheer embarrassment. "Yeah, I'm fine." That vodka really was messing with my head. Maybe I drank too much of it, but my pussy was aching for dick, and Tony was looking fine as hell in that sharp, black suit. By then, all I wanted him to authorize was me squeezing his bare ass while he fucked the back of my throat with his cock. I started thinking about what his dick was like, but then the bastard interrupted me.

"You sure you're okay?" he asked.

"Um, yeah ... yeah, I'm cool, Tony"

"I'll let myself out," he said. "Uh...." He cleared his throat. "Keep me posted on your progress."

"Will do." I giggled a bit. Then, I went and plopped back down on the sofa. I was glad he left because that was one hell of an awkward situation. Something's seriously wrong with me. I don't think it was Tony at all--okay, it was Tony a little bit--but I never thought about him like that before. Maybe it's because I never knew he had a girlfriend. Soon as he told me she was talking marriage, my pussy got really wet. It never fails. I always want the guys I can't have. I looked down and realized just how much I drank out that bottle. I was tipsy and losing control once again. I looked at my watch. It was after midnight.

"Go ahead," she said.

"Huh?"

"I know you wanna get fucked, but you're scared, so go ahead and have another drink, it's alright, sexy."

"I hate you bitch, get out of there!" I grabbed my head with both hands and closed my eyes tight, but I couldn't get her voice out of my mind.

"Remember what we did in college?" asked Blondie.

"Shut up!"

"Remember what we did with her?" she asked.

"SHUT UP GODDAMMIT, JUST SHUT THE FUCK UP!" I snatched the bottle of vodka and turned it up to my lips. I was trying to drown that blonde trick to death, and at first it seemed to be working, but it had an unfortunate side effect. I got so drunk and horny I couldn't see straight.

I ripped my clothes off and licked my fingers until they were nice and wet. Then I played with my clit and fingered my pussy for a while. I thought masturbating would calm me down, but it didn't, and I was beginning to feel that burning sensation deep inside again. I was so hot I couldn't think about anything else. I jumped up, threw on a short dress, some heels, and a coat. I stuffed my badge, gun, cuffs and cell into a purse and left the apartment.

"Ms. Southerland!" yelled Ralph. "I haven't seen you in a while. Hey, you don't look so good, are you alright?"

"I'm fine Ralph. Can you get me a cab?" I asked, walking right past the desk.

Ralph circled around and ran ahead. He held the door open for me and then came outside behind me. He spotted a cab and sprang into action. He stepped into the street, whistled and waved. The cab driver pulled over to the curb.

"Thanks Ralph." I handed him a twenty.

"Any time, Ms. Southerland, and thank you," he responded, holding the cash up for a brief moment.

"Alex," I reminded.

"Thank you, Alex." He held the cab door open while I climbed in.

"Where to?" asked the cab.

Ralph shut the door.

"East 54th street," I ordered.

The cab driver started the meter and pulled off. He seemed to be taking the scenic route, but I didn't care. I had a buzz from the drinks back at the apartment. When we got over to East 54th, I told the driver to stop the cab. He pulled over to the curb. I got out and paid my fare. Then, I walked down the street towards this club I'd been to before.

I could hear the music thumping as I approached the entrance of the club. Evidently, it was reggae night. There was a line at the door, but I walked right up to the front and opened my coat. It was cold outside, and I was extremely horny, so my nipples were poking through my thin dress. The doorman looked me up and down, and then waved me on in.

I checked my coat and walked up to the bar. I ordered myself a drink, Courvoisier, straight up. As always, I downed it fast. I got ready to order a second when a gentleman approached. I was kind of feeling him because that brother stepped to me and got right to the point.

"I'm going to buy you a drink, and we're going to dance," he predicted.

I smiled. I liked his attitude. It was real "New Yorkish". He was seriously good looking too, well-built and dressed nicely. I leaned into him and said, "You're wrong big boy."

"Oh, you think so?" he asked.

I put my lips to his ear. "You're so fuckin' wrong baby."

"How's that?" he asked.

"You're going to buy me another drink, but we won't be dancing tonight."

"Really?" He started grinning big. "So, what's the plan?"

I pushed him away a little. "Hey, don't be a fuckup!" I yelled. Then, I put my finger in my mouth and sucked it. I was convinced he got the message.

He leaned in and whispered in my ear. "I'm here wit' my homeboy ... let me tell that nigga to go catch a cab."

He was about to walk away, but I grabbed his jacket. "Is he ugly or something?" I yelled.

He laughed. "Fuck you askin' me for shawty?"

I shook my head. "Nah, good looking boy like you ... you ain't gone be hanging around no busted mufuckas ... what's the matter, you can't handle competition?"

"Yo, fuck dat son!" he replied.

"Hey, I don't care about your little pride, baby I need dicks not a dick. Your boy can fuck, or he can watch. That's the deal. You got a car?"

"Yeah." He flagged down the bartender. "One more ova here!" he yelled.

I drank another cognac as he rounded up his boy, who by the way was finer than hell. That nigga was all big, dark and chocolate, and his legs were like tree trunks, damn near busting out his slacks.

"This her?" asked his buddy.

I shot him a bird. "Keep running your mouth, slick, and you'll regret it."

He laughed. I sucked down the last of my drink and leaned my head back slowly. I started rubbing my chest. I thought those two clowns were gonna jack off right there at the bar. I hopped down and started walking to the door, swinging my hips left to right, playing with the bottom of my skirt. I grabbed my coat and walked outside to wait for those two idiots to come out. Finally, they did. The first guy I met ran over to his BMW 745. He got in and started the motor.

"So, what's your story," asked the tall, really hot looking one.

I rolled my eyes. "You ask way too many questions, are you retarded or some shit?"

"HEY, FUCK YOU BITCH!" he exclaimed.

"That's more like it slick," I teased.

"Yo, the name's-"

I put two fingers over his lips. "Shhh ... don't mess this up for me, okay?"

"Yo, you psycho, man!" he responded.

"Look at my ass...." I turned around and pulled my coat and skirt up. I wasn't wearing any underwear. I looked back and watched his eyes get big. "Like I said, shut the fuck up and don't blow this for your boy."

He shut up just like I told him to. His buddy pulled the car around. I got in up front and immediately started rubbing the driver all over. I stuck my hand in his shirt and rubbed his hairy chest. Then, I put my tongue in his ear and reached down, rubbing the inside of his thighs and gripping his balls in the palm of my hand. His dick grew big in his pants. It was nice and hard, thick just like I like it. My head was spinning from those last two drinks. That cognac plus the vodka I drank earlier had me feeling just right. At first, his boy was just standing there watching through the window. Finally, he got smart and got in.

"Damn homie!" he exclaimed, climbing into the back. He closed the door and leaned forward to see me doing what I do best.

"He talks too much," I whispered. "Tell him to shut the fuck up so you can have this pussy first."

The driver turned around like he was ready to shoot that fool in both kneecaps. "HEY, DON'T FUCK THIS UP NIGGA, SHUT THE FUCK UP!"

"Ooh, good boy," I said, giggling. "Now, take me home and get this good pussy."

Without saying another word, he sped us off into the night. You would've thought that man was an Indy car driver because he was rolling, dipping left and right through traffic. I continued teasing him the entire way. I even let his boy feel up my tits from behind.

They took me to his apartment in Brooklyn. It was kind of a bad neighborhood, but the inside of the apartment was nice—not as nice as mine, but nice enough for what we were going to be doing. The three of us went inside straight back to the bedroom, which was quite clean and neat for a bachelor. I didn't waste any time. I threw my purse in the chair in the corner and stripped off my coat and dress, but I left my heels on to create the proper effect.

I walked over and jumped up on the bed, got down on my back and immediately started playing with my kitty. It was completely shaved and already wet from the drive over. They were both standing there like they were awaiting orders, so I gave them one.

"STRIP!" I yelled. "...NOW!"

They looked at each other a little strange, but then complied. I guess it was the first time they'd been naked together, but neither was willing to take a chance on some homophobic trip and miss out on my treat. The big dark-skinned one ran up to the bed, his love rod already hard as steel, standing at complete attention.

"I'm 'bout to get in that pussy ma!" he announced.

I stuck my foot out and stopped him from getting close to me. "Sit over there!" I commanded, pointing to a chair near the bed.

He reluctantly walked over and sat down with his dick in his hand. I pointed to his friend and beckoned him over to the bed. He walked up stroking his dick. He wasn't nearly as big, but he was big enough, and his body was absolutely beautiful. They both had nice bodies. I sat on the edge of the bed and reached around, squeezing both his ass cheeks and pulling his swollen member up to my lips. The cologne he was wearing was nice. It smelled good, not sweet or real strong, but definitely good. I put my tongue under his cock and teased him a little before pulling it completely into my mouth.

"Oh, fuck!" he groaned.

As I licked and smacked all over his dick, I stared at his buddy. I wanted him to know I was punishing him for his arrogance and disobedience. The sight of us excited him, and he began stroking his dick. I pushed the light-skinned brother to my left and pulled him down onto the bed. I slowly came down with him, still sucking him off and squeezing his balls a little. Then, I spread my legs and smacked my pussy so hard I nearly hurt myself. His boy jumped up and ran back over to me.

"That's right boy, do as you're told," I mumbled, my mouth completely full.

Out of nowhere, he pushed the head of his dick up against my pussy lips, so I kicked him right in the stomach as hard as I could. I still had my shoes on, so I know it had to hurt. He doubled over a little, so I reached down and pulled the back of his head until his face was buried in my dripping wet snatch. I was the master that night, the head mistress in charge, and I had to teach that boy a lesson. He fought me a little at first, but then he gave in and started lapping up my endless supply of creamy love juice. His chocolate ass was just fine as hell, so I called him Cocoa—mmm yeah, Light-Bright and Cocoa—they were so yummy.

As Cocoa tasted me between my thighs, I realized his cock wasn't the only thing supersized. His tongue was long, and he pushed it deep in my pussy, in and out like a penis. It felt so good having those two big boys attacking me at the same time from top to bottom, I didn't know what to do. Light-Bright was humping my face while Cocoa was down there making a hot sticky mess of my pussy.

Out of the blue, Cocoa made me cum, and I didn't like that, so I decided to punish him more. I pushed him away and climbed up on top of Light-Bright, leaving Cocoa down on his knees with his mouth open and his tongue wagging. I hiked my ass up and reached back, guiding Light-Bright's cock up to the entrance of my love tunnel and sat back on it. I closed my eyes as his shaft slid all the way inside. Then, I started rocking my hips, slamming down hard on his cock, moaning as I French-kissed him like an angry lover.

After a good five minutes of riding, I reached back and slid my fingers into my asshole, pulling it to stretch it and get it ready for Cocoa's giant cock. I looked back and saw him jerking his dick, damn near drooling at the sight of my round ass. I smacked my asshole, still riding Light-Bright. "Spit on it!" I commanded.

Cocoa leaned down and spit right in my ass. I didn't have to tell him what to do next he was already on his job. He took his cock in his hand and pressed the head tightly up against my asshole. Then with all his might, he forced that big black dick deep inside my ass. It was so big, he almost pushed Light-Bright out of my pussy, but we fought together to keep it all in. Then, they got into a rhythm of pulling and pushing me up and down on their hard cocks. I started cumming and squealing like a Brazilian porn star.

"FUCK ME YOU LITTLE FAGGOTS!" I yelled.

Cocoa pulled my hair and banged my ass harder. I thought he was going to rip me apart, but I continued to mock him.

"PUSSY!" I screamed, flinging my hair back at Cocoa. "FUCK MY ASSHOLE LIKE A MAN YOU LITTLE FUCKIN' BITCH!"

"BITCH, HUH? I'LL SHOW YOU A FUCKIN' BITCH, BITCH!" He grabbed my ass cheeks and rammed every inch of his cock up my ass.

"OH SHIT, MY ASS, YES FUCK, MY ASS!" I dropped down and tried to suck Light-Bright's tongue out of his mouth. "GRAB MY TITTIES! OH ... OH SHIT, OH SHIT!"

We were sweating all over each other, and Cocoa's balls were so big, each time he thrust into my ass, they slapped up against my pussy and of course Light-Bright's dick, but it didn't seem to bother either of them at all, and naturally it made me even hornier. I clinched my pussy lips around Light-Bright's rod and tightened my asshole. They both exploded simultaneously inside me, screaming and hollering like little girls. I couldn't help myself, I just started laughing.

Cocoa pulled that big anaconda out of me and damn near fell backwards. He walked around and sat on the edge of the bed. I kept on riding Light-Bright, until his cock was completely limp. As soon as it slipped out of my pussy, he kind of just fell into a trance.

"You got a joint?" I asked.

He could barely open his eyes. "Top drawer ... hey dog, blaze one up man."

Cocoa rushed over to the nightstand and pulled out a fatty. He lit it up and took a few puffs. I climbed off Light-Bright and walked around to Cocoa. He put his big arms around my waist and handed me the blunt. I smoked it while he sucked on my nipples.

The weed made me want to fuck again. Evidently it made Cocoa horny again too. His mammoth-sized dick, still dripping with cum, was beginning to grow again. All of a sudden, we heard snoring. We looked over at Light-Bright and he was knocked out.

"Goddamn!" Cocoa snickered, lowering himself down on the bed, "you got that nigga fucked up yo!"

I climbed in Cocoa's lap with my knees bent and pressed my aching pussy against his cock. I put my arms around his neck and whispered in his ear. "Put it in."

He reached around and forced his half erect cock inside my pussy. I alternated between sucking his earlobe and puffing on my joint. Each time I licked his ear, his dick grew bigger inside me. In a split second, he jumped up and slammed my back against the wall. He held me up in the air with his arms under my legs and gripped my ass with both hands. He launched up off the bed so abruptly, I ended up dropping the joint on the sheets, and they started to catch fire.

I was drunk and high, so of course Blondie was in control, and she knew exactly what she was doing with her evil ass. I fought her for a few seconds, but then gave in. Neither she nor I warned that fool at all. We just giggled and watched the blunt burn a hole in the sheets. I was kinda hoping it started a blazing inferno while Cocoa pumped my pussy. Sex in a burning room? Now that's hot. Unfortunately, it burned out before any real damage could be done. Since Cocoa made me drop my joint, I figured it was time to punish him again, so I dug my nails deep in his back.

"GODDAMMIT BITCH, WHAT THE FUCK?" he yelled.

I squeezed my thighs tight and kept digging the nails on my left hand into his back as I pulled his curly hair with my right. I was really trying to hurt him. He looked up at me like he wanted to punch me in the eye, but instead, he just fucked me harder and harder, grunting and moaning in ecstasy. When he was ready to cum again, he lifted me off his cock, tossed me onto the bed and squeezed his dick until my tits were completely covered in his milky love juice.

"FUCKIN' BITCH!" he yelled triumphantly as if he'd just conquered the world.

I laughed loudly as Cocoa dropped face first down onto the bed. After I got my tickle over and done with, I was ready to get cleaned up.

"Shower?" I asked.

"Second door on the right," he replied.

I got up and ran into the bathroom. My ass was on fire from that big behemoth's cock. "Son-of-a-bitch it burns!" I whispered.

I tore open a new package of soap and jumped into the shower to get all clean. When I got out to dry off, the room was so steamy I could barely see a foot in front of me. I rummaged around in the drawers and found some deodorant. It was some hardcore man stuff, but I just needed to get back across town, so I sprayed it on and tried not to cough. It was strong. When I went back into the bedroom to get dressed, Light-Bright was still out, but Cocoa was up, running his damn mouth again.

"You one nasty white bitch!" he blurted.

"And you're a stupid mothafucka!" By then, I had my dress back on. "Hand me my coat."

He sprung up and helped me put my coat on. "I wanna see you again, shawty."

"No, you don't." I walked over and grabbed my bag.

"Damn, that's cold," he said.

I didn't say anything else. I just hobbled my swollen ass up out of there and caught a cab back to my apartment.

By the time we hit Wall Street, I was kicking myself. Of all the stupid things I could've done, I think that one took the cake. I didn't even feel drunk anymore. I just felt like a dirty whore. I ran a hot bath and put some Epsom salt in the water because my booty felt like it was broken in half. I'm pretty sure it felt good at the time— it's hard to remember—but goddamn if I didn't regret it after. And, what the fuck was I thinking letting all those strange men cum in my pussy? *Birth control or not, I gotta start buying some condoms.*

"We don't like condoms remember baby!" said Blondie.

"Oh, not you again ... fuck! Look what you did to my asshole bitch!"

"You liked it," she said. "So, stop actin' like a little punk and let's get a drink."

"NO!"

"You better," she warned, "or I'll never let you get back to work. You'll be the nastiest slut in the Bureau ... how'd that be, huh?"

"FUCK YOU!" I jumped up out of the tub and ran into the kitchen, slipping and sliding all over the floor. I opened the fridge and grabbed a Heineken. I used a bottle opener to get the top off and then drank half of it. "GET OUT OF THERE DAMMIT!" I yelled, slapping myself upside the head. I took another sip of beer before running back into the bathroom and jumping in the water. "OUCH!" I yelled, bumping my head against the back of the tub. "Shit, I'm trippin." I shook it off and lit a scented candle. Then, I sunk down into the tub up to my neck.

My bubble bath was very relaxing. I stayed in there for about an hour. When I got out, I went into the living room and sat down on the sofa. Before I left the club, I'd turned my phone off, so I got it out of my bag and powered it back on. I figured I missed a few calls, and I had. There were two voicemails. Both calls were from Dom. He said he was beginning to get concerned I hadn't checked in. I called his cell phone to put his mind at ease.

"Top, what's going on?" he answered.

"Everything's fine," I responded, my speech slurred a bit. "I was with Tony, and he's going to see what he can do to help. But um ... uh ... yeah, we'll proceed with negotiations until something else turns up, buddy."

"You need me to pick you up?" he asked.

"No, stay put," I replied, "I'll be in my apartment if you need me, and I should be back at the command center Sunday."

"Okay," he said, "be careful, this guy seems to be all over us."

"Copy that. I'll see you later Dom." I hung up and stretched out across the sofa. I picked up a magazine and read it for a while, but soon fell fast asleep.

The next day, soon as I woke up, my mind was stuck on one thing—seeing my little brother. I stood in the bathroom staring at myself in the mirror while I brushed my teeth and formulated a strategy. My mother kept him away from me for years, but that Saturday, nothing in the world was going to keep us apart. My ass still hurt from the night before. I kept wiggling and squirming, trying to get in a comfortable stance so I could finish brushing my teeth. *Note to Blondie ... no more anal for a while—a long while.*

I finished washing up and grabbed my laptop from the living room. I went back into the bedroom, so I didn't have to work sitting down on my ass. I unfolded my laptop and stretched across the bed on my tummy. I logged in and did a search on Chris, his personal info, licenses, everything I could find. I even got a recent photo of him. He looked just as I remembered only bigger. I printed everything and gathered it all up into a neat file. Then, I pulled down directions to Princeton.

Once I had my plan set, I showered, did my hair and got dressed. I wanted to see him because I missed him, but with all that was going on, I also needed to check on him. I wanted to see with my own eyes he was actually safe. Who knew, Aker may have had him tied up in the Embassy too. The bad guys always seem to know exactly who to get and just how to exploit you. They're always one step ahead somehow. As far as Aker was concerned, deep down inside,

I knew there would be no reasoning with him. He was playing chess, not checkers, and I had to guard every piece on the board if I was gonna even come close to winning this deadly game.

Chapter 10

I must have been some kind of doggone idiot running to New Jersey unannounced. But I didn't trust anyone else to check on Chris, not even my ex. If Bill told me everything was fine, I'd still be worried until the case was over. If you've ever been a detective or investigator, you know that's not a good thing. You going to keep your mind clear in the field and stay sharp, or you'll find yourself on the wrong end of an armor-piercing sniper round. In light of the situation, I wasn't taking any chances. As a field operator back in Brazil, sometimes I didn't even wear a bra, but that day, I had my Kevlar strapped on under my blouse. I was also toting three guns-one on my hip, a backup in a concealment holster in the small of my back, and another in my ankle holster. I was totally weighted down, but with Mr. Aker and all his bullshit, I couldn't afford to take any chances.

I gathered up my notes on Chris, grabbed my laptop and left the apartment. I went down to the garage and got in my DBS. When the techies loaded up my car, they were kind enough to give me one of those little laptop cradles, so I could drive and do what I needed to at the same time. Between my wireless internet and the car's GPS, I was always headed in the right direction. I strapped my laptop in, opened it, and plugged in the broadband wireless card. Then, I started the car and pulled out the garage.

From Wall Street, I took South Street over to FDR Drive. Then, I took I-478 towards Jersey City. I followed the Staten Island Expressway into New Jersey and headed south on the Turnpike. I got off on Nine to get into New Brunswick. Route 1 took me all the way down to Princeton.

Then, I made a right on Washington, which put me just a few miles away from the school.

I thought for a moment about calling Bill to let him know what I was up to, but I figured he'd try to convince me to fly down to Atlanta the next time Chris came home instead, so we could all be together—one big happy family. I wasn't trying to hear that shit though because I knew if I was in Atlanta long enough, I'd end up whooping Theresa's ass one good time. Don't get me wrong, I don't necessarily want to kick Theresa's ass, but Blondie keeps score, and there's no way she's gonna let our beef with Theresa go unchecked. You know how we do it; my ass would be down there starting a brawl, and I'd just as soon avoid that drama right now. Speaking of Blondie, that freak is gonna be the death of me. My asshole still hurts and guess what; I've never smoked weed before this year, but now because of her, I can't seem to stop. She's gonna get me fired and or put behind bars.

It only took about an hour to get down to the school. I should've paced myself, but I always drive like a bat out of hell. It was still early in the morning—only 9:30 a.m. On a Saturday morning Chris probably didn't have any classes. I figured he may have been sleeping in, but there was only one way to find out. Only, I didn't want to bust in and scare the hell out of him and his roommate if he had one. It was early, so I decided to hang back. Besides, I didn't know where Chris was exactly. I still had to find him inside the dorm, and that would take some doing.

All of a sudden, out of nowhere I got nervous about seeing him—anxious even. I was worried how he might react to seeing me. *What if he's like Theresa?* I'd be so embarrassed and hurt. I was really tripping, so I decided to stop somewhere, calm down and pull myself together. Once I made a left onto Nassau, I spotted a Pancake House named PJ's on the right, so I parked near the curb and got out. I wasn't really hungry, but I figured some coffee would help take the edge off, so I walked through the cute little red French-looking doors and grabbed a table. As soon as I sat down and looked at the menu, my stomach started growling. Guess I'm hungry after all. Out of the blue, I was starving, so I ordered the old fashion buttermilk pancakes and a coffee. After eating, I paid the bill and just hung around for a while.

I didn't want to wait too long, just long enough for Chris to get up and get moving. So, around 10:15, I walked out of the restaurant and got back in the car. I sat there for a minute thinking about how crazy I was for doing what I was doing. I thought, *Hell Chris probably doesn't even remember what I look like, more less give a shit about anything I have going on. What the fuck am I doing here?* It didn't matter though because I was there. Come on Alex ... let's get this over and done with.

I cranked up and pulled off the curb, driving slowly down Nassau. I made a left onto Princeton University and just kinda crept down the street to have a look around and get a feel for the campus. It was kind of spooky to me being back on the college scene, even if I wasn't a student. I tell you one thing, school's really changed, or maybe it was just Princeton. I remember back when I was in school you couldn't drag my black ass out of the bed before noon on a Saturday, but those kids were up and about, doing all kinds of productive-looking things.

I got stare after stare as I rolled down the block; mostly from boys. They were looking at my car, pointing, yelling and whistling as if they were watching a topless cheerleader with big nipples do cartwheels down the yard.

The campus was massive and highly populated. I took the scenic route down Elm past the tennis courts all the way back to Chris' dorm. It's a good thing I kept Bill's letters from earlier in the year. I thought about throwing them away several times, but I guess I kept them for good reason. They sure came in handy that day.

In one of the letters Bill sent, he told me everything about Chris' first year. Well, probably not everything; you know boys will be boys. I guess at this point Bill's probably like a dad to Chris, or at least maybe a good big brother. From the looks of the letters, Bill had a lock on everything from the day Chris was accepted to the major he took on and housing. Obviously, the housing info came in handy since I just so happened to be looking for my lil bro that day.

Bill was so cute with his letters. He told me what building Chris was in and even his floor. He said Chris was on the Butler campus up on the third floor. That's one thing I always liked about Bill, he was thorough. Only thing I didn't have was Chris's room number, but I figured I'd just ask around. Not trying to brag, but if he's anything like his oldest sister, he's well-known and popular.

There wasn't any parking near the dorm, so I made myself a space. Basically, I just pulled up and stopped right in front of his building. I got out and walked up to the door. It was wide open, so I made my way in and took the stairs up. There were kids all up and down the hall, looking at me like I was somebody's mother. I started to wonder if I actually looked that old. Some of the rooms were closed, but most weren't. I peeked in door after door, hoping I'd get a glimpse of Chris, but I didn't see him. After strolling down a couple more hallways, I started asking around.

"Excuse me...."

"Yes?" replied a young man.

I held up a photo of Chris. "You know this kid?"

He shook his head. "Sorry, lady."

"What about your friend?" I showed it to him too.

He stared and squinted at the picture for a moment. "Yeah, he's down the hall on the right ... uh, I forget his name, but-"

"Christopher?"

"Yeah, Chris," he responded, "somethin' like that. Just go down the hall and make the first right. He'll be on the right."

"Thank you." I followed his instructions. That hallway was just like every other one with room after room lined up and down each side. I was curious what college kids were into these days, so I did my nosey detective bit. I poked my head into each open door on the right. I came across one door that was closed, so I went ahead and knocked. Just as soon as I pulled my fist back for a second knock, the door swung open and a young skinny white guy in sweats greeted me.

"Hey!" he said, grinning. "You've come to the right place!"

"I certainly hope so," I responded. "I'm looking for Christopher Southerland."

He turned around and looked back into the room. "Hey Chris, some lady's here to see you."

"What she look like?" yelled Chris.

The boy looked me up and down from head to toe. "She's hot man!"

"Then, I'll be right out," he said.

The boy leaned against the doorjamb. "He'll be right out," he said, still checking me over. "So, what's your name, sweetheart?"

I pulled my jacket back so he could see my badge, and he sprung up to attention.

"Oh, uh ... yeah, Chris, yeah he's gone be right out." He spun around and ran back inside with his tail between his legs, letting the door shut in my face.

I chuckled a little. He was funny to me. After a few minutes, Chris came out of his room, pulling a sweater over his head. He was gorgeous and tall, taller than me. He had some little muscles too! And, he had this thin mustache. Oh my God, he looked like a little grown ass man. I was beyond overjoyed to see him, but I tried to contain myself. As I suspected, he didn't recognize me, and I didn't want to spook him, so I just played it cool.

"Christopher Southerland?"

"Yeah, I'm Chris," he replied, sticking his hand out.

I shook his hand. "Chris, is there somewhere we can talk?"

"What's this about?" he asked.

I didn't know what to do, so I flashed my badge. "Just need to ask you a few questions."

"Is it going to take long?" he asked. "I have somewhere I need to be."

"Not long at all," I said, fighting to keep from grinning ear-to-ear.

"We can go downstairs," Chris said.

"Lead the way."

Chris stuck his head back in his room and yelled, "Hey man, I'll be back in a minute."

I followed him down the hall and we walked down the stairs to the first floor. He opened the door for me, and I walked through. After a few steps, I got the feeling I'd lost him, so I turned around. He'd stopped walking and was just standing there, looking at me with his head cocked to the side and his mouth wide open.

"Sis...?" he asked slowly.

A tear streamed down my cheek. I didn't want to get all emotional, but man I couldn't help it.

"HOLY SHIT!" He ran up and damn near tackled me, hugging me and kissing my face. "Alex, what the hell are you doing here? Holy shit man! My God, look at you, you're beautiful sis, just like I remember!"

I was blushing so badly it was embarrassing. "It's been a long time little bro."

Chris said, "Shit man, you scared me half to death with that badge, I thought I was in trouble."

"I'm sorry I just didn't know what to say ... I-"

By then everyone was looking at us being nosey.

"Come on," said Chris, grabbing my hand and tugging me down the front steps.

We stood outside in the yard and just hugged each other a little while longer.

"I love you, man!" he said, "I miss you for real."

"I miss you too, lil boy." I wiped my tears with my fingertips. "How 'bout we go somewhere we can sit down and catch up? That cool or you got something else-"

"Nah man, fuck dat!" he replied. "I'm just meeting some people at the library, but that shit can wait."

I smiled. "Come on man let's go."

"Fuck yeah!" he exclaimed.

I guess my big fat mouth rubbed off on him because he sure seemed to curse a lot more than I remember. More likely though, foul-mouthed Theresa was to blame; he'd hung around her a helluva lot more than me. That tactless twit was famous for making sailors run for cover. I'm trippin really. I didn't care he was cursing. I was just happy he was doing alright. I could tell he was a good kid too. I can't exactly say how I knew. I just knew. I could feel it. We walked together towards the car.

"Damn, is that your ride?"

I smiled.

"What the fuck?" he jumped up and down a bit. "Oh, shit, you gotta be kiddin' me!" He ran up to the car and slid his hands over the hood line, looking in through the front windshield, since the sides and rear hatch were tinted pitch black. "This thing's like $100,000 dollars, you rollin' like that?"

I shook my head. "Two-hundred and sixty thousand, but don't get excited, I have this arrangement with the dealership."

"Can I drive?" he asked, enthusiastically.

I raised an eyebrow. "I don't know ... can you drive?"

"Hell yeah!" He stuck his hand out. "Come on sis, please!"

I thought about it for a second. Then, I reached in my pocket and took the key out. I put it in his hand and said, "Don't do anything stupid, got it?"

He snatched the key. "Yeah, yeah whatever, come on!"

Chris ran around to the driver side like a kid would run to his first bike. He pressed the button to unlock the doors and we both climbed in.

I pushed my laptop up and out of my way. Then, I strapped on my seatbelt. Chris was staring at the dashboard with a painfully lost look on his face, so I figured I'd help him out.

"Look, you got the clutch down?"

"Yeah," he responded.

"Okay, you've got the key turned, so just press the little red button."

"You gotta be fuckin' kiddin' me man!" He laughed really loud.

"No, actually I'm not. Just press the little button there."

Once the motor turned over, his eyes swelled. "Damn, you feel that?" He was cheesing big time. "V-12?"

"Yup!" I chuckled a bit.

"Shit, I'm nervous now," he said.

"Don't be Chris. Just take it easy. There's not a lot of clutch, so take your time to get used to it."

Chris put the car in gear and turned the wheel left. He gave it a little gas and came out of the clutch, but he did it too fast, and the motor stalled out. We rolled a few feet down the road, and then he started the motor again. This time when he got ready to pull off, he was a little more patient with the clutch. The car shook as he took his foot completely off the clutch pedal and simultaneously tapped the gas.

"THIS IS UN-FUCKIN-BELIEVABLE!" he yelled. Then, he made a right out of the dorms and pulled up to Washington Road. He came to a complete stop, and then looked over at me as if to ask my permission to open her up.

I smiled and put my hands up. "Go for it, kid."

He turned the wheel to the right, put the car in first gear and launched us out onto the street, slamming into second gear and then third. I didn't care. It felt good to see him having fun. No wait, I put that a little too mildly. Chris was having a ball behind the wheel of that supercar.

"Goddamn!" he yelled. He was pushing it, so we came up on the next intersection in no time. As soon as the light changed, he gunned it again, speeding down the bridge over Lake Carnegie.

"You eat yet?" I asked.

"Nah, not yet," he replied, shifting into fourth gear. "Man, this bitch is hot!"

"Well then, pick a place, Mario Andretti," I said, "I'm buying."

"Cool. There's a Saladworks down off Hightstown," he said. "It's kind of early, but I know this girl Tiffany that works there. She'll hook us up."

"That'll do it for me man."

I watched him as he played with the car like it was a brand-new toy. I think he touched nearly every control in there from the radio to the power seats and windshield wipers. I was just happy to see him; happy he remembered me, but most of all, I was happy he was more like me than Theresa. Chris seemed real cool—a little wild, but still he had a laid back, chilled persona, and I liked that very much.

That boy whirled the car into Saladworks' parking lot like he was high on crack cocaine or something. The tires squealed as we came to a screeching halt right on the line between two parking spaces.

"Think you might want to straighten up?" I asked.

"Hell naw, man!" he exclaimed. "Car like this, you don't want these idiots out here slamming their doors into it. Ain't nobody gonna fuck with it like this, please believe me." He laughed hard.

"Chris, you truly are my baby brother."

We walked inside the restaurant, and a young lady greeted us at the door.

"Welcome to Saladworks," she said.

Chris leaned in to her and whispered, "Is Tiffany here yet?"

The young woman smiled. "Yes, she's here, hang on a minute." She ran into the back, and after a few minutes, reappeared with young Tiffany, who walked right up to Chris and gave him a hug that seemed a little more than just friendly.

"Hey Chris!" she said, excited to see him.

"Hey babe," he replied.

Then, she looked over at me and frowned. "You eating, baby?" she asked still looking directly at me.

"Yeah," Chris replied. "Hey, this is my sister Alex."

Her entire demeanor changed. "Oh, I'm sorry, hey gurl, how you doing?" She laughed a little bit.

"Just fine." I shook her hand.

"Oh, yeah, I see it now," she announced. "You guys look alike."

"You gonna hook a brotha up?" Chris asked.

"Don't I always?" Tiffany smiled. "Come on back. I'll get you something to drink and then bring out some wraps. That cool?"

"Hell yeah!" exclaimed Chris. "Make mine a buffalo chicken."

She looked back at me. "And what about you?"

"Uh, I'll just take a Coke."

"You not hungry?" she asked.

"I stopped at this Pancake place and had breakfast."

"What PJ's?" asked Chris.

"Yeah, I think that's the one."

Tiffany smiled. "Okay, well, you guys can sit down right over there, and I'll bring you a coke and Chris I'll get you some lemonade."

"Perfect." Chris said.

We sat down at the table. Chris just kept staring at me.

"You think we look alike?" I asked.

He nodded. "Yeah we got some similar features going on. You just so damn bright and shiny, lookin' like a piece of notebook paper without the stripes."

I broke out laughing. "Hey watch it boy!" I said, jokingly. Then, I got serious. "I thought you might be mad at me," I said.

"I was for a long time, but I know the deal Alex. I mean, I'd have to be dumb, deaf, blind, and stupid not to see what mom was doing."

"I heard she passed."

"Yeah, I went down for the funeral," he said. "Bill pretty much took care of everything because Theresa was a zombie."

"Are you sad?" I asked.

He shook his head. "Yeah ... I love her, but she was having a lot of trouble, I mean, she was in a lot of pain. I'm just glad she doesn't have to go through all that any more, you know?"

I didn't know whether to smile or cry. I swear he was just such a little grown man. I reached across the table and touched his hand. "I saw her right before she died."

"No shit?"

I smiled. "No, seriously, I went down and saw her at Crawford Long." I dared not tell him our dirty little secret. I figured I'd just keep that to myself.

Tiffany came back with our drinks. "I'll be right back with your food Chris."

"Thanks babe," he replied.

I took a sip of my Coke. "Yeah, we talked for a while. It was good to see her, but..."

"What? Shoot Alex, I can't believe that. She was mad salty at you every day."

"Yeah, I know. But she was writing to me. Bill wrote me too, which is how I knew you were here. When I saw momma, she was just so weak and frail it didn't seem like her to me at all."

"You know what she told me?" he asked.

"Nah, what?"

"She told me you left for the Navy because you blamed her for dad dying ... said you didn't love us, so you didn't want to be around."

I shook my head. "That's not true at all. I love you guys ... I love her too. I miss her a lot, but there were some things going on between her and Dad that made it difficult for everybody."

"You mean he cheated on her, right?" he said.

"How'd you know?"

"She told us ... me, Bill and Theresa right before she died. I guess it was something she just needed to get off her chest."

"What else did she tell you?" I asked.

"That was about it," he replied. "Bill said the night before she died, she was talking about you, telling Theresa that you loved her and for us to take care of you."

I smiled.

"Theresa hates you with a passion though," Chris said, taking in half his lemonade in a single gulp. "If I even mention your name, she goes slap off."

"T and I are gonna be okay," I said.

"I know, Alex. You guys were always tight."

I asked, "What about Bill?"

Chris kind of frowned. "I know what happened," he said. "Nobody wants to tell me, but I know something had to happen. Bill was with you and now he's married to Theresa ... I mean, that's some fuckin' bullshit, you know?"

I dropped my head a little. "It's all good."

"Nah man, fuck that!" Chris was beginning to get excited. "I know shit happens, but you don't do that to your sister. I blame Theresa, but Bill should've known better. He and I have words from time to time, but for the most part we're cool."

"They taking care of you?" I asked.

"What, you mean with money and stuff?" he asked.

"Yeah."

"Here you guys go," said Tiffany, standing over us with two plates. She set one down in front of Chris and the other on my side of the table. "I know you said you weren't hungry, but I had them make you a wrap just in case. I got you the Chicken Caesar though, 'cause I don't like all that hot spicy stuff, and you look so proper."

"Well, thank you Tiffany, I think."

She laughed loudly. "I'm just saying the boys like all that hot stuff. Anyway, if you don't like it, I can switch it out, and if you don't eat it all, I can box it up for you ... just let me know, and don't worry about it, it's all on me."

"Sweetie, you don't have to do that," I said.

"No, I insist," said Tiffany. "It's not every day I get to meet my man's family." She cleared her throat loudly and obviously on purpose.

"Yeah, yeah, yeah," Chris replied.

I smiled. "Thank you, that's very nice of you."

"You're welcome," she responded in a chipper tone. "I'll be back to check on you guys later." She batted her eyes at Chris, and he winked back at her.

Watching him interact with Tiffany, I could tell he was a player. I could see it in his eyes. No telling where he got that from since I am so innocent and Quaker-like. Yep, he was definitely a free spirit—a free thinker—and I loved it. I hoped somehow that I had something to do with that. I watched him attack his little spicy wrap like it owed him money. You would've thought he hadn't eaten for weeks. *Boys*.

"So, Bill and Theresa are handling all the money okay?"

"Yeah," he replied, his mouth full of food. "They pay for school and everything, got me a car, and they give me some spending money every month."

"What kind of car you get?"

"Mercedes," he replied. "I think Bill has something going on with Benz cause that's all he wants to buy now. It's silver, got some size to it, it's a 500."

"Well, that's a nice car."

"It's a piece of shit!" exclaimed Chris. "That thing stays in the shop more than on the road. I'm always driving that little stupid courtesy car, you know the hatchback with the dealer's number stamped across the back window in big white letters?"

I laughed. "They don't make 'em like they used to."

"You can say that again!" he exclaimed. "Speaking of money, I take it Mom finally hooked you up, cause you lookin' like a million bucks," he said in a high pitch.

"Thank you, but no it didn't go down that way. I'm assuming Bill and Theresa are controlling her estate and whatever money she had. I just wanna make sure they keep you taken care of."

"So, you're rich, right?" he asked.

"I got a little somethin' saved up." I picked up my wrap and took a bite. "Wow, that's good."

"I told you my girl would hook us up!" Chris exclaimed, proudly.

"She's you're girlfriend?" I asked.

He whispered, "She's a good friend." Then he gave me this big shit-eating grin. "You know how we do it ... I got one here, one there, but I ain't trying to get tied down."

"You've grown up so much," I shook my head, "you're one handsome boy."

If he could've I think he would've blushed. "You trippin' man."

"I'm serious!" I exclaimed. "I'm proud of you too. I mean, Princeton...? Good grief man, give me a break."

"Well, one does what one can," he replied.

"Ain't that the truth Chris ... ain't that the truth."

"True dat."

"Hey, look lil bro, I'm sorry ... sorry for being away so long, I just had to-"

"You don't have to do that, sis," he said. "Unlike Theresa, I remember what it was like back home. Man, you couldn't please Momma if the baby Jesus came down and said it should be so. She was a trip, I mean, I ain't trying to talk about the dead, but she always had her ways, and she was stuck in 'em, you know?"

"Yeah, she was a trip, no doubt."

Chris got serious. "Man, I was young and all, but I remember some days, Momma would just be sitting around talking to herself, and then out of nowhere, she'd be ready to kill somebody, and she'd go looking for you. I used to try to distract her and get her to pay me some attention, but she was just zoomed in on you."

"I took a lot of beatings, but you know what...?"

"What?" he asked.

"I'd do it again as long as it meant you and Theresa never had to deal with all that shit."

"It's funny 'cause Theresa acts like you never did anything at all for us," he said.

"Chris, Theresa's gotta find a way to deal with all that mess from the past. There's nothing I can do to change the way she remembers things ... I just have to love her from a distance."

"You know they had a baby, right?" he asked. "Her and Bill."

I replied, "I saw she was pregnant when I was down there. I assumed it was his."

"Yeah, they had a little girl," he said. "She's cute man ... got a lot of hair."

"Bill always wanted kids ... I'm happy for them."

"Don't you want kids someday?" asked Chris.

I shook my head. "No, not me ... I'd screw up a little kid, seriously. That's the last thing I need man."

"Personally, I think you'd make a great mother," he proclaimed.

"Chris, I appreciate the vote of confidence, honey, I really do, but I think the world would be much better off without another Alex running around."

He chuckled a little. By then, he'd finished his food, but I was still working on mine, gradually getting hungrier the more we talked.

"You know who I miss?" Chris asked.

"Dad?" I guessed.

"Yeah," he said softly.

"I'm glad you remember him. He was so good to us."

"Shit yeah man." He started cheesing super big. "I mean, you know it's like I remember certain things, like how his cologne smelled or the time he took me out in his squad car. I remember his tattoos, especially the one on his arm-"

"The Navy Seal one?"

"Yup, with the bird and all." Chris smiled as he continued to reminisce. "I remember he used to call you pork chop all the time. Oh, and he knew like everybody in the neighborhood."

"You know what I miss most about him, Chris?"

"Nah, what?" he asked.

"His voice."

"Really?" he asked.

"Yeah man. His voice was soft, but strong. Even when he was fussing at us or arguing with mom, his voice still seemed calm, almost soothing, you know?"

"Like you knew he really loved us." Chris got sad for a moment.

"Yeah," I shook my head, "it's still hard to believe he's gone. You know I had a chance to work with some of his buddies from back in the day."

"No shit?" Suddenly, Chris cheered up again.

"Yeah, a guy named David Chandler and another guy named Tony Crane."

"You still talk to them?" Chris asked.

"Actually, I still work for Tony. I used to work for David, but he got killed on the job. We were working this case together and this crazy ass lady shot him."

"Damn, that's fucked up," he said.

"Yeah, but it's all good. They knew a side of him we didn't, so hanging around them, in a way, it's like dad's still around."

"Yeah, I can see that." Chris took another big gulp of lemonade. "So, what you doing here in New Jersey ... I ain't complaining, I'm glad you came, but did you need something in particular or you just wanted to see your little brotha doing it big, baybay?"

"You so silly! Nah, I just wanted to make sure you were alright."

"I'm good man, I'm good."

"Chris...."

"What?"

Tiffany was back again. "You want me to box that up for you?"

"Please," I replied. "Thank you it was very good."

She picked up Chris' empty plate along with what was left of my little chicken Caesar wrap. "I'll be right back," she said politely.

I lowered my voice. "You know I still work for the FBI, right?"

"Yeah, I saw your badge," Chris said.

"I'm working kidnappings up in New York now ... it's dangerous, you know?"

"You being careful out there though, right?" he asked.

"Well, yeah, but ... see, the thing is ... some of these kidnappers are pretty desperate to get what they want, and they'll do anything to get it ... even try to hurt the negotiator or do something to their family to try and force their hand. You understand what I'm saying?"

"So, you're a negotiator?" he asked.

"Yeah ... Chief Negotiator on my team." I sighed. "Look, I don't want to get you upset or paranoid or anything, but-"

"Nah, you ain't even got to tell me, I'm straight," said Chris. "I ain't like these white kids, man—no offense—but, somebody come fuckin' wit' me, they gone have to take me out."

I laughed. "Chris, you are definitely my little brother. Listen, I just need you to be a little extra careful around here. Keep your eyes open, and don't deal with people you don't know ... just take some extra precautions until I close this case. I'll let you know when everything's alright on my side."

"Yeah, no problem, sis," he said.

I smiled and touched his hand again. "Good deal ... God, you're a good-looking boy."

"Thanks, you're not so bad yourself. When my roommate said you were hot, he was right, man you been working out or something?"

"I like to run."

"Yeah, I play ball," said Chris.

"Basketball?"

"Hell yeah, Alex, I'm like Jordan out on the court. You don't wanna fuck wit' me."

"That's good. How's school though?" I asked.

"Made the Dean's List," he replied.

I squeezed his hand. "I'm so proud of you. Look Chris, if you need something—anything at all—I'm talking money, somebody to listen to your problems, hookers, whatever—I got your back ... I'm just kidding about the hookers though."

Chris laughed again.

"Seriously, I'm a good listener, so talk to me. And, if you see anything go down that doesn't look right to you or you feel threatened, I want you to give me a call first." I slid a card across the table. "My cell number's there along with my office line and my email address. Emails come straight to my phone too, so if you can't get me on the phone, just send a message. I'm only about an hour away, so I can be here in a flash if you need me. What's your number in the dorm?"

"Here, you got another card?" Chris took a pen out of his pocket.

"Yeah." I gave him another business card.

"I'm just glad to see you," Chris said, writing his dorm and cell phone number down on the back of the card. "It's been what, like ten years?" He slid the card back over to me.

"It's been a long time ... too long, baby brother. It's good to see you again. I'm so proud of you, Chris, and I love you with all my heart."

"I love you too," he replied. "You gotta go?"

"Yeah, I probably need to get back," I said reluctantly. "You okay with pocket money?"

"Yeah, I'm good."

"Well, let's get you back so you can make your library date."

He held up the key to the DBS. "I'll drive," he said, grinning.

"I just bet you will Mr. Christopher Southerland. Hang on, let me leave her something." I took a ten dollar bill out of my purse and put it on the table. Tiffany was a good waitress, especially considering we weren't paying for anything. She saw us get up and ran back over to the table with my to-go box.

"Here you go," she said, handing me the doggy bag. "It was nice meeting you, Alex."

"Tiffany, I assure you the pleasure was all mine. Thank you very much."

She smiled and Chris grabbed her around the waist. He kissed her lips and said, "Thanks girl. I'll see you later?"

"Yeah baby." She kissed him back.

Chris and I left. He drove back to the dorm like a crazed street racer. He parked the car in the same spot as before and we got out. I looked in his eyes and just couldn't stop smiling. He was my little brother, but to me he was like my own child. I loved him so much. It was cool because after all those years and all that woman's lies, there wasn't any distance between him and me at all. Going there and seeing him was nothing like I expected. I was so afraid he'd be bitter towards me like Theresa, but he wasn't upset at all. He was cool as hell. We stood beside the car and I locked him up in a big bear hug until my arms got tired. I made him bend down so I could kiss his forehead, and then we said our goodbyes.

"I love you sis," he said. "You stay safe out there."

"Will do, and hey, don't forget Chris, call me first if you need anything or if you just need to talk."

"No problemo ... hey, I gotta run." He squeezed my arm. "Love you. I'll call you this weekend."

"Looking forward to it, man." I watched him run his tall, lanky ass back into the building and my heart filled with joy and happiness. It's funny, he looked so much like mom it was ridiculous. He had her dark brown skin and everything. I was glad to know he was doing fine. Seeing him made all my worries go away. Chris was cool, but I could tell he had attitude just like me. If any of Aker's boys tried to get the drop on him, I suspect they'd have one helluva problem on their hands. I felt relieved.

I jumped in the car and headed back home, satisfied everything was gonna be fine. Chris genuinely seemed happy to see me, and I was damn sure glad to see him after so long. He was a lot more mature about all our family problems than I thought. He was a little old man, which was completely funny to me. I was surprised he wasn't torn up about Mom dying because he was always right up under her everywhere she went. Maybe he already got his crying out the way, or maybe they weren't as close as I thought.

After that day, nothing my mother had done to me really mattered anymore. In the end, she may not have been my mother, but Chris was definitely my little brother. There's no doubting that. I love him so much, and I know now how much he loves me. In a way, I think that alone gave me reason to wanna live and do better. It's a trip because up to that point, nothing anybody said made a damn bit of difference to me. But, being around Chris ... I don't know, I just wanna live long enough to watch him walk down the aisle.

I flipped through the CDs I'd loaded into the car's disk changer earlier. After a few disc skips, I settled in on Tina Marie. I listened to that talented white woman sing, yell and drop me off into some funk all the way back to New York. Listening to Honey do her thing was the icing on the cake of a good day. I may have been going through some difficult times in my life, but that was one of the best days I'd had in a while. I think it even topped my little shopping spree.

As I sang along with Tina and navigated the streets of New York, I thanked God for everything in my life. I thanked Chris for still loving me. And, I guess I also had to thank Bill too. If it hadn't been for his persistence and him trying to stay in touch with me and all, I wouldn't have been able to find Chris so easily. "Thanks Bill ... believe it or not, I still love you," I mumbled.

Chapter 11

Have you ever had a thought so insane, so wild— I mean a thought so messed up that it makes you sick to your stomach? That's how I felt after a few phone calls in the car. I was almost back home from visiting Chris when my cell rang.

"Southerland," I answered.

"Top, it's me, Deb."

"What's going on Deb?"

"I've got Mr. Amadi and his brother requesting permission to leave the premises. They want to go out for dinner and drinks."

"Okay, where's Dominic?" I asked.

"I'm not sure," she replied. "He left not too long after you did."

"And he didn't check in?" I asked.

"No," she said.

"Well, did he say where he was going?"

"No," Deb responded.

"That's not like him."

"Yeah, I was a little surprised too," Deborah said. "He just told me he had to go take care of something."

"I'll follow up with Dom. As far as the Amadi brothers are concerned ... they can go out, long as they have a babysitter."

"They're requesting to go alone," said Deborah. I could hear the hesitation in her voice. Finally, she dropped the bomb. "The brother insists on it."

"I knew he was gonna be a problem," I said. "Look, either they roll with a chaperone or they stay in, got it?"

"I got it," replied Deborah. "I already told them, but they keep pushing and I wanted to give the courtesy of running the request up the chain."

"I understand Deborah. You have trouble with those two, call me first okay?"

"Will do Top," she responded.

"Keep me posted."

"Copy that," she said.

I hung up and immediately dialed Dom's cell phone, but he didn't answer, so I hung up and redialed him. By the time I pulled into my parking garage, I'd called Dominic nearly 10 times. Finally, he answered.

"FBI, this is Harris." His voice echoed even though it seemed he was whispering. It sounded like he was in a great hall or trapped inside a shipping container.

"Dom...?"

"Yeah, this is he."

"Dom, it's Alex."

"Oh, hey Top, what's up?" His tone completely changed.

I just played it cool. "Checking in ... how's everything going with Amadi?"

"Good," he replied, clearing his throat. "Everything's good. He and his brother are going out on the town, so I gave them the green light ... Chuck's going to go with them. I stepped away to go to the house ... one of the girls is sick, so I'm going to get her to the hospital."

"Oh, I'm sorry to hear that," I told him. "You need anything?"

"No ... nah, we're good. I'll be back on site soon."

I asked, "Do I need to get back to the command center?"

"No, not at all," he replied. "Deborah's in charge ... I'm confident she can handle it."

"You sure?"

"Absolutely," he confirmed.

"Alright then, I'll see you guys tomorrow," I said.

"Okay, bye."

I hung up and sat there in the car feeling like some dark cloud had come over me. How did Dom know about Rahid and Gamba wanting to leave? And, Deborah acted like he just left without saying a word. That's completely unlike him. Was Deborah messing up again? Did she forget Dom already sorted this thing out with Amadi or was something else going on? If you can't trust your own people, you're pretty much fucked. Thing is, I trusted Dom with my life. I toiled over it in my head for a few minutes, but then decided it had to be just a little mix up. That or the Amadi's were just trying to play Deb. Either way, you know that bad thought I was talking about earlier? Well, that was it, and it stuck with me.

I got out of the car with my wrap from Saladworks and picked through it, munching on little pieces of shredded lettuce and chunks of chicken, on the way up to my floor. I got off the elevator and walked down to my apartment. As soon as I walked through the door, my phone rang again.

"Southerland," I answered.

"Alex, it's me," came a voice.

"Bill?"

"Yeah, thanks for picking up the phone this time," he said.

"Yeah, well ... ... I neglected to check the caller ID." I put my purse down on the table and went into the bedroom to get undressed.

"Well, thanks anyway," Bill said. "Hey, I just talked to Chris. He said you stopped by the school ... thanks for going to see him."

"I didn't do it for you, Bill."

"I know," he replied. "Still, it means a lot to me. Chris is a good kid."

"Yeah, you guys did good with him."

"Thanks," Bill responded.

"So, what do you want, Mr. Mom?"

He chuckled. "Nothing at all, just wanted you to know I appreciate what you did and hope we all see more of you."

"Bill, I'm not ready for all this closeness. I mean I got a lot going on, and ... I ain't trying to be an ass about it, but I got my own problems to deal with."

"Yeah, I know Alex, but that's what I've been trying to tell you since high school ... we all need help and we all need to try and help the people around us that we love. But, if you don't let nobody help your stubborn butt, then you and the people around you will have this empty void, you understand what I'm trying to say?"

"I gotta go Bill."

"Can we talk again next week?"

"NO!" I exclaimed.

"Alex...?"

"WHAT?"

"ALEX!" he yelled.

"Fine goddammit, but I have to deal with this fucked up case first, so I need a few weeks, maybe months. Just don't hold your breath Bill, that's all I'm saying."

"I understand. You got a lot on your shoulders Alex. Just don't forget about us, and even if you don't call me, try to call your little brother every once in a while."

"I gotta go," I said, and then I hung up. Bill was naggy as ever like an old wife. And, every five minutes, he's always trying to give somebody a speech. He gets on my damn nerves, but at the same time, it's refreshing to know somebody actually cares. Truth be told, I always enjoyed punishing him—sometimes for no reason. He used to just turn red and start whining like a bitch, but not anymore. He took my verbal assault like a man. I guess lying to your girlfriend, fucking her sister, and generally pissing on her already miserable life has the potential to put chest hair on the sissiest of sissies.

It would seem the dynamics between me and Bill had totally changed. Oh, what a good sport he'd become. He was taking whatever I could dish out, and I wasn't holding back either—well for the most part. If I let Blondie have her way, she'd be the first to say we're letting him off easy. She'd call him a punk ass bitch repeatedly and convince me to open up a can of butt whoopin'. She was itching to tear into his ass too, but I ignored the voice inside my head and all her suggestions to fly down and smack Bill around. Instead I listened to the alcohol demons that insisted I was thirsty. So, I undressed down to my bra and panties and went down the hall into the kitchen to get a drink.

"FUCK, I'M COMPLETELY OUT!" I yelled at the top of my lungs. "FUCK, FUCK, FUCK!" I rummaged through the fridge and all the cabinets in the kitchen but came up empty-handed. "I'm tired of this shit, I mean WHAT THE FUCK? A bitch can't even have one goddamn drink up in here? GODDAMN, MUTHAFUCKIN', SON-OF-A BASTARD-ASS STANKY BITCH! FUCK...! I BET TONY DID THIS!"

I stood in the kitchen with all the cabinets and the refrigerator doors wide open, throwing a major temper tantrum. I was losing it for real, getting angrier with each passing moment. After arguing with myself for a while, I realized I had no other choice but to go to the store. However, taking in account the cab ride, time in the store, and the ride back, it dawned on me just how long it'd be before I had something good to sip on. As a result, I completely lost it. I unleashed some kind of built up, Kung Fu fury style aggression on all the cabinets, jump kicking, punching and back handing each of them closed. I felt much better after I finished my Bruce Lee, *Dragon* bit, but I still needed a drink, so I ran into the bedroom to get dressed.

I threw on a t-shirt and some jeans. Then, I put on some sneaks with no socks and stuffed my gun down the back of my pants. I clipped my badge to my belt and grabbed some cash from the top dresser drawer. Then I put a coat on and ran out. I took the elevator down to the first floor.

"Ralph, do you ever go home?"

"Man's gotta eat, right?" He smiled.

"Guess so. Hey man, where's the nearest liquor store?"

"You need me to-"

"No, I can get it," I interrupted, "just point me in the right direction."

"Well, okay," Ralph replied. "Hmm, there aren't a lot of liquor stores on Wall Street. But I tell you what ... I'll get you a cab. Have the driver take you over to a place on Lexington Ave. They got a decent selection and probably the better prices in the city."

"I'm familiar with Lexington," I said. "Is it one of those Mr. Patel joints though?"

Ralph burst out laughing. "Hey, this is New York," he reminded.

I giggled. "True dat, Ralph, true dat."

He came around the counter. "Give me a second and I'll get that cab for you."

I handed him a few bucks. "Thanks Ralph, you're a gentleman and a scholar."

"Thank you, Alex," he responded, holding the money up and smiling.

I watched him through the glass doors. He whistled a couple of times and did that little New York wave as if to say, *hey dammit pull that fuckin' cab ova, I got shit to do!* I swear I'll never get used to seeing that. It totally trips me out, but it works like penicillin on an STD—not that I would know anything about that, I'm just speaking to its general known effectiveness.

Ralph was the cab-hailing king, and his performance was always impressive. Hell, I'd be out there all day and damn near have to fall down in front of a speeding car before they stop for me. As soon as a car pulled up Ralph opened the door for me and waved for me to come out.

"Thanks Ralph. I won't be gone long," I yelled running up to the car. I climbed down into the back of the cab. "You'll be here when I get back?"

"Absolutely ... I ain't going nowhere," he said sarcastically, laughing a bit as he closed the cab door.

"Where to lady?" asked the driver, rudely.

"There's a liquor store on Lexington not too far from here, you know the place?"

"There are several liquor stores," the driver replied, "which one?"

Asshole. "I don't care, pick one."

"Yeah, I got it," he replied.

"Quick as you can," I ordered.

We got there pretty fast all things considered. I was starting to calm down a little because I could finally see the light at the end of the tunnel. I walked into the store and picked up a basket—yup, a basket—I had to stock back up. Ralph was right, they had it all, but the prices weren't that nice. I didn't care though, I was just happy to be there.

"Come to momma!" I commanded under my breath as I started loading up my basket. I got everything I wanted, and then walked back to the front to check out. There were a few people in line at the counter, but there was also this strange-looking man at the front, who caught my attention. At the time, he was bending all over the counter. He wore all black and had a skullcap pulled down on his head. I mean, I know it's a little cold out, but damn that dude looked like he was getting ready to jack somebody. I didn't pay him much attention at first because I was too busy fantasizing about getting drunk in the depths of my mind, but after a while I started wondering what was taking so long. I think everybody else in line was wondering the same thing, but we soon found out the worst way possible.

The man was mumbling, but his voice slowly escalated into a serious roar. Before long, he was yelling at the top of his lungs.

"STOP FUCKING AROUND!" he told the man behind the counter. Then, he stepped back and drew a pistol from his coat pocket. "I'll fuckin' blow your brains all over the place!"

"I be goddamned," I whispered, "dis nigga's trying to rob the place ... I can't believe this shit. I just want a goddamn drink!"

A little Asian lady tried to creep towards the door, but he caught a glimpse of her out the corner of his eye and turned around.

"DON'T ANYBODY FUCKIN' MOVE!" he commanded, swinging his gun around at all of us, and she froze in her tracks.

I guess I should've sprung into action. Law enforcement officers are supposed to be on duty even if we're off duty. If we see something illegal going on, we're trained to do something about it, but honestly, I just wasn't feeling it that day. I wanted him to do his thing and get out so I could get out too. I was really starting to get impatient too. Either he or the cashier was dildoing around, taking forever, and that was just pissing me off.

"Will you just hurry the fuck up please?" I didn't realize I said that aloud until everyone turned around and looked at me. "Shit," I mumbled, shaking my head.

The bad man in black ran up to me, gun first. "I WILL KILL YOU BITCH!" he exclaimed. "GIVE ME YOUR

PURSE, NOW!" He pointed his gun right in my face to make sure I knew he meant business.

So, there I was looking down the barrel of a gun once again. If I didn't want a drink so bad, I probably would've given in, but I needed my little cash. I should've just shut my mouth, but instead, I completely nutted up. It was like a scene from *Lethal Weapon*. Instead of complying with his demand, I started pushing him around.

"I'M JUST TRYING TO GET DRUNK!" I yelled. "THE FUCK KIND OF LOSER ARE YOU COMING IN HERE TRYIN' TO ROB THIS JOINT? STUPID ASS!"

"SHUT UP BITCH! SHUT UP!" he exclaimed.

"What were you thinking? I mean goddamn! Where the fuck's your mask?"

I could see the people ahead of me in line. Some were slowly moving back towards the door, others were mouthing and motioning for me to be quiet, but I didn't. In fact, I got even louder.

"FUCKIN' PIECE OF SHIT! GET THAT FUCKIN' RUSTY BULLSHIT OUT MY FACE! I SAID GET THAT FUCKIN' GUN OUT MY FACE MAN!"

He looked confused for a second. Then, he drew back and hit me on the side of my face with his gun. It wasn't a hard blow, just hard enough for me to get the point. My head kind of swung around to the right.

"HERE!" yelled the clerk, holding up a brown paper bag full of cash.

The bandit spun around and took two steps forward, taking his attention off me for just a few seconds. It was all the time in the world I needed. I dropped my basket and drew down on the gunman before it hit the floor. I aimed right for his shoulder and looked deep to make sure I had a clear shot. Then, I squeezed the trigger. The blast echoed throughout the store. The would-be robber dropped his weapon and fell limp down onto the floor. Everyone else hit the deck too. The Asian lady started screaming.

I winged the crook square in the middle of his shoulder blade—close range. Some of his blood spurted back onto my shirt. I looked down at my basket and sighed.

"See what you made me do dumbass?"

When the basket hit the floor, most of the bottles broke open, so not only did I have his blood on my shirt, my pants and shoes were covered in liquor—good liquor that should have gone home with me.

"GODDAMMIT!" I yelled, picking up his gun with the sleeve of my coat. "TRYING TO ROB A LIQUOR STORE IN THE MIDDLE OF THE DAY ... WHAT KIND OF FUCKERY IS THIS?" I put his gun in my pocket.

"Bitch shot me, man!" he cried, squirming around on the floor.

"Everyone just calm down," I said, waving my badge around. "I need you all to get up slowly and move back towards the wall over there. Nobody leaves, alright? Just take it easy everybody."

One-by-one, each of the patrons got up off the floor. Then, they moved over to the large refrigerators where all the beer was. I dropped to my knees to pat the perp down. He didn't have any I.D; just some cash, a little vile of crack cocaine, and a bag of weed, which I wasn't too proud to stuff in my pocket when no one was looking. I figured the idiot owed me something after messing up my Saturday afternoon, so yeah, I took his weed. Then, I continued to agitate him.

"Stupid ass," I said softly, "it's broad fuckin' daylight out here. And, again I ask, where's your mask? Shit man, if you're gonna be a criminal be a fuckin' criminal, dummy!"

"Fuck it hurts, man!" he yelled, face down on the floor with my knee in the middle of his lower back.

"SHUT THE FUCK UP!" I exclaimed. "Stupid ass, you could've been out of here with the cash, but noooo, you had to go put your little grimy fuckin' hands on me."

"SHE SHOT ME MAN! POLICE BRUTALITY!" He looked up over at the clerk for sympathy, but the man didn't seem willing to lift a finger to help that fool. "Y'all see this, fuckin' police brutality man?"

"I'm not the damn police, stupid. What's your name?" I asked.

"FUCK YOU BITCH!" he yelled, coughing. "UNNECESSARY FORCE ... UNNECESSARY FORCE!"

"Fuck me? Oh, okay ... I got your unnecessary force right here...." I stood up and kicked him so hard I thought I'd draw back brain on the tip of my shoe. He was out like a light bulb. Good thing too, because I didn't have my cuffs and I was tired of him flopping around down there on the floor like a fish out of water.

I walked over to the counter. "What's your name?" I asked the clerk.

"Vikram," he replied.

"You good?"

"Yes, but you're bleeding," he said, pointing at my head.

I touched the left side of my temple and checked my fingertips. He was right. The nameless bad boy broke some skin when he pistol-whipped me. Vikram gave me a paper towel, which I pressed against the side of my head.

"Thank you." I picked up my cell and dialed 9-1-1.

"9-1-1, what's the nature of your emergency?" answered an operator.

"This is FBI ASAC Alex Southerland, number zero-seven-zero-eight-six-four-four. I have an attempted armed robbery at a liquor store on Lexington Ave-"

"We just received reports of gunfire on Lexington."

"Yes, I fired one shot ... suspect is in custody--black male, approximately twenty-five years of age ... has a single gunshot wound to the shoulder. I need paramedics and NYPD units dispatched immediately."

"Yes ma'am," replied the 9-1-1 operator. "I'm routing police and emergency services to your location. ETA approximately three minutes. Agent Southerland, are there any other injuries?"

"Negative."

"And the number you are calling from, is that the best number to reach you?" she asked.

"Yes," I responded.

"Agent Southerland, I need you to stay on site until officers arrive."

"Copy that," I replied. I hung up and looked back over my shoulder. The perp was still unconscious, bleeding all over the floor. "Vikram, here give me some more of those paper towels. Better yet, you have a real towel or something like that?"

"Yes." He reached down behind the counter and took out a hand towel.

"Thanks. Hey, make sure nobody leaves the store."

"Yes, okay ... thank you Agent," he said.

"Just doing my job, Vikram ... make sure everybody's alright over there--no heart attacks or nothing."

He smiled and came from behind the counter to check on his customers.

I walked back over to our inept robber and lifted his wounded shoulder up off the ground to have a peek. Amazingly, the bullet didn't go through. It was still lodged in there somewhere. I dropped him back down and used Vikram's towel to put pressure on the entry wound.

"Where am I?" he mumbled, as he came to.

He was disoriented, but he kept trying to get up, so I sat down on his back to keep him on the floor.

"Fuck you doin' to me man?" he asked. "Hey, whose blood is that? IS THAT MY FUCKING BLOOD? WHAT HAPPENED, YO?"

"You've been shot, it was very tragic," I said sarcastically. "Just take it easy, the ambulance is on the way."

"Man, my chest hurts when I breathe," he said.

"Take some slow deep breaths, you'll be fine. It's not as bad as it looks."

I pressed harder on his shoulder, and he screamed out in agony. You would've thought somebody just cut his balls off with a rusty axe. I had to hold back my laughter. I didn't feel bad about shooting him at all. But, by the time the cops and medics arrived, that fool was really starting to wince. I don't think he was faking it either. Maybe the bullet bounced and hit something major. Hey, shit happens. *Better him than me.*

The medics ran in and immediately began treating his wound. Then, the cops helped roll him over onto his back. As soon as he saw me, his memory kicked in.

"Hey man, I'm the victim here!" he exclaimed. "This bitch right there, man, she fuckin' shot me, robbed me and kicked me in the fuckin' face, fuckin' bitch!"

"HEY, SHUT UP!" warned one of the officers. "You're in a lot of trouble son, so just shut your mouth."

He looked over at me, but I was giggling a bit.

"Can I talk to you for a minute?" asked the officer.

"Sure, come into my office," I replied.

We walked a few feet away to talk while the other officer handcuffed the suspect and helped the medics get him ready to move.

"I'm Officer Brown," he said, smiling.

"Agent Southerland, FBI." I showed him my badge.

"You know I gotta ask, Agent Southerland."

I smiled. "Yeah, I know, but you sure you want to hear the answer?"

He nodded and cocked his head to the side a little. "Well, did you?"

"Of course, I did ... he came in, tried to rob the store, and he pistol whipped me, I mean look at my face." I pointed to my left temple. "Obviously, he meant us all harm. He wasn't wearing a mask or anything. For all I know, he wanted to kill everyone here. As soon as he hit me and turned back towards the clerk, I had a clear shot, so I took him down. Then, he was being belligerent, so I kicked him—knocked him out—hell, I didn't have my cuffs. As for stealing from him ... come on Brown, he's a crook, crooks do lie, my friend."

He leaned over and looked at the side of my face. "You need to get that looked at," he said. "Hey Lisa, come over here for a second, bring your bag."

"Hang on a sec," Lisa responded. After a few moments, she ran over to us. Brown and I continued talking while she patched me up. She was a damn good paramedic, very thorough and fast. Once she finished, she put a bandage over my cut and walked back to check on the perp.

"Hey Brown," yelled the other officer. "He ain't doing too good. We're gonna go ahead and get this guy out."

"No problem," he replied. "I'll finish up here." Then, he asked the one question I knew would come back later and bite me in the ass. "So, did you have to shoot him?"

I paused for a second to gather my lies. "Look at that big fucker, Brown... he's twice my size, and he was angry as hell. He said he'd kill me. I think he meant business."

"FUCKIN' BITCH ROBBED ME!" the robber said, coughing, as the officer and paramedics struggled to drag him out of the store.

"See what I mean?" I asked.

"How many rounds did you fire?" asked Brown.

"Just one."

Brown asked, "So, when you kicked him, was he standing up or was he already down ... I mean, was it like a spinning kick or jump kick or something?"

Well, make that two questions that would come back to bite me in the ass later. "Yeah, about that," I said. "It happened so fast ... I believe he was down, but he was definitely trying to get back up. As soon as I made sure the clerk and everyone else was safe, I called it in and tended to him. I took a towel and put some pressure to the wound." I figured the whole Good Samaritan bit was sure to score me a few points with NYPD.

"You on duty?" he asked.

"Well, ain't that a loaded question ... no, I am not."

He leaned in a little and sniffed me. "You been drinking today?" he asked.

"When the perp hit me, I dropped my basket. Some of the bottles broke and it got on my jeans."

"Well, it was a good thing you were here," said Officer Brown. "It could've been a whole lot worse."

I nodded, hoping he'd just keep going in that direction— good off-duty FBI agent takes down bad man, nuff said.

"Robberies in this area have gone up, big time," Brown said. "You gotta be careful. Most times we tell people just to let them go and call us, but you being law ... you did the right thing. I'm glad you took some action, and I'm sure those folks over there are too."

"Hopefully, the powers to be will see it the same way. I'm sure he'll be trying to sue us."

"Pardon my French, but fuck 'em, ya know?" he replied in a serious tone.

"Couldn't have said it better myself, man."

"How long you been with the Bureau?" he asked.

I said, "Just hit eight years."

He smiled and nodded as if to say he totally approved. Brown wrote down all his notes from our conversation in his little memo pad. "This joker got a name?" he asked.

"I didn't find any I.D. on him, and he wasn't giving up the goods."

"Well, whoever he is, he's going down for attempted armed robbery, assault with a deadly weapon, and assaulting a Federal Agent. You gonna stick around while I interview everyone?" he asked.

"Nah man, I trust you," I responded. "I'm gonna pay for whatever's not busted up in my basket and go home. Here's my card if you need a statement or something."

"'Preciate it," he responded. He took my business card and pushed it under the clip on his clipboard. "The D.A. may need to get with you. You'll be available, right?"

"Yeah, sure. I'm in the New York Field Office."

"Alright then." He stuck his clipboard under his arm, and we shook hands. "Thanks for your help Agent Southerland, we need good-"

"Oh, shit, I almost forgot!" I turned to the side and pulled my coat pocket open. "Perp's gun is in here."

"Yeah, we might need that." He laughed.

"Careful man!"

"I got it." He took the revolver out and unloaded it. Then, he placed it and the bullets into an evidence bag. "Thanks Agent Southerland. Now, you get home safe."

"Hopefully my cabbie's still out there."

Brown glanced out through the window for a second. "I didn't see any cabs out front when I pulled up. He probably left when he heard the shot. You need a ride?"

"Can you?" I asked.

"Yeah, hang on..." He grabbed his radio and pressed the talk button. "Dispatch, this is Brown."

"Go ahead Brown," came a voice.

"I'm on location at the liquor store. I need transportation for the FBI agent who called it in."

"Copy that Brown, I'll send an officer to your location."

"Ten-four," he replied.

We immediately heard the call over the radio. An officer responded, saying he was only about a block away, so I gave Brown a final handshake and picked up the only bottle in my basket that hadn't gotten busted. I walked back over to Vikram to pay for it.

"No, take it," Vikram said. "We are in debt to you. That piece of shit robbed us two weeks ago."

"Thanks!" I held the bottle up and smiled.

"No, thank you, officer. You come back when you need another bottle, and you ask for me."

I smiled. "That's not necessary I was just doing my job."

"Please, I insist," he said.

I touched his shoulder. "Take care, buddy. I'll see you around."

"Goodbye," said Vikram.

I walked outside with my little bottle of cognac. I flagged down my driver and hopped into the passenger seat of his police cruiser.

"Hey, I'm Rick," he greeted. His accent was by far the heaviest New York accent I'd heard in five years. He was straight up Brooklyn.

"I'm Alex Southerland." I closed the door, put my seatbelt on and secured my cognac between my thighs, gripping the top with both hands to make sure I didn't lose it on the way home. It was all I had left.

"Where can I drive you?" asked Rick.

"Financial District ... 55 Wall Street."

"Seriously?" he asked, grinning.

"Yup."

"I thought you were an FBI Agent," he confessed, turning off his flashing lights as we pulled away from the curb.

I shrugged. "And?"

"Well Alex, that's like a pretty expensive part of town, you know what I'm saying?"

I laughed. "What, don't you think the government pays well, Rick?"

"Government don't pay me well," he retorted, "I'm getting like a few pennies a day."

"Well, maybe I saved a lot of my pennies."

"Get outta here!" he said, chuckling loudly. "I heard you got that fucking guy back there, pardon my French."

"Yeah, I think we slowed him down a bit," I replied.

"Good for you," said Rick. "But he'll be back on the streets before the week's out."

"We just lock 'em up, my friend ... rest is up to the courts."

Rick looked over and stared at me for a second. "Ain't that the fucking truth?"

"So, you married, Rick?" I asked.

"Divorced," he said angrily, "she took me to the fucking cleaners too. You know how you ladies do it."

"I have no clue what you're talking about," I said sarcastically. "You got five bucks on you?" I broke out laughing, and so did he.

"You guys are bad news," he said.

"Who us? No way man, didn't they tell you ... we're cute and caring."

"Well, my wife was a cute monster," he said, laughing, "nothing caring about her at all, forgetaboutit!"

I giggled. Rick was funny as hell. He had mad personality, but he was kinda chubby for a beat cop. I imagined him sitting in roll call, his clean-shaven face sticky with doughnut icing dripping off his chin. *Okay, let me stop, I'm going "there" again.*

I hadn't ventured that far off, so it didn't take long for Rick to get me back to my apartment.

"Well, here we are," he said, "55 Wall Street."

"Thank you, Rick."

"Forgetaboutit," he replied. "You take it easy, Southerland."

I smiled. "You too."

I got out and walked into the building with my little bottle of cognac. Ralph looked at me like he wanted to ask what happened, but I just waved him off and ran into the elevators.

I spent the rest of the day sipping Courvoisier and watching TV. For those few hours, I felt completely free—no worries whatsoever. It'd been some time since I had a nice relaxing Saturday, and short of foiling a robbery, I guess that day wasn't too bad. I had nothing at all to do for the rest of the day; not a single thing, and it felt really good. I just kicked back and relaxed.

Chapter 12

The following Monday was business as usual. I was on the case back at the Amadi command center with the rest of the team. As soon as I walked through the door, I pulled Dominic to the side.

"What's up, Top?" he asked. "Whoa, what happened to your face?"

"It's a long story...." I paused for a moment and looked him right in the eye. "Anything you need to tell me, Dom?"

"No ... no, I'm good."

Over the course of my life, I've probably lied to thousands of people. I'm not saying I'm a liar. I'm just saying I have some familiarity with the subject, and I know when somebody's coming up short with me on the truth.

"You sure?" I asked.

"Seriously, Top ... everything's fine."

I nodded a little. "How about your daughter?"

"Yeah, she's back in school today," he replied. "Some kind of stomach virus. Guess it was just a 24-hour bug ... she's good now."

I smiled and tapped him on the shoulder. "Okay ... okay." I nodded. "Where are we on everything?"

"We're good."

"What about Rahid and Gamba ... they get out this weekend?"

"No, they decided to stay in," said Dom.

"Interesting ... seemed like they really wanted to get out and get some fresh air."

"Yeah, I guess they changed their minds." Dom seemed extremely detached—distracted even. He was definitely not himself that day.

I scratched my head. "Alright, then ... go on do your thing. Get back to work dude."

"We're gonna get through this," said Dom. Then, he walked back into the office.

I went outside and placed a call back to the office from my cell.

"FBI," Tony answered.

"Tony, it's me."

"ALEX!" he yelled.

"Yeah?"

"GODDAMMIT, WHAT DID I SAY?" he asked angrily.

"Uh ... I don't know Tony, you say a lot."

"ALEX, I TOLD YOU TO KEEP A LOW PROFILE!" he exclaimed. "DIDN'T I SAY THAT? I KNOW I SAID IT BECAUSE I REMEMBER SAYING IT!"

"Yeah, you did." I knew what he wanted to talk about, but he was gonna have to drag it out of me.

"AND...?"

"And, what, Tony?"

"YOU SHOT A MAN!" he yelled. "SATURDAY, YOU SHOT A MAN IN THE BACK. THEN YOU KICKED HIM!"

"Tony, it was just a little scratch."

"SCRATCH MY ASS!" he shouted. "HE'S IN THE HOSPITAL IN ICU WITH A DEFLATED LUNG!"

"No shit?" I asked.

"YEAH, NO FUCKING SHIT!"

Tony never actually cursed directly at me, so I could tell he was really pissed.

"I'm not sure what you want me to say, Tony, I...."

"I WANT YOU TO SAY YOU'LL STOP ALL THIS FUCKING BULLSHIT!" he exclaimed. "I spend half the day cleaning up your mess, and the other half hearing about it. DAMMIT, I got a whole office full of agents that don't give me any of this shit! And, then I got you."

"But Tony, none of those other jokers are anywhere near good as me. Look, I saved—hell I don't know—six or seven people in that store. That guy was a maniac—probably high on some shit. He had illegal drugs ... he had an illegal firearm, oh and did they forget to mention the fact he was robbing the place? On top of all that, he pistol-whipped me. What was I supposed to do?"

"ALEX, YOU SHOT HIM IN THE BACK!" Tony exclaimed. "How do you think that makes the Bureau look?"

I sat quiet for a moment.

"THAT'S RIGHT!" exclaimed Tony. "WE LOOK LIKE ASSHOLES THAT WILL POP A CAP IN THE BACK OF YOUR ASS AT A MOMENT'S NOTICE! This is bad. I've already got Director Mullen halfway up my ass ... just ... fuck it, I'll call you later." Tony hung up.

"Well he sounds pissed," I said, rolling my eyes.

I stepped back inside and bummed a cigarette off Deborah. She had the strangest look on her face, almost as if to say, *Holy shit, if you're smoking, then we're all about to go to hell in a hand basket, wearing gasoline drawers.* I didn't say a word I just took the cigarette and went back outside. I fired it up to recharge my nicotine supply. Halfway through, my cell phone rang. It was Tony calling back.

"Southerland," I answered politely.

"Alex, it's Tony again."

"Tony, I'm sorry, I-"

"Forgetaboutit, it's taken care of," he said. "When was the last time you were in therapy?"

"It's been a minute."

"You're back in there tomorrow morning!" he commanded.

"I can't, I-"

"OPR orders," he replied, "nothing you can do about it ... you should've thought about that while you were shooting up liquor stores."

"That's not fair, Tony!"

"Be that as it may, you're in with OPR tomorrow, no exceptions. And, Alex...."

"Yes."

"Remember what we talked about before?" he asked.

"Yeah, I remember."

"I gotta go." Tony hung up.

It seems Tony had taken yet another shot in the bottom for me. I swear I don't do this shit on purpose. I didn't wake up that day and go out to get robbed. This sort of thing just happens. It's like I'm a goddamn high polarity drama magnet. Mothafuckas seek me out to start some shit. I felt bad Tony was getting flack over the situation though. Guess I should've handled it differently, but that son-of-a-bitch made me mad when he hit me. Next time, I'll just put a suspect in a chokehold or kick him in the balls and save my bullet.

I hadn't seen Stephens since I first started working the Amadi case, but I was certain she'd been sitting around sharpening her knife, waiting for me to get back in there so she could get her hands on some fresh, slightly dark meat. She was like an evil fucking shark, circling in the water, hoping my little raft would spring a leak. I'm sure many had fallen at her little scaly hands, but I am not without some skills. I had a plan. I was tired of hearing all that "turn the other cheek" crap Tony jabbers about; the hell with that. It was time for me to put my foot where the sun doesn't shine. I had it all planned out in my head what I'd do, and I couldn't wait for the next day to come.

I spent the rest of the day just kinda watching everyone. I knew there was dissention in the team and some folks weren't happy with all the decisions up to that point, but I couldn't imagine them doing anything below board, especially not Dom. If I could depend on anyone, it was him. He was always on point.

For some reason, Mondays seem to fly by as if all the clocks in the world are pumped up on speed and running double-time. Before I knew it, the night was upon us, and it was almost time to talk to Aker again. As the hour drew near, I could feel the tension in the air, but not from me. I was totally calm. Evidently, I'd worked all the drama out of my system earlier that day. That or I finally found a more effective way to ignore Blondie's foolishness—live target practice in urban environments. *I am so going to hell for that.*

I drank a few cups of coffee and got ready for a long night. Mike was kind enough to brew a fresh pot to make sure we were all running at a hundred and fifty percent. He knows I'm a coffeeholic. I think we all were. None of us were any good without a fresh pot nearby.

At 10:45 p.m., I took my phone off the charger. "Guys, it's almost eleven," I said. "Let's get everything online and checked. Let me know when we're ready ... Deb...."

She got up and walked over. "Yeah. Top?"

"Come with me," I whispered.

We walked through the house and out the front door.

"What's up?" she asked.

"I need a no-bullshit answer from you ... Did Dominic know about Rahid and Gamba leaving this weekend?"

"I don't think so," she replied, shaking her head. "Like I told you, he left right after you. It was way before they even got up Saturday morning."

"Why'd they decide not to go out?"

"What?" She seemed surprised and confused.

"Rahid and Gamba, they didn't go out, did they?"

She looked funny. "Yes, they did. They were out for almost four hours."

"Is that so?"

"Yeah," she replied. "I had Mike follow them and check out the locations they visited before clearing them to go in."

"Did Mike stay with them the whole time?" I asked.

"Yes, but he waited outside in the car after he checked the locations. He followed procedure. Why, what's going on?"

"Nothing ... I think maybe Dom's just a little distracted. His daughter was ill."

"Oh ... well is she doing better now?" asked Deborah.

"Yeah, she's fine."

"So, we're good?" she asked.

"Yep, go on in ... oh, wait, can I-"

Deborah held up a cigarette. I smiled and took it from her. I held it to my lips, and she lit it up for me with her lucky gold lighter.

"Should we be worried?" asked Deb.

I frowned, puffing out a cloud of smoke. "This is my second one in a year!"

"No need to get testy, Top," she said smiling, "you take it easy with that now you know how hard it is to-"

"I'll be in there in a second Deb," I snapped.

She didn't press the issue. She turned around and walked back into the house.

I finished my cigarette and flicked the butt over into a nearby empty flower pot. I turned around and walked back in. Halfway down the hall, my phone rang. It was him.

"Hello."

"Agent Southerland," came a voice.

"Aker, please, call me Alex. How can I help you this fine evening?"

"Compliance Alex, compliance will do just fine," said the man.

"How's Keon?" I asked.

"Right down to business, eh?" said Aker. "No, no, no, I don't think so. This is not the way we will work together. We will take our time and get to know one another. I assure you the boy is safe and sound. We have all the time in the world."

I walked around the corner into Rahid's office. Everyone was in there holding a headset up to their ear, including Rahid and Gamba. I could tell we were gonna have a hard time keeping those brothers on the right track. They definitely seemed to be on edge.

Parents always have such high expectations, but I try to warn them early on that the negotiation process is long and arduous. Things can go well, but more than not, things don't go our way at all, and you're just on an emotional rollercoaster, going up and down when you least expect it. My gut told me those two brothers had something else going on; something they weren't telling me. Even if everything was above board, I had the feeling they lacked the patience to go the distance. Rahid wanted Keon back fast, but I didn't blame him. Wouldn't you want to do everything you could to get him home if it was your child? I sure as hell would. I think that's what keeps me going even when the shit hits the fan.

Aker continued smooth-talking me while I kept my ears wide open for any little shred of information I could use against him to help give us an edge.

"I'm a very interesting person I assure you," Aker revealed. "Wouldn't you like to get to know me, Alex?"

"I'd like that very much." I sat down and got comfortable.

"Well, I like you Alex, very much so—to use your terminology," he confessed. "Tell me, why do you think I like you so much?"

"Hmm, let me guess ... you need a date this weekend, and I look good in a ball gown?"

"Sarcasm," said Aker, "you are fascinating! But no. I like you because you are just like me."

"Really? And, how's that Aker?"

"You are a ruthless black hole," he explained. "You care more about getting the job done than how people perceive your actions."

"Am I that transparent?" I asked.

Aker replied, "Let me tell you a story ... growing up in South Africa, we were not wealthy like some whites, but we were not poor either. We lived on a farm. It was a good place to live, but the neighboring townships were a different story. No clean drinking water, gangs, killings, there was hardly any food at all, and AIDS literally everywhere. It was lovely as you can imagine. I remember coming home one day from school. I was 13, the oldest of seven children. I sat with my mother, who looked me in the eye, tears streaming down her cheek, and told me my father had been beaten to death and beheaded. Coloureds took my father's life. No one knows why they killed him, but they did—heartlessly I might add. Now, my mother knew she couldn't maintain the farm and support the family all on her own, so you know what she did?"

"No."

"I followed her into their rooms," he said in a solemn tone, "and, she made me watch as she took their lives, all six of them. Some she shot with my father's revolver. As for the younger children, she suffocated some and stabbed the others to death. She bathed in their blood. Even today, I can still hear their screams. You see, these coloureds, these mixed breed bastards like you, Alex ... they took my father's life and destroyed our family. My mother knew she had to do something, and so she did. After slaughtering my brothers and sisters, she gave me a rifle, and we went out and killed our white neighbors and took their land. Then we spread out into the slums. Together we killed many, niggers—niggers like you, Alex."

I knew he was trying to bait me in with all that *nigger* talk, so I just remained calm and listened to him carefully.

"We took whatever we could from them," said Aker, "and I learned everything I know from that woman. She told me just as my father's life was theirs for the taking, so was everything else as far as the eye could see. She told me fools fear progress, but men use their power for gain. I was nothing like my mother. She was strong, but I ... I was a coward, and I didn't have the stomach for it. I eventually turned away from her. I tried to have a normal life ... tried to love instead of being full of hate every day. I met a young woman who instantly captured my heart. I would meet her in secret, at night or whenever I could get away, but after a while, my mother discovered my little secret, and you know what she did next?"

"I can only imagine," I replied.

Aker said, "She challenged me ... challenged my right to live and my right to be with the woman I loved. One night, she made me watch as her men ravaged my love, tearing her limb from limb. She told me real men stand up for what they believe. She taunted me, but I was no real man ... I didn't fight for her ... I didn't fight for the only woman I ever loved. Those men raped and killed my girlfriend like she was an animal right before my very eyes, and I was powerless to stop it. They laughed as they mutilated her body and spit and urinated on her. It was horrible, but I learned a valuable lesson that day, and when the time was right, I took mother's advice ... I stood up for what I believed, and I believed she deserved to die a horrible death. I waited until she was good and drunk with wine, and I raped and beat her, the same way those mongrels did my love. I took a large knife and cut off her breasts, and just before I slit her throat from ear-to-ear, you know what she did...? She smiled. She was filled with so much hatred, she was actually proud of the evil monster she'd created in me. Do you know why I am telling you this, Alex?"

I tried to hide the horror I was experiencing inside from his sick story. "Somehow, I take it you're gonna enlighten me, Aker."

He chuckled. "I tortured and killed my mother because she challenged me. Since then, I have killed many men, women, and children. I have filled this world to the brim with hate from my black heart. I have spewed its darkness out from my mouth until there was no one left who dare challenge me. But I think about my life now, and I know full well I am surrounded by men who believe I'm old, frail, and weak. I think about today, and I know I am faced with you, a woman who carries my mother's spirit deep inside her. I can see it, I can hear it in your voice, and I needed you to know something, Alex ... I wanted you to hear what happened to my mother because I need you to understand if I can do that to my own mother, who gave birth to me, imagine what will happen to you and your family if you challenge me in any way. I will start with Bill and you will watch as he is humiliated and reduced to nothing. Then I will make him watch as I take Christopher apart, piece-by-piece. Do you understand?"

"I understand Aker, and I can hear your mother's sadness in you. Your father was a great man, wasn't he?"

I think I hit a nerve. He got quiet as hell for damn near a minute.

"Aker ... you still there?"

"How did it feel when you shot that man in the back Saturday?" he asked. "I wonder if you felt sadness then. No ... I think you thoroughly enjoyed pulling the trigger didn't you, Alex?"

"How'd you know about that, Aker?"

"I know everything," he replied. "So, tell me, did you get blood on your face? Could you smell it? Could you smell the blood, Alex?"

"I think you believe you already know the answer to that, don't you?"

He sighed. "It's time," he said.

"I agree. Why don't you tell me about Keon?"

"Oh, not yet!" he exclaimed. "Not until I get what I want first. So, we don't have any problems, allow me to tell you how I work ... I will give you a figure. Mr. Amadi will provide this money in the denominations I specify, and this money will be delivered in accordance to my requirements. If there is one mistake, my men will castrate the boy and we will start again whether the money has been received or not. It is important you understand that all things must be done properly. Once my instructions have been followed, we will release the boy from the Embassy. As we speak, your superiors have put us under surveillance. Now, you may be thinking about storming the Embassy or the Consulate, but I assure you my soldiers will kill your men, leaving you alive, and we will castrate the boy and start over again. If he has already been castrated due to an error on your part, we will move to his hands, feet, and other appendages. Do you understand?"

"I don't think your protocol will present a problem," I replied, "but I need to know that the boy is still alive and in good health."

"Our time is up," he said.

"Aker, you sound like my therapist."

"You mean Dr. Stephens of the FBI's Office of Professional Responsibility?"

I got quiet.

"There's nothing you can do I won't find out about," he said in a spooky tone. "There's nowhere you can hide from me, Alex. As far as that cunt Stephens is concerned ... well, let's just say if I actually gave a damn, I would kill her for you. Personally, I think you should do yourself a favor and slit her throat tomorrow during your session."

I jumped up out of my seat and damn near dropped the phone.

"We will talk tomorrow night, Alex. Goodbye." He hung up.

We all looked at each other as if we'd just seen a ghost.

Rahid put his headset down. "I don't understand," he said.

"Get them out of here now!" I ordered.

"Come on guys," said Chuck.

"NO WAIT!" yelled Gamba. "We have every-"

"OUT NOW!" I yelled.

Chuck and Mike escorted Rahid and Gamba out of the room.

"What's going on, Top?" asked Deborah.

I stood there looking at my phone, my mind was wandering all over the place.

"Top...?"

"What is it, Deb?"

"How did he know-"

"Hang on," interrupted Dom. I think he could tell I was pissed, so as usual he acted like a buffer between me and the rest of the team. Deborah took a deep breath and calmed down.

"Tear this place apart," I said. "Start with this." I tossed Deborah my phone and walked out.

Chapter 13

After my little talk with Aker, I had to take time to collect my thoughts; thoughts that kept leading me down the exact same path. Sure, he might be able to get general information about me and my family, my little brother, maybe even where I went to school, but my meeting with Stephens that's on the books? I just found out about that earlier from Tony. All this could mean only one thing. We had a leak in the department—a big fucking leak.

I walked into the living room where Rahid, Gamba, Chuck and Mike were. I sat down on the sofa and looked directly at Rahid.

"I need you to be straight with me," I said.

He threw his hands up. "I have told you everything-"

"BULLSHIT! I NEED TO KNOW THE WHOLE STORY ... I KNOW YOU'RE LEAVING SOMETHING OUT."

Mike and Chuck closed in on him. He looked up at both of them like he was about to shit a brick. Rahid was clearly nervous, but his brother Gamba on the other hand was cooler than a fan in December.

"Why'd they kidnap Keon?" I asked.

"It is for the money," said Gamba, "they just want the money."

I shook my head. "I don't buy it. This Aker guy knows what I had for breakfast, and there's no way he's that fucking good. He's got help from the inside ... help from inside this house, NOW TELL ME THE TRUTH GODDAMMIT!"

"I believe they mean to kill me," said Rahid.

Suddenly, Gamba got all excited. "THERE IS NOTHING TO SUGGEST THAT, YOU ARE JUST PARANOID, BROTHER."

Rahid closed his eyes for a moment. "I believe someone in my organization means to kill me and take over. This is why I moved my son here to America. My wife has already been taken from me, now I urge you to let my brother-"

"Agent Southerland, if you were doing your job instead of bowing down to this false god, then we would-"

"What...? What would we be doing, Gamba?"

"DO YOUR FUCKING JOB!" He stood up and stormed out.

Mike looked at me. I just shook my head.

"Let him go," I said, running my fingers through my hair. I moved over and sat beside Rahid. "Look me in the eye and tell me this guy will take the money and return Keon unharmed."

Rahid sighed. "He will draw me out into the open, and his men will kill me. I believe my son is already dead."

"Don't say that Rahid!" I looked up. "Guys, can you give us a minute?"

Mike and Chuck left the room.

I touched Rahid's hand. "I don't like to lose. I know you don't trust me, but trust in the fact I don't lose, alright? We'll get through this I promise ... you and me together ... we will get Keon back home safe, I give you my word."

He sighed. "Young lady ... I fear we have already lost."

"No Rahid, we're just getting started." I smiled and tapped his knee. "It's late. Come on, get some rest for me."

Rahid stood up and walked off, slowly. Of all the things I could've asked him to do, I think that was the most difficult. It's easy for me to take a nap and recharge. Hell, all I had to do was my job, but it's never that simple for the family. Some do better than others, but Rahid was totally restless. You can't blame him. After losing his wife, Keon was all the family he had left.

I slept for about five hours and then got back up to go run. Actually, I ran several times that day. I had a lot of energy to burn off, and evidently so did the team. By the time I got back inside from my last run, they'd turned every single screw, nut, and bolt in the house. Dominic caught me coming in through the back door.

"Top...."

"What's up, Dom?"

"We're finished," he replied.

"So, lay it out for me."

"House is clean, but...."

I raised an eyebrow. "But what, Dom?"

He replied, "Your phone's been compromised."

"How?" I asked.

"We don't know, but it's active right now," said Dom.

"Shit!" I snatched my cell phone from him.

"What do you want me to do, Top?" he asked.

"Can you use the phone to trace him?"

"We already did. The source is the Consulate ... check this out." He handed me a file. "Aker is actually Ivan Ashbie, Consul, South Africa Consulate General, right here in New York. He's tied into crooked deals all over the world. From what I can see, he's a goddamn maniac."

I asked, "How's this even possible?"

"He's gotta have some kinda help from the inside," said Dom.

I looked at my watch. "Shit man, I gotta go see OPR."

"What's the deal with that, Top? I thought all that was over."

"I shot a guy this weekend, so I gotta see the shrink within 48 hours. House rules, and the house always wins, Dom, the house always wins. See you later tonight." I started walking off.

"Hey...."

I turned back to him. "What's up?"

"Be careful."

I nodded. "Call me if you need to but use the radio until I get this phone to the guys in the lab."

He gave me a thumbs-up, and I left immediately. I drove straight back to the office. I dropped off my phone with the lab before going up to see Stephens. As always, she was free, as if she had nothing better to do with her time than to sit around and wait for me to show up.

"Agent Southerland." She appeared to be gloating about something. "Please have a seat."

I walked over and took my usual spot on the couch.

"You've been quite busy since the last time we spoke," she said.

I smiled.

Stephens stood up and took a file off her desk. She walked over and sat down next to me. I have to admit I was feeling a bit uncomfortable. Last time I was that close to her, I was butt naked in the shower. *Don't ask. It's a long story.*

"Alex, we haven't spoken in months," she reminded.

"Like you said, I've been busy Dr. Stephens," I replied with a smug look on my face.

"Do you know why you're here?" she asked.

"I shot someone, so I have to see a shrink."

She didn't say anything.

"No Doc...? Okay then, I guess I'm so sexy, you can't go without seeing me for extended periods of time," I said, laughing out loud.

"Sexuality and shock is your shelter, isn't it?" she said. "I wonder if all that will help you now." She leaned in to me and opened the folder. "Have a look at this."

"FUCK ME!"

"Oh yeah, that's right," she smiled.

It took all my might to resist from strangling her right there on that couch and running out the door. "What do you want, Stephens?"

"Well, let's see here," she said, holding up a picture. "That's you shaking hands with a known drug dealer. No telling what you were doing with him, but I suspect a drug screening will let us know." She continued flipping through the photos. "You should remember this one? I believe you and a couple of gentlemen from a bar performed a number of illicit acts that night." She let out a laugh that was chilling. "Thermal imagery is simply amazing. You know, it wasn't the sex that did you in. The drugs, on the other hand, are a different story. I don't even have to give you a drug test now. This picture says it all. I've spoken with both of them already. They had no clue you were an FBI agent. They are willing to testify against you to save their own asses. Did you know one of them was married...? Yeah, the big guy ... oh my goodness, would you look at that, he is big!" She held a photo up and tilted her head to the side, staring at it. "You don't see something like that every day, do you?"

I shook my head. "You been surveilling me?"

"Here's what I want to know," she said, "how is it you can afford a car like this and an apartment on Wall Street?" She had pictures of my DBS and my apartment building. "I guess it doesn't matter. Once we get authorization to investigate your financials, we'll find out."

"THE FUCK DO YOU WANT?" I yelled.

"I tried to help you," said Dr. Stephens. "For years, I've tried to be your friend, but you spat in my face every single time. So, I've been building a case against you."

"You can't do that ... client privilege!"

She shook her head. "Not if I deem your actions illegal and a threat to the Bureau. You've committed felonies. I have collected enough evidence to prove to my superiors and a jury that you should be terminated and prosecuted to the full letter of the law. You're a bad agent Southerland. I just need one more thing to paint the right picture. When you lose the Amadi case—and you will lose the Amadi case—I'm gonna put you away forever. If by some miracle you recover the victim, it's just a matter of time before you slip up again, and I still get what I want."

"Why all the bullshit," I asked, "just do what the fuck you gotta do!" I stood up and walked towards the window. That bitch was making my head hurt.

"I WANT CRANE!" exclaimed Stephens. "There's nowhere you can go that I won't be."

"Yeah, I heard that one before," I mumbled.

"Southerland, I'll follow you into hell if I have to," she threatened. "The good news for me is, obviously, you can't control yourself. So, I guess you have a choice to make. Either give up your boss, testify against him, or you're going down this time."

"GO FUCK YOURSELF, SHRINK!" I yelled.

"Shame to see you behind bars," she retorted. "We don't even want to talk about the video surveillance from the liquor store this past weekend. I've seen the footage." She shook her head and made a few strange noises. "It's unbelievable."

I just stood there staring outside. "I'm gonna need that file Stephens," I said.

She smiled and said, "You'll get a copy of everything once we indict you."

"I don't think so."

I turned around, held up my little pocket recorder. As soon as I pressed play, Stephens dropped the file and lunged towards me. I guess hearing her career slipping away all in her own voice was too much for her to handle. I put my hand on my gun and she stopped dead in her tracks. I'd recorded the entire conversation. *I may be crazy, but I ain't stupid.*

"Well, good doctor," I teased. "I think this just might be enough to get you up outta here."

"THIS CHANGES NOTHING!" she yelled.

"It changes everything. Now, I'm a gambling girl, and you're right, I have done some pretty screwed up things, but that doesn't make me a bad agent—I'm certain of it— and I'm willing to put it to the test. So, here's the deal, you slimy piece of white trash." I smiled really big. I was enjoying myself. "If I bring the Amadi case home, then you back off—forever. Clear me off OPR's radar. Tell Cross whatever you have to but get OPR off my back and keep 'em off for as long as I'm here. This shit ends now. If I don't get Amadi back, then I'll face the charges willingly, but I won't testify against Tony. That shit's out of the question. You want a snitch? You need to find somebody who actually gives a shit."

"YOU BITCH!" she exclaimed.

"Oh, Dr. Stephens, such language, but that changes nothing. So, what's it gonna be...?"

She was so pissed she kicked her trashcan across the room.

"Oh, don't be like that sweetie." I giggled. "What'd you think would happen? You thought you'd just come in here and roll all over me? If I'm such a bad agent, then you had to know it was gonna be tougher than that. If I'm so bad, wouldn't you just have a tragic accident...? You know what your problem is doc...?"

She crossed her arms.

"Ambition," I explained. "You're far too overzealous." I walked over and sat down at her desk. "So, I've got a laundry list of violations on tape here, and even if it doesn't hold up in criminal court, it's enough for my boss to barbeque your skinny little ass. You'll never work again in the government or even as a therapist for that matter. I'm guessing your little *all access OPR* pass will get revoked the same day this thing goes public. And, yeah, sure, Tony's a nice guy, but I promise he'll pulverize your ass."

I think I could see steam rising up from the top of her forehead.

"Come on doc, if I get the boy back, we'll trade, my file for your tape. If not, then we'll both take our chances."

She thought about it for a second. "FINE!" she yelled. Then, she walked over to shake my hand.

"No, we kiss on it."

"What?" She stepped back, looking completely disgusted.

"That's right," I said, "I don't shake on deals, I kiss on 'em. Anybody can shake hands, but if you kiss me, then I know you're serious."

I held the recorder up again and waved it back and forth. I was fucking with her and loving every minute of it. She looked like she wanted to pick up her envelope opener and stab me. Her face was beet red.

"Let's just get this over with!" she exclaimed.

I beckoned her with my finger. "Come closer...."

She slowly and reluctantly walked up to me and leaned over. I spread my legs and pulled her down on me, putting my mouth over hers and forcing my tongue inside. She tried to push away at first, but I grabbed her ass and pulled her in tighter. After a second, she closed her eyes and started kissing me back, so I immediately pulled away and moved my head beside hers.

"For you to be a shrink, you're so stupid," I whispered in her ear.

She stood up, wiping her mouth and straightening her hair. "I know what you're thinking. You think if I'm subjected to a polygraph you can discredit me, but just remember, Agent Southerland I'm OPR, and I have friends in high places. Now, our time's up, so get out of my chair, and get the fuck outta my office!"

"I'll be looking for my file soon." I laughed.

"Don't count on it," she retorted. "You don't know the half of what's going on around you."

I smacked her on the butt before leaving, which seemed to piss her off even more. As soon as I got out of there, I ran down to Tony's office. Thankfully, he was in.

"Come in and close the door," said Tony.

I pushed the door shut and sat down at his desk.

"What's the deal?" he asked.

"We got a bit of a problem Tony, I-"

"Did you miss the mirror this morning, Alex?" he interrupted.

"Huh?"

He pointed to my mouth. "Your lipstick's smeared all over your face ... well, it's a different color actually. Soooo .... what's going on?"

I touched my lips. "Oh, yeah, I just made out with Dr. Stephens."

Tony tried to put his hand on his head, but it never made it. He just kept reaching for his forehead and putting his hand back down like he was in shock or something. He started shaking his head from left to right. Then he put both hands up. "I... I," he stuttered, "I can't deal with you right now!"

"No, Tony, she was trying to get me to squeal on you, and-"

"SO, YOU FUCKED HER?" he yelled. "MY GOD ALEX WHAT THE HELL-"

"Lower your voice Tony, Jesus! No, I didn't fuck her, I don't swing that way."

"Well, thank God for little miracles," he said.

I twisted up my lips and frowned. "Come on Tony ... here, I got her on tape trying to blackmail me." I slid the recorder across his desk.

He took a deep breath and frowned. "You know, it's like a goddamn soap opera with you."

"What, like Dallas?" I smiled.

"No, one of the really bad ones," Tony retorted.

"I made a deal with her," I explained. "If I get the Amadi kid back, she won't try to get me fired, and I promised I wouldn't give you this tape."

"But you're giving me the tape now," he said, raising an eyebrow.

"Everybody needs a backup plan," I replied.

"Alex, what possessed you to do this?"

"I knew she was going to try to get to me, especially after this weekend, but I didn't know what she had on me."

"What does she have?" Tony asked.

"You don't want to know," I said bashfully.

"Jesus, Alex!"

"Anyway, I got her to play ball. All I have to do is focus, get the job done, and I'm through with her ass forever. I just hope she'll keep her word."

"She will," said Tony. "She's a scheming, conniving asshole, excuse the expression, but she won't break a deal once she's made it."

"Well, she's after you like white on rice, on a paper plate in a snow storm."

"What?" He seemed surprised.

"She's trying to get someone to testify against you. So, what up wit' that, sir?"

"It's a long story," Tony replied. "Basically, she stepped over the line dealing with one of my fellow agents a long time ago, I mean years back. She was hungry for promotion but was trying to get there by stepping all over everybody. She had someone from OPR approach me, but there was no way I was gonna give up my partner. I ended up testifying against Stephens, and based on my testimony, she was recommended for termination. Instead of giving her the boot, OPR swooped her up. From what you're telling me, sounds like she's up to her old tricks."

"She's definitely got a grudge against you, Tony. Better watch your back man."

He laughed. "I doubt there's any more room after all the knives you've stuck back there."

I frowned. "That ... tha ... that's not nice."

"Here...." He handed me his handkerchief. "What the hell were you doing making out with her?"

I took the hanky and wiped my mouth. "Oh yeah, I kissed her instead of shaking on the deal."

"What?" He squinted hard at me.

"Hell yeah man, I had a tongue showdown with shrinky," I said giggling. "She was starting to get into it too. I told you those OPR jokers are sick in the head. If she tries anything, I'll just testify she's an angry lover during the hearing. We'll have to take a poly and, can you imagine the results on that?" I laughed out loud.

Tony held up his hand. "Could you just do me a favor, please?"

"Tony, I know-"

"No!" he interrupted, pointing his finger at me. "You don't know ... you think this is a game, and it's not."

"But, I-"

"Just cut the bullshit, okay Alex? It stops now! I mean everything. You finish this case, by the book, or you won't have to worry about OPR, catch my drift?"

Suddenly, I got serious. I think my feelings were hurt. Tony actually threatened me. I sat up in my chair. "You're serious, aren't you?"

"Alex, look at me."

"I'm looking at you, Tony."

"Alex, I love you like you were my own daughter, which is probably the problem ... you think you can get away with anything. Don't get me wrong, your work is impeccable, but you've gotta cut out all this other shit. If you think I won't fire your little smug ass, then you are sadly mistaken. All this is hanging over my head now, and I will make an example out of you."

I hung my head down low. "Okay ... I'm sorry, Tony."

"Just take it down a few notches," he said. "Can you do that for me?"

"Yeah, I guess so."

Tony smiled at me. "Get out of here and bring that boy back alive."

I stood up, saluted Tony and ran out while he was in a halfway decent mood. I never like it when he's upset with me. He was right though, in a way, we were like father and daughter, and something inside me always looks to test his limits you know, see how far I can go. Obviously, it was keeping him up at night though, so I figured I'd try to behave going forward.

On my way back out, I almost forgot to go down to the lab, but I remembered just as soon as I reached for my phone to make a call. Thank God I was still in the building because I probably would've left that shit behind if I was already in the car.

I strolled down to the lab and busted through the doors. Everybody turned around, looked back at me and frowned. I had this kind of love-hate relationship going on with them, especially with this technician named Matthew Perkins, who I called Matt or Perky when the mood struck. He looked right at me and twisted his little face into the biggest frown ever.

"PERKY!" I yelled. "WHAT UP PERKY?" I said, sounding like a ghetto hoochie momma from the dirty South.

"Somehow I knew this was your phone, Alex," he said, sighing heavily.

In a very annoying tone, I replied, "Err, uh, what gave it away Perky? The phone book? The call log? How 'bout my name in there as the frickin' owner?"

I walked over and sat on the edge of his desk. I was always doing stuff to piss him off. He was so neat and organized, so plopping down on his workstation was just too good of an opportunity to pass up. I kinda wiggled my ass around on top of his desk until I was comfortable. With each gyration, he squeaked and squirmed in his chair. Boy, that frown of his looked like it was gonna be permanently stuck in place. I was thoroughly enjoying myself, so I went ahead and started scooting back towards his papers.

"NO!" he yelled, moving his things away from my butt. "It wasn't the phone data," he whispered. "It was the fact you're always the source of some National Security breech!"

I frowned. "Seriously?"

"No, just joking."

"Fuck you Perky, goddamn lab rat!" I giggled.

Matt laughed, but his peers looked at me like they were totally disgusted.

"How'd these geniuses crack my phone Perky?" I asked.

"I hate it when you call me that!" he exclaimed, frowning up again. "Look." He spun around in his chair.

I leaned over the desk to see what he was talking about. He unlocked his computer and pulled up a window.

"See that right there?" he asked.

"Yeah, what is it? Is it part of the board?"

"Nope, it's transmitting," he replied.

"But, how...? It's like microscopic."

"Maybe nanotechnology ... Alex, I've never seen anything like it."

"Then, how'd it get in my phone?" I asked.

"I don't know," he replied. "I can't even figure out how it's connected. Alex, this is the weirdest thing you've brought down here. It's got to be expensive though."

I thought for a moment. "Government issued?"

"Can't say," he replied, "but I'd guess it's private or ... maybe it's Japanese." He grinned really big.

"Smartass."

Matt rubbed his chin. "Just what the heck are you mixed up in this time?"

"I don't know Matt, but how long will it take for you to identify it?"

"Hours ... days, maybe never," he replied. "I'm going to have to get it to my supervisor. I mean honestly, I don't think we'll ever figure out what it is ... probably just lock it up somewhere."

"Meanwhile, I don't have a phone," I reminded.

"How bad do you want one?" he asked, grinning big.

I smiled and said, "Mmm, I'd be willing to do really nasty, downright dirty things for it Perky," in my deep sexy voice, breathing hard.

His entire head turned red. He took a new cell phone out of the box. "You're crazy!" he exclaimed. "Here's a new phone, I already put your SIM card in it and transferred your address book. Any chance you can keep this one clean?"

"Give me the phone smartass. I thought you were transferring to San Diego anyway."

That instantly got him grumpy. "Yeah, I'm still waiting on the paperwork."

"You mean they have a lab out there that's actually big enough to hold your fuckin' head?" I laughed.

He picked up his ruler like he was going to smack my knuckles with it.

I waved my new phone in the air. "Thanks, Matt."

"You're welcome, Alex."

I hopped down off his desk and was about to walk away when he grabbed my arm.

"Hey."

"Yeah?"

"Be careful, alright? I ... I'm just saying, you know ... take it easy."

I leaned down, grabbed his neck and hugged him, which just about drove him nuts. He totally disapproved. Matt has one hell of an obsessive-compulsive disorder, so he wasn't a big fan of physical contact. He squirmed and twisted in his chair until I let him go.

"Uh ... yeah, oh ... okay, thanks Alex, thanks a lot." He straightened out his glasses.

"Don't leave without seeing me, Perky ... I will fuck you up! Understand?"

"Bye, Alex."

I darted past the ladies sitting near the front in their little shiny white lab coats. They were still rolling their eyes at me, but I just dismissed their stuck-up butts and went on 'bout my business.

I ran back out of the building down front where I was illegally parked. My car was still there, and I didn't get a ticket thank God, so all was good. I hopped in and cranked up, just in the nick of time. After a few raindrops hit my windshield, the sky just all of a sudden opened up. It took a while for me to find my windshield wipers; I hadn't used them since I got the car, so I had to look for them. After a few passes across the dashboard, I finally found them and got them turned on. I needed to make my way back across town to the command center, and didn't have enough fuel, so I stopped at a gas station on the corner.

I pulled up to a pump, got out, and swiped my credit card. By then, the rain was really coming down. It had to be blowing sideways because I was a couple of rows in and was still getting wet. The pump authorized my card and I pushed the start button for ultimate. I stuck the nozzle into my gas tank and set the handle to run automatically. I'm not sure I ever noticed how much fuel that thing took, but I did that time. It sucked down almost $35 dollars. I checked my receipt to make sure I wasn't seeing things, and sure enough, it was thirty-four seventeen. I was totally disgusted, almost ready to go back to driving the company Benz—maybe, even that damn BMW. My Beemer was old, rusty and only ran every other day, but it got good gas mileage. Then again, I wasn't paying for the Aston Martin anyway. That said, I came to my senses and got back in the car with a smile.

I drove to the command center and got myself ready to deal with that sick bastard Aker. The last call didn't go my way, but I had an idea of how I was going to make up for it. This time, I'd be ready for him.

Chapter 14

Honestly, I've encountered a lot of assholes in my career that I could've done without, but I also met a lot of good people. I've got a lot of experiences to draw on, and I try to make use of them when I need to draw a reasonable conclusion. Personally, I hate having to do that though. I don't think it's the right thing to do because most times you just end up prejudging people. But hey everybody does it, so I'm not about to stop now. Anyway, one thing I noticed in all my years of experience is the difference between good and evil. Take Star Wars for example. Luke Skywalker and Han Solo—good guys, right? So, if they were so good, why the hell were these jokers stuck working with substandard equipment every goddamn mission? They're out there flying old shuttles with expired Imperial access codes, living in remote ice wastelands on the outer rim of the galaxy, and riding filthy, stinking animals around. But, on the other hand, Darth Vader was rocking all the goods. He had a fly, black suit with a cape and buttons that lit up with gadgets all over the front. He had a massive Death Star weapon that could blow up a planet, a fleet of star destroyers, and an unlimited supply of completely faithful stormtroopers. If somebody didn't see things his way, he just waved a few fingers in the air and crushed their windpipe—just like that. Nothing stood in his way, but the heroes always suffer until they make the impossible possible.

Aker, A.K.A. Ivan, had a few things in common with Darth Vader. He is sitting in his little ivory tower up on East 38th Street—untouchable—having teatime. He's connected all over the place, and he himself has a bunch of stormtroopers, only angry little ill-tempered African ones.

So, move to the other side and ask, well, what does Alex have to fight with? Hmm, let me see … how 'bout my wits and my tongue, which of course I can do some tricky things with, but that too can only go so far. All I'm saying is where the hell are my stormtroopers? I've got little nerdy sissies that bitch and whine when their vacation accrual isn't showing up right on their paycheck. *This is a goddamn Greek tragedy!*

Honestly, I just think I'm in the wrong line of work. Maybe I should ask Aker for a job. Knowing my luck, he'd hire me just to rape and dismember me like he did his momma. *Can you believe that sick bastard?* It's hard to imagine there are people like him walking the earth free. Maybe he wasn't telling the truth. Maybe it's just a scare tactic, but it sure as hell sounded real to me, and it worked. I was so scared, you could hear my knees knocking together.

I stopped talking crazy inside my head and checked my watch. It was almost that time again, so I had to get my game face on.

As always, Aker called right on schedule at 11:00 p.m. You could set your watch to it with confidence you'll always have the correct time. The phone rang and I picked up but didn't say anything. This time I let him talk first.

"So, Alex, did you kill her?" he asked.

"You could say that," I replied.

"Good for you," he said. "Remember, there's always more than one way to end someone's life."

"I'll keep that in mind," I replied. "So, Ivan, what's a nice guy like you doing working for a bunch of lunatic Freedom Fighters…? You know, all those niggers?"

"Alex, your sarcasm never ceases to amaze me. You are fascinating indeed. However, it is a legitimate question I suppose. The truth is that I have more power than God himself. I don't need more power, but one can never have enough money these days. Plain and simple, I do it in part for the money, but mostly because I am good at it."

"Interesting."

He asked, "I see you have discovered my identity, yes?"

"That would be true," I replied. "I also have your location."

"Good, that will save us some time," he responded. "Now, I'm assuming at least one of the five agents monitoring our conversation has something to write with. Perhaps Michael or Charles?"

"Give me a second." I covered the receiver and looked around a bit. At that point, the cat was outta the bag. There was a real, live rat in that room. I knew Ivan had help from inside the department, but I'd hoped my suspicion about someone helping him from inside the Amadi house was just my imagination getting the better of me. I was wrong. Somebody was screwing us big time, and I had to find who fast.

Before I could complete the thought in my mind, I was already stacking the chips up against Deborah. I just don't buy that whole *I'm a little incompetent grandma* bit. My patience had worn thin with her. She was definitely hiding something. And, that whole thing she did trying to mix up Dom and make him look bad? What's up with that? *Maybe she's jealous I made him team leader*, I thought. I glanced back over at Rahid and Gamba too, but I couldn't imagine either of them giving up info to the man who had their own blood. My gut told me it had to be Deborah, and like Tony always says, I'm right more than I'm wrong.

"Alex...?"

"Okay, Ivan, we're ready ... go ahead."

"Excellent," he replied. "Friday, a warehouse in Brooklyn will receive a shipment at-"

"Whoa, hold on their Ivan, aren't you forgetting something?"

"Absolutely not," he responded. "Listen, you have my requirements, you know how I work, so I-"

"Ivan, you said, you'll hurt Keon if we don't follow instructions, and that's fine, but only after we receive the instructions, which I'm not ready to receive. First we need proof of life."

"That will never happen," Ivan said, "you'll have to take my word the boy is fine."

"Mr. Amadi believes his son is already dead and based on your unwillingness to deliver proof of life I'm actually beginning to give in to the idea."

"So, you're already beginning to challenge me?" Ivan's tone was spooky and sinister.

"Ivan...?"

"Agent Southerland...?"

"Listen to me very carefully," I said, slowly, "proof of life on my desk, or you can go fuck yourself like you did your mother, you sick bastard!" I slammed the phone down, walked over to Mike and terminated the call.

Gamba nearly climbed up the wall. "WHAT IN GOD'S HOLY NAME ARE YOU DOING YOU FOOLISH WOMAN?"

"Calm down Gamba," I replied.

Rahid didn't move an inch. I think he'd been spending the past few days coming to grips with the idea Keon was already dead. He knew all they were trying to do was lure him out in the open to meet his doom. I knew it too. I just refused to accept our fate. I had to try something.

"He'll call back," I said, calmly.

"THIS IS BULLSHIT BROTHER! SURELY SHE WILL BE THE DEATH OF US ALL!"

Rahid shook his head. "It is out of our hands now brother. We must trust in God."

The phone rang again. I looked up to the ceiling and took a deep breath. Then, I picked up. "Hello." No one said anything. "Hello," I repeated.

"I assure you Alex, you don't want to make a habit of this," Ivan said. "Now, I don't want to drag this thing out any longer, so I will allow you to speak with the boy."

"That's not what I asked for, and you know it Ivan. Listen, it's simple, you give me what I need, so we don't have issues getting the money together. It's in your best interest to do it this way. I can't go forward without it."

"I will make a deal with you," he said. "I will take some time to consider your request if you guarantee Mr. Amadi will be present during the exchange, whether I provide proof of life or not ... the ball is in your court."

I pulled the phone away from my head and looked over at Rahid, who at the time was still holding his headphones up to his ear. He heard Ivan's deal, so he knew the danger. He stared at me for a moment, and then nodded. Gamba ran over and grabbed his arm, trying to dissuade him, but Rahid pushed him away.

"Ivan, you're giving very little, but you're asking for a helluva lot, so what do you want me to do here?"

"The question, Alex, is how much is it worth Mr. Amadi to see his boy alive."

I sighed. "Okay ... agreed."

"Extraordinary. You will know my decision soon. Now, let's talk about something more pleasant."

"Like what?"

"I'd like for you to tell me about Karla Charles."

"I'm sorry Ivan, but that's classified."

"The case is over," he replied. "I don't understand."

"Well, it's complicated."

"You saved the day, you received a promotion," he said. "I don't see the complication."

"What do you want to know, Ivan?"

"Heroically, you nearly took your own life to save others," he said.

Everyone looked directly at me.

"That's ancient history Ivan. Nobody wants to hear about that."

"You're right Alex," he replied. "I don't want to know about that at all. Actually, I want to know about the crime scenes."

"You're a sick man, Ivan. You need help, and, no, I can't talk about that either."

Ivan said, "Your hostage negotiation training specifically states you are not to tell the hostage taker *no*. Am I not a hostage taker?"

"What can I say, Ivan, I'm a slow learner. Look, you're asking for something that, even if I wanted to, I can't give you. You're a sick fuck, that's why I hung up on you before. What makes you think I'll give you what you want this time around?"

"Because if you tell me what I want to know, and you do not cheat me out of the gory details, I will give you my answer."

"Proof of life?" I asked.

"I give you my word that you will have my answer," he responded.

I thought about it for a moment. "Fine, what do you want to know?"

"I want to know about the first victim, how she looked, what you saw. This killer fascinates me, and you are the only one, who can give me satisfaction."

"Jesus Christ...." I took a deep breath and rubbed my face. "Look ...." I sighed. "I was a rookie, working serials for the first time. I was foolish and ambitious. I thought ... I thought I could take on the world—handle anything—you know what I'm saying, Ivan?"

"Indeed, I do," Ivan replied. "Please, continue."

"I got the call in the middle of the night. It was late, and I was in bed."

"Did you know you were going to get the call?" he asked. "Were you expecting this assignment?"

"No, it took me completely by surprise. I got dressed and drove to the crime scene. The girl had been murdered in the master bedroom of a mansion in Atlanta, Georgia. When I walked into the room, I could smell something, but I wasn't sure what it was. The smell was lingering at the tip of my nostrils. I sniffed and took a few deep breaths, but it was sticking to me."

"You smelled the body?" Ivan asked.

"No."

"Then, what was it you smelled, Alex? ... ... Alex, are you there?"

"It was death ... it was ... I smelled death in the air."

He breathed heavily into the phone. "You are as intriguing as you are beautiful," he said, eloquently.

"Who me...? A coloured?"

"We all have our flaws," he retorted, "please continue."

"The body was right on the other side of a sofa. When I cornered the sofa, I saw it all at once ... her pain ... her death ... it was like all of the hatred and evil from around the world came into that house simultaneously and murdered her in ways I....” I paused. “It looked like they killed her in ways I never imagined, physically, mentally and spiritually.”

“I know such a sight,” said Ivan. “I have seen it many times in my country. Describe the body for me.”

I sighed heavily. “She was naked,” I said slowly, “bound to a makeshift cross-”

“The crucifix,” he interrupted. “Tell me, what did the killer call himself.”

“Constantine ... John Constantine.”

“Yes ... yes, go on, please.” Death seemed to excite Ivan.

“He’d hurt her really bad. There was blood everywhere. He stabbed her many times ... just completely destroyed her abdomen to the point where her insides were hanging out. Her face was badly swollen too. He beat her badly.”

“And what did you take from this virgin experience?” he asked.

“Death.”

“Explain, please explain, Alex.”

“I don’t know what death feels like, or even how it looks, but I know what it smells like. I can tell when someone around me is about to die. I know it because I can smell it. It’s indescribable.”

“I envy you,” Ivan said.

I asked, “How’s that?”

“You are still afraid, Alex,” he replied. “You are filled with evil, yet you hold on to your fear. It’s your heart that keeps the demons at bay. I can hear it in your voice. You have killed, but not with malice in your heart. You have hurt, but not with hate because you still fear hate. On the other hand, I do not. I no longer fear anything at all. You see, once you cross the line ... when you decide you are willing to take a man’s life—not for freedom or justice, but for personal gain—you will be faced with a choice. You can either hold on to your fear or release it. See, there are two types of people in the world ... those who hold onto fear, who turn to guilt and go on to repent for their sins like the good book commands, and then there are those like me, who unleash the product of their fears upon humanity. It is the latter who rule the world. The question I present to you is ... how will you choose when you are faced with this decision?"

"Honestly, I don't know," I said.

"You will never truly know power until you have completely released all your fears."

"Tell you what Ivan ... how bout you come down here, and we'll see if your theory's right."

He laughed loudly. "Oh, Alex, you slay me."

"I gave you what you wanted now it's your turn."

"You will have my decision soon enough." Then, he disconnected the call.

"SHIT, DEBORAH, GET HIM BACK ON THE LINE!" I yelled.

She tried but wasn't able to get through.

"SON-OF-A-BITCH!" I yelled, slamming the phone down. Then I started nodding. "It's cool y'all," I said, "it's alright ... we're making progress here. Don't anybody get upset just yet ... we'll get him again tomorrow."

This time, Deborah didn't wait for me to ask. She proactively walked over with two cigarettes and looked at me like she was about to fall into little pieces all over the floor. I figured it was a good time to chat with her and feel her out, so I casually accepted her smoke break offer. After that call, I needed a quick fix anyway. We walked out to the garage this time.

"Man, that was intense," she said, firing up her cigarette. She held mine up to the end of hers to light it.

"Thanks, Deb." I put that little cancer stick in my mouth and sucked like my life depended on it. I quickly felt the nicotine rush, and suddenly, all was good again.

"You okay?" I asked.

"Yeah, I'm good, I just-"

"Never had to look at or even think about dealing with a dead body before?"

"God no," she replied. "How do you get used to it?"

"You don't," I said. "You just kinda accept it and move on."

She took a few more puffs. "How does Ivan know so much about you?"

"I've been wondering that myself, Deb."

"Someone in the department?" Deborah was chatty all of a sudden.

"Could be, what do you think?"

"I just don't know." She shook her head. "Your phone was being tapped, and Dominic has been acting strange. I'm just an old lady who wants to make it to see my grandbabies grow up and graduate from college."

I giggled a little.

"No, I ... I'm serious!" she exclaimed.

"I've seen your file, Deborah. You're good. No, I take that back, you're damn good. How'd you end up here?"

"What here in New York?" she asked.

"No, here on this team," I responded. "I mean it looks like you were up for a promotion, SAC. Why didn't you go for it?"

"You're suspicious of me?" She took a real big long puff and let it out slow. "Listen Top, I can't fight anymore ... I lost it."

"I don't understand," I said.

"Yes, you do," she said. "You just handle it differently. I try to go for the politically correct responses. I also try to stick to the rules no matter the situation. But, if you do that around here, with all this corruption and sexist bullshit, it'll drive you bananas. My health started to deteriorate. After a while, I just said, hey, enough's enough. I put in for a less prestigious position and disappeared into the crowd."

"So, you don't care about getting promoted?"

"It sounds bad when you say it that way, doesn't it?" She smiled.

"A little, but I guess ... I guess it depends on your goals?"

"You're absolutely right, Alex. I finally realized at the end of the day, once the Bureau has used you all up, you'll be left with only yourself, and what will you look like? Sure, maybe D.C. can use you a while after. Maybe you find yourself on a subcommittee or something, but who will you be around? How will they feel about you? Will they even know who you are? And, then comes the most important question of all, young lady ... will you know who you are?" Deb had gone from subordinate to mentor all in a flash.

"Damn, that's deep," I said solemnly, taking another deep puff. I sucked in and held it in my lungs, and then breathed out slowly.

Deborah threw her cigarette butt on the ground and stepped on it to put it out. Then, she blew out a big cloud of smoke. "Wow, thanks for the chat Top, I feel better now. I was really tripping. Sorry, but I gotta run back in there, I been holding my water for the past hour." She laughed and skipped back inside.

I guess a quick smoke was all she needed to get back in the game. As for me ... well, I needed a little bit more. I believe Deborah had given me an honest answer. I can tell when people are lying, and I think she told me the truth about why she didn't want a promotion. So, if she wasn't all disgruntled about Dom's supervisor deal, then that pretty much kills any motive for her to give us up. So, I had to canvass my recent conversations. Maybe I wasn't looking for a sinister manipulator after all. Maybe I was just looking for a liar. Perhaps it was that simple. So, who was the only one that had lied to me so far? I thought about it for a minute and came up with just one name—Dominic. Deborah passed my lie detector test, but I felt like something just wasn't right with Dom. I couldn't put my finger on it, but my undying trust for him was starting to fade slowly.

Chapter 15

Days passed, and we didn't hear a peep from Ivan. But, on the third day, he resurfaced. It was about eight o'clock in the morning, and I got a call on the radio.

"Command, this is unit one," radioed Chuck from the front gate. He sounded frantic.

I grabbed my radio. "Go ahead unit one."

"I have a diplomatic motorcade requesting access," he said.

"Copy that unit one, who is it?"

"You're not going to believe this," he said, "it's Ivan Ashbie from the South African Consulate."

"FUCK, YOU GOTTA BE KIDDIN ME!" I pressed the talk button down again, "Unit one, hold them at the gate. Attention all units we are code red, I repeat we are code red."

The team scrambled, pulling on their vests and breaking out their MP5 submachine guns. They geared up and ran out to the driveway. I dashed into the kitchen where Rahid and Gamba were having breakfast.

"What is all the commotion?" asked Rahid.

"NO QUESTIONS GENTLEMEN!" I yelled, "you have to move to the back of the house, right now!" I pulled my vest over my head and Velcroed it together on both sides. "COME ON LET'S MOVE! NOW!"

I pushed them both back towards the rear of the home. There was a room beside Rahid's office that didn't have access to the outside, so I told them to go in there and lock the door.

"AGENT SOUTHERLAND YOU NEED ME!" Gamba desperately exclaimed.

"INSIDE!" I shouted. "Lock the door and don't come out. If you come out, I'll shoot you myself." I slammed the door and ran to the front of the house.

"Unit one, Command." I radioed.

"Go ahead Command."

"Let them in, but cover them from the rear, do you copy?"

"Copy that, Command," he confirmed.

"Okay, I'm coming out now guys."

I walked out the front door into the driveway and stood behind my agents. We watched as three black armored cars came to a stop in the middle of the driveway. Several men dressed in military gear jumped out and stood beside the cars, gripping their assault rifles.

I just shook my head. "This is fucked up," I whispered.

"That's an understatement," Dom replied.

We were at a standoff for nearly five minutes with Ivan's hoard of stormtroopers halfway up the driveway and me and my four little Jedi, standing at the top of the hill.

Finally, Ivan showed himself. My team drew down on him as he approached. He was smiling with this shit-eating grin on his face as if he and I were familiar or something. I moved a few steps in front of my crew. Ivan walked up with five soldiers behind him. He was tall, had curly hair and a full beard. His suit was white, and it was squeaky clean from his shoulders to the little cuffs in his pants. He was the devil in white, and with this unexpected visit, he was clearly overconfident, and my guess is he was up to no good.

"Agent Southerland," he greeted, grinning. "Or, may I still call you Alex?"

"You may."

He reached out his hand, but Dominic sprung up and put his gun in Ivan's face. Ivan's men immediately responded, surrounding Dom and me.

"Gentlemen," said Ivan, still smiling. He looked around. "Put your weapons down," he commanded.

His men were well trained and loyal. They lowered their guns all in unison.

"Now, aren't you going to offer me some tea, Alex?" Ivan asked.

I looked over at Dom. "Pat him down."

Dom pulled his MP5 by the strap up onto his shoulder and grabbed hold of Ivan, checking his pockets, and his jacket inside. Then, he frisked Ivan all the way up and down his pants legs.

"He's clean," said Dom.

"Come on Ivan," I said. "You can bring one of your men with you."

"Top, I-"

I shook my head and Dom shut up.

"Come now, that won't be necessary, Alex. We're all friends here. Besides, I trust you."

I held up my radio. "Unit one, maintain the perimeter. No one gets in or out."

"Copy that, Command."

"Mike, Deborah ... keep these gentlemen company," I told them.

"Roger that Top," said Deborah.

Mike nodded. "We got this," he replied.

I looked in Ivan's eyes. "Alright now, no funny stuff, got it?"

"Wouldn't dream of it," he replied.

We walked inside the house and into the kitchen. I poured Ivan a cup of tea as requested. Then, I poured myself a cup of coffee and sat down with him. Dom hovered over us with his gun pointed right at Ivan.

"Is this really necessary?" asked Ivan, looking up at Dom.

"Ivan, you killed your own mother, of course it's necessary!" I exclaimed.

He smiled. "Mr. Amadi has a very nice home, though I'm not surprised. He's quite a wealthy man."

For some reason, we engaged in small talk about the weather and world news. But after a few minutes, I'd had enough.

"This is highly irregular Ivan," I said. "Have you come to your senses and brought Keon back home? Is that why you're here?"

He laughed, sipping his tea. "I have brought you something alright." He reached in his jacket pocket and pulled out a photograph. He placed it on the table and stood up. "Thank you for the tea, Alex ... good day."

He walked to the door and out of the house. Dom and I followed him, watching as he walked down the driveway. Halfway down, he raised his fist, and all the soldiers jumped into formation, protecting him all the way back to the cars.

"Command, unit one," came Chuck's voice over the radio.

"Go ahead unit one," I radioed.

"They're getting ready to move ... what do you want me to do?" asked Chuck.

We stood there cautiously watching every move Ivan and his men made as they loaded up.

"Let 'em fly, unit one," I responded.

He hesitated at first, but then gave in. "Copy that, letting 'em fly."

I turned my attention away from Ivan's motorcade and held up the picture he'd left behind. Of course, the image was blurry as hell, but I could tell it was Keon. He was sitting up in a chair, gagged with his legs bound and his right arm tied behind his back. One thing immediately caught my attention though. Keon was holding up a newspaper with his left hand. "This guy is a trip," I said.

"What is it, Top?" Dom asked.

"Proof of life," I replied. "Here Deborah, process this. I need to make sure it's real, and I need to know what date is on that newspaper." I handed the picture to her.

"You want me to get it to the lab?" she asked.

"No, do it here."

"It's gonna take longer, but I-"

"You got fifteen hours." I turned around and stormed back into the house. As soon as I found a quiet spot, I picked up my phone and called Tony.

"FBI," he answered.

"Tony, it's me," I whispered.

"What's up, Alex?"

"Guess who just showed up at the Command Center."

"Who?" he asked.

"Ivan Ashbie."

Tony didn't respond.

"Tony...?"

"Yeah?"

"You hear me?" I asked.

"Yeah Alex, I heard you."

"He brought proof of life. Looks like Keon is still alive. I have Deborah processing the photo now."

Tony said, "Look, I'm working on something ... I think we can get some support from D.C., but I need time."

"I'm trying to close this up ASAP, Tony."

"How long do I have?" he asked.

"I'm thinking three days."

"Daylight's burning," said Tony. Then, he hung up.

I knew what that meant. It was David Chandler's favorite catchphrase. He used to say it to me all the time, and basically, it means one of two things—shut up and do what you're told or leave me the hell alone I'm doing everything I can. In this case, I believe Tony meant the latter. We needed help from the top of the food chain—a bigger player than Ivan himself. I didn't know what Tony could do, but if there's something that could've been done, he was the only one who could make it happen.

Later that night, Ivan called, but this time he was thirty minutes late. Guess his trip out to the Amadi house earlier got him off schedule. I picked up after about the third ring.

"Ivan, you're late," I answered, "I was beginning to worry."

Mike handed me a cup of coffee, which I sipped, pacing around the room, wearing my wireless headset.

"Alex, I apologize for the delay," he said. "May we get started?"

"Absolutely."

"I trust your agents were able to validate the authenticity of the photo, yes?" asked Ivan.

"They were. Thank you for keeping your word."

"I told you, I am a man of my word," he said. "Now, I wonder ... are you a woman of yours?"

"If keeping my word brings my victim home, then yes."

"And, outside of work?" he asked.

"I've been known to tell a little white lie or two."

He laughed. "Alex, your candor is refreshing ... alright, no more chit chat."

"You're right Ivan. I've got what I need, so let me help you get what you need."

"Ninety-five million dollars USD," said Ivan. "The cash must be delivered in unmarked bills no larger than $20s-"

"Hang on there, Ivan, your client isn't holding Bill Gates ... you've got a business man's son. There's no way Mr. Amadi can raise that kind of money, and you know it."

"Then that is a problem isn't it?" Ivan replied. "The proof of life I gave you will be followed by proof of death ... is that what you want, Alex?"

"What I want is for your client to consider a figure that's reasonable—one that we can deliver in a reasonable time frame. Reasonable is the way to go here."

Ivan was quiet for a moment. He seemed a little different that night. I don't think he was distracted, but his tone suggested a lack of concern for our negotiations. His reputation preceded him, so obviously he was good at what he did, but I could tell he wasn't playing with his poker face on that night.

"What do you suggest, Alex?" he asked.

That was just the question I'd been waiting for, and along with that came the real beginning—our first day of negotiations. It always plays the same, like a deadly game of cat and mouse with high stakes. I thought about my response to Ivan's question very carefully. Too much, and they'd say, *thanks for the down payment*, but too little and they might think we're not taking them seriously. No matter what I said, Ivan would not be happy with the figure, so I went as low as I could in good conscious.

"Two million," I replied. I knew it wouldn't close the deal, but I was hoping it'd be enough to keep the negotiations going. If this really was just a standard gig, the kidnappers weren't going to turn down two million and chop the boy up. After all, business is business.

"That's absurd!" exclaimed Ivan. "We have Mr. Amadi's financial records. He is worth nearly a billion-"

"Yes, but how can he raise that much cash in a day or two."

Ivan didn't respond, so I turned up the heat.

"You know how things work here in the U.S., and your clients should've thought about that. If they wanna wait for Amadi to try and make that number—if you know me like you say you do—you know by then I'll find a way to get into that Embassy and get Keon out legally. Bottom line, your men are committing acts of terrorism on U.S. soil, so I imagine their interest here is of a time-sensitive nature. I have people working around the clock on finding a way in. Now, you think I'm bluffing, Ivan?"

"I think you lack the capacity," he retorted. "However, you and I both know, they are on sovereign Nigerian soil, which is why you are powerless to act."

"Ivan, I think we should work together to end this thing quickly and on a positive note."

"Do you know why I came to see you this morning, Alex?"

"You think I can't touch you," I replied.

"Well yes, that too," Ivan responded. "However, I came to see you because I admire your spirit. I believe you and I have a future together."

I shook my head. "Mr. Amadi can get two million quickly."

"Tell me something, Alex...."

"What?"

"Do you still believe this is a kidnapping?" he asked.

I stood silent for a moment. All my fears were coming true. I knew it wasn't a simple kidnapping. I just didn't believe he'd ever admit to it. Something big was going on.

"I believe you're a man of your word," I finally replied.

"Two million will not suffice," said Ivan. "I will return to my client to discuss options. Alex...."

"Yes?"

"Pray to whatever god you pray to that my client does not wish to send Keon Amadi home early."

"Ivan, I know you're a man of your word. Convince your client to settle on an amount we can all work with, so we can complete this transaction."

"Remain by the phone for the next few days," said Ivan. "I will call at any time."

"Thank you," I responded.

He hung up.

I looked over at Rahid. Gamba had his hand on his shoulder and was leaning in whispering something in his ear.

"So, is there anything we can do at this point?" asked Mike.

I turned to the team. "Nah, we wait," I replied. Then, I looked over at Deborah. "Good work on the photo."

"Thank you," she replied.

"Mike, go relieve Chuck on the perimeter."

"Roger that." He picked up his submachine gun and ran out.

We stayed up straight through the night, all of us pumped up full of coffee and cigarettes. The next day was a long one too. With little or no sleep things get hairy real fast. We impatiently awaited the next battle of wits with our sinister foe, Ivan. After a long grueling morning, he finally called again that afternoon. His clients had dropped the ransom from $95 million to $60 million, but I continued to negotiate.

Over the next three days, I spoke with Ivan several times. He'd make an offer, and I'd make a counteroffer. I pushed as long as I could, pulling every trick in the book to buy more time, but each time I talked to Tony, he seemed less confident a diplomatic solution was plausible.

On the eve of the fourth day, I realized we were going to have to go through with the transaction and hope for the best. I'd been grouchy all day, which wasn't helping the situation, but something that was stuck in the back of my mind still bothered me—a question Ivan asked the other day. He asked if I still believed it was just a kidnapping. After all his dancing around, I'd already come to the conclusion it was not, but that wasn't the problem. I suspected early on they were going to try and kill Rahid. In hindsight though, I realize now I casually signed his death certificate the moment I asked him to deliver the money and he agreed. It was easy for us both to make that gamble when we thought Keon was already dead. *What the fuck was I thinking?*

Lately, I'd been spending quite a bit of time with Rahid, and I could see in his eyes what he refused to speak aloud. He was a very spiritual man—wise and well-studied. I think he knew death was drawing near. As for me, I was starting to smell Karla Charles when I was with him. Unless I pulled a rabbit outta my hat, Rahid was as good as dead.

I continued working with Ivan. By the fifth day, my counteroffer was up to fifteen million, and I had a feeling we were getting close to the mark. All I had to do was keep pushing them in the right direction—that and figure out a way to flush out a filthy rat. That situation was getting crucial too because Ivan had so much up-to-date information on us, it seriously inhibited my ability to negotiate.

I was getting desperate, so I did what I imagine anyone in my position would've—I proceeded as if the entire team was guilty. I put a call into Tony and had him send a replacement team. Then, I had another team transport us straight back to the office—no stops, and no communications whatsoever. I sent my folks into a conference room to wait further instructions—all of them, including those who weren't even at the Amadi home. It seemed like a waste of time, tying them up for hours when we could've been out doing something constructive, but in my mind, it was a necessary evil.

Satisfied they were sufficiently tired, I sent them in, one-by-one, for a polygraph. I watched each of them as the technician administered the poly. As soon as I got the results, I went back down to see Tony.

"We gotta talk," I said, shutting his office door.

"Have a seat, Alex," said Tony.

I walked over to his desk and sat down in a guest chair. "They're all clean," I said.

Tony sighed, tapping his pen on his desk. "Tell me about the negotiations."

"They're good. I think we'll be able to close at twenty million."

"How's your team?" he asked.

"A little pissed off with me, but I think they understand what's going on."

Tony frowned. "What about your family?"

"I've been checking in on them. For now, they're fine."

"Tell them to go somewhere safe, somewhere out of sight," said Tony. "And tell them to leave right now."

I sat up straight and grabbed hold of the edge of his desk. "What are you talking about Tony?"

"You have to close down negotiations with this Ivan character tomorrow. You're under orders to stand down, and you are not to communicate this to him. You must continue negotiations tonight as planned."

"What's going on, Tony?"

"Unofficially, President Wood's involved.

I squinted at him. "What?"

"I wasn't getting anywhere, so I met with Deputy Director Kirsten, who pulled in Director Mullen. Mullen spoke with the President and Secretary of Defense Harold Richardson. With all the soldiers and illegal activities, they immediately classified this as an act of terrorism, so it falls under the Patriot Act. Nigeria's cooperating too. They don't like Ivan and they're trying to capitalize on the situation ... Alex, they're selling him up the river. Attorney General McNamara and his staff are working up language as we speak to authorize a special inspection of the Nigerian Embassy and South African Consulate plus a potential strike based on the outcome of the search. The president of Nigeria has given authorization."

"This is bullshit! If we send inspectors in there, they're just gonna move the boy. He's as good as dead. WHAT THE FUCK, TONY! And, what exactly did we have to give the Nigerian government for this fucking bullshit?"

Tony rolled his eyes. "It's out of our hands now, and the answer to your question is way above your pay grade—mine too—so drop it."

I shook my head. "Then, I'll do what I have to-"

Tony smacked his fist on the desk and pointed his finger in my face. "NO! You will do as you're told. Don't go near that Embassy."

"Okay." I stood up.

Tony yelled, "YOU GO NEAR THAT EMBASSY AND I WILL PERSONALLY-"

"You don't have to threaten me Tony! I give you my word ... I will not go anywhere near the Embassy."

"We still have eyes up on the Embassy, so if they try to move him, we'll know about it and I'll have a team intercept."

I headed towards the door. "Then, we'll go back and relieve the other team."

"No, you won't," said Tony.

"Tony, I gave you my word that-"

"I DON'T TRUST YOU, ALEX," he interrupted.

I almost jumped four feet off the floor. "WHAT?"

"I don't trust you to follow the rules," Tony said, "and I don't give a shit if your team passes 14 polygraphs, you've got a leak. The backup team stays in place. You go out tonight, and make Ivan think everything's still in play. I will debrief your team. The Attorney General needs 'til the morning to get the legal stuff in order. It is imperative that our inspectors show up unannounced. I can't risk this information getting out to Ivan."

"Give me one team member," I said.

"NO," he snapped.

"Tony, the backup team doesn't know the command center. They make one mistake, and Ivan will be alerted anyway. It'll just be a matter of time before he and his contacts inside the department figure everything out and flip the script on us."

Tony rubbed his chin. "Fine, pick one teammate, but the others go down to holding until I debrief them after the inspection tomorrow."

"FUCK YOU TONY!" I blurted out.

"YOU CAN GO TO HOLDING TOO, AND I'LL TAKE OVER THE NEGOTIATIONS!" he screamed.

"I can't believe you're doing this to me!" I yelled. "You know they're gonna kill that boy, and OPR's going to be all up my ass Tony."

"Well, you should've thought about that a long time ago. I may not agree with the President's call, but it's not my place to override him. And if you violate a Presidential order, then there's nothing I can do for you … it'll be considered treason. Shit Alex, this thing could escalate into military action against Nigeria. Ivan is a goddamn diplomat. You do this one by the book, or you're done for. I can't protect you anymore. Now, I-"

"Don't say it Tony, I don't want to hear it." I could see sadness grow in his eyes almost instantaneously, but I didn't care. I'd made my mind up, and there was nothing he could do about it. "Is that all, sir?"

Tony looked at me with a blank stare. "Don't fuck with me on this, Alex."

"Yes, Sir," I replied in a dry tone. "Is that all, sir?"

Tony slumped back down in his chair. "You're dismissed."

I walked out the door and stood outside his office for a moment, trying to put together my next move. While I was standing out there, I heard Tony make a phone call. He actually put a tail on me. Soon as he finished with that, he radioed the agents onsite. He told them I was to return to the command center to close negotiations, and they had orders to bring me back in immediately afterwards for debriefing. I knew Tony wasn't playing around this time. He was serious, but he wasn't the only one. I ran back to the conference room. Federal police officers were already rounding up the team.

"WAIT!" I yelled. "Hold on."

"Agent Southerland," said an officer, "we're under orders from Director Mullen to-"

"No, I just talked to SAC Crane, and he told me I could use one of my agents to brief the backup team at the command center."

"I didn't get that order," said the officer.

"CALL HIM!" I demanded.

The officer squinted a little, hesitating to respond.

"I swear I just came out of there. Call him and verify it."

"That's okay," he said, "I believe you … which one?"

"I need my team supervisor, Special Agent Harris."

The officer nodded to Dominic, who walked over and stood beside me. The officers directed everyone else out the room.

"You alright?" asked Dom as we watched them herd the rest of the team off to holding.

"Yeah, but if we don't do something fast, Keon's dead. I'm sorry about hauling the team in. I seriously thought for a minute you were selling us out, Dom." I frowned and looked away from him for a second. "Jeez, I'm sorry man."

He cleared his throat. "Trust me, you shouldn't be."

I didn't realize what he meant by that, so I just dismissed it. "Look, I need your help Dom."

"You know I'm here for you, Top," he said.

"I need you to understand something though ... if you do this, you're fucked."

"I'm already fucked," he replied. "Last time I checked, I worked for the Bureau just like you."

I smiled. "Come on, we got work to do. Get a car. I'll brief you on the way."

Chapter 16

Dominic picked me up around the front of the office in a Crown Victoria. I jumped in and we sped back to the Amadi home. I was taking a big risk involving Dom, but Tony made it clear which side his bread was buttered on, so I didn't have anyone else I could turn to.

"I'm sorry 'bout all this, Dom," I said.

"Top, we can make up later," he replied. "Right now, let's get the boy back."

"The President's declaring this an act of terrorism. He's getting authorization to send inspectors into the Embassy to look for Keon."

"Shit, Top!" he exclaimed. "They'll kill him and dump his body in the river before the inspectors get on site."

"That was my point," I responded, "but Tony's not hearing it. We gotta do something."

"When are the inspectors going in?" he asked.

"Tomorrow morning soon as AG McNamara gives the okay."

"Shit, how much does Amadi have like $30 million?" asked Dom.

"Uh ... yeah, I think. I'm not sure."

"You thinking what I'm thinking?" he asked.

"No, what?"

Dom suggested, "We tell Ivan-"

"Whoa!"

"Just hear me out, Top," said Dom. "We make the drop tonight, you, me and Amadi. We get the boy back before sunrise and it's all over."

"And we go to jail?"

We looked at each other for a second. Then, Dom turned his attention back to the road.

"We do what we gotta do," he said. "Look, it's up to you, but you know I'm down for whatever ... whatever it takes."

I asked, "What about your wife, and the girls?"

"My family will be taken care of," he replied. "Besides, what would we do if it was one of my girls or your little brother? Top, we gotta do the right thing here, even if no one else will."

"And, what about the backup team?"

"I'll think of something," he promised.

I could see the wheels turning in Dom's head. I was fresh out of ideas, but I trusted his judgment, and I knew he'd help me seize the right opportunity. We'd find a way to get out of there safely without harming our coworkers. We had to for Keon's sake.

As soon as we got back onsite, Dom and I introduced ourselves to the backup team. ASAC Anderson was without doubt an anal-retentive asshole. Anybody else and I would've tried to solicit their help, but I knew there was no getting through to him, so I didn't press my luck. Tony always talks about doing things by the book, but Anderson acted like he is the book. He was fucking irritating. He even looked irritating to me—average height, thin mustache and dark hair, which he kept all neatly trimmed up in an army style crew cut.

"ASAC Southerland," greeted Anderson.

"I'm Southerland and this is Special Agent Dominic Harris."

"I know who you are," said Anderson. "You are confined to this command center. You're hereby ordered to continue negotiations with the terrorists as planned and await further instruction. My men are posted all over this property. Agent Southerland, your reputation precedes you ... I'm warning you, do not question my authority."

"Wouldn't dream of it," I replied.

Soon as we shook hands, I immediately started plotting against Agent Anderson in the depths of my mind. Dom and I couldn't really say anything to each other because the house was flooded with agents, but I could tell by the look in his eyes he was thinking on fast-forward.

Man, when Tony sends a team, I mean he really sends a team. We had at least one agent looking over our shoulder and listening in every room.

Rahid and Gamba grew restless as the evening progressed. No one was talking to them, and they were getting extremely worried. I figured that was a good excuse to start making some moves, so I grabbed a Kevlar vest and walked over to Rahid.

"Agent Southerland, what are you doing?" asked another agent.

"Just a routine conversation with Mr. Amadi before I go online tonight."

"And the vest?" he inquired, suspiciously.

"Well, if you must know, we always put Mr. Amadi in body armor as a precaution before we start the negotiations ... there a problem?"

The agent looked at Rahid, who looked like he was about to blow my little charade at first, but then he played it cool. Then, the agent looked over at Anderson, who looked back at me and stared for a moment. Finally, he nodded, giving the okay.

"I need to brief Mr. Amadi," I said, "so we'll be upstairs for a while." I grabbed Rahid's hand and pulled him out of the office. He hesitated at first, but then he came on. He followed me upstairs and into the master bedroom.

"What is going on, Agent Southerland?" he asked.

I pushed his back against the wall and shut the door. "Lower your voice," I said. "We don't have a lot of time."

I ran around and closed all the blinds. It was almost night time, so with the windows covered and the lights out, the room was very dark. I walked back over to Rahid, still standing near the door.

He grabbed me by the shoulders. "I need to know what's going on, now Alex," he whispered. I could tell by the cold stare in his eyes he meant business.

"You and I have spent a lot of time together recently," I reminded, "I know it's hard for you, but you're gonna have to trust me. You need to know that my team is being pulled off this case. The President of the United States has ordered us to stand down. They are going to send inspectors into the Embassy to find your son."

A tear streamed down Rahid's cheek. He struggled to respond. "But ... but, they will kill Keon." He looked up at me and just fell apart. "God help my son," he whispered up to the heavens, weeping.

I stood there, watching this big, strong man cry like a baby for his only son, and it moved me. I dropped the vest on the floor and reached around to the back of his head, pulling him down onto my chest. He sobbed right there in my arms for what seemed like an eternity. No one could deny he loved Keon with all his heart. For Rahid, the thought of losing his son was too much to bear. I rubbed his neck and back and pulled him close to me.

"Forgive me," he murmured, "I-"

"Shhh!" I lifted his head and wiped his tears with both hands. "Don't do that," I whispered.

"But, what-"

I pressed my lips against his and his eyes got big. I kissed him repeatedly, and finally, he kissed me back. I sucked on his bottom lip and then licked it. He closed his eyes and pulled me completely into him, offering his tongue to me. I hungrily accepted his invitation, opening my mouth wide to receive him. He flicked his tongue around in my mouth, and it was big and long just like his cock, which by then was poking against my tummy. I rubbed the front of his pants and tongue kissed him passionately. It sounds crazy, but I think I could feel his pain; his fear of losing his son was as close to me as his body. Right there in the dark, I felt his soul and mine become one. Without skipping a beat, I gave myself completely to him.

I lifted up his shirt and pulled it over his head. His body was ripped and muscular like that of a 20-year-old. His shoulders were broad and thick. I traced the lines of his chest with my fingertips all the way down to his navel. I kissed his chest while he fondled my breasts, one-by-one, and then both at the same time. I pulled off my jacket and dropped it on the floor. Then, I unbuckled his belt and pulled his pants and shorts down. The sight of his long, slender rod was overpowering. I cupped his balls in the palm of my hand and squeezed them gently. Then, I moved up to his cock, stroking it slow and easy. I made note of Rahid's body language, and I was most pleased. Before, he would argue just to be arguing with me, but with a gentle touch of my hand, he completely submitted to my will.

I cleverly switched hands on his cock as I pulled my arms out of my top, side-by-side. Then, with one hand, I unhooked my bra in the front and my breasts popped out like they'd been held captive for a decade, waiting for the touch of a mature man who'd appreciate them. When he saw my perfectly round tits, he got excited. He reached down and picked me up. His thighs, chest, and arms flexed as he lifted me over to a desk to the right of the door. He hobbled over, stepping out of his pants and leaving them on the floor. Then, he gently set me down on top of the desk. I used my hands to lift myself up as he pulled my pants off over my heels. He carefully laid my pants down, making sure my gun, badge, and other heavy items on my belt didn't make any noise on the hardwood floor. Then, he grabbed my head and pulled me in for a deep, breathtaking kiss as if we were long-lost lovers.

As he pushed his tongue further and further into my mouth, I stroked his big, black cock. I could barely breathe. I was asphyxiating on his desire for my body and it made me feel all woman—the way Bill used to make me feel.

I touched between my legs. I was so hot and wet. I rubbed my pussy through my panties, which were soaked through in the front. You could smell the intoxicating scent of hot passion between my thighs. We stopped kissing and he pulled back, staring me right in the eyes. He was breathing erratically and so was I. He reached under my knees and pulled me towards him until my booty was right at the edge of the desk. Then, he pulled my panties to the side and took hold of his long hard cock, which he carefully guided to the entrance of my pussy. I don't know what was wrong with me, but I was rubbing my clit really fast and I came before he put it in. That made my pussy even wetter. I had to bite my tongue to keep quiet as he slid his supersized love tool deep inside my pussy. He worked it in until it would go no further, and we both moaned in ecstasy.

I leaned back and pulled his head down to my breasts. Rahid licked and smacked on my nipples as he pumped me hard and slow. The lamp and several other items on the desk shook and fell over as he thrust his cock inside me over and over again.

I squeezed my breasts and moaned, "It feels so good."

Rahid looked up at me. I couldn't believe he was still crying.

"It's okay," I whispered. "It's okay baby."

I put my arms around his neck and my legs around his small waist, pulling him deep into my pussy. I nibbled on his ear as he swung his hips in a circular, upward-thrusting pattern. I was dripping all over the desk, and my ass began to slide around in my own love juices.

Out of the blue, Rahid started speaking Swahili. I didn't understand a word he was saying, but I didn't care. That man was giving me good loving, slow and passionately like a husband would his new bride. I came all over his pulsating cock, gripping my pussy lips around it and working my hips round and round to meet his.

"It's okay," I said again. "It's alright, sweetie."

Suddenly, Rahid shuttered a little. I can tell when a man is about to cum. He tried to pull out, but I fought him. My legs are strong, and I easily overpowered him, locking my ankles together and lifting myself up onto his cock as he tightened every muscle in his body and exploded inside me. It was so warm, sticky, and intense. Rahid pulled me up off the desk and took a few steps back, but I held on with all my might. He grabbed my ass with both hands, and I rode him with my legs latched around his waist until I was certain he'd injected every ounce of his hot cum into my throbbing, wet pussy.

He held me in the air for a moment. I wiped the sweat off his brow and the tears from his eyes. Then, I softly kissed his lips. I waited until his cock slipped out, and then slowly lowered my feet to the floor. He rubbed my chest and squeezed my breasts a few more times. Then, we just stared at each other for a moment, smiling.

"We should not have done this," whispered Rahid.

I moved into him, wrapping my arms around his waist and pressing my face against his sweaty chest. His sticky cock, completely covered in my love juice, felt so good pressed against my skin.

"This was a mistake, Alex."

"Why?" I asked softly.

He rubbed his fingers through my hair. "I do not love you."

I closed my eyes for a moment. "You love your son?"

"With all my heart."

I sighed. "Then, that's enough for me."

He pulled my head back and looked deep into my eyes. Then, he smiled and kissed me one last time.

"What was that for?" I asked.

"I have to go," he said. "I need to prepare for my son's funeral."

I shook my head. "No, you don't."

"I don't understand." Rahid looked confused.

"We're going to get your boy back," I said.

"How?" he asked.

"Put your clothes on, Rahid."

I walked back over to the desk and started getting dressed.

"There's nothing we can do," he said.

"I told you before, you have to trust me."

I zipped my pants and buckled my belt. Then, I pulled my top over my head and put my jacket back on. I checked the mirror on the wall to make sure everything was still in place. Aside from a little sweat, I was good to go. By the time I finished, Rahid was dressed too. I walked back over to the door and picked up the vest I'd brought up.

"Here put this on."

Rahid bent over and I guided the TAC-3 vest over his head. I helped him secure it in place, and then I gave it a few tugs to make sure he was good.

"I need you to stay close to me," I whispered. "I don't know how this is gonna play out, but I promise, we'll get Keon back. I give you my word, Rahid."

He nodded.

"Come on, let's go back downstairs. Be ready to move when I give you the signal."

"But what is the signal?" he asked.

I smiled. "I don't know yet, but you'll know it when you see it."

We walked out of the bedroom and back down the stairs. Gamba was standing at the bottom of the stairs waiting for us with his arms crossed. His face was all frowned up.

"Brother, what are you doing?" he asked abruptly.

"Nothing," said Rahid, "leave me alone."

Gamba grabbed him by the collar. I just watched as he went into his tirade.

"Bullshit! She is going to get Keon killed and you know it.'

"I told you before-"

"How can you let this half-breed whore destroy our family?" asked Gamba. "How can you let her come between us, brother?"

I didn't say a word.

"I SMELL HER STINK ALL OVER YOU! YOU HAVE BETRAYED US ALL."

Rahid grew angry. He pushed Gamba back. "WHAT HAVE YOU DONE FOR THIS FAMILY GAMBA? You have profited off the death of our father, but you have done nothing to help secure the future of our family—of our bloodline." Rahid pointed his finger in Gamba's face. "You are my head of security, but you have failed me. YOU ARE TO BLAME FOR ALL THIS, NOT THE FBI."

"YOU SAY YOU ARE A MAN," Gamba yelled, "BUT YOU ARE NOTHING! MANY WILL DANCE AROUND YOUR GRAVE, BUT I WILL SPIT ON IT!"

Their argument drew a crowd. Suddenly, Dom and a mob of agents converged on us—everyone including ASAC Anderson.

"The hell is going on in here?" asked Anderson.

We all looked over at him, all except Gamba, who I noticed from the corner of my eye was backing up towards the door.

"Sir, I am having a conversation with my brother, and if you-"

Suddenly the phone rang. I knew it had to be Ivan, but we were standing in a stale mate out in the hall. Suddenly, the lights went dark, and something or someone fell to the ground. Then, all I could hear was a bunch of clicks as the agents around us disengaged the safeties on their firearms. I instinctively squatted to get out of the line of potential crossfire.

"HOLD YOUR FIRE," yelled Anderson, "NOBODY SHOOT GODDAMMIT!"

Rahid scrambled around in the dark and finally found the light switch. When he turned the lights back on, there was an agent down on the floor, unconscious, and his gun was missing.

"Attention all units," Anderson radioed. "Brother's on the run, I repeat we've got the brother on the run. He's armed and dangerous. Lock this place down and bring him back to me."

Everyone scrambled except me, Rahid, Anderson and Dom.

"PHONE!" I yelled. "Goddammit, we missed it, it's gotta be Ivan."

Anderson looked at me and asked, "Will he call back?"

"Maybe."

"WELL, GET IN THERE!" commanded Anderson.

The four of us ran into Rahid's office, hoping Ivan would call back. If he didn't, then we were all fucked. The other agents hustled outside to find Gamba. Thankfully, the phone rang again, so I picked up.

"This is Southerland," I answered.

"You are lucky I like you, Alex," said Ivan.

"I'm sorry, I missed your call. I was otherwise engaged."

"Is everything alright in there," asked Ivan.

"Yes."

"Alex, you are lying to me."

"Yes."

Anderson wasn't monitoring the call, so he couldn't hear the other side of the conversation. He, Dominic, and Rahid were all just crowded around me.

"Then, the rumors are true. They will attack us?" Ivan asked.

"Yes."

"Can you complete the transaction, Agent Southerland?"

"Yes."

"You will be a marked woman." Ivan paused for a moment. "If you deliver the $30 million, then I will guarantee the boy's safety."

"How?" I asked, anxiously.

"He is not at the Embassy," said Ivan. "He is here with me at the Consulate, but you must act now."

"Give me instructions," I responded.

"No more instructions," he said. "Come to my office. Bring the money. My client will be here."

"Okay."

"That's not it, Alex. You must trade more than just the money. My clients require Mr. Amadi's life, and I require your services."

I stood there silent for a moment.

"The boy's life will be spared," Ivan promised, "but you must turn the father over to my client, and you must turn your life over to me. I will teach you how to shed your fears, and together, we will show the world what true power is."

I wasn't in a position to say much of anything with Anderson standing right in front of me, so I played it as smart as I could.

"If we agree, how can I be sure you will keep your end of the bargain?" I asked.

"You have my word, and you have two hours to deliver, or the boy dies. Good luck, Agent Southerland." Ivan hung up.

I put the phone down.

"Well, what's the situation?" asked Anderson.

I closed my eyes for a split second, and then drew down on him.

"WHAT THE FUCK ARE YOU DOING?" He reached for his gun, but Dominic drew his weapon, and Anderson finally got the message we weren't playing around.

I shook my head. "I'm sorry, Anderson."

"You're under orders from the President of the United States of America, Agent Southerland. It is your duty to-"

"SHUT THE FUCK UP!" I yelled. "Dom, get his gun."

Rahid just stood there in shock, but as usual Dom was a man of action. He grabbed Anderson's weapon and took his handcuffs too.

"YOU TWO ARE GOING DOWN FOR THIS!" exclaimed Anderson.

Dom cuffed his hands behind his back. "Like the lady said, shut the fuck up, old timer."

"DOM, CUT THE PHONE LINE AND GRAB A COUPLE OF MP5'S FROM OVER THERE!" I yelled.

He pushed Anderson down into a chair and walked over to the equipment lined up on the table. He pulled the power cords and cut all the data cables, stuffing a section of each one into his pocket. Then, he came back over with two MP5s and a bag of extra magazines.

"You know how to use one of these?" he asked Rahid, offering him Anderson's pistol.

"Yes," Rahid replied, stuffing the gun down in the back of his pants.

"Safety's off," said Dom. "Just point and shoot."

"I understand," said Rahid. "Agent Southerland...?"

"Yes?"

Rahid said, "I know what you are doing ... thank you."

I gave him a slight nod. "Come on guys ... Rahid, stick close to me. Dom get those cases down to the Crown Vic. Put 'em on the floorboard in the back behind the passenger seat. Rahid and I'll be right behind you."

"Copy that, Top." Dom tucked the two metal briefcases full of cash under his left arm, still gripping his gun in his right hand. He had the MP5s and the bag of magazines slung over his shoulder too. He was a bad boy.

"Move it Anderson!" I pushed him forward and we exited the house—right out the front door—and made our way down the driveway.

Before long, every FBI agent on the property had abandoned their search for Gamba and turned their attention, and their guns, to us. We were completely surrounded. There were too many agents to count. I pressed my gun hard against Anderson's neck and moved him along. Rahid was right behind me. Every time an agent got close, I dug my gun harder into Anderson's neck.

"DON'T SHOOT!" he yelled. "HOLD YOUR FIRE! I REPEAT, HOLD YOUR FIRE. SHE WON'T GET FAR!"

"Shut up, Anderson!" I ordered.

Dom put the cases in the car and backed up the driveway. He stopped right in front of us. I tapped on the trunk and he opened it up.

"Get in the passenger seat Rahid," I said.

He circled the car and hopped in. I pulled Anderson around to the driver side of the car and opened the back door. I got inside and pulled him halfway in, still holding my gun to the side of his neck.

"Tell them to put their radios and cell phones in the trunk."

I held his radio up to his lips. "All units place your cell phones and radios in the trunk," he said, "no questions, okay, no questions."

I watched out the rear window through the gap between the bottom of the trunk and the body of the car as each agent reluctantly complied with my request. The last agent closed the trunk. They each took a couple of steps back, their weapons still drawn, pointed directly at my head.

"Now, tell them to turn around and go back into the house. TELL 'EM!" I nudged him with the barrel of my gun again.

"OKAY, OKAY." He leaned in to the radio, but I didn't even press the button. "All units return to the house. I repeat, all units return to the command center immediately."

"THEY CAN'T HEAR YOU STUPID THE RADIOS ARE IN THE TRUNK!" I exclaimed.

Anderson stood up and stuck his head up out of the car. "GO BACK INTO THE HOUSE!" he yelled. "NOW, GODDAMMIT, GET BACK INTO THE HOUSE RIGHT NOW ... DO NOT FIRE, I REPEAT HOLSTER YOUR WEAPONS AND RETURN TO THE COMMAND CENTER!"

One-by-one, they started backing up. I pulled Anderson back down inside the car with me and reached over him to close the door.

"Anderson, I will shoot you. You know that, right?"

He gave me a cold stare. "It certainly seems that way Southerland."

I tapped on the back of Dom's seat. "Let's go, buddy."

Dom shifted into drive and floored it down the driveway, busting through the front gate and out onto the street.

"You're not gonna get away with this," Anderson warned. "What exactly do you think you're going to accomplish with a stunt like this?"

I replied, "President doesn't know dick about K&R, and you know it. By the time those pencil pushing jerk-offs get around to searching the Embassy, we'll find Keon's head in a park somewhere."

"That's not what this is about, Southerland!"

"Yeah, well what is it about, Anderson?"

"It's about doing your job. You have a job to do, and it's not too late. Turn this car around, and I'll pretend this never happened."

"You believe this guy, Dom?"

"Fuckin amazing, Top," Dominic replied, calmly.

Anderson said, "Agent Harris, I'm ordering you to turn this car around."

Rahid spun around and yelled, "THEY ARE GOING TO KILL MY SON. DON'T YOU CARE ABOUT THAT?"

"It's not my job to care. You'll be a fugitive too, tried and hanged for treason. Would your son want that? YOU'LL ALL BE DEAD! YOU HEAR ME I SAID-"

I swung my gun hard enough to knock a baseball out of Yankee Stadium. I slammed the side of it into Anderson's head. I knocked him up against the window and his head kind of rebounded back until he was slumped over. He was out cold.

"THANK YOU!" exclaimed Dom. "Fucker was gettin' on my last nerve."

We heard the call come over the radio. One of Anderson's crafty little agents either kept their phone or was able to rig up the phones in the house. The dispatcher said we'd kidnapped Agent Anderson and she gave a description of the vehicle. By then we were several blocks away from the house. Dom pulled over into a lot and parked next to a Chevrolet Tahoe.

"What the hell are you doing, Dom?" I asked.

He rolled down both driver side windows and hopped out. Then, he opened Anderson's door and removed his handcuffs.

"Dom?"

"TRUCK'S OPEN!" he yelled, tossing the keys to me. "Get in, you drive."

Rahid and I jumped out and got into the SUV. Meanwhile, Dom cuffed Anderson's hands through the windows and around the pillar of the car between the front and rear doors. Like I said, Dom was a bad boy. Who would've thunk it? He had a damn government issued getaway car parked close by just in case I suppose. Whatever the explanation, that white boy never ceased to impress me. The cops had a description of the Crown Vic, but at that point it was useless. Dom drug the cash over and threw it in the back of the Tahoe. Soon as he hopped in, I slammed on the gas and wheeled out of that parking lot.

I hurried up and got us the hell out of Nassau County. That place was crawling with cops. I jumped onto I-495 West, headed towards East 38th street. I tried to punch the accelerator through the floorboard. Even though it was the middle of the night, there was still traffic, so I switched the blue lights on and kept the pedal to the metal. I was exhausted from the night before, but I kept driving. I didn't have any choice. I had to keep going. Dom offered to take over, but I didn't let him. I needed to make sure we got there in time, and I just didn't trust anybody else to do it— not even Dom.

We continued to hear a lot of radio chatter. NYPD was dispatching all available units to the Nigerian Embassy. They didn't know it, but we weren't going anywhere near that place. I was smart enough not to say anything while we were in the car with ASAC Anderson. Sure, we thought he was unconscious, and maybe he was, but he could've been faking it just to pick up some intel. Waiting until he was out of the picture meant no one outside of Rahid, Dom, and I knew where Keon was. I hoped it would buy me enough time to figure out what to do next. The only thing we had to worry about was entering the Consulate and getting Rahid and his boy back out alive. I didn't give a shit what Ivan had to offer, I gave my word. Even if I didn't make it out, I'd make sure they did.

As I drove through the damp streets of New York City, I started thinking about my family. I wondered if I'd ever see them again—Bill, Theresa and Christopher—I wondered if they knew how much I love them. I always thought nothing, and no one, could come between me and my sister, Theresa, but someone did, and that someone was Bill. No matter what revelations develop, I don't think we'll ever be the same again, but I still love my sister. I'd give anything just for one more minute with her. I would hold her and kiss her forehead and tell her how much I love her. Then, afterwards, knowing us, we'd probably try to kill each other.

I kept looking at my watch. We had about an hour and 45 minutes left. I paid the toll and pulled over onto the shoulder of the road right before the East River. I parked the truck and shut off the lights. Yeah, it was a stupid thing to do because if anyone was looking for us—and everyone was—we were sitting ducks out there. Still, I couldn't go any further without breathing in some fresh smog, which was the closest thing I had to a blunt. I turned the motor off and got out. Dom hopped out too and followed me around to the back of the vehicle.

"Top, you alright?" he asked.

I put my hands over my face and took a deep breath. The night air was cool, and the breeze was strong. I felt a chill in my bones, so I paced around for a few seconds rubbing my hands together.

"Top...?"

I put my hands on my hips and gave Dom a blank stare. "I don't feel good about this man," I said, shaking my head, "something's not right."

"You having second thoughts?" he asked.

"No, I just ... I don't know."

Dom sighed. "Look, it's over for us, you know that, right?" he said softly.

"What are you talking about, Dom?"

"Alex, even if we get the boy back and nobody gets killed, they're going to lock us up and throw away the fucking key, and there's nothing anybody can do about it, not even your precious Anthony Crane ... he's gonna wash his fucking hands of the whole situation, and you know it!"

Dom really seemed to be shook up. It wasn't like him.

"So, what are you saying, Dominic?"

"I'm saying this Ivan guy is throwing us a life-line, and I think we should take it."

"No, we can't do that." I shook my head.

"Alex, think about it," Dom reasoned, "he's got a helluva lot more pull than anybody on our side. He's deeper in the department than you can ever imagine. This guy's a monster, and-"

"DOM, I SAID NO! WE BOTH KNEW WHAT WE SIGNED UP FOR. WE DO THE CRIME, WE FACE THE TIME! Yeah, shit man, it sucks, but that's how it is. I'll do whatever I can to keep you out of this."

I sighed deeply, shaking my head. The thing is, deep down, I knew Dom was right. They were gonna crucify us, and Tony already told me where he stood. No matter which way you looked at it, or how we turned, we were proper-fucked to say the least.

"Top, all I'm saying is-"

"That's enough, Dom...." I touched his shoulder. "Come on, let's get ready to roll. Can you take us in?"

"Yeah, I got it." He turned to walk away.

"Dom."

He stopped in his tracks but didn't turn to face me.

"Don't worry. We're gonna make it," I assured him.

He nodded his head, and then continued on around to the driver seat.

I stood behind the truck for a few more minutes. I was in a bit of a daze. The whole situation didn't feel right. It's like going to eat at one of those buffet places with a bunch of snot-nosed kids running around, sneezing and coughing all over the bar. You walk into those joints and pay like $10 or $15 dollars to get all you can eat, but it never works out that way. Either the food is cold, or they don't have a good selection out, and you end up sitting at the table with some fat mothafucka leaning the back of his chair against yours as you stare at your plate, pretending you made a good decision. That pretty much summarizes how I felt about our options. It was all my fault too. Once again, in a blink of an eye, I decided to defy the man in charge, only this time, it was the President of the United States, Mr. Commander in Chief himself. Hell, it seemed like a good idea at the time, but I was having second thoughts for sure.

Standing there looking out at the East River, I was faced with yet another decision. It was kinda like at the buffet table. You can either pack it up and go running back with your tail between your legs or look down at your plate and pretend you made a good decision. I think I would've seen the answer more clearly had I had a cigarette. I needed a fix bad, but no such luck. I was on my own that time, and you know what happens when it's like that? Nothing good most times.

Dom started the truck back up. The rumble from the exhaust snapped me out of my trance. I shook myself back to reality, circled around to the passenger side of the vehicle, and climbed into the back.

"You good?" I asked Rahid, squeezing his shoulder.

"Yes," he replied. "Is this real?"

"As real as it gets, my friend," I said. "We're gonna go get your boy back now."

He closed his eyes for a brief moment and took a deep breath. "And what will happen to you, Alex?"

"Don't worry, Rahid, we're big kids, right Dom?"

Dom turned and smiled. "Yes ma'am, we are. Ready to roll?"

"Let's do it," I responded.

Dominic shifted into drive and pulled back out onto the street. We crossed the East River and took Tunnel Exit Street to 39th. The closer we got to East 38th, the quieter it was inside the truck. I don't know if there's a way to get more silent than dead silent, but we were so quiet you could hear a rat pee on cotton in there. Despite our earlier optimisms, we knew the worst was inevitable.

The further we traveled, the more it seemed like we were frozen in time, waiting for a comet to crash into the earth's crust, splash sea water up our asses, and kill us with a deadly nuclear winter all in a span of about two minutes. I know that sounds extreme, but there's no doubt about it, we were rolling full speed ahead into certain death. There was no way I'd let them take Rahid, and there was no way I was gonna ride off into the sunset with Ivan the Terrible, so one way or another, it would end badly.

We never said another word to each other, but I could feel the worst was near, and I suspected Dom and Rahid felt the same. Even if we did the impossible and made it out of there with Keon alive, our lives would never be the same. We were traitors—fugitives, running from the law, and like Dom said, no one's coming to the rescue this time—not even Tony.

Chapter 17

We finally made our way over to our destination—East 38th Street. The Consulate was a few blocks up on the left. Dom pulled right up to the front door. I'm not sure what I was expecting. I guess I was expecting for somebody to be smart enough to figure out where the hell we were going. At first, I thought we might have to blast our way in, but we didn't; the place was like a ghost town. Funny thing is the door was standing wide open in the middle of the night—in New York of all places. Did Ivan really have it like that? Maybe Dom was right. Maybe we should've taken a job from that joker. *Uh, yeah, that thought lasted all but two seconds.* It's possible, Ivan was a master of the universe, but a more likely explanation was it was just the boys in blue. Anytime something appears too good to be true, it is. The place wasn't deserted at all. It was under surveillance. Somebody had eyes up on it, which meant our window of opportunity was limited. One step inside and they'd come running.

We took one last desperate look at each other and then hopped out the vehicle all at once. Dom grabbed the briefcases of money out of the back of the truck and we moved in. Slowly, we crept up to the door with our guns drawn. We were prepared for the worst. I'd holstered my Glock and was carrying my MP5, which I pointed straight ahead as we moved inside the building. Ivan's office was on the ninth floor, so we snuck across the lobby towards the elevators, being careful to avoid the guards.

Dom hit the up button and we crouched against the wall to wait for an elevator, using the trashcans as cover and trying our best to stay off camera. I could tell Rahid was beginning to lose it. His hands were shaking badly, and he was starting to sweat. For me, it was just like being back on deployment. I was feeling rather nostalgic actually, but Rahid on the other hand was doing a fair amount of second guessing.

"You okay?" I whispered.

He nodded, but then the bell for the elevator rang and he tumbled over backwards. I rushed to him and helped him to his feet. Dom held the doors open while Rahid and I got in. Then suddenly, things got complicated fast.

"Hold the elevator," said a guard, rushing down the hall to get to us.

Dom let the doors go, hoping they'd shut before the guard made it. We were sure those doors were going to close, but somehow, the guard managed to stick his hand out and stopped them just in the nick of time. He was in such a rush I don't think he even noticed who we were or what we were doing. If he'd been just a second slower, he would've missed it, but no, he had to make like O.J. Simpson, running down the hall doing hurdles over garbage cans to get in that elevator with us.

The guard looked over and pressed the button for the fourth floor. Then, he turned around and glanced back at us. Oh, what a sight we were, standing against the back wall with automatic rifles. He instantly got nervous and turned to face the elevator doors. He was whispering something to himself, but I couldn't make it out. Maybe he was praying for his life. He didn't know it, but we weren't there to hurt him. At the same time, we couldn't afford for him to alert the rest of the guards. I thought about just knocking him out from behind, but he wasn't making a move, so I figured we'd take our chances. Hell, the entire world was on its way anyway, so what difference did a few more guards make.

Out the corner of my eye, I saw Dom inching up, getting ready to take the guard down, but I shook my head and raised my fist. Dom backed off. When the elevator came to rest at the fourth floor, the guard squeezed through the doors before they could open all the way. We watched as he hustled down the hall, looking back over his shoulder and desperately radioing his supervisor. The three of us burst into laughter. I laughed so hard, my sides were hurting. The doors closed and we continued to ascend, cracking up.

"Stay sharp," I said, still giggling as the elevator arrived at the ninth floor. The doors opened and I reminded, "Rahid, you stay close to me, got it?"

"Alright," he replied, nervously.

Dom and I checked the hallway before moving out. Then, I waved for Rahid to catch up. The entire floor was dark except for the office at the far end of the corridor. We started down the hallway, but I stopped abruptly, reaching out for both Dom and Rahid to hold their position because my hip was buzzing. I pulled out my cell and looked at the caller.

"I don't need this shit now," I whispered.

The guys looked at me like I was crazy for taking the call, but I had to because it'd probably be the last opportunity I had to speak with the caller. I could smell it in the air. Death was dangerously close.

"Tony, I'm right in the middle of something," I whispered, pressing my phone to my ear with my shoulder.

"Surveillance at the Consulate made the call," he said. "NYPD's on the way. Alex...?"

"Yeah?"

"So is Secret Service," he warned.

"Fuck me!" I snapped.

Tony cleared his throat. "They have orders to take you into custody. I'm sorry, Alex."

"What about my team?" I asked.

"You've got less than 20 minutes."

"Tony, what about my-"

"They were just following orders," he replied. "Alex, I'm-"

"Tony, I hope you understand why I'm doing this."

He was quiet for a second. "You ... you're doing what we all wish we had the courage to ... I really am sorry, Alex."

I shut my eyes for a moment. "When I see David, I'll tell him you said hey."

I heard Tony sniffle, but I didn't wait to hear him cry. I just hung up. I closed my phone and clipped it back on my belt.

"Who's David?" asked Dom.

"Old friend ... he's dead."

"SHIT, TOP!" he exclaimed.

I shook my head. "Come on, let's go. Dom, take point, Rahid, stay behind me."

We moved down the hall all the way up to the office at the end. Rahid and I got in position on the hinge side of the door, while Dom cracked it open. He peeked in, and then opened the door all the way. He stood up, pointing his gun inside the room, and then slowly entered. Rahid and I followed right behind him.

"There's no need for that Mr. Harris," said Ivan, holding up a glass and smiling. "We're all friends here." Ivan was wearing another all white getup, but this time, he had on a black shirt.

Even with all that was going on, I'd be less than Alex if I didn't notice Ivan was one sharp dude. I most certainly approved of his attire. He looked good.

"Please, come in, sit," he said.

We moved further into the room, still drawing down on the man.

"Always with the guns," Ivan said, chuckling. "Make yourselves comfortable. May I offer you a drink or some water?"

"No thanks," I replied. "Where are all your stormtroopers, Ivan?"

He looked at me and started laughing. "You're referring to my security staff?"

I scanned the entire room, looking for any sign of a trap. "Yeah, where are they?"

He took another sip of his drink. "My security detail will not be needed tonight, and I appreciate your promptness. You made it here before my clients. I couldn't have chosen a better apprentice."

"You assume too much, Ivan."

"And, you take things too seriously, Alex. Come now, play nice ... put the guns away."

I lowered my weapon, and after a few seconds, so did Dom, but Rahid was another story. He took two steps forward and pointed Agent Anderson's Glock 40 at Ivan's head.

"Where is my son?" asked Rahid, forcefully.

"My clients tell me you are a cowardly man, Mr. Amadi," said Ivan. "Are you willing to take my life the same as we took your wife's?"

Rahid gasped.

"Your wife was murdered because we could not find you," Ivan revealed. "She was unimportant, but her untimely expiration was useful. It drew you out into the open, right here in America where my power and reach is even greater thanks to such amazing laws and civil liberties. Knowing this, does it make you want to kill me?"

Rahid started to cry. "Yes."

"Put the gun down Rahid," I said softly. I started closing in on him. "He's just fucking with you, man."

"I take pride in my abilities," said Ivan. "I assure you Mr. Amadi, I took pride in personally dismembering the love of your life in hopes of this very moment, where you and I stand face-to-face. And, even now, knowing that I am the one who killed her, you are powerless to act. This is why my clients require your life. Your planned entrance into the political arena jeopardizes my clients' operations in your country and mine. People must be controlled. Your idealistic thoughts of democratic carryings-on sicken me. You are weak Mr. Amadi, weak at the very moments in your life where you must be strong, when others depend on you. You want something from me? Why should I even allow you to look upon Keon with your wretched, worthless eyes?"

Rahid sniffled and wiped his tears. "You are right Mr. Ashbie ... I am not a killer." He kneeled down and placed the gun on the floor. Then, he pointed at Dom. "In those cases that Agent Harris is holding, there is more than thirty million dollars. It is not a gift, it is a ransom. You have taken from me. I am here to take back what is mine, and to give to you what is yours."

I nodded at Dom. He walked over to the desk and put the cases on top. He opened both of them, so Ivan could see the cash inside. Ivan carefully inspected both cases, searching for some sort of booby-trap, but of course they were clean.

Rahid stood tall and stared Ivan directly in the eye. "I am prepared to do what is necessary for my son, but I assure you that neither you nor your clients have power over me and my family. Your reign will be but a speck of dust in time compared to your eternal damnation. You see Mr. Ashbie, you may take my life, but in the end, you will lose."

Ivan smirked. "I've heard enough of this spiritual babble. Agent Harris, there is a conference room, two doors down the hall. The boy is inside ... bring him to his father."

Dom turned around and walked out.

"Where are the clients?" I asked.

"They will be here soon, Alex. Are you ready to fulfill your destiny?"

"NYPD, FBI, and Secret Service are all gonna storm this place in less than 15 minutes. We can discuss it later, right now we need to complete this transaction."

"Always business first," he said, smiling, "I like that about you. I like that very much."

"Fuck you Ivan." I walked over to Rahid and grabbed his hands. I looked up into his big brown eyes and said, "I'm sorry. I just-"

He shook his head. "Alex, there is no other way."

"I love you," I whispered. "You and I we're more than just-"

"I love my wife, but she is gone, so I would've done anything to get my son back. If being with you gave me the opportunity to see his face again—even just for a moment—then it was the most beautiful wrong thing I've ever done in my life. I too am sorry."

I smiled and shook my head. "No, I don't want anything from you. You're a good man. I know it's hard to understand, but I do love you, and I am sorry for this."

"Do not feel sorry for me, Alex." He stood tall and even prouder than before. "Tonight, I will dine with the angels."

Ivan got a call on his cell.

"Hello," he answered. "Yes ... yes, that's excellent ... someone will meet you in the back hallway in five minutes." He hung up.

By then, Dom had returned with Keon. My heart nearly jumped out of my chest cavity. I was filled with joy, and so was Rahid. Keon was very sluggish, but it looked like he was alright. Rahid ran over and hugged and kissed his boy.

"MY SON!" exclaimed Rahid. It was clear he didn't ever want to let him go again.

Keon was in a daze, but I could tell he knew he was in the presence of his father. I walked over and stood by them.

"ALEX, THIS IS MY SON!" Rahid exclaimed.

"He's a handsome boy," I said smiling, "like his father." I touched Rahid's shoulder for a second while they embraced, but then I backed off to give them some room.

Dominic and I walked back over to Ivan, who was pouring himself another drink.

"Now's the time to decide, Alex," Ivan said. "My clients will be at this back door in less than a minute. Will you be the one to greet them as my new protégée?"

"And if I don't?" I asked.

"Then, one way or another, you will surely die," he responded.

I had to buy some time for a couple of reasons. First, I still had to figure out a way to get Rahid and his son out alive, and second, I noticed Ivan was pointing Agent Anderson's gun at my stomach. That sneaky bastard picked it up off the floor when we weren't looking.

"Do we have an agreement, Alex?" asked Ivan.

"Yeah," I mumbled, turning my head to the left.

"I'm sorry, I didn't hear you."

I turned back and stared him down. "I SAID YES!"

"Good then. Here...." Ivan handed me the gun, which I stuffed in the back of my pants. Then, Ivan leaned in and whispered, "There is a member of my client's entourage who must not leave this consulate."

"Who?" I asked.

"You will know him when you see him," Ivan replied. "I hear he's a bit unhappy with you right now. Our contract requires his termination. Kill him, deliver the money, and return here to finish the rest of the job, understood?"

"And, what if I clip the wrong guy?"

"Then they will kill you," Ivan replied, "and most likely Agent Harris too. Choose wisely for nothing is as it seems."

"Fuck you Ivan," I whispered. "Don't think for a second I don't hate your fucking guts." I shook my head, "I'm gonna fucking kill you."

"You are mine now," he reminded, "and before you kill me you will do as you're told. My threats are not idle, and they do not stop here in these walls. Your family is now my family. As long as you work for me, and you do as you are told, they will be taken care of beyond their wildest dreams. The day will come where the apprentice will kill the master. But, until that day, if you fail on your end of the bargain for any reason, then you will have sent them to their graves, understood?"

I rolled my eyes. Then, I placed my MP5 down on the desk, grabbed the cases and drug them towards the door in the back of the office. With all that money inside, those cases were heavy as hell. I don't know how Dom was lugging them around so easily with one arm. That little man was strong. I limped to the back of the room, struggling with the cases and cursing at myself. "What the fuck are you doing here stupid? Taking orders from a known terrorist, a killer, a goddamn psycho maniac? Fuck me ... FUCK ME ... FUCK ME!"

I opened the back door and pushed the cases out into the hall together under the first light. Then, I started pacing from side-to-side, back and forth and around the cases. After a few more circles, the door at the other end of the hallway opened up. There were five men approaching from the shadows. I positioned myself to the far right and drew my gun. I held it down and out of sight near the back of my thigh.

The man in the middle of the group was walking fast and pointing. He started shouting, but I couldn't make out what he was saying at first. His accent was thick, and his voice echoed down the hall. I put my finger on the trigger of my gun and tightened my grip, getting ready to fire.

"BITCH, YOU FUCK MY BROTHA! YOU THREATEN MY FAMILY! AND, NOW YOU WILL DIE!"

I squinted. "Gamba?"

Yes, it was him, and not only was he furious, he was armed with a twelve-gauge tactical shot gun. I didn't respond I just stood there watching as he approached, cursing and yelling at the top of his lungs. Gamba was so fixated in on me he didn't even notice his four cohorts had stopped walking. They pulled back and moved out of the line of fire—two on each side of the hall. At that point I had an epiphany. Ivan was talking about Gamba. Obviously Gamba betrayed Rahid, but the Rebels in turn betrayed Gamba, and now they wanted him dead too. Ivan told me to kill him, but I couldn't do it, I just couldn't. Nothing I'd done up to that point had turned out right. There was no way I could keep my promise to Rahid. It was my time—time for me to go.

Gamba was my angel of death, and I could smell my end coming near as he approached me in the hall. But somehow, before he could pump his shotgun slide, I'd already put two in his chest, and I didn't even realize what I'd done. Gamba had no clue he'd been shot until his body hit the floor.

To this day, I still don't know why I shot him like that. It was clear he meant to kill me, but I didn't necessarily mean to kill him. I don't know. I really only wanted to wound him, but I did what I did. Now, I have yet another mark on my soul—another deed carried out by request of the devil himself. I was already doing Ivan's dirty work. Surely, I was doomed. I should've just let Gamba take me out. It would've been a hell of a lot simpler, but Gamba was gone for good, and I was poised to complete a transaction that would further empower the scum of the earth.

The four remaining rebels cautiously approached. The men were carrying weapons, but didn't seem very hostile, and they certainly were not interested in me. They wanted the money. I didn't move an inch, but I continued pointing my gun down the hall in case they got any bright ideas.

The men stepped over Gamba's lifeless body and walked towards me. I took two steps backwards away from the money, keeping a sharp eye on their hands as they drew near. Once they were within a few feet of me, I was confident they meant me no harm, but then I heard a gunshot, and then another, and another. They all came from behind me, from inside Ivan's office. When I heard the first shot, I jumped back a little, and so did the men in front of me in the hallway, but none of us fired. I quickly turned back and opened the door. As soon as I did, the men in the hallway grabbed the cases and took off running.

I pointed my gun down the hallway after them, because there was no way in hell I was getting shot in the back. When I let go of the door, it closed again behind me. As I watched the rebels flee with the money, my heart rate increased tenfold, and all I could think about was who fired those shots. I started to panic and prepared for the worst. I knew Ivan was not to be trusted. I'd heard three shots. In my heart I feared Ivan had killed Rahid, Keon, and Dom.

I watched the men exit out the door they came in, and then I turned back towards Ivan's office. I took a few steps back away from the door. Then, after few deep breaths, I ran full speed ahead, leaning down low and smashing the door open with my shoulder. I rolled into the room like SWAT, came to my feet, and pointed my weapon at Ivan, but he wasn't moving. Dom looked over at me with this expression on his face I'd never seen before. It was disturbing, as if I'd just caught him red-handed and elbow deep in the cookie jar.

I slowly moved over to Ivan, who was sitting at his desk, with his brains all over the back of the chair and floor around him. He was dead, but I checked his pulse anyway just to be sure. I kept my gun on Dominic the entire time.

"I need to ask you something, Dominic...?"

"Yeah, Top?"

"How did Ivan know how much ransom money we had? There were only four people who knew that ... Rahid, me, Tony ... and you. When I spoke with Ivan, he already knew about the $30 million. How did Ivan know about the money?"

I circled behind Ivan, being careful not to slip up in the puddle of blood and brain fragments back there. I cornered the desk and looked on the floor. Rahid was bleeding all over the place, and Keon was unconscious down on the floor beside him. I didn't know what to do. All I knew was I had to keep Dom talking.

"I don't know, Alex, Tony, must've told him."

"Why'd you kill Ivan?" I asked.

"He tried to-"

"SAVE IT DOM, HE'S STILL HOLDING A FUCKIN' DRINK NOT A GUN!" I ran my fingers along the edge of the desk, moving towards my MP5. "What are we doing here, Dom?"

"You don't understand the half of it ... DON'T FUCKING DO IT TOP!" he yelled, advancing and aiming at me.

I put my hands up. "You don't wanna do this, man."

"YOU DON'T KNOW ANYTHING ABOUT ME! NOW, TOSS THE PISTOL AND THE RIFLE ONTO THE OTHER SIDE OF THE DESK, SLOWLY!" he commanded.

I put my gun down on the table and pushed it along with the MP5 across the desk right past Ivan's dead body. They made a thud on the floor as they hit the carpet.

"Alright Dom, you're holding all the cards now," I said, taking a few slow steps forward. "Come on man, lay 'em out for me."

"See, it's like this," said Dom, "I made a mistake long time ago, and I've been trying to set it right, but the more I try, the more screwed up everything gets. Top, I'm trying to set this right for both of us."

"The hell are you talking about?"

"Alex, I'm OPR," he confessed.

"WHAT?"

"Funny huh?" he said, grinning. "Yeah, I bet you didn't see that shit coming! I've been helping Dr. Stephens build a case against you and Crane. I've been OPR for months now. Those pictures of you with those men, I took 'em. I've been the one running surveillance on you."

"SON-OF-A-BITCH!" I exclaimed.

"Yeah, I know, right?" he said, chuckling. "Thing is though, Ivan came to me, just right after OPR did, and he made me an offer I couldn't refuse. He had my little girl. They killed her teacher ... the substitute teacher's one of

Ivan's men. That's just one way how he keeps an eye on your entire family. He makes you do what he wants, or he kills your family, but now, I've killed him, so it's over. I'm not a rat ... I couldn't stand giving him information, but you see I had to ... they were gonna kill my little baby girl. I put the entire team in jeopardy, but I just couldn't do it anymore. I've been planning this for weeks, right under you and Crane's noses. By now they have evidence of my involvement with Ivan, so there's no going back for me. Do you see, Alex? We have to go underground. There's no turning back for us now."

I raised an eyebrow. "Us?"

"HEY, DON'T DO THAT!" he screamed. "I can't go back now. Look..." He pointed his gun up towards the ceiling. "Video cameras," he said. "It's just a matter of time, and you're in this as much as I am. Shit, you're deeper in it than me. You just killed the brother, Gamba. I merely killed a terrorist."

"So, what are you saying, Dom?"

"I'm saying we fulfill the contract. We kill the boy. Rahid will bleed out. We make it all look like a family dispute. Clients are satisfied, they take over Rahid's petroleum company, and I take over Ivan's operation. Everybody wins."

"You?" I asked.

"No, we ... us, together, you know ... you and me, Top."

I heard sirens, and then I could see flashing blue lights reflecting against the windows.

"Top, we don't have a lot of time here," he said, laughing and still pointing his gun at my head, "I sort of need your decision now."

"This is crazy, Dominic," I said. "Come on man, we can talk about-"

"NO GODDAMMIT, YOU'RE EITHER FOR ME OR YOU'RE AGAINST ME!"

Out of nowhere, Rahid, reached up and grabbed Dom's pants leg.

"SHIT!" Dom jumped back, pointing his gun at Rahid's head and shifting his focus away long enough for me to pull Agent Anderson's pistol out of the back of my pants.

I aimed straight for Dominic's heart. I had the perfect shot, but I hesitated to take it.

"PUT THE GUN DOWN, DOM!"

He looked up at me, with a sheepish grin. "Where the fuck did that come from, Southerland?"

"Put it down, Dom ... I don't wanna shoot you, man!"

"UNGRATEFUL BITCH!" he exclaimed. "I did this for us!"

I shook my head. "NO, YOU DID IT FOR YOU DOM! OPR's got your head twisted, and you saw a way out with Ivan ... shit man, you took the easy way out."

He kept raising his gun, slowly but surely.

"DON'T DO IT, DOM! PLEASE, DON'T MAKE ME DO THIS!"

"I knew it," he said, "I knew the great Alex Southerland wouldn't go against the Bureau. Fucking amazing to me 'cause you been nothing but a sick, twisted whore the entire time I've known you ... now all of a sudden you're too good to be with me? I thought we were better than this."

"Dom, we have to-"

He laughed. "Right ... truth is Top, I'm tired." Suddenly, he had this really crazy look in his eyes.

"It's okay," I said, moving to my left. "It's okay. The call earlier, it was Tony ... he promised me you're in the clear ... everything's okay with you, they're after me, not you."

"It doesn't matter," said Dom. "I didn't turn my report over to Stephens. Even if I don't go down for this, OPR's gonna bring charges against me if I go back. I can't go to jail."

"Dom, you're no terrorist, and you're no traitor ... you're a good agent."

"I WAS A GOOD AGENT!" he exclaimed.

"Come on, dude, we did this together, we got the boy back! Let's go in together. You don't wanna live your life on the run, do you?"

"And who's going to take care of my family when I'm in jail, you...? Nah, Top ... nah, you're gonna have to let me get out of here. Look, I'll slip out the back. Tell Crane whatever you wanna tell him."

"I can't do that," I responded. "Wrong is wrong, Dom, NOW PUT THE GUN DOWN!"

"Then, you gotta take me out Top," he said, "For my kids ... you gotta do this for me."

"NO!"

He became extremely angry. "If you don't shoot me, Top, I'm gonna fucking murder you!"

"Dom, you're a good person. You won't shoot me, and I'm not gonna shoot you. Nobody else is gonna die today, alright?" I lowered my gun a little, hoping he'd give up, but I was wrong.

All of the muscles in his body flexed as he drew down hard on me. He got a shot off, but so did I. He missed me, but I never miss. I hit him directly in the abdomen. He clutched his stomach and fell to his knees. He sat there on all fours with blood spilling out of his gut and mouth. I ran over and grabbed him by the shoulders. I gently helped him lay on his back. I ripped off my jacket and balled it up, pressing it against his stomach to try and slow the bleeding, but I must've hit something major, because his mouth was full of blood. He was dying fast.

"Thank you," he murmured, blood gurgling in the back of his throat.

"Shhh." I started crying.

Dom smiled and closed his eyes. I knew he was almost gone. I could see his soul slipping away. His light was dimming, and there was nothing I could do to bring him back. I just sat there on the floor and pressed on his stomach until he stopped wiggling.

"FUCK!" I yelled, falling over onto his chest.

I cried for my friend Dominic briefly, but then I got right to business, cleaning up the crime scene. I wiped the blood off my hands and ran back over to Ivan. I moved the glass out of his hand, replacing it with Anderson's gun. Then, I moved around behind him and used his finger to fire a shot to make sure he had GSR on his hand. Finally, I went through Ivan's desk and Dom's pockets, checking for any incriminating evidence. I didn't find anything, so I ran back over to Dom, and started administering CPR for the audience I was about to have. Before long, they had arrived.

"SWAT!" yelled officers, busting through the doors with a force unknown to the average man. They used all the standard flash bangs, smoke bombs and every other breech method the law allowed. I was surprised they didn't throw in a little CS gas just for kicks and giggles. I closed my eyes and covered my head with my arms. As soon as the smoke dissipated, I got back to my CPR charade.

"POLICE, GET DOWN ON THE GROUND, AND PUT YOUR HANDS ABOVE YOUR HEAD!"

"FBI," I yelled, "I GOT AN AGENT DOWN."

"Get on the ground and put your hands on your head or we will fire!"

I immediately dropped to the floor, rolling over onto my stomach. I slowly raised my hands above my head, just like they told me to. An officer ran over and put his knee into the back of my neck while another zip-tied my hands behind me.

"I'M AGENT SOUTHERLAND, FBI," I yelled. "I'M F, B, I!"

It was hard to breath with two-hundred and 20 pounds of man pushing my face deep into the carpet. He called me every kind of cunt and trailer park bitch in the book. Then, he picked me up by the shoulders and slammed me face down on top of Ivan's desk.

"SHIT, IS THAT NECESSARY?" I asked, squirming.

"SHUT UP CUNT," he yelled, grabbing me all over.

All while he patted me down, I stared at Ivan's exploded head. It was horrible, the entire room smelled just like Karla Charles. It's funny, even when completely surrounded by death I still somehow manage to narrowly escape it—a gift and a curse all at the same time.

"WE GOT TWO CIVILIANS DOWN, OVER HERE!" yelled another officer. "One still breathing ... no wait, they're both breathing, but the adult male has multiple gunshot wounds. GET THE MEDICS UP HERE NOW! COME ON, MOVE!"

My cop spun me around, and then drug me across the room. "CLEAR!" he yelled, tossing me over onto the sofa in the corner.

I watched as NYPD SWAT ran all over the place, yelling, "CLEAR" over and over again. But the only thing that was clear was how messed up I was. Everybody was dead and hey, who in the world would believe a rogue FBI agent, turned fugitive, slash terrorist. Not to mention the goddamn security cameras. My little ruse may have fooled SWAT, but once they check the video footage, it's over. I'll be in pine-oil-heaven by the end of the week.

"Man, what I wouldn't give for a fuckin Quarter Pounder with cheese, some fries, a coke, and a pound of bud," I whispered.

"SHUT UP!" said the officer.

I didn't want to agitate him, so I just sat there thinking to myself what a mess everything was. Nothing had worked out the way I saw it unfolding in my mind earlier, especially not with Dom. He was my boy, the only one I thought I could trust, but he was a trickster in true form— an OPR snitch and a traitor to his country. I sat there on that couch watching the EMS crew hustle to save Rahid. I couldn't help but think about Dom. I chose him without looking back, so what did that make me?

After a few minutes, everyone spilled into Ivan's office-- more medics, CSI guys, and NYPD Detectives. I fell asleep waiting for the big kids to arrive and the real show to begin. When I woke up, I looked over and there was a man sitting to my right. I looked across the room at Dom's body, and Tony was standing there, hovering over him. I could tell what he was thinking. I'd gone too far, and an agent was dead. More than that, somebody was gonna have a field day with this one. The situation was beyond reparable.

"Agent Southerland," said the man to my right.

I turned and gave him a nod.

"You're finally awake," he said. "I'm Special Agent Stephen Billings, United States Secret Service. You and I are going to be spending a lot of time together."

Chapter 18

Agent Billings of the United States Secret Service and I sat on the sofa in Ivan's office for a while, watching as the paramedics worked on Rahid. They patched him up, and then put him on a gurney and administered oxygen. By then, Keon was fully alert. I guess whatever drugs they had him on had worn off. He stood by his father's side the entire time, not leaving him for a moment. As they lifted Rahid up and rolled him towards the door, Keon walked alongside him, squeezing his hand. When they got to the door, Rahid struggled and leaned forward a little. He looked at me and raised his fist as high as he could. I don't know how, but I'd done it—I kept my promise to him. He and his son made it out alive.

I was happy for them both, but their struggle was far from over. The transaction was not complete. Petroleum is big business, and Rahid's business was thriving. Plus, I remember what Ivan said about Rahid's political aspirations, a huge piece of the puzzle Rahid neglected to mention. My gut told me Ivan's clients would never back off no matter how much cash they took. Those two good men—father and son—would be fighting for their lives and the people they love for a long time. God be with them.

Rahid and Keon, with a whole lotta help from the man upstairs and a little bit of help from my dumbass, had escaped tragedy. Ivan and Dom weren't so lucky though. They went home in body bags. We watched the officers do their thing. They processed the crime scene right in front of me with Secret Service Agent Billings sitting by my side the entire time. After a while, I didn't want to delay it any longer I just wanted to get it all over with.

"Come on, help me up," I said.

He looked over at me. "Sure."

He stood up and helped me to my feet. Then he turned me around and cut my plastic restraints with his pocket knife. I was waiting for him to do his thing, but he just stood there looking at me.

"So where are you taking me?" I asked.

"Taking you, ma'am?" He seemed confused.

"You have orders to take me into custody, right? So, let's go and get this over with."

"I have no such orders ma'am," he replied.

"What...? Then, why are you here, Agent Billings?"

"I'm here on orders from the Vice President of the United States. I've been assigned to your detail."

"Detail...?" I responded. "What are you talking about man?"

"I'll be with you twenty-four hours a day until further notice," he explained. "I'll need to be privy to your schedule, and my team will coordinate transport to the White House at the appropriate time."

I squinted and looked hard at him. "What?"

Billings nonchalantly replied, "The Vice President would like to have a word with you soon."

"So, you're telling me I'm not under arrest?"

"Um, no, yes ma'am." He shook his head, and seemed a bit confused by my question. "I'm not here to arrest you. I'm here for your protection."

I laughed out loud. "YOU GOTTA BE FUCKING KIDDING ME!"

"No ma'am, I am not," he replied. "Listen, sometimes this can be difficult, but I recommend you try to go about your day as you normally would. I will always be within five paces of you, and I'll clear any room before you enter."

"So, you're gonna stay in my apartment with me?" I asked.

"Everywhere you go, I go, until I'm reassigned," he explained.

I squinted at him. "Which would be when?"

"That's up to the Vice President."

"Shit man...." I kept giggling, which was probably inappropriate, crime scene and all, but shoot fuck it, I was a free woman.

"Is there something wrong ma'am?" he asked.

"No, but I guess we need to get to work." I looked around the room. "HEY!" I yelled. Everyone looked up. "WHO THE HELL HAS MY GUN AND CREDENTIALS?"

Tony looked surprised. "Over here," he said.

I walked up to him and Billings followed right on my ass. Tony looked at him for a moment.

I was grinning like an idiot. "He's my bodyguard," I said, looking back over my shoulder.

"Agent Billings, United States Secret Service, sir." He offered Tony a handshake.

"I know who you are," said Tony, refusing to shake his hand. "Are you taking my Agent into custody?"

"No, Sir," replied Billings.

"Don't mind him," I said.

"Well, can you give us a minute?" asked Tony.

Billings looked at Tony briefly. Then, he looked at me and said, "I'll be right over here, ma'am."

"THANKS!" I yelled as he walked away. I turned back to Tony, giddy as hell. I guess I was just happy I was still alive and not on my way to jail. "Boss, before you say anything, I just want to say that I did-"

"Agent Harris is dead," he interrupted, "what happened?"

"Ivan shot him."

"Really?" Tony asked, suspicious of my answer.

"Yeah see, I was at the back door delivering the money, when Rahid's brother Gamba drew down on me with a shot gun. I fired a couple of shots, but then I heard several shots back here in the room, so I ran back in. Ivan was in his chair, Dom shot him, but he got a few shots off ... he hit Dom in the stomach. When I came in the room, I helped Dominic down on his back and tried to apply pressure to the wound, but it was too late. Dom's a hero ... he saved our lives. Ivan shot Rahid too, but Rahid was wearing a vest, so he just took a few shots in the side. If Dom hadn't responded so quickly everyone would be dead."

Tony sighed. "So, Alex ... let me get this straight ... you're saying the bullets they're gonna remove from Rahid will match Ivan's gun."

"You mean Agent Anderson's gun," I corrected.

"How did he get Agent Anderson's gun?" he asked.

"He took it from me."

"Okay," Tony said, "you're telling me Ivan managed to take Agent Anderson's gun away from you?"

I nodded. "That's exactly what I'm saying, but the ballistics won't match."

"Jesus, Alex," Tony whispered.

I lowered my voice and moved in closer. Tony leaned in to me. "Dom's been working with Ivan," I explained, "and believe it or not he's OPR too ... he was the leak."

Tony pulled back and was about to blurt something out.

"Shhh! Come on Tony, he was a good agent," I whispered, "You know he was a good agent, and if we paint him out to be one of them, his family will get nothing."

"You shot him?" he asked, quietly.

I nodded.

"And the brother?"

I nodded again.

"And what about Ivan?"

I shook my head.

"Dom?" he asked.

I nodded.

From the look on Tony's face, you would've thought I was draining the life blood out of him.

"You wanna sit down, boss?" I tugged at his coat.

Tony looked down at me and sighed a few times. At first, he didn't want to move, but then finally gave in. He followed me over to the sofa and we sat down together. Agent Billings adjusted his position so he could keep an eye on us from across the room. He was something like a secret agent man, for sure.

"What the hell are we going to do?" asked Tony. "And, why the hell are you so goddamn happy?"

"I don't know." By then I was really cheesing, big time. "I'm alive. I'm not in handcuffs. That's a good thing, right?"

"OPR's been up my ass all day long," said Tony. "They want somebody's blood, and guess whose?"

"Hey, fuck 'em."

"I can't go down with you on this one, Alex."

"I trust you'll do what you can for me," I replied.

Tony just rolled his eyes.

"I know this is off the subject, Tony, but why do I have a Secret Service detail?"

He shook his head. "Fuck if I know. This is a goddamn mess. What the hell are we going to do about Harris?"

"Look, it's my word against Rahid's-"

"What about the money?" asked Tony.

"What money?" I asked.

"Alex, the $30 million?"

"Gone, shit man, the clients took it. They wanted the money, plus they wanted to kill Rahid and his son, and then take over the company. They got their money, but we managed to save the father and his boy, thank God."

Tony replied, "Jesus, man ... well that's gotta count for something, shit! I'm glad you told me that. Amadi looked bad when I got here, and I was so busy looking after Dominic I didn't notice them roll him out."

"Yeah, he was still alive," I told him. "He waved at me. They both made it."

Tony seemed extremely relieved all of a sudden. "You did good kid, I can work with that ... yeah, you did real good."

"I do what I can, when I can, sir."

"Alex, I thought I'd never see you again," Tony whispered.

I touched his hand. "Evidently, I'm not going anywhere yet."

He smiled a little. "You better not, or you'll have to answer to me ... listen, Alex, we're going to have to clean this up."

"Make sure everything goes to us," I whispered. "I'll work with Matt down in the lab to process the evidence, especially the goddamn tapes. You gotta get these tapes, man. Send out a memo that everything goes through me, and I can make the necessary adjustments. Oh, and Ivan had a man watching Dominic's daughter—it's her substitute teacher at school. That's what they were using as leverage against him to make him play ball. We need to get some agents in there and bring him in before he realizes Ivan's dead and kills the girl. Maybe we can put some pressure to him and make some arrests."

"Alright, I can do that," Tony said, "but do you think you can trust Perkins with all this?"

"He's about the only one. Besides, he's on his way out the door, transferring to San Diego. By the time he figures out I tampered with the evidence—if he ever even realizes—it'll be irrelevant. I'm just worried about OPR."

Tony said, "You did the right thing, but they're going to walk all over you, and I'm fresh out of favors, understand?"

"I gotcha. Hey, don't worry Tony, I'll be fine. By the way, why the hell does the Vice President want to see me?"

He raised an eyebrow. "The U.S. Vice President?"

"Yeah, that's why Billings over there is hanging around."

He shook his head. "I haven't heard anything, but I can make a few inquiries."

"Okay ... thanks, Tony... look I'm tired man, here, help me up." I raised my arm.

Tony sprung up and pulled me off the couch.

"You're gonna have to go see Harris's family," Tony ordered, "and I expect you to be at the funeral."

"What? Wait, no ... no, I don't ... I don't do funerals."

"You went to David's!" he snapped.

"That was different."

Tony asked, "How so?"

"David wasn't a fucking terrorist!" I exclaimed.

"Lower your voice," said Tony. "You asked me to cover for him, so now you're going to pay the price right along with me." Then, he yelled to a group of FBI agents, standing on the other side of the room. "Gentlemen!"

They turned and looked in our direction.

"This one's ours!" Tony announced. "EVERYTHING GOES THROUGH ASAC AGENT SOUTHERLAND FIRST, NO QUESTIONS! We lost a good agent, and I want to make damn sure we get this one right!"

They each raised their hand, acknowledging Tony's order, so he turned his attention back to me.

"I'll send out a memo as soon as I get back to the office," he said in a low tone. "Take the rest of the day, go home and get your mind right. Understand, OPR's on the rampage."

I straightened out his collar. "Thank you, Tony."

He smiled and walked away. I waved at Billings, who was, as promised, about five paces away. He walked over to me.

"You got a car?" I asked.

"Yes ma'am," he replied.

"Then, let's go."

We started walking towards the door.

"Where to?" he asked.

"Home."

He held up his hand and talked into his sleeve. "Flamingo's on the move, I repeat Flamingo's on the move."

I followed him downstairs and outside. We got into his black Chevy Tahoe and headed back to my apartment. I sat in the back and engaged in some useless small talk with him while he drove us towards the Financial District.

"What was your name again, Billings...? Your first name?"

"Stephen, ma'am."

"Oh, okay ... well, as you can see, I had a rough day today Stevie." I was already fucking up his name, but he didn't seem to care, so I just kept right on doing it. "I lost an Agent ... a good man."

"That can be tough, ma'am," he said.

"You said it, Stevo. You got family?"

"No ma'am," he replied.

"No brothers or sisters?" I asked.

Billings replied, "No ma'am. I'm an only child."

"So, when do I get to see the man?"

He looked up in his rearview. "You mean the Vice President?"

"Yup."

"He'll send word. Until then, we'll carry on, business as usual."

"I have a lot of personal issues Agent Billings ... you gonna be able to handle all that?"

"Ma'am, in this job, there's not much I haven't seen," he replied.

I liked Steve. He was like a grown ass imaginary friend. He was polite as hell, but he looked like he could put a foot in King Kong's hind parts without breaking a sweat.

We made it back to the apartment just before sunrise. Billings had a long list of questions about my cars, my schedule and daily habits; everything. We covered several of his questions down in the parking garage, but then he continued with a barrage of them the entire way up to my floor. I was really tripping because he had all his gear with him too—a duffle bag, a suit bag, notebooks, and all sorts of little gadgets. All while we were talking it was hard to keep from humming the *Mission Impossible* theme song in my mind.

Up in the apartment, I showed him around, and then went down the hall to take a shower. I took my time and washed the dirt, grime and all the other bad stuff from the day off me. I think that shower was far more emotional than it was physical. I got nice and clean, sprayed on some "smell good," powdered myself up and put my Falcon's jersey on. Then, I strolled back down the hall into the kitchen. Billings was sitting there writing up his situation report. He was stiff as a board, but at least he'd taken his jacket off. The apartment was kind of warm, so I adjusted the thermostat to make sure it was comfortable. It was the least I could do.

Billings spent a few more minutes explaining how he worked, but I didn't care, I just thought the whole thing was cool. I felt like Chelsea Clinton or a Kennedy. And, perhaps I was being a tad bit childish about it but give me a break. It'd been one helluva week so far—losing Dom and all. I needed something to feel good again even if just for a brief moment in time.

After Steve and I finished chatting, I got up from the table and headed towards the bedroom.

"I'm going to bed," I shouted back over my shoulder.

"I'm here if you need me," he said.

"There's some food in the fridge, Stevie ... make yourself at home."

"Thank you, ma'am," he responded.

"ALEX!"

"Thank you, Alex."

"Any time Steve ... night, night."

I walked into the bedroom and closed the door. I shut the blinds and took off my jersey, tossing it over the back of a chair. Then, I pulled back the covers and jumped into bed. "God this feels good," I said, closing my eyes.

That night, there was no sign whatsoever of my insomnia. Soon as I shut my eyes, I fell asleep. When I woke up, it was after five o'clock in the afternoon, and I was hungry as hell. I sat up in the bed and sniffed a couple of times.

"Damn, something smells good!"

I jumped out of bed and grabbed a short silk robe from the closet. I ran down the hall to brush my teeth at lightning speed. Then, I double backed down the hall in the other direction to the kitchen. When I walked in, I almost fell onto the floor laughing. Stevie was in there with one of my aprons on, cooking chicken of all things. I thought I was still asleep and dreaming, but no, my man was doing it Rachel Ray style. I walked around the corner and started being nosey, lifting up tops to see what was going on. He had grilled some chicken and made asparagus and potatoes. It was a trip to me because that shit looked good as hell.

I giggled. "I didn't know white men could cook like this."

He smiled. "It's ready. Please have a seat."

I walked over to the table and sat down.

"I don't do this often," Steve confessed. "Usually we order take out, but I saw you had quite a few things in your refrigerator, so I just pulled something together."

I replied, "Yeah, the maid brings all that stuff up and keeps the fridge stocked, but I usually don't cook much.

With a few flicks of his wrist, he plated up the food and brought it over to the table along with a couple of bottled waters. He took off the apron and hung it back up in the kitchen. Then, he came back over to the table and sat down.

"Alex, would you like to do the honors?" he asked.

"You're joking, right?"

"No ma'am, I never joke about that," he responded.

We bowed our heads and closed our eyes. It'd been so long since I prayed, I almost forgot where to start. Surely, I wasn't going to embarrass myself in front of company, so I mustered up something from deep down inside. I think it was the shortest prayer in the history of mankind.

"Dear heavenly Father, thank you for this food we're about to receive, in your name we pray, Jesus, amen."

I looked over at Billings for a moment to see if he approved. He smiled. I guess he figured my prayer was enough to cover a little piece of chicken, so he moved on. He picked up his fork and dug in.

I was eager to try this version of dinner in New York, courtesy of the Secret Service. I swear I can't make this stuff up. I cut a small piece of chicken, stabbed it with my fork, and then used my teeth to pull it off onto my tongue. I just let it sit there for a second to get a good feel for the taste. To my surprise, it was good, well-seasoned and everything.

"Wow, that's good, Steve."

"Glad you approve, ma'am," he replied.

"I do, thank you, and it's Alex, remember."

"You're welcome ... Alex." He was so polite.

We sat quietly together and ate. I finished my plate and then got up for a drink. I poured myself a scotch and offered Steve one, but he refused, saying he was on duty. I could tell he wanted it though. I thought I saw him smack his lips for a second there. No problem, that just meant more liquor for me. I hadn't had a good drink in days, and I needed to feed the demons, so I wasn't shy at all.

After dinner, Steve cleaned up the kitchen. I told him not to worry about it, but he insisted. Once he finished, he got right back on the clock, doing whatever it is a Secret Service agent does. As for me, I knew I'd be facing the axe the next day, so I didn't do much of anything at all. I watched a little TV, read a book, and then hit the sack around 10:00 that night.

Chapter 19

I didn't sleep at all. Now, sometimes people say that after having only a couple of hours of sleep, or being up half the night, but I didn't sleep one bit. My sleeplessness was back with a vengeance. The whole night, I just lay there in the bed, staring up at the ceiling. All I kept envisioning was Dominic walking around with a big hole through his stomach. He was dead, and I was his killer. To make things worse, we were covering it all up. Sure, it was for good reason, but it still felt downright rotten. I was at an all-time low. I sat up and put my feet on the floor. Then, I remembered I forgot to clean my gun. I had fired it back at the Consulate and needed to clean it before OPR got their grimy hands on it and started drawing all kinds of fucked up, yet accurate, conclusions. I jumped out of bed and grabbed my cleaning kit from the closet. Then, I spread a towel out on the corner of the bed.

As if I haven't already made a big enough fool of myself, I guess I'll keep it going and share my next sickness with you. I like to clean my gun in the nude. Yup, that's right. I get completely naked, spread everything out, take my gun apart and go to work. It's not a sexual thing, I can't exactly explain it, but there are benefits to doing it this way. First off, I like to wipe my hands on my clothes. Yes, I know it is a stupid, nasty habit, but a habit nevertheless. I think I probably got that from my mother. She'd eat a cookie or something, and then use her pants leg to kind of dust the crumbs off her fingertips. I still do it all the time, but when you have gun oil on your hands, you can imagine what that does to a nice pair of pants. The next one's kind of an excuse, but I prefer to clean my gun in the morning, and since I sleep naked, there's no point in going through the trouble of putting anything on just to take it off again to shower. Finally— and probably the most important of all— once I'm finished, I snap the slide back into place, hop off the bed and stand in the mirror with my gun pointed straight ahead, whispering, *FBI, Agent Southerland, bitch!* And, yes, I do that pretty much over and over again. It definitely helps keep me on my toes.

Just thinking about that sight usually makes me feel good, but it wasn't working that morning because I wasn't very happy with myself at the time.

Whenever I wake up on the wrong side of the bed, Blondie always manages to find a way out of her cage. As soon as that happens, it's all downhill from there. Next thing I know, I'm knee deep in trouble, drowning in alcohol, and letting some poor unfortunate soul stick his johnson in places that would give any self-respecting member of the female species a complex. It doesn't matter with her either she'll have me stuck up in a janitor's closet actin' a straight fool. She doesn't care she just wants what she wants—sex, drugs, alcohol, and random violence all the time. *I do need help.*

I fought the urges as best I could while I got my gun in tip top order. I just tried to put them completely out of my mind. I showered, did my hair, and got dressed. Then, I walked into the kitchen and threw my suit jacket over the back of a chair. Mr. Handyman of course was already up, shaved, starched down from head to toe, and having coffee. That man was unbelievably neat and clean. I couldn't even tell he'd been in the bathroom before me. Maybe he was in there at the same time and I didn't realize it. It's like the Amazing Stevie Copperfield just went invisible on me. I'm starting to wonder just what they teach those guys over at the Secret Service, and why the rest of the men on the planet aren't required to go through similar training.

"Good morning, Stevie," I greeted.

"Morning, ma'am."

"ALEX!" I exclaimed.

He smiled at me.

I was still amazed at how messing up his name didn't bother him at all. As for me, well that just made my day.

Perhaps he called himself getting back at me by continuing to call me ma'am though. *Sneaky bastard!* I grabbed a mug and poured myself a coffee. Then, I sat down with him at the table.

"Just give me a few seconds to get some coffee in me and we can go."

"Take your time, ma'am," he replied. "We run on your schedule."

I finished my coffee and we left for the office. I drove my DBS and Stevsy followed in his SUV. We made it in right before nine o'clock. After clearing security, we headed straight to my office. Now, I've been known to raise a few eyebrows around there, but with Stevo and his ear bud, hot on my trail, I was a goddamn spectacle. There's no telling what stories my peers were conjuring up, but I'm sure they probably involved me in the chain gang getting whipped. No one gave me any shit though. In fact, they were quite kind all things considered.

As I walked through the office, everyone gave their condolences for Dominic. They all adored him, and so did I. In my mind he was a good man, no matter what had transpired. I know he made a few bad decisions, and he turned out to be a traitor, but he did it for his family. Well, he agreed to be an OPR puppet in a hat to save his own little skinny ass, but Ivan was threatening his baby girl, and that's a totally different story. Any man that makes a sacrifice that big for his family is a good man in my eyes. In the end, I think Dominic just let all the money and power, or maybe even just the sexiness of Ivan's operation, go to his head, and it drove him overboard. Hell, I can't pass judgment. Who knows? I may have done the same if it were me. I sure as hell thought about it. I dare not condemn Dom. I just hope he's in a better place than this shithole of a planet we call home.

My team was out of holding and hovering around my office, so I took a detour over to Tony's. I didn't want to deal with them just yet. Tony wasn't in, so I waited for his assistant to get off the phone. As soon as she put the phone down, I stepped up to her desk.

"Hey Janet, is Tony here?"

"Good morning Agent Southerland," she greeted, "yes, but he's in a hearing. They're expecting you too."

"What?" I was shocked.

"Yes, Assistant Director Cross asked me to make sure you were in before nine o'clock. I called your cell, but it went straight to voicemail."

I touched my belt on both sides. "Shoot, I forgot my cell phone."

"You're late," she said, "you better get in there now."

"Thanks, Janet."

Agent Billings and I hustled down to the hearing. Every now and again, I'd look back over my shoulders to make sure he was still there with his little visitor's badge stuck to the left side of his chest. For some reason, he was just so cute to me. When I walked into the hearing, it was just like before, only this time, Tony was in the hot seat. Cross looked up at me and smirked.

"Good of you to join us, Agent Southerland," she snarled. "Take a seat we will be with you momentarily."

I sat down on a bench in the back, and Steve stood right beside me.

"Please answer the question, Agent Crane," Cross ordered.

Tony leaned forward to the microphone on the desk. "No, the operation was not sanctioned."

"So, Agent Southerland and Agent Harris acted alone and without your authorization," she asked.

"Yes," Tony replied.

Cross looked over the rim of her glasses. "SAC Crane, with all your years of service to this Bureau, I implore you to answer the next question honestly and in its entirety. A Presidential Order, prohibiting any action be taken against these terrorists, was violated by one of your Assistant Special Agents in Charge. As a result, one of our best agents was killed, a foreign citizen injured, and his brother killed. The man responsible for this—along with a string of other kidnappings—was killed as well, leaving no opportunity for questioning and further investigation. Did you give the order for ASAC Southerland to lead a deadly assault on a foreign consulate?"

"No," Tony answered. "On the day in question, I met with Agent Southerland at which time I ordered her to stand down. I placed the remainder of her team in custody until such time as the inspectors could complete the search of the Nigerian Embassy. I instructed Agent Southerland to return to the command center and continue negotiations in order to avoid raising suspicion."

"I have been with this agency for many years, SAC Crane," said Cross. "Like you and many others, I started as a Special Agent, in the field. I was taught quickly that there is a big difference between what I call a managerial request and a hardcore command. An agent may feel they have the latitude to deviate from the details of a request, and many times rightfully so, but a direct order in my eyes should be followed without question. SAC Crane, it is the belief of this review board that, on the day in question, you deliberately failed to establish this difference with ASAC Southerland, thus empowering her to violate a Presidential Order."

Tony said, "Assistant Director Cross, it's no secret, I did not agree with the President's call. However, I cascaded the order down as commanded, and I established mechanisms to prevent team members from violating that command."

"But, SAC Crane, these mechanisms you speak of did not suffice," said Cross. "You had no measures in place to deal with the most problematic member of your team."

I was looking at the back of Tony's head, but I could only imagine the expression on his face.

"ASAC Southerland," he cleared his throat, "in fact has been the most productive team leader and performed well as an ASAC. However, I deployed ASAC Anderson and his team to the command center as a precautionary measure that-"

"THAT DID NOT WORK!" exclaimed Cross. "SAC Crane, according to ASAC Anderson's testimony before this review board yesterday, ASAC Southerland kidnapped him, assaulted him, and restrained him inside an abandoned vehicle."

Tony cleared his throat. "I cannot condone these actions, but I believe it would be prudent to allow Agent Southerland the opportunity to give her side of the story."

"You're not exactly helping here Tony," I mumbled under my breath.

"She will have such an opportunity," said Cross. "SAC Crane, this board again notes your years of service to the Bureau, and we appreciate your cooperation regarding this inquiry. We feel your actions, as always, were consistent with proper behavior as a member of the leadership team. We thank you for your appearance today. This review board just has one more question ... on the night in question, records indicate a call from your office to Agent Southerland's mobile phone. I'd like to know what transpired during this call."

Tony replied, "I contacted ASAC Southerland to warn her that additional units were being dispatched to her location."

"And, did you again command her to stand down?" Cross asked.

"No," he answered.

"What did you say to her during this call?" asked Cross.

That's it! It's all over. Tony was about to give up the goods. He was about to cover his ass and let the steamroller have its way with me. I was dead meat.

"I told her that she was doing what we all wished we had the courage to do," said Tony, reluctantly.

Everyone in the hearing got quiet, and I nearly sprung up out of my seat. I couldn't believe he told the truth. He really was the poster boy for the FBI, a genuine Boy Scout, and my only friend in the world. Cross looked like she wanted to say something smart, but she didn't.

"Thank you, SAC Crane," she said. "Is there anything else you would like to add?"

"Yes, Assistant Director. This was not our brightest day. I'm solely accountable for Kidnapping and Recovery, and I take full responsibility for the outcome of this situation and the loss of a good agent. Although I disagree with her methods, I believe ASAC Southerland acted in the best interest of the victim, this agency, and our country. Yes, our team experienced a great loss, but the victim was recovered unharmed and we were able to avoid what could have resulted in an international incident. All of this is a direct result of ASAC Southerland's actions."

"Duly noted," she said. Then she started talking really fast. "Thank you again for your cooperation, SAC Crane. Agent Southerland...." She looked across the room and stared at me once again with her cold, judgmental eyes.

I stood up and so did Tony. We crossed paths as I walked towards the table and he headed for the exit. We made eye contact, and he gave me a look that spoke volumes. I knew exactly what he was thinking. The whole situation was hanging on by a thread and a prayer, so I just needed to keep my fucking mouth shut. If he could've told me that, he probably would've. I'm certain I read him right. In fact, I think he would've spin kicked me if he could've snuck one in without the review board seeing.

Any other time, I'd be a hard headed, irritating asshole, but with all the events leading up to that hearing, I would've been pushing my luck big time. I didn't give Cross a bad look or anything. I just sat my butt down, pulled the microphone forward, and kept my big mouth shut.

"So, here we are again, Agent Southerland, only this time, you've been promoted, which evidently enabled you to cause even more mayhem than previously. Since you last appeared before this review board, you've managed to shoot a man—in the back—in public. As if that were not cause enough for extreme disciplinary action, you now have violated a Presidential Order to stand down on this case. We are awaiting the preliminary report from crime scene processing, but based on your record, I'm willing to bet the circumstances surrounding Special Agent Harris's death are questionable to say the least. This review board has many questions for you today, but we will begin there. ASAC Southerland, did you know that Agent Harris was conducting an investigation on behalf of OPR?

"No," I replied.

"Were you aware that Special Agent Harris was in fact assigned to OPR?"

"No."

"Are you sure, ASAC Southerland?" Cross asked.

"Yes," I replied.

Cross reached to her left and another member of the board handed her a stack of papers. She flipped through them for a second and then held the papers up. "According to SAC Crane's testimony this morning, you told him at the crime scene that you were in fact aware that Special Agent Harris was OPR."

I couldn't believe my ears. I didn't know what to say.

"Southerland, it is your duty to respond truthfully before this review board," Cross reminded.

I spoke up but responded carefully. "Yes, as I stated, I was not aware that Special Agent Harris was assigned to OPR. However, before he died, he told me that OPR was building a case against me. He did not, in any way, tell me that he was the one building the case. But, him having knowledge of this, if indeed a case was being made, led me to speculate he might have been OPR. My speculation, combined with what Agent Harris told me after he'd been shot, was not grounds enough for me to definitively say before this review board that I knew he was, in fact, an OPR informant."

"ASAC Southerland," Cross replied, frowning, "your ability to skate around issues continues to amaze me. Allow me to be more specific ... our Agent was killed, before he could report his findings on you, and he was shot with an Agency issued weapon that, according to ASAC Anderson's testimony, was in your possession."

I replied, "Assistant Director Cross, the weapon in question was not in my possession at the time of Agent Harris's unfortunate death. The terrorist, Ivan Ashbie, seized Agent Anderson's firearm, which he then used to shoot Special Agent Harris." Having said all that, it was pretty much over for me. It was official. I was going straight to hell.

"I see," said Cross.

Then, the strangest thing happened. All of a sudden, a bunch of men busted into the room. Cross looked completely disgusted, but she didn't say a word. One of the men walked right up to her. She leaned forward and covered her microphone so they could not be heard. He whispered something to her, and she immediately became angry, rolling her eyes and speaking harshly to the man. I couldn't hear what was said, but it didn't seem to matter to the guy. He said what he had to say, and then turned and walked out. The rest of his men followed. I didn't know who they were, but I knew someone who did. When they all barged in, I looked back and Agent Billings didn't move one inch. He had to know who they were, and I was betting they were Secret Service.

Cross sighed and rolled her eyes, collecting her thoughts and regaining her composure. Whatever she was about to say, it looked like it was rather painful—like it drained her to get it out.

"ASAC Southerland," she bellowed, "it is my belief that Agents like you are poisonous to this agency. No matter your successes, I personally feel you are a disgrace to your superiors and your peers. However, through some mechanism I am unaware existed and one that I do not understand, you will continue to be an FBI Agent for a very long time ... you are hereby ordered to report to the White House in Washington, D.C. after first meeting with your approved OPR therapist, Dr. Stephens. Your file, and all events surrounding your recent and future field operations, have been deemed classified and are no longer relevant for this inquiry." Cross took her glasses off and set them down on the desk. Then, she sat up straight in her chair and took a deep breath. "Make no mistake about it ASAC Southerland, if it were up to me, you would never wear that badge around your neck again."

It didn't take a rocket scientist to figure out what had happened. Somebody high up the food chain liked me all of a sudden, hence Stevo and the get out of jail free card. In light of all that, I responded to Cross in kind.

"Assistant Director Cross ... I sincerely thank God that it is not up to you."

Her jaw dropped, but I didn't hang around to see it hit the floor. I stood up, spun left, and drug Stevie out by his wrist.

Cross really fucked up telling me that shit man. In a split second, I went from timid little Alex to Blondie on a fucking rampage, stampeding directly to that trick, Dr. Stephens' office.

I busted through her door like a crazed maniac and zoomed in on her. Agent Billings was trying to come in behind me, but I turned around and pushed him back.

"PATIENT-DOCTOR PRIVILEGE!" I exclaimed.

He paused for a second and looked around the room. "I'll wait outside," he said.

I slammed the door in his face and turned back to Stephens, who was standing right in front of me, nose-to-nose. I tried to move back enough to punch her lights out, but she grabbed my wrists. I tried to struggle free, but that white woman was stronger than she looked. She had a serious grip on me.

"I know why you're here," she said.

"Fuck are you psychic now too, let me go!" I exclaimed.

She said, "You think it's my fault Agent Harris is dead, and ... you're right."

I immediately stopped squirming and just listened to her.

"Way back, your boss, Tony Crane, did something to me, something I never forgave him for, and I grew dark. All I could see was getting back at him. That's in part why I joined OPR. It got so bad, I was willing to do anything to have my revenge. Six months ago, I recruited Dominic off of a simple administrative scenario. I should've dropped the charge, but he got me closer to Crane than ever before. When he refused to turn in his report, I stole it from his home. That's the file you saw the last time you were here in my office. Dominic was a good Agent. I took advantage of him, and now he's dead. I went too far."

I leaned to my left to look around her. There were moving boxes all over the place.

"So, do you still plan to hit me?" she asked.

I shook my head.

She smiled. "So, if I let you go, are we going to be okay?"

I nodded.

Stephens said, "I've made a lot of mistakes—more than you think. I can't stay here." She let go of my arms. "Officially, this is your 24-hour visit. At least, that's how I'll mark it down. We're supposed to meet for an hour, but I don't have a lot of time. Since this is an official session, and we have doctor patient privilege, I will share something with you. Years ago, when we first met, I was so jealous of you ... you were a free spirit. You still are. I don't think torture would make you stop doing what's right, even though sometimes you do it the wrong way. Do you understand what I'm trying to say?"

"I think so," I replied.

"I was just jealous, plain and simple," Stephens explained. "Anyway, I thought you should know today is my last day. My marriage is nearly ruined. I have to find a way to tell my husband I'm carrying Dominic's child."

I gasped.

She smiled. "Like I said, I've made a lot of mistakes. So where does this leave you and me Agent Southerland?"

"There is no you and me," I said, sighing. "Look, I'm sorry about Dominic. You're right, he was a good agent, but he's gone now. So, what about you and me...? We still have business. I tell you what, give me the file, and I'll give you my word I'll destroy the tape recording."

Out of nowhere, Stephens shoved me by the shoulders back up against the door and kissed me like no one has ever kissed me before. She caught me completely off guard. We locked lips for nearly half a minute. Then, she stepped back and wiped the lipstick off her mouth.

"Kiss on it, right?" she said, smiling.

I felt violated. I wanted to be pissed, but damn she was actually a good kisser! Blondie was jumping up and down, so I had to smack some sense into her. I cleared my throat, and mumbled, "Can I have my file please?"

She walked backwards slowly, her legs crisscrossing as she moved her feet one-by-one behind the other. She was swinging her arms back and forth like a school girl after her first kiss on the playground. I watched as she slid all the way across the floor and picked up a folder off the corner of her desk without even looking back.

She smiled. "You mean this file?" she said, holding it up.

I walked over and took the file. I opened it and started thumbing through it.

"It's all there," she said, holding up a compact and redoing her lipstick.

"So, I'm not gonna be on the news with my bare ass on full display?" I asked, very seriously.

"If so, it won't be because of me," she replied. "Those are the only copies, Alex."

I smiled a little. "I know I'm going to kick myself later for saying this, but I think I'm gonna miss you."

"Pleasure doing business with you." She stuck out her hand.

I reached for it and paused for a second. "Look Doc, you're a good kisser and all, but if you try to kiss me again, I'm gonna beat you."

She smiled.

"No, not like that, I mean really beat you."

She smirked, and I went ahead and shook her hand.

"I realize now I was wrong about you, Agent Southerland," she said, "but be careful ... not everyone who acts friendly to you is your friend. You remember that and stay safe."

I nodded and turned. I walked out of there without looking back. I stepped into the hall and pulled her door closed behind me. Then, I leaned back against it, closing my eyes tightly, and sighing heavily. After a few seconds, I opened my eyes again. Steve was right there looking at me as if he wanted to ask, *what the hell did you do?* Yeah, believe it or not, I did it again. I ran out of a closed door with two shades of lipstick smeared all over my face. I was a walking administrative nightmare.

"You okay ma'am?" he asked, sheepishly.

"Yes."

He handed me a hanky, which I used to wipe my mouth clean.

"It's not what you think, Stevie."

"Ma'am, we have to go," he said. "Chopper's standing by."

"What...?"

"The Vice President will see you now," he replied.

"But, I-"

"We don't want to keep him waiting," he warned.

"Shit, how do I look?" I started tugging at my clothes.

"Just fine," he replied. "Now, come on, we'll take my vehicle." He held up his right sleeve. "Flamingo's moving to the helipad, ETA approximately thirty minutes."

Agent Billings and I hustled out of the office and down to his truck. We climbed in and he started the motor. Then, he turned on the lights, and drove me directly towards the next chapter of my ridiculous life.

I'm not sure if I should've been worried, scared, or what. I just didn't know how to feel, but one thing's certain, everything around me was changing fast. I knew I wasn't ready for it, but at the same time, I was. It's hard to explain. The only thing I can say is life's a journey, and even though I was facing uncharted waters, I knew I was still on the right track. I feared the worst going into that hearing, but as it turns out my morning wasn't that bad after all. As we approached the helipad, I kinda felt like I'd won my life back from OPR. God really does look after babies and fools.

Chapter 20

Have you ever been to the White House? I haven't—not a single day in my life. I didn't get the chance to go on any of those little cool trips in school because my mother kept me out and made me study. I also never had a reason to go there as an adult until now. After all my years in the military and law enforcement, I never once stepped foot on the White House lawn, so I didn't know what to expect. I didn't actually get nervous until I could see the White House from a distance on approach in the helicopter. All the noise from the chopper wasn't helping either. With little or no warning, my stomach started doing flips and turns, and my spine felt like it was made of Jell-O. I'd been optimistic up to that point, but I started thinking whatever Vice President Keller wanted to talk to me about wasn't so good after all. Maybe that's how they treat all Federal agents who willfully commit acts of treason—kill you with kindness and then lock your ass away for 10 20-year consecutive sentences. That or they'll lead me down to the backyard and run me over with the Presidential Hummer while Keller yells, *just an accident people—nothing to see here!"*

I gazed at the amazing landscape as the pilot moved in closer and closer, turning the bird sideways to touch down. The scenery was unbelievable. You can see it in a book or on TV, but those images just don't do it justice. It was extraordinary. What a day. I was nervous at first, but once I saw that place up close with my own two eyes, I forgot all about it.

After a few more tilts and turns, we finally touched down on the lawn. Agent Billings and I hopped down out of the chopper and he led me in through the back of the building. We went through checkpoint after checkpoint. Then, Billings handed me off to Mike Fletchman, White House Chief of Staff. Fletchman was a very shrewd-looking politician, one you might notice slithering up over your shoulder when you least expect it, flicking his little forked tongue in your ear and whispering absolutely nothing at all.

"Special Agent Southerland. How are you?" he asked.

"Fine, thank you."

He smiled. "I trust the trip over was good."

"My first helicopter ride, Mike."

He looked at me for a moment, and I stared right back at him. Then, I smiled, and finally he seemed to get the punchline.

"Ah, good sense of humor," he replied, chuckling. "Vice President Keller will be pleased. This way Agent Southerland."

"So, what am I doing here?" I asked as we walked down the hallway.

"Not sure," Fletchman replied, "I just know it's important he speaks with you. Vice President Keller is ... have you ever met the Vice President?"

"No."

"He's an amazing man," Fletchman said.

"Well, that's what I hear."

"You'll meet in here." He pushed open a door and held it for me.

I walked in and was taken aback by the room—the walls, the ceiling, the furniture, the carpet, everything was beautiful and immaculate. Fletchman walked in behind me and shut the door.

"Vice President Keller is finishing up a meeting with the President and Secretary of Defense. He will be with you soon. Is there anything I can do for you while you wait?"

"No thanks ... I'm fine."

"Alright then. Please have a seat and make yourself comfortable. The Vice President is on schedule, so he should be here in less than 15 minutes. My office is right down the hall on the left. Please feel free to come get me or give me a call if you need me." He gave me a business card.

"You can use the phone over there between those chairs. Any questions?"

I shook my head. "No."

"Then, good luck to you Agent Southerland," he said.

"...Thank you," I replied.

After Fletchman left the room, I immediately got down to business, which meant I instantly started being nosey.

That room alone looked like a modern-day palace. I walked up and stood in front of the big mirror over the fireplace. I took a nice soft brown pencil out of my purse and outlined my mouth. Then, I used a lighter colored lipstick on my lips. I smacked my lips to make sure I was all good. I fluffed my hair out a bit, but then I looked down and realized I was standing on a seal. I cocked my head to the right a little to read the words around the edge of it. I wasn't standing in some random meeting room. I was in the office of the Vice President himself. All of a sudden curiosity got the better of me, and I started really nosing around, checking out every square inch of that place.

The coffee table first caught my eye. On top of it was a vase full of beautiful red roses. There was a ring of chairs surrounding it with a big blue sofa to complete the circle. I walked further into the room towards Keller's desk. The hutch on the right was filled with books, and I'm talking real works of art. He had a huge map hung on the wall and flags on both sides of his desk. The chandelier that hung down in the middle of the room from the high ceiling looked as if it belonged in a large dining hall. Oh, and don't get me started on his actual desk. It was solid, not like that bullshit we have over at the Bureau. No, this was the real deal. I pushed down on the desktop with both hands to prove my theory, and sure enough, it didn't budge one bit.

Keller's office was nice. Aside from the little dancing figurines back on the table, I was really digging the man's style. I guess I wasn't too surprised because whenever you see him on TV, he's always sharp as a tack and very smooth talking. Keller had the whole package, but it was more than just that—he had skills. He was a decorated war hero, had been a senator for years, and he chaired the Armed Services Committee. He was one hell of a VP. His only flaw in my mind was he was a Republican, but he didn't seem to let that get in his way of helping others. He was a good man.

I continued circling the room. There were several paintings on the wall, but I didn't pay much attention to the old geezers on display. The painting that caught my eye was all the way on the other side of the room. It had a thick gold frame, and though the painting itself was of a simple nature scene, it really did something for me. It was—how can I say this—it was tranquil, like it possessed the essence of peaceful bliss. Somehow, the artist managed to transfer pure serenity onto that canvass. The landscape was very detailed, and the colors were vibrant—green with red, and a lovely blue sky. I don't know much about art, but I certainly took a liking to that particular piece.

"That's my favorite one too," came a voice from behind.

I was a little startled. I was so into that painting, I didn't realize someone had snuck up on me. I turned around, and it was Keller himself. He was wearing a navy-blue suit and a silver tie, looking very presidential with his full head of gray hair neatly combed to the back. He was as clean shaven in person as he looked on television; only in person, he had this weird kindness thing going on all over his face. It wasn't an expression or anything like that. I don't know, maybe it was just he had an aura about him—something respectable—something that said, *Hey, you can trust me.*

"Um, I'm sorry, Sir, I didn't mean to-"

"It's alright, Agent Southerland. I'm glad you're looking around. Actually, I'm glad you're finally here." He had a file folder with him.

"Well, Sir, about that ... I'm actually wondering why I'm here."

"Please, call me Jack. Here, have a seat." He pointed to the blue sofa.

I walked over and sat down. He was such a gentleman. He waited 'til I was seated, and then he joined me. He took a seat on the right side of the sofa about a space over. Soon as he got comfortable, he put his file down between us.

"So, tell me about yourself Agent Southerland," he said, smiling and maintaining direct eye contact the entire time.

"Alex," I corrected.

"Oh, very good. Now, tell me about yourself, Alex."

"There's not much to tell." I felt stiff and rigid. I was sitting up straight and clinching my hands together. He made me so nervous.

"Alex, you wouldn't hold out on your Vice President, would you?"

I smiled.

"Just relax," he said, "nobody here but you and me. No need to be nervous, you're with a friend."

"I have to be honest, sir, I thought I might be in a bit of trouble."

"Absolutely not," he replied, "...does that make you feel a little better, Alex?"

I nodded. "A little."

"And, if that were actually true, would it make you feel even better?" he asked.

Right, then, I knew what was going on. It's called BOHICA—*Bend over here it comes again!* "Well, probably," I replied, frowning.

Keller paused. He was about to say something, but by the time he parted his lips, he seemed to have changed his mind. "Tell me about your family ... are you married?" he asked.

"No, I was engaged once—well kind of, but it didn't work out."

He genuinely seemed concerned, but I had to remember he was a politician.

"What about your parents?" he asked.

"Oh, they're both dead."

"I'm sorry to hear that," he said very sincerely.

"My father was killed in the line of duty, and my mother recently passed. She had cancer."

He nodded. "Were you close to them?"

"I was close to my father."

"And was he an FBI agent too?" he asked.

"No, sir-"

"Jack," he reminded.

"Sorry ... Jack, no he wasn't FBI. He was a police officer—a Sheriff down in Georgia."

He smiled. "Ah yes, you're from Georgia, right?"

"Yes, I am."

"Great state," said Keller, "you know, I had an opportunity to go down and help raise some money for Governor Russell last year."

"He won by a landslide," I reminded.

"He's a good man, Alex," said Keller, "a fine young man. So, do you have any brothers and sisters?"

"Yes, I have a younger sister and a baby brother, who's attending Princeton."

"Wow, a Princeton man!" he exclaimed. "You must be proud."

"I am ... we all are," I replied.

"So, you're very close to them?" he asked.

I shook my head. "Not exactly."

"I see. Tell me something, Alex ... have you ever met the President?"

"No, I haven't, but I know he's serious about kidnappings and homeland security."

"Yes, yes he is," replied Keller. "He and I spend a lot of time together. He's a good friend. You'll hear me say that a lot, not because he's our Commander-in-Chief, but because it's true. He really is a good friend. We've worked together for years. When he asked me to run with him, I told him I'd think about it, and I did ... about 30 seconds later I said *yes*," he told me, laughing loudly, "and we've been making progress ever since. So, you want to know why I've brought you here, and I think it's time I told you. There's something the President needs to know, but unfortunately, he can't ask you himself."

My eyes got big, and I put my hand over my chest. "He wants to know something about me?"

"Yes."

"Mr. Vice President, I'm just an FBI agent, I-"

"Jack," he reminded, smiling that chiseled smile of his.

"Jack, I just don't really have-"

"Alex," he interrupted, "your President has tasked me and me alone with asking you a very important question. But I must warn you in advance, I need you to give me an honest answer. No matter what, it won't impact what happens today. Can you do that? Can you give me your honest answer?"

I didn't know where all this was going, but I remember the last time I had to be perfectly honest with someone— my mother. She asked, "Alex, do you think you should be goofing off right now or doing your homework? Now, no matter what you say, I won't get mad." *Imagine that.* To an eighth grader, that's like a wet dream, and stupid me believed her. I dug my heels into the carpet in the living room, looked up at her and said, "I have some stuff I could be doing, but I'm sick and tired of studying all the time, so I'm going out to play." You can imagine this didn't work out too well. Five minutes later, I found myself choking down a knuckle sandwich with a supersized side of five-finger slaps. More than 20 years later, now I'm faced with the exact same dilemma, only it's the Vice President of the United States asking. Clearly, the stakes were much higher. We're not talking about homework here. This was obviously a matter of National Security. I hesitated for a while, but then I finally answered.

"Yes, I think I can give you an honest answer," I replied.

"Good. Alex, the President wants to know if you are prepared to do what you have to do to serve your country."

I just sat there and stared at him totally confused.

He gave me a solemn look and said, "I'd appreciate your honest answer now."

I didn't really mean to, but I started shaking my head slowly, stuttering saying, "I... I think, I... um, what I'm saying is that I think you picked the wrong person."

"Alex are you refusing your Commander-in-Chief?" he asked, slyly.

"No, I just-"

"Then, are you prepared to serve your country?" Keller asked.

You'd think I would've gotten the message back in grade school with my mother—just tell people what they wanna hear and keep moving. It would seem there are some things in life, I'll never learn. I love my country, and I'd do just about anything to keep it safe, but my little voice told me I was about to get fucked again, Keller style, and I was tired of getting fucked. So, I took a deep breath, looked him in the eye, and said, "No sir, absolutely not."

Keller wasn't the least bit concerned. He was the confident type. And, who the hell was I anyway, right? So naturally he stepped right up to the plate and swung hard.

"I spoke with Admiral Zimmel," said Keller. "He told me there was one man he trusted implicitly with his life, and that was no idle compliment. I talked to this man, Captain Riggs...."

Keller paused to get my reaction, which was impossible to conceal. I damn near came undone, sighing and all but crossing my arms and poking out my lip.

"You two have history, right?" he asked.

"Yes, we do," I responded, nervously.

He said, "I asked Captain Riggs to recommend a former Seal team member who was capable of enduring long-term, specialized deployments—someone, who may not have a shining record, but a man who could get a job done right the first time. I expected to receive a file of a young, brave sailor, but he sent me yours instead. He said he'd bet his life you were the ideal candidate for this special operation. Why do you think he did that?"

"With all due respect, sir, I believe there's been a mistake. Riggs would not recommend me, and besides, I wasn't a Navy Seal. I was just an intelligence officer—a dumb, lucky one at that."

Keller dug into his inner jacket pocket and pulled out a tri-folded piece of paper. He reached across the sofa and offered it to me. I unfolded the letter, and the contents shocked the hell out of me.

Riggs had written an official memorandum, detailing my training and field capabilities. He also indicated due to the sensitive nature of the operation, a woman would be best suited for it and could operate virtually free of suspicion. Basically, he'd given me a stellar endorsement, but I wasn't convinced it was authentic or out of the goodness of his heart. Deep down, my gut told me it was just more of the same. Riggs couldn't manage to get me killed all those years ago, so now he's back to finish the job. I put the letter down on the sofa.

"With all due respect, sir ... Jack ... this is bullshit."

"I have to admit, Alex, I was a little concerned myself. Riggs is a decorated officer, but perhaps he's getting old. Maybe he mixed up the names, it happens to the best of us. So, I sent for him. We could've just spoken over the phone, but I needed to see his face and look into his eyes. We sat down together, and I asked Riggs if he was certain. I told him we had no room for error, and you know what he told me?"

"I'm afraid to ask," I replied.

"He said, and I quote, 'even when every inch of her body tells her to stand down, she will never back down from a fight, she will never falter, and she will not fail the mission.'"

I chuckled a little. "You think I don't know what's happening here? I see what's going on. I was supposed to go under the guillotine with OPR today, but magically, majestically, all of that just—POOF—went away, and now I'm sitting here with you, the Vice President of the United States, in a private meeting after I violated a Presidential Order. It's obvious you want me to do something that won't be in my best interest, something that'll be done in secret, under the radar, and with great risk. You want me to put my life on the line or else. Otherwise, we'd be having this meeting in the dining hall."

"Riggs was right you are very perceptive," said Keller. "Alex, I was born in a little town called Lynchburg in Virginia."

"Lynchburg...?" I frowned.

"Yes, yes I know, but it was a long time ago." He grinned really big again. "I'd like to tell you a story about me growing up there if that's alright with you..."

"Doesn't seem I'll be going anywhere anytime soon, so-"

"Thank you." He smiled again. "It was 1949, four years after World War II. I remember I was ten years old. We lived on the lower end of College Street right across from Lynchburg College. Best thing about our street was this old deserted mansion at the corner of Westwood Avenue, I'd say about a block up the road from my house. Running along the back side of that mansion was a bamboo thicket, and it was really dense. I remember my grandfather used to sneak on to that property, go into that thick blanket of bamboo, and find the best pieces he could cut down. We'd use it to make fishing poles. See, we'd go fishing down on the college lake. Back then, I walked or rode my bike everywhere—to the store, school, it didn't matter—I just liked being out there, you know?"

I nodded.

Keller continued. "Problem was there was this little brick house right next to the old mansion. I never knew who lived there, but even today, I can remember that little house, it stuck in my mind. It was a small, one-story red brick house sitting up on a hill. It looked like a real nice home, but there was one problem—actually, two problems—a couple of big Great Danes, I mean big drooling angry monsters. Now, I was in the fourth grade, so they both outweighed me, and they howled like hungry bloodhounds. They were nowhere to be found around morning time, but in the evening, if I was out too late, they'd come running, searching for fresh meat. Now, if you can imagine what was going on in my young mind, I thought these two wild beasts had razor sharp teeth and jaws strong enough to tear through steel. I was terrified of them, so terrified, I'd take the long way around, through the woods, or down the next street over. Now I was never really a smart feller, but I had a good memory. What I remembered most about the yard those two big dogs were in was it lacked a very important safety feature—a sturdy fence. When the sun went down, those dogs ruled College Street, and everybody knew it. What do you think happened to me, Alex?"

"You got bit?" I speculated.

Keller chuckled. "I must've circled around the block at least a hundred times to avoid those big bastards. No matter what the situation was, I just couldn't bring myself to walk past that yard. I was afraid—afraid they'd see me and make a snack out of me. Sometimes, I'd just stand and watch 'em from a distance. They'd run around in the yard, fighting each other, generally being mean and nasty. Hell, I figured if they treated each other like that, I knew they'd make mincemeat of me if I gave them the chance. But, then one day it happened ... I met her ... the love of my life. She had pigtails I imagine only God himself could've combed together." Keller smiled, reminiscing. "She was an angel, but she lived around the corner on the next street over. I faked her out as long as possible, but eventually she started asking why I always took her street home. Now, I couldn't tell her I was scared of a couple of mangy mutts, but she also wasn't falling for my lie about taking a detour just to see her. I realized at that point, if I was ever gonna see 1950 through the eyes of a man versus those of a scared little boy, I had to take those dogs head on. So, I drew up a little will on the back of a piece of cardboard. I planned to leave my new Rawlings fielder's glove to my best friend, 'cause even though I felt brave, truth is I was no match for those lapdogs of Satan."

I wanted to burst out laughing, but he seemed so serious. I just held it inside while he continued with his story.

"I got my affairs in order, and then left the house," he said. "I took my usual route, but this time, instead of going on to the store, I waited around the corner ... I waited ... and, then, I waited a little longer till the time was right. The sun was going down, and I knew those dogs would be out on schedule, hungry and hunting for a young, tender meal. I walked back down the street, staying close to the curb, and as I drew nearer to the little brick house, I stopped to arm myself with a good-sized branch from an oak tree. I pulled the leaves off and swung it around a few times to make sure I'd picked the right one, and it was good, so I proceeded. As soon as I walked up to that yard, all hell broke loose. Those dogs tore ass out from the side of the house, headed right for me, drooling, barking and moving faster than a bullet train. I was as good as dog food. My knees began to shake, but I stood strong, gripping my little tree branch as if it were my Louisville slugger, which would've been a far more effective choice of weapon, but I guess hindsight's 20/20. Now, this was almost sixty years ago, and I never been so scared in my entire life. I knew they were going to kill me, but I was gonna get one good lick in before they took me out. And, you know what happened next, Alex?"

"No, what?" I asked.

"Nothing," he confessed.

I smiled. "Nothing?"

"Nothing at all," said Keller, "dogs stopped right at the edge of the yard and just stood there, growling and barking. I was frozen stiff there in the street, petrified with fear, but it turns out I was in more danger of being run over by one of my buddies on his bike than those big dogs taking a plug outta me. Thing is, those dogs were trained, they knew not to leave their yard, and I realized at that point, there was no real danger in walking up and down that street past the old magnificent mansion we'd all come to love, even with those loud barking dogs. Afterwards, I felt good about myself. I was glad I finally faced my fear. I never ran past those dogs again. In fact, I slowed down as I passed by and took my time. I'd just about stick my tongue out at 'em 'cause I knew they weren't coming up out that yard ... I was completely and totally safe from those mongrels."

"So, you never got bitten?" I asked.

He nodded, "Oh yeah," he laughed, "I got bitten alright, by a goddamn two-pound Chihuahua! Son-of-a-bitch jumped up and clamped his teeth right into my leg, hanging on like a bloated tick until his owner jumped down and wrestled him loose. It was horrible. That little dog took a chunk clean out of me. I still got the scar today, and every time it starts itching, you know what it reminds me?"

"What?"

He replied, "It's not the big dogs that bark loud and make a lot of noise that get you, Alex. It's the little ones you never even suspect, and their bite is always bigger than their bark." Keller opened up the file he'd set on the sofa between him and I. He spun it around, so I could see it right side up. "This file contains everything—everything Agent Harris collected on you plus authorization for a warrant for your arrest in connection to his murder—least that's what we'll call it. We also have documentation regarding a number of federal charges, including obstruction of justice, tampering with evidence, tax evasion—mind you—and possession of illegal drugs. We found the weed in your apartment. You throw treason in on top of it, and if a jury doesn't send you to the chair for that alone, you'll never see natural sunlight again. The moral of this here story is OPR's the big barking dog, but they have to stay in their yard. Me on the other hand, well I'm that little dog, the one who takes a big chunk out of your ass ... I guarantee you, Agent Southerland, you will never recover from my bite. Every time it itches, you'll think of me, only you'll be locked down so goddamn tight you won't even be able to scratch it ... ... my offer is simple ... you can do your job—serve your country—and this file is yours to keep tonight, or you can get ready to bend over." He crossed his legs and sat back. "So, what's it gonna be?"

I just looked at him and squinted for a moment. I couldn't believe it. That little old dude was extorting me, right there in his bullshit office, and what the fuck was I gonna do? I couldn't even think of anything to say. I knew the game, I'd learned it from the best a long time ago. It was the only way a girl like me could survive at the Bureau for eight years. I'd mastered my craft too, I mean hey, just look at how I handled Dr. Stephens. This time I'd been beaten though—beaten at my own game by an opponent, who, even if I found a way to stick it to, would just pull a trump card. You can imagine what a man in his position could do if he were so inclined. Keller was a slithering fork-tongued, son-of-a-bitch, and I wanted to cuss his ass out, but who was I kidding? This wasn't Tony or Bill or Theresa—it was the goddamn Vice President of the United States of America. I didn't have a snowball's chance in hell of coming out of this thing with both hind cheeks intact. I thought about my response for a minute and then decided to do what I always did in situations like this—press my luck.

"You can't do this," I told him.

"Attorney General says I can," he replied. "Since he had so much time on his hands after you stormed the consulate, he took the liberty of drawing up some language to indict you. Of course, you're more than welcome to take the matter up with him, but I'm willing to bet you just might see this as an opportunity."

"Is that so?" I crossed my arms.

"That's right," Keller replied. "Young lady, it's an opportunity to do whatever you can to serve your country again and make up for the lives you've taken and the trail of a mess you've left from Atlanta all the way up to New York."

"How do I know there aren't copies of this file floating around?"

"You have my word," he assured.

"THE WORD OF A POWERFUL EXTORTIONIST?" I exclaimed.

"The word of the Vice President of the United States," he retorted. "I didn't get here by making enemies. I gotta tell you Alex, right now, I need a friend more than ever. I'm asking you to be my friend. You have to admit, it's a much better deal than the alternative, isn't it?"

I shook my head a few times.

"No...?" His left eyebrow shot up to the ceiling. "Very well then...."

Keller reached for the file, but I was faster. I snatched it out from under his hand and held it to my chest. I let out a big sigh.

"What do you want me to do, Keller?"

He smiled really big. "Jack," he reminded. "Captain Riggs told me he trained you in the field as if you were one of his Navy Seals, is that true?"

"Yes."

Keller said, "He also said you took out a number of strategic targets while undercover."

"I did, but that was a long time ago."

"Fact still remains you killed for your country," said Keller.

"I was asked to kill for my country," I corrected.

"Your country is asking again." Keller stood up and walked towards the map on the wall.

I got up as well to see what he was after.

"A storm's brewing," said Keller, "right here on American soil. A cloud of poison is making its way from

Miami, to D.C. and all the way over to the Western Seaboard. You should know the President is not happy about the Amadi case. Very simply, you threw egg on his face and undermined him on a highly public, political situation. He wants to charge you with treason. I only tell you this because what we're asking you to do will be extremely dangerous. Those responsible for this reign of terror are heavily armed and they don't like the law. There's little chance you will survive this mission, but instead of being known for your treason, you'll die an American hero. This is your last chance, Agent Southerland. Are you ready to make a sacrifice to protect those who cannot protect themselves?"

"Yes, but on one condition," I replied.

"What's that?" asked Keller.

"Show me the scar."

"What?" He chuckled.

"SHOW ME THE SCAR FROM THE DOG BITE!" I exclaimed. "Way I see it, you're either being forthcoming or you're bullshitting me Mr. Vice President. If you're being straight with me, then your little chihuahua story's true, and you shouldn't have a problem letting me see the evidence."

He gave me a really strange look.

"Hey, this ain't my first time being blackmailed, so you're not the only one calling the shots here. Show me the scar, or I take my chances with the courts."

He shook his head. "Young lady, I see we're going to have a very rocky relationship."

"THE SCAR, MR. VICE PRESIDENT!"

"Alright, alright," he said sighing. He looked down and started unbuckling his belt. "This is ridiculous," he said, shaking his head.

He was right. It was ridiculous, but he was doing it. He pulled his pants down, and turned to the left, exposing the backside of his leg. Sure enough, there was a nice half-moon shaped scar right there on his little hairy hamstring.

"I need to know exactly what it is you want me to do," I said, staring at the back of his leg.

Keller pulled his pants back up and completely turned his back to me. "Have a seat at the desk."

I walked over, pulled back his chair and sat down.

"We have to protect this country from all threats," he said, "foreign and domestic. Last week, a shipment of valuable cargo arrived on the West Coast. The goods were hijacked, mid-transport on their way to Virginia. We have definitive evidence the man responsible for this terrorist attack is still at large in the U.S. Take a look at the photo on my desk." Keller paused for a moment.

I looked down. It was a picture of a man named Peter Tesh. He looked like a black man, but I could tell he wasn't. I could also tell it wasn't his real name. Judging from his facial features, he was most likely Middle Eastern.

Keller said, "You are to find the target, and neutralize him by any means necessary even if it means taking your own life. I'm authorizing you to utilize any weapons and, or resources within our military arsenal. Effective immediately you have been granted a number of Top Secret, SCI, and SAP clearances providing specialized access to classified information from all agencies. Now, your unfortunate behavior has cost us all dearly, and despite SAC Anthony Crane's shining record, he will suffer as well."

"No, he didn't have anything-"

"I don't make the rules around here, young lady," Keller interrupted. "It's too late for him now. He'll be stripped of his command and the only reason he'll keep his job is to keep an eye on you. He'll be forced to make a lateral move to Counterterrorism, and you will continue to report to him for appearance sake. On paper you'll be military. For your cover, you'll continue to report to Crane, but you will work directly for me ... understand?"

"Yes."

"The President and I will be the only two people living privy to your assignment," he said. "No one can know, not even your priest. However, I will grant you a one-time get out of jail free pass. Your codeword is *containment*. You say that along with your full name over any open line of communications, and it will trigger an extraction unit home or abroad, but I suggest you use it wisely. Communication protocol will be provided by Secret Service. And, as far as the file is concerned, I'll do you a favor ... you can have it right now, no strings attached, but I'm gonna hang on to the Treasury documentation. Consider it motivation. If you abort your mission, you'll be arrested and prosecuted to the full letter of the law for tax evasion and-"

"Wait a minute," I interrupted, "what is this tax evasion stuff?"

Keller explained, "Secret Service's inquiry revealed you own a holding company in New York City that has generated quite a bit of profit from numerous business ventures and investments. You have not shown this activity on your Federal returns. There are more than ten years unaccounted for."

"NO, THAT'S NOT RIGHT!" I exclaimed. "I just found out about these businesses ... my father had his friends set everything up. Besides, the accountant is filing amendments for prior years, so you've got nothing on me."

"It's your word against my agents'," Keller replied. "I have enough evidence to send you to a Federal prison while it all gets sorted out. You and I know what they do to women in those detention centers—especially cops."

I just shook my head.

"Stay focused Agent Southerland," he said. "You have a short window of opportunity to complete your mission. Initially, you will be the only asset in place, but I will personally recruit and deploy other assets to assist and ensure you stay on task. If you succeed, and you make it home alive, you will have earned your freedom. However, I reserve the right to utilize this Secret Service report and make an example of you, so I suggest you do everything in your power to get on my good side. Do you have any questions?"

"Can I keep this photo of Tesh?" I asked.

"No ma'am," he replied, "you're on your own."

I stood up with my file tucked under my arm. "Am I dismissed?"

He nodded. "Dismissed."

I circled around his desk and headed towards the exit. "Alex...."

I stopped. "Sir?"

"I am sorry for all of this, Alex," he said, "I truly am. I'm sorry for asking you to make such a great sacrifice for your country. I hope one day you can forgive me. Now, I know it's gonna take some time for you to understand why all this is happening to you, but I am hopeful one day you'll have the wisdom and courage to see things from my perspective. Until then ... good hunting, sailor."

I nodded and left the room. Turns out my first trip to the White House wasn't so great after all, but it was damn sure memorable.

Later that night, I took my time, carefully and thoroughly working my incriminating file deep into the pit of a roaring fire, page-by-page. I stood in front of my fireplace, creating the most liberating pile of ash I'd ever seen. I was free, but I felt like a fugitive getting ready to run, only it wasn't the law I had to hide from—it was me. I didn't know how long it would take, but at least for a while, Alex Southerland could be no more. I had to get as far away as possible from the people I loved and become completely detached from everything that meant anything to me. My life depended on it.

Something told me my time with the Bureau was coming to a close whether I wanted it to or not. From where I was sitting, that wasn't so bad. In fact, the thought of being a private, law abiding citizen was beginning to have new meaning to me.

I realized that night, after all the drama, there was one thing I really wanted that no one—not even the Vice President—could offer me; a simple life. It may sound stupid but destroying that file and deleting my awful past closed one door and opened up a new one. I realized at that point what I needed most. Maybe it was a way for me to prove my parents wrong. That even through troubled times, family is the most precious thing in the world. I envied Rahid Amadi and the love he and his son shared. Suddenly, I wanted it all for myself. I longed for a real home, a husband, and a child—a family. That was the new prize, a prize I was more than willing to fight for and even ready to kill for. I knew then that a family of my own was the only thing that could really complete me once and for all. There was just one thing standing between me and my newfound happiness—a dead man.

www.ingramcontent.com/pod-product-compliance
Lightning Source LLC
Chambersburg PA
CBHW031659170626
46808CB00005B/1525